W9-BUA-117

SAVOR THE DANGER

Savor the Danger

Lori Foster

This Large Print edition is published by Thorndike Press, Waterville, Maine USA and by AudioGo Ltd, Bath, England.

Thorndike Press, a part of Gale, Cengage Learning.

Thorndike Press® Large Print Romance.
The text of this Large Print edition is unabridged.
Other aspects of the book may vary from the original edition.
Set in 16 pt. Plantin.

LIBRARY OF CONGRESS CATALOGING-IN-PUBLICATION DATA

Foster, Lori, 1958–
Savor the danger / by Lori Foster. — Large print ed.
p. cm. — (Thorndike Press large print romance)
ISBN-13: 978-1-4104-3883-6 (hardcover)
ISBN-10: 1-4104-3883-X (hardcover)
1. Large type books. I. Title.
PS3556.O767S28 2011
813'.54—dc22 2011021440

Published in the U.S. in 2011 by arrangement with Harlequin Books S. A.
Published in the U.K. in 2012 by arrangement with Harlequin Enterprises II B.V.
U.K. Hardcover: 978 1 445 83828 1 (Chivers Large Print)
U.K. Softcover: 978 1 445 83829 8 (Camden Large Print)

Printed in the United States of America
1 2 3 4 5 6 7 15 14 13 12 11

ACKNOWLEDGMENTS

To the Animal Adoption Foundation, a no-kill animal shelter in Hamilton, Ohio. Continued gratitude to the shelter for the remarkable work you do for animals. Gremlin (brother to Liger, featured in *Trace of Fever*) is one of the cats that my son adopted from you. Gremlin has a quirky personality, a smoker's meow and a purr that will melt your heart. Thank you for "rescuing" him so that we could make him a part of our family. The AAF will always be one of my "pet projects" whenever I do fundraising.
To learn more, visit www.AAFPETS.com.

Dear Reader,

I'm pleased to give you *Savor the Danger,* book three of my new series of über-alpha hunks featuring private mercenaries who are big, capable, a little dangerous and (I hope) oh-so-sexy. If you read the first two books, *When You Dare* and *Trace of Fever,* then you already know why I call them my men who "walk the edge of honor."

Please note — each of the three books is a stand-alone, so they do not need to be read in order. You will meet characters from the previous books, but the relationships are briefly explained so that the books are independent. My novella in the anthology *The Guy Next Door* got things started by introducing you to characters related to the heroine of *When You Dare.*

To see more about the books, including how they're related and more on the characters, visit my website at www.LoriFoster.com and feel free to chat with me on my Facebook fan page — www.facebook.com/pages/Lori-Foster/233405457965.

I'm very excited about these books, so I hope you enjoy them! Do let me know. My email is on my website.

Lori Foster

Chapter One

Wakefulness brought a crescendo beat of pain piercing his brain. He tried to swallow, but the desert at high noon couldn't be as dry as his mouth.

What the hell was going on?

Disoriented, in agony, Jackson Savor got one eye open.

The source of his sharpest pain was a blinding ray of Kentucky's morning sunshine slicing through the part in his bedroom curtains.

His curtains. So he was in his own apartment.

With one question answered, he closed his eye again and struggled to take inventory.

Had he been captured? Tortured?

Slowly, very slowly, he moved his right hand. His arm felt like lead, but he lifted it.

Sluggish, a little weak, but not bound, thank God.

He tried to move his left hand and realized that something warm and soft kept him pinned in place. He inhaled . . . and recognized the enticing, undeniable scent of woman.

Oh, shit.

Staying very still to avoid alerting anyone to his cognizance, Jackson opened his hand and . . . felt.

He didn't need a clear head or his vision to know he palmed a very sweet female backside.

Huh.

The body beside him stirred. A slim, smooth leg came over his, gliding up and over his crotch. Inside he jolted, but outside he stayed perfectly still.

A woman purred, "You're awake?"

Both eyes shot open with recognition. He snapped his head around so fast that pain nearly blinded him.

The knee resting over his dick shifted as the woman readjusted to better see him. "Is something wrong?"

Shit, shit, *shit.* Carefully, his eyelids scraping like sandpaper, Jackson peered to his side and found none other than Alani Rivers. Sleepy, warm, soft. She watched him with sated, golden brown eyes, her pale hair spread out around her — on *his* pillows.

She had the unmistakable look of a woman who'd spent a satisfying night doing the nasty.

With him?

Though no words came from his parched throat, the hand on her ass contracted. Yeah, so his brain wasn't quite working — his instincts were fine and dandy.

Blushing, Alani ducked her face and rose up to an elbow.

The sheet pulled to her waist, giving him an up close and personal view of her *really* beautiful breasts and rosy nipples.

His thoughts cramped. So did his balls.

"So quiet this morning," she murmured as she bent and kissed his mouth. "Especially after last night."

Meaning . . . *what?* Had they been noisy? Had he been chatty?

She chewed her bottom lip. "Are you feeling as shy as I am about the things we did?"

Shy? Never. *What the hell had they done?* He tried to sort it out, but beyond the pain and the confusion was the mind-boggling fact that he had Alani Rivers in his bed.

Naked.

Affectionate.

Replete.

And he didn't know how any of it had happened.

Acid crawled around his guts and squirreled up his throat, making his stomach pitch. Groaning, he threw back the covers.

Didn't matter if his head fell off, he would *not* puke in front of her.

In only a few long strides, he made it to the connecting bathroom where he dropped to his knees in front of the john in just the nick of time.

He felt vile. Worse than that even.

What the hell had happened?

"Jackson?"

He looked up to see Alani in the doorway. Naked.

He groaned again. "Go away."

"But . . . can I get you —"

"Out!" He kicked at the door. It hit so hard that it bounced open again. He saw her shock and hurt, but damn it, no way in hell did he want her to see him like this.

Luckily for them both, she turned and strode away.

When the nausea finally subsided, he flushed the toilet and, feeling weaker than a newborn, used the edge of the sink to haul himself to his feet. His legs shook. His head thundered.

He turned on cold water, splashed his face, rinsed his mouth, and after a few seconds of mental searching that left him blank, he turned to stagger out.

Alani stood there yet again.

Still naked.

Jackson swayed. He tried, but he couldn't take it in. For a hell of a long time, he'd wanted her. Now she was here, but . . . how? Why?

His burning gaze zeroed in on her neat triangle of golden brown pubic hair. Another question answered — but it had nada to do with his current predicament.

She folded her arms under her breasts, which had the effect of getting his riveted attention off her lower body and up a little — as far as her chest anyway.

Ah, damn, so pretty. Had he touched her breasts? Kissed her nipples?

Dizziness assailed him. The possibility of passing out or puking more loomed near.

But God Almighty, she looked fine. Better than fine.

She looked like *his.*

Face red, voice high, she snapped, "Real nice, Jackson."

Picking up on the acrimony, he managed to meet her gaze through a fog of emotions. Uh-oh. She looked both hurt and pissed.

Her lips tightened. She gave one fleeting glance at his body, but when he remained mute, her eyes narrowed and she tossed her head, sending back her long fair hair. Like pale liquid, it poured over her smooth skin, mostly behind her shoulders, though one long strand trailed over her breast.

Mesmerized, he took a moment to realize she was talking to him.

"I *told* you this wasn't a good idea," she said. "I told you it would never work."

Looked to him like it had worked just fine.

But to make sure they were on the same page, he rasped, "It?" Bracing one hand on the door frame, the other squeezing the bridge of his nose, he started on a great admission. "Thing is, I don't remember —"

"Talking about it?"

Anything. "Uh . . ."

"Big surprise there, right?" Her attention tracked down over him, then jumped back to his face. "You were too busy getting me naked to listen to reason."

Sounded like him, he had to admit.

"Too busy racing for the bed," she complained, "to even think about my concerns, about what I said."

The words resonated over and over. *He'd gotten her naked and in bed.*

And then what?

Nothing rational came to his spinning brain, so Jackson just shook his head while again looking at her body. If it wasn't for the door frame supporting him, he'd be on his face on the floor, but he couldn't *not* look at her.

Wounded, disgusted, Alani turned on her heel and stalked back to his bed. Seeing the bounce of her rounded backside gave him a whole new reason to wish his vision wasn't so blurry.

"Alani . . ." With no idea what to say, Jackson started to follow her. One jarring step was enough to warn him not to leave the dubious convenience of the bathroom.

His stomach did jumping jacks. In the nick of time he dropped back down in front of the toilet again.

This time when he finished, his stomach muscles ached but his guts felt a little quieter, as if he'd gotten some foul poison out of his system.

Unfortunately, Alani was now fully dressed and marching toward the front door.

Feeling like a weak, mewling pup, he stumbled behind her. "Wait."

Pausing, she looked back at him — and all over him.

It suddenly dawned on Jackson that he was completely naked, too. He held on to the wall and willed away the pulsing agony in his noggin. "Let's . . . talk."

"So you can get sick again with . . . regret?

No thank you."

Regret? There was more to regret beyond the fact that he couldn't remember shitola?

She jerked his front door open but didn't storm away. With her back to him, her voice quavering, she said, "Don't worry about it, Jackson. I'm naive, I know, but I'm not dumb. I understand what happened."

"What?"

"I won't say a word to anyone and since this will never happen again, you can just forget all about it."

The slamming of the door almost took out his knees. Slowly, he sank down to the cool hardwood floor in his hallway. His eyes closed, but he could still see Alani naked.

He didn't want to forget a damn thing.

He wanted to *remember*.

Alani stayed busy as long as she could. She'd shopped, cleaned her car, had a light breakfast, seen an early matinee . . . but no amount of distraction had helped. Her chest still hurt with the weight of thick emotion.

Humiliation vied with regret.

Why had she believed him?

Why had she allowed herself to be so easily swayed?

Fool!

What could have been the most amazing

night of her life now felt like the most degrading. Not that she could blame Jackson for everything. She'd been so infatuated with him for so long, it had required very little from him to win her over. A few small words and . . .

The groan vibrated out, heartfelt, sad and angry.

She'd done things with Jackson that she'd never before considered. He'd encouraged her to speak her mind, to be totally open and honest about what she wanted, what she enjoyed — and he'd done the same. With him, she'd reveled in her sexuality.

And then, with the morning light, he'd taken one look at her and rushed off to be ill.

Her face flamed.

All along, from the very first day she'd met Jackson Savor, she'd known he was trouble. Over and over again she'd resisted him because an involvement with any man who worked with her brother, especially a man too much like her brother, seemed impossible.

Her cell phone rang, and she glanced at the caller ID. Speak of the devil . . . Her brother had already called several times, but she wasn't up to speaking with him.

She waited until the ringing stopped, then

checked her voice mail. Trace said, "Where are you, Alani? I've called three times now. I want to talk to you. Call me back."

She knew Trace fully expected her to do as told, but she couldn't talk to him right now. If she tried to, she'd get emotional, maybe even weepy. God knew Trace had always been protective, but since her kidnapping more than a year ago, he'd been insane with caution. If he knew she was upset, he'd be on the warpath in minutes. She had no intention of telling him about her misguided — and obviously brief — liaison with Jackson, so there'd be no point in getting him caught up in her personal drama.

By necessity, given the responsibilities inherent in his work, Trace was autocratic by nature, occasionally overbearing and always too confident.

Jackson was the same.

Actually, so was Trace's friend, Dare, who had worked with Trace from the inception of the business.

They had typical personalities for lethally honed mercenaries — how else could they remain so successful in their efforts to help others?

Of course, Trace, Dare and Jackson were the only mercenaries she knew. And while each of them was different, they were also, in the most basic ways, the same.

They were men who smiled while squaring off with danger, men who didn't flinch when put to the test, men who, without a single second of hesitation, would protect others with their own lives.

They were good men.

They were scary men.

Most people, even without knowing of her brother's vocation, still feared him, and with good reason; Trace emanated danger and capability. To meet him was to be wary of him, and so dating had never been easy for her. Guys took one look at her brother and decided it was safer to keep their distance.

But . . . Jackson wasn't like most guys. Because he was on a par with Trace, not much ever intimidated him. In fact, he felt at ease jesting with Trace, even taunting him on occasion with his good humor. Knowing Trace and Dare counted on him in the most dangerous situations, Jackson had promised her that his job security wouldn't be affected by their involvement.

But then, he'd also sworn that it wouldn't be awkward. Now she was on her own, and it was so excruciatingly awkward that her face continued to burn.

Unfortunately, Trace called yet again as

she parked in the driveway. The phone rang four times and then went to voice mail. Alani just knew Trace would show up on her doorstep if she didn't touch base.

Hating to fib, but feeling she had no choice, she sent back a text message saying only, "I'm at the movies. I'll call you soon."

Then she turned off the phone.

After gathering the clothing bags from her trunk, she started around the walkway that led from the driveway on the side of her small but perfect house to the front door.

She drew up short at the sight of Jackson sprawled out on her porch steps, a cowboy hat on his head, mirrored sunglasses hiding his eyes.

He didn't move, and neither did she.

For half a minute she stood there frozen, unsure what to say, what to do.

He had an utterly relaxed look about him, but then, Jackson had perfected a deceptively indolent pose that hid razor-sharp reflexes and phenomenal speed.

Last night, *all night,* he'd been far from indolent.

Breathing fast, Alani studied him. His continued stillness suggested sleep. Even when she shifted her bags and inched closer, he didn't move.

The tall oak in her front yard offered

plenty of shade, but Jackson hadn't removed the hat or the sunglasses. He was now clean-shaven. A snowy white T-shirt pulled across his wide chest and shoulders and hung looser around his taut abs.

Age had worn out his faded jeans in select places, such as at the knees, the hems and where they cupped his sex.

Even now, so tranquil, he looked . . . impressive.

The bombardment of awareness stiffened her knees.

Memories of touching his body, tasting his hot flesh, sent a tide of sensation through her veins. She remembered wrapping her hand around his erection, how he'd groaned all deep and rough, the insanely sexual things he'd whispered to her as suggestions and encouragement, how he'd covered her hand with his own, showing her how hard to squeeze, how fast to stroke. . . .

His total lack of inhibition had left her free to be less inhibited.

She swallowed audibly — and stared some more.

He sat with his long legs loose, one foot braced on a step, the other stretched out, his elbows back, his breathing deep and even.

Alani licked her lips and started to slowly,

silently retreat.

"Don't make me chase you, darlin'."

Shock snapped her shoulders back. The big faker!

He'd been watching her watch him . . . *Ohhhhh.* "I thought you were asleep!"

"And so you figured you could rape me with your pretty eyes? Or will you deny that?"

If she had a rock close by, she'd throw it at him. Teeth set, Alani asked, "What are you doing here?"

"Whatever it takes." Lazily, he sat upright. Muscles flexed. His shirt pulled tight. With a thumb, he tipped back his hat. Sweat dampened his temples, leaving the ends of his dark blond hair curly. "Where you been anyway? I've been baking out here for hours."

Something in his tone sounded . . . off. He was just as outrageous as always, but the cocky edge had waned, almost as if he was sick or worried, or both. *She didn't care.*

"It's none of your business, Jackson."

The barely perceptible curling of his mouth alarmed her. "Full of spice this afternoon, huh?"

Determined to brazen her way through things, Alani put back her shoulders and charged forward. "I'm full of disgust."

His mouth firmed. "At what we . . . did?"

Uncertainty didn't suit him at all. "At myself, actually." Breath held, she stepped around Jackson, but he didn't touch her. At the front door she shifted the bags into one arm and, with fumbling hands, fished her keys from her purse. "I should have known better than to —"

His mouth skimmed the back of her neck. Low, sultry, he suggested, "Let's talk about what we did."

Fire raced down her spine, and her legs turned to noodles. In an instant, Alani's mind took her back to his bed where he'd kissed her nape just like that while he slowly took her — doggy-style, he'd called it — from behind, burying himself deep, his arms around her, his hands holding her breasts. . . .

"Stop it!" She shoved the door open and tried to slam it closed again. It bounced off Jackson's shoulder.

She raced in.

Of course he followed.

Making a beeline for her kitchen, she said with as much venom as she could manage given the fluttering of her stomach, "Get out."

Not more than two steps behind her, his boot heels sounded on her tile floor.

Her packages held in front of her like a shield, Alani spun around to face him. She sounded far too panicked when she screeched, "I mean it, Jackson!"

He stopped and stared at her. Tension crackled between them.

For a few seconds there, Jackson looked as if he might leap on her, but instead, he chewed his bottom lip, then retreated a step, moving as if not to startle her.

Cajoling, he said, "Take it easy, okay?"

Given the riot of emotions clamoring inside her, *taking it easy* wasn't an option. "Don't placate me!"

Without a word, he set his hat on the counter and tipped his head. Fists low on his lean hips, expression enigmatic, he studied her, all of her. Suddenly her casual, comfy sundress felt insubstantial. Around Jackson, she needed a damn suit of armor.

The concentrated scrutiny left her fidgeting, too warm and vulnerable.

In a rough whisper, he said, "God's truth, darlin', I don't mean to ride roughshod over your feelings, but I need to see you again." And before she could react to the hunger in his tone, he added, "I don't suppose we could put this little confrontation on hold long enough for me to appease my curiosity?"

Curiosity? He'd already seen her in great detail throughout the long night. He hadn't been shy about looking, either.

Where Trace and Dare treated her with kid gloves, Jackson just treated her like a woman he wanted. It was sort of nice in small doses . . . when he didn't go overboard.

In light of all that had transpired, his outrageous suggestion was way over the line. Alani threw the clothing bags at him.

The packages landed against his chest and then hit the floor.

He barely flinched at the assault. "I take that as a no?"

"No!"

He cocked a brow at her outburst and then caught her as she tried to shove around him. He was so big and so solidly muscular, it proved too easy for him to wrap her up in his arms and lock her in close, her back against his chest, his forearms under her breasts. "Shh, baby. Don't."

Those sultry memories, along with his heat and scent and sex appeal, enveloped her as surely as his body did. Desperate, almost panicked, Alani demanded, *"Let me go."*

She felt him flinch, wrapped tight around her. "Sorry, love. Can't."

Love. He would dare to use that word now? Her throat tightened in a panic. *"Jackson —"*

His breath moved past her ear as he whispered, "Give me just a sec, okay?"

She heard the pain in his words, and that calmed her struggle.

"Better," he breathed and relaxed his hold.

Worry overtook outrage, and she tried to twist to see him. "What's wrong?"

The tension intensified, and then he said, "I don't remember a damned thing."

"About what?"

He rocked her a little, and his voice lowered even more. "Everything. I'm . . . blank."

She didn't understand, but she picked up on his agony, so she stopped straining away from him. "What are you talking about?"

"I don't know what happened, honey. With us, with anything." He hugged her, his chin on the top of her head. "Yesterday is just . . . gone."

Disbelieving, Alani jerked around to see him. Standing in the circle of his arms, her hands on his chest, she had to tip her head way back to see his face. "What do you mean, gone?"

Ill at ease, he shrugged. "All I remember is waking up with the king-daddy of all migraines, a wallop of confusion. . . ." He shifted, drawing her closer to his body. His voice went hoarse. "And there you were, in the raw beside me."

Her heart almost stopped. "But . . ." She shoved him back accusingly. "You told me you hadn't been drinking."

"Did I?" He ran a hand through his dark blond hair, then pulled off the sunglasses. "Because I don't remember that, either. Hell, I don't even remember talking to you."

Immediately sidetracked, Alani strangled on a breath. "Oh my God, Jackson." Never had she seen eyes so bloodshot. Sympathy welled up. "You look —"

"Like shit, I know. Feel like it, too, believe me." He pinched the bridge of his nose, squeezed his eyes shut a second, then snapped them open again. "We had sex?"

Good grief, he had a one-track mind. But then she'd found that out last night. She winced as she took in his expression. The whites of his eyes looked blood-red, making the green seem more vivid. But even miserable, his direct gaze managed to keep her snared. "You honestly expect me to believe you don't remember?"

One large, warm hand hooked her nape, lifting her to her tiptoes so he could kiss her once, hard and fast. "I woke up with my vision dicked, my brain on fire and my guts brawling. And then I saw you, in bed, beside me." He went gruff with arousal. "You looked so incredible, it's a wonder that didn't send me right over the edge."

"But it did, remember?" She went nose to nose with him and prompted, "You threw up."

Rather than retreat, he moved in until he surrounded her with his size and his determination. "Woman, there is no way you think you were the cause of that."

She should have put space between them, but it felt so good being close to him again. It seemed that last night had left her addicted; all morning long, her body had mourned the loss of his scent, the heat of his touch. With less conviction than she intended, she asked, "No?"

"Hell, no." Restless, his hands kneaded her back. "You looked so hot, I wish I'd taken a photo. I wish I had you painted on the ceiling. Looking at you buck-ass might revive me, and it'll definitely give me wood, but it would never repulse me or —"

Flustered by his brazen language, Alani smashed her fingers over his mouth. "Just . . . stop."

She felt his relieved smile.

And then she felt his tongue.

Quickly, she tucked her hand behind her. When his strong fingers wrapped around her wrist, keeping her in that vulnerable position, she realized her mistake.

"Let's put it to the test." He leaned in, his hot breath brushing her cheek, the top of her shoulder. "Let's get you out of this little dress and we'll see how I react."

"Oh, for the love of —"

"I swear, darlin', I might implode . . ." His mouth opened on her shoulder in a stirring love bite. "But I won't be ill. Not even close."

"Jackson, *please.*" She tried to retreat two steps — and he reluctantly released her. "I don't understand any of this. You need to give me time to think."

"Maybe you'd think better naked." He touched the hem of her dress and murmured more to himself than to her, "It'd be pretty easy to get you out of this —"

Infuriated, she slapped his hand away and glared at him.

"Okay, okay." Frowning, he gestured his subdued agreement. "Think away."

How could he not remember *anything?* What he'd said, what he'd done . . . All the things *she'd* said and done, the things she sort of regretted now.

"How is this possible?"

"I don't know."

"So just like that," she asked with skepticism, "you've lost the details of last night?"

"That's about it."

Humiliation hung with her, but knowing he had no memory of it alleviated a big part of the regret. She gave him a sideways look. "This is sort of convenient."

He shook his head. "I hear the suspicious tone, babe, but I'm not firing on all cylinders today, so you'll have to spell it out for me. No way in hell does any of this seem convenient to me."

Could he be telling the truth rather than dodging responsibility for his actions of last night? Maybe. After all, she'd left him with no obligation, and she'd promised not to tell anyone. He had no real reason to pretend he'd forgotten it all.

Thinking aloud, she said, "It's just that it's so unreal." What would explain such a thing?

"Tell me about it." Gaze hot and far too intense, he bent his knees to search her face. "Did I get inside you, sugar? I'm dying to know."

Wide-eyed, Alani turned to give him her back. Jackson's effect on her was enough that, even with so many unanswered questions, she wanted to rush him into the bedroom and do it all again. But that would be dumb. *If* she slept with him again, she wanted the time to talk and clear the air first.

Besides, he didn't exactly look able to do all those awesomely amazing things again. But on the tail end of that thought, he stepped closer again and she felt a solid erection nudging her backside.

"Jackson!" Never in her life had she done so much screeching. "What do you think you're doing?"

"Suffering. You gotta tell me something here, Alani. Please."

Frustrated, she snapped, "Can't you turn it off for just a minute? We need to talk."

"You're kidding, right?" Red-eyed and a little shaky, he still sounded and looked on the make. It was there in his voice, the set of his hard shoulders, the probing way he watched her. "Since the day I laid eyes on you, I've wanted to get you out of your panties. You know it, because I wasn't shy about it."

"Certainly not." He'd been overwhelmingly obvious.

"And now it seems like I finally did, but damn it all, I can't remember it. Before you can expect me to concentrate on anything else, you gotta put me out of my misery."

Her mouth pinched; she forced herself to face him again. "Okay, so maybe you don't remember, but still you know." He wasn't an idiot. Waking up with her naked, wrapped around him, *smiling* like a satisfied sap, had to be a pretty good clue.

His gaze stroked over her features. "I'm assuming." His interest settled on her mouth. "I'm *hoping.* But I need the details." He caressed her shoulders. "Damn, woman, do I ever need the details."

Yes, to some extent he probably did. That'd only be fair. But she'd be judicious. She'd tell him only the basics. All the rest, her overblown moans and begging, the things he'd done to her, the things she *loved* him doing . . . no way would she tell him any of that.

Not looking at him helped, but just a little. She swallowed and whispered, "You . . . we . . ."

"Had sex?"

Sex didn't quite cover it, but she nodded and took a breath. "Yes."

Muscled arms came around her once more, cuddling her close, his hold somehow pleased and possessive. "It was good?"

Could Jackson Savor be insecure about his performance? Actually, that'd make sense for anyone who couldn't remember.

She nodded.

He growled low, "Did you come?"

She tried to lurch away, but instead she found herself turned into him, her breasts against his chest, his heartbeat matching her own.

As if he already sensed the answer — and liked it — he got that seductive, lazy look about him. "Did you?"

Face hot, she nodded. "I . . . yes."

Mouth curling the smallest bit, he whispered, "A wimpy little come, or a really smokin' hot, screaming orgasm?"

Memories battered her, wearing her down until her mouth went dry. Rather than admit too much, she settled on saying, "Um . . . not wimpy."

He expanded on a deeply indrawn breath. "Did I go down on you?"

Oh, lord. She felt it all again, that insane spiraling of pleasure, growing tighter and tighter, the touch of his cool hair and rough jaw on the insides of her thighs, his velvet tongue, the gentle bite of his teeth.

The tugging of his mouth as he sucked on her most sensitive flesh.

Her breath labored, and . . . she nodded.

Jackson's muscles bunched, his nostrils flared. His voice going thick and hot, he asked, "Did you come then, too, darlin'?

With my mouth on you?"

Her orgasm had been so incredible, she'd wept. But she couldn't bring herself to be that explicit. She licked her lips and, in a mere breath of sound, admitted, "Yes."

Putting his forehead to hers, Jackson groaned like a man in agony.

Alani touched his chest. Heat, strength, safety. He was all of that and so much more. But why couldn't he remember? "Were you sick, Jackson? Is that why you can't remember?" Looking at the morning in a new way, she realized he'd been seriously ill.

And she'd stormed out on him.

Flushed with shame, she cupped a hand around his neck. "Are you all right now?"

"All right? Hell, no. I'm tortured by what I can't remember." He covered her hand with his, lifted it to his mouth to kiss her palm. "After all that time of me wanting you so bad, and you turning me down flat, how the hell did I finally manage to win you over?"

Chapter Two

It wasn't easy for Alani to accept that he truly couldn't recall a single detail. She'd suffered so much angst over her gullibility, over behavior that, for all intents and purposes, no longer mattered.

Except that she wanted to do it again.

Unwilling to expose her heart, she shook her head. "I don't know."

"C'mon, darlin'. Something swayed you." He tried a strained half smile. "Help me out here."

Because Jackson looked so agonized, she tried to give him the simplest of truths. "It doesn't matter anymore, but it was the things you said as much as anything you did."

"Yeah?" He brought up her chin, leaving her no choice but to look into his deep green eyes. "Like what?"

He kept touching her with an implied intimacy, stroking, nuzzling. She'd just spent hours coming to grips with the idea that she'd succumbed to a one-night stand, yet he acted as though they'd just begun a long affair.

She discounted everything he'd said last night, but still . . . did he want more?

If so, how much more?

He trailed his fingers over her cheek, around her neck, over her bare shoulder.

She shivered. Jackson might be sick from whatever had taken his memory, but he was still the quintessential primal male. Always.

At least . . . that's how he always was with her.

Was he like that with every woman? Probably. Even Dare's and Trace's wives had noted Jackson's good looks and sex appeal.

Shaking her head, Alani refused to think about it. "It was just . . . things you said. That's all." Things he'd promised, commitments he'd insinuated. "I guess it's the stuff guys say to women when they want to talk them into bed."

That made him frown. "Like what? Compliments? Big deal. When have I ever *not* complimented you?"

Sure, Jackson did a lot of sweet-talking — while on the make. "No, this was different." This had felt more genuine, wrought from emotion and not just lust.

"How?" His attention drifted to her chest. "I bet I told you how damn sexy you are."

Resisting an eye roll wasn't easy. Later he had called her sexy, but at that point they'd already been on a heated path to lovemaking and she'd *felt* sexy.

She wasn't sure she could pinpoint the moment that she'd known she would sleep with him, but that day he'd been different. Not more intense, because that wasn't possible. Jackson was *always* intense.

But from the second she'd walked in the door, he'd looked at her, touched her and spoken to her differently.

He'd spoken from his heart — or so she'd thought.

Renewed embarrassment made her defensive. "Actually, you said I'm pretty." And that was both sweeter and more touching than claiming her "hot" or "sexy." Those sentiments had been expressed by the men who'd taken her, the men who'd manhandled her, restrained her, touched her, the men who'd planned to —

"Hey." As if he sensed the direction of her thoughts, Jackson pressed a tender kiss to her forehead, the bridge of her nose. Sounding much as he had last night, he said, "You are pretty, Alani. So damn pretty." His mouth brushed her ear. "All over."

Face warm, she shook off the remnants of old emotion, fear and desolation from her kidnapping, discomfort from her naiveté last night.

"Thank you." Dare had killed her kidnappers, and her brother now focused on destroying all human traffickers. She wasn't with those men anymore. She was with Jackson, and he was about all she could handle right now. "You also said I was sweet."

His burning gaze zeroed in on the notch of her thighs. "God, I bet you are."

Her knees went shaky, so she pushed back from him. Hoping for a few calm moments to think, she said, "We have to figure this out, Jackson, so leash the lust."

His chin went up as he stared down at her. "Woman, you ask the impossible."

"Do it anyway!"

Sighing, lifting his hands from her as if in surrender, he stepped back. "This is me trying."

Though the situation couldn't be more skewed, he remained strong and capable. She envied him that. "What do you think happened? *Did* you drink?"

"Doubt it." He shook his head. "I can't remember, but I'm not much of a drinker." And then with a shrug, "Never have been."

She knew that about him. It was a control

thing. Her brother and Dare . . . they disdained alcohol because it could throw off reflexes or perception, and they were all about control — of themselves and others. If Jackson imbibed much, they wouldn't trust him.

She didn't know the whole story of how Jackson came to join their team, but not long after she'd been recovered from Tijuana, they'd brought him on board. Obviously they trusted him, and that meant Alani could trust him, too — at least about this.

With anything more personal, like a romantic relationship, she just didn't know.

He watched her every move. "I rummaged through my apartment, even the garbage, but I didn't see any empty bottles. No sign of a drinking binge on my end."

Suspicions crowded in, but for the moment, she pushed them aside. "Did you maybe fall and hit your head?"

That insulted him. "No." He snorted. "Course not."

"But you don't remember, right? So how do you know?"

Roughly tousling his own hair, he said, "See? No bruises, no bumps." He moved in again. "In fact, other than a few scratches that I'm hoping came from you, I don't have any marks — no bruises or cuts or anything."

"Scratches?"

His mouth quirked sensually. "On my shoulders. Small half moons right where a woman usually holds on tight when she's —"

"So." Interrupting seemed the safer course. "You probably weren't involved in a scuffle, then."

He shook his head. "Let's talk about what might've happened . . . after."

Would his possibilities mesh up with her suspicions? Likely. "After what?"

He pointed a finger at her. "Maybe you don't understand how it is for me, how it'd be for any guy, but especially for me since I've been hot on your tail for a while now."

The things he said, and how he said them, were both insulting and somehow . . . flattering. "Jackson . . ."

"To make sure there aren't any misunderstandings, let me clue you in, okay? I've got a bad case for you."

"Sexual chemistry. I know. You've told me." Last night it had felt like more, but last night didn't exist for him.

"Call it whatever you want, doesn't matter to me."

Sadly, what they called it mattered a lot to

her. "I see."

"Don't go twisting my words, okay?" Jackson thrust out his chin. "Bottom line is that I *have* to know what we did. All of it."

"I already told you."

"We had sex, yeah. Got it. But that could mean a whole range of things. I need the particulars, like if it was nice and slow, or fast and furious."

Oh. She peeked at him. "Both?"

He went still, then clasped his head and groaned again. In a croak, he asked, "Good old missionary, or did we mix it up a bit? Bedroom or living room?"

The first time had been in his bed. Then his shower. And later in the hall, against the wall. "All of the above."

His nostrils flared. "How many times did I have you, anyway?"

She bit her lips then ventured . . . "All night?"

Jerking away, he stalked three steps, then rushed back to her. "Lights on or off?"

"On." He'd insisted, but at that point, she hadn't cared. She had enjoyed the concentrated way he'd looked at her, and she'd wanted to see him, too.

Not only had she forgotten any shyness over her nudity, she'd also forgotten about the past, about men who'd taken her and looked at her, handled her like property. With Jackson, she'd overcome a lot of hang-ups. Maybe too many, considering the night had been built on fraud.

His expression a mix of pleading and demand, he grabbed her shoulders. "Damn, baby, I need to see you again. All of you. I need to know how you sound when you're excited, and when you come." His busy fingers went to the shoulder strap of her sundress, touching almost idly, playing with it as if it tempted him greatly. "I need to taste you, smell you —"

Stunned, flustered and a little turned on, Alani grabbed his wrist. She hated to disappoint him — and herself — but she saw no other choice. Not right now. "Jackson," she said gently, "you can't seriously expect me to put aside everything that happened and just . . ."

"Pick up wherever we left off? Yeah." He searched her gaze. "God, yeah."

"*Not* happening." But he looked very endearing in his need. No one had ever wanted her the way Jackson Savor did.

He also looked ready to collapse. Worried for him, she touched his jaw and forced her mind onto more immediate matters. "Have you eaten?"

He scowled. "No. Screw that." He drew

himself up. "You think I could wake up with you naked, soft and smiling one minute, pissed off and storming out the next, with no clue why or how, and I'd just go about my day?"

Yes, well, that did sound absurd. "Sorry."

"After you left, I suffered through a cold shower, choked down three aspirin and prayed for even a kernel of memory. I got jack-shit. Nothing."

And yet, when he should be resting in his bed, all he wanted was . . . her.

Her heart softened more, and her reservations waned. "Why do you think you've forgotten?"

Frustration clenched his jaw. His head dropped back on his shoulders, eyes closed. "You're not going to let this go, are you?"

How could she, especially with him looking so sick? "Of course not."

His eyes narrowed, and that, too, looked painful, prompting her to change tactics.

"This is ridiculous. You need to sit down." She took his hand and led him back to her living room. At the couch, she stopped and pressed against his chest. "Sit."

After a heartbeat where he looked as if he might argue, he more or less fell into the cushions, his strong limbs lax, his entire demeanor devastated. And the enormity of it all hit her, really hit her.

Even the strongest of men had moments of weakness. Jackson always seemed so indomitable, so confident.

But for right now, he needed her, in more ways than one.

Maybe she hadn't been the only one played last night.

Sinking down next to him, Alani touched his forehead. As if surprised, he went very still.

"No fever." She cupped his jaw, and felt it firm under her fingers. "Although you are warm."

Warily, Jackson watched her.

She smoothed his unruly blond hair. It was a little too long, bleached by the sun. Cool and silky. Such a contrast to his inner strength and his external hardness.

Alani made up her mind. "We're definitely going to talk about this, Jackson, you can believe that. But first I'm going to get you something to drink, and then something to eat. When did you take the aspirin?"

One eye twitched in rebellion. "Don't start mothering me, Alani. That's not what I want from you."

She smiled at his surly tone. "Consider it friendly concern, okay?"

"Call it whatever you want, but I'd rather

you lift up that dress, skim off those panties and straddle my lap."

His audacity stole her breath and her aplomb. "Forget that idea."

"With you touching me? Not likely."

"It's not my touch that's doing it." Playful, hoping to tease him into a less sexually aggressive mode, she nudged him with her shoulder. "It's from all the provocative talking you're doing."

Slowly he shook his head. "It's from you, babe. Talking to you, thinking about you." His eyes closed for only a moment as he whispered, "Remembering you naked." He rested a big, hot hand on her thigh, just under the hem of her sundress.

"You need to focus, Jackson."

"I'm focused, believe me."

Boy, was he ever. "On something *other* than sex."

"I'm focused on you, and thoughts of sex automatically follow." He tugged her closer. "But you know, I could be a lot more cooperative if you'd help me take the edge off first."

And exactly how did he think to do that?

His hand slid higher while his voice went lower. "Just let me touch you —"

She grabbed his wrist. *So thick, so solid.* Dangerous waves of desire weakened her resistance. “We can’t do this.”

“We sure as hell can.” And then, “We already did. Right?”

Unnerved by how tempted she felt, Alani shook her head. “*I* can’t do this, not right now. So tell me, when did you take the aspirin?”

He stared at her mouth, and his fingers contracted. “Before I headed here, ’bout three hours ago.”

Relieved that he’d finally let up, she released a tight breath. “All right. I’ll get a couple more. Do you want to take off your boots?”

Slowly he nodded. “And my shirt.” His gaze came up to snare hers. “Maybe my pants, too.”

That was his most tempting offer so far. She hadn’t gotten nearly enough time to look at him last night, and this morning . . . well, he’d been vague, sick, and she’d been so insulted. . . .

To remind herself as much as him, she said, “Forget it, Jackson. You’re not up for it.”

“Wrong.” His hand slid around to cup behind her knee. He tugged her leg toward him, over one of his thighs. “Trust me, I’m up.”

Don’t look, don’t look — *Unbelievable.* A

full erection strained the worn denim of his jeans.

"Jackson." Before things could get completely out of hand, Alani pushed up and away from him. "Be right back."

She heard Jackson groan as she more or less fled the room.

When she returned minutes later with the aspirin, a cola and a sandwich, Jackson looked to be sleeping again. He had his head back, one forearm over his eyes, his body relaxed.

She wasn't fooled; he still had an erection, so she knew he was wide-awake. "Here you go."

Lowering the arm, he tracked her every move as she set the plate of food on the coffee table and sat down beside him to hand him the aspirin.

He eyed the glass of ice and foaming cola. "You open a new can?"

"Yes."

He didn't accept the aspirin. Showing his teeth in the semblance of a smile, he said, "Let's strike a bargain."

Given the look in his eyes, Alani already had an idea what he'd say. She had tried to use her time in the kitchen to collect herself. One look at Jackson, and she was lost again. "What kind of bargain?"

He caught her wrist and tugged her toward him. "Kiss me, and I'll take the aspirin."

She wanted to so badly. "Only a kiss?" she asked doubtfully.

"For now."

She hesitated. He didn't.

Taking her lack of denial as agreement, he drew her closer saying, "C'mon now, you can at least give me that."

"I . . ." Was it even possible to resist him? She didn't think so. "All right."

She'd barely gotten the words out before his mouth covered hers in a kiss that was soft, hot.

Deep.

Before she knew it, he had her on her back on the sofa. He still held her wrist as he settled between her legs, pinning her down with his big body. He turned his head for a more complete fit, his tongue moving past her teeth, teasing hers.

Alani quickly lost the fight, already wanting him, needing him — and he freed her mouth.

Balanced over her, he dragged in a breath. "I'm coming on too strong."

"Yes." But she actually liked it.

He sawed his teeth together. "Just so you know, honey. You can trust me. No means no to me. If you say it —"

"I will."

Panting, he pushed up on stiffened arms and said, "Give me the damn aspirin." But he didn't wait for her. He took them from her hand, tossed them back and reached for the drink. After downing half the glass, he plunked it back to the coffee table and stared at her. "We going for round two?"

"Round two?"

He gave one sharp nod. "You want me to eat, you gotta kiss me again."

Forget bargains. His obvious need made everything else unimportant. Already reaching for him, she said, "Okay."

His eyes blazed. He lowered himself to her.

And a knock sounded on her front door.

Alani went stiff with apprehension.

Jackson cursed under his breath.

The knock sounded again, more urgent this time, and then she heard the unmistakable sound of a key in the lock.

Ohmigod. That had to be her brother; no one else had a key to her place. She shoved frantically at Jackson's shoulders. "Jackson, move!"

On a ragged groan, he started to do just that — and the door opened.

They both swiveled their heads.

Not only her brother stood there, but

Dare, too. Both men froze.

Alani's heart shot into her throat. She was trying to think of what to say, how to ease the awkwardness, when Jackson sat up and pulled her into his side.

As if awkward situations didn't faze him at all, he said, "I'd shoot you both for rotten timing, but I guess we had to do this sooner or later."

His face drawn from his surprise, his eyes narrowed and his demeanor mean, Trace slammed the door. "Yeah," he said, and he started forward. "Let's do this now."

Jackson was more than a little amazed when, before he could even decide if he wanted to face off with Trace or not, Alani jumped up to stand in front of him. She spread her slim arms wide and braced her feet apart. "Knock it off, Trace. Right now."

Furious, Trace drew up short. "I *knew* you were fibbing when you told me you were at the movies."

"Sorry about that." Alani squirmed in guilt. "I just . . . I needed some time."

"So I see."

Brows climbing high, Dare leaned around Trace to see Jackson. "She's protecting you?"

Suffering his own surprise, Jackson settled

back into the couch. "Guess so."

With his first good look at Jackson, Dare recoiled. "Jesus, man. You look like —"

"Shit. I know." He caught Alani's waist and plunked her down . . . right into his lap. Her backbone went stiff, probably from shock at his daring.

To her brother, he said, "Get a grip, Trace. We need to talk."

Held back by Alani's displeasure and probably his own sense of fair play, Trace locked his jaw. "It hardly needs explanation."

" 'Fraid it does."

Stiffening even more, Alani gasped and jerked around to face him. "Don't you *dare*."

Her appalled tone quadrupled Dare and Trace's curiosity. Trace asked, "Don't dare do what?"

Jackson didn't want to embarrass her, so it was with a lot of regret that he said reasonably, "They have to know, honey."

"Jackson . . ." she warned.

"One of you better spit it out," Dare said. "My imagination is in hyperdrive."

"I think someone drugged me."

Dare and Trace pulled back. "Well, hell," Dare said. "Didn't see that one coming."

Alani tried to leave him, but Jackson held

on, and short of causing a scene, she couldn't.

Trace, never one to miss a thing, glared.

Dare sat on the edge of the chair, patience personified. "All right, let's hear it."

Alani struggled anew, and that prodded Trace's anger. In a deadly whisper, he ordered, "Let her go."

His deadly whispers didn't faze Jackson. "Not happening."

Trace started forward.

And just that quick, Alani stopped fighting him and instead went back to defending him. "Stop right there, Trace! I mean it."

Trace pulled up short, his left eye twitching.

No sense in dragging this out and making it worse, Jackson decided. "I woke up this morning with —"

"Jackson!"

"— Alani in bed with me."

A collective breath-holding took place. Hell, he could almost hear heartbeats, it got so damn quiet. Jackson looked at Dare and then Trace.

Giving Alani a slight hug, he said, "Thing is, I have no recollection at all of getting her there."

Beyond their slack-jawed surprise, neither Dare nor Trace reacted.

Jackson shrugged. "For a few hours this morning I was sick as hell, seeing double, light-headed, weak."

Alani looked guilty, probably because she'd stormed out on him. But he understood her reaction. Always, whenever he'd considered getting her under him, he'd thought in terms of gentleness, easing her into things, showing deference to her lack of experience and the trauma of her past.

Had he been gentle with her? God, he hoped so, because her proverbial "morning after" sure had sucked. It'd been memorable — for being so awful.

Jackson hugged her again. Of course Dare and Trace both noticed.

"All I can think is that someone drugged me, but I don't know who would do that, or how or why. Far as I can remember, I spent the day working on my house." The place was livable but far from complete, so he preferred to stay in his current residence still. His plan had been to get Alani involved, using her expertise as a professional decorator. Whether she'd accepted it or not, he knew the sexual spark was there between them, and time together, alone, would only work in his favor.

But now . . . hell, he could maybe use the plan to soften her up after whatever had transpired yesterday.

"You see anyone while you were working?"

Jackson shook his head. "Not that I can remember."

Silence reigned.

Since Alani burned with embarrassment and Trace looked lethal, Dare took over.

"If you were drugged, it could've been Rohypnol. Easy enough to slip that into a drink. It's a sedative, so it could make you sick, and it can cause that amnesiatic effect."

Jackson's brain throbbed even more. "A date-rape drug? Seriously?"

Alani panicked. "We need to take him to the hospital!"

"No." Jackson held her when she started to stand. He had no intention of getting on anyone's radar. When he found out who had done this, he'd handle it himself, without the interference of local officials.

"Don't be an idiot," Alani told him with venom.

"Too late," Trace said.

Jackson ignored the insult. He got where Trace was coming from. Alani's brother didn't like being blindsided with the idea that his baby sister was in a sexual relationship. Understandable.

Jackson only wished he could remember

the sexual relationship.

Again, Dare interceded. "I'm not sure the hospital would do him much good, hon. Urine screens don't look for Rohypnol. A blood test would be better but usually hospital labs don't have the equipment to screen for it, so it'd have to be a send-out — and that takes time."

"And by then, I'll be fine," Jackson told her. He ran his hands up and down her arms, hoping to reassure her. "I'm already feeling better, in fact." A lot better, given how she'd kissed him, how quickly she'd melted once he got his mouth on hers.

Soon as he could get rid of Dare and Trace, he'd show her how great he felt.

Course, he needed to get it together. He absolutely couldn't continue the hot and heavy relentless pursuit. Alani could take it as a lack of respect, maybe think he only wanted one thing from her, when in fact, he wasn't sure how much he wanted.

Sex, definitely. Conversation, sure. He wanted to protect her, and he wanted her to trust him. What all that meant, he couldn't say. He refused to jump the gun and mire himself in emotional restraints.

Once he had her, he'd be able to regroup and become a gentleman again. Maybe. With the way she pushed all his buttons, he couldn't be sure —

Alani fretted. "I don't know . . ."

"If we're assuming he was given a roofie, then he can ride it out," Dare told her.

"Well . . ." She looked at Jackson again, full of soft concern and maybe even caring. "Okay."

Trace shook his head in disgust. "It wasn't really up to you, Alani."

No, it wasn't. Never would Jackson let a woman dictate to him. It wasn't in his nature. But to soften that reality, he said, "Trust me, Alani, I'm okay."

Her censuring gaze swept the room. "As if any of you would admit to needing help."

Dare took that as her agreement. "Great, then that's settled. Now on to the rest." He gave Alani a pointed look. "You spent the night with him?"

Her chin went up. "Yes."

"What time did you get to his place?"

At the no-nonsense questioning and lack of condemnation — at least from Dare — she calmed a little. "Around dinnertime yesterday."

"He was okay when you got there?"

"He was . . ." She glanced at Jackson, lifted a shoulder. "I suppose so. That is, he seemed a little off, but still —"

Trace suddenly lost it. With disbelief, he

said, "*Jackson,* Alani? Really?"

She shouted right back, "Yes, *really.*"

"Without a single date? Without a damn clue? Or is that something you've kept from me?"

"No!" Then she flushed and cast a harassed look at Jackson. "That is . . ."

"He knows what it is, honey." Not about to let her brother badger her into ending things before he even had a chance to figure out what he wanted, Jackson narrowed his eyes. "Get used to it, Trace."

Dare held up a hand. "Do you think we could keep it civil so we can figure out what happened?"

Jackson shrugged. "Fine by me." Never mind that he'd been slipped a mickey, that his head still pounded and his strength hadn't completely returned. Alani was a warm, soft weight on his lap.

With every breath, he inhaled the unique perfume of her body. For the first time ever, he was able to stroke his fingers through her long blond hair, as he did right now. He could touch her skin, kiss her — and he did, lifting her delicate hand to brush his mouth over her knuckles.

She shivered, but otherwise tried to pretend the kiss meant nothing.

Trace looked apoplectic, but what the

hell? Jackson couldn't stop himself. Her brother was damn lucky he hadn't already thrown him out so that he and Alani could get back to business.

But then again, why kick Trace out when his presence goaded Alani into showing her true feelings?

At any other time, having a woman — having *anyone* — act protective would insult the hell out of him. He could damn well face any problem head-on without help; he'd been doing it all his life. He didn't need anyone shielding him.

But Alani wasn't just any woman. She was special, so he relished this new twist. It beat the hell out of her telling him "no" any day.

Dare said to Trace, "Well?"

"Fine. But let's get on with it."

"Stop rushing him. He's been through enough."

Jackson hid his grin. When he'd first met Alani, he'd known she wasn't the faint-hearted flower her brother made her out to be. Sure, she was a delicate little thing, especially compared to his height and physicality. But she had the same strength of character, the same conviction, stubbornness and independence as Trace.

Losing their parents young had to have been rough. But Trace had overcompensated. He'd sheltered Alani more than she needed, pampered her beyond reason.

And then she'd been taken by human traffickers, and . . .

Jackson put his arms around her and pressed his face into her neck. He hadn't known her then, but he couldn't think about it without wanting to kill men who were already dead.

Mistaking his reaction for something altogether different, Alani touched his hair with a gentle hand. "Jackson, are you okay? Do you feel sick again? We can put off the inquisition until later, if you need more time."

Trace growled in annoyance.

"He's fine, Alani." Dare gave Jackson a pointed look until he sat up straight again. "But he won't be if he doesn't start explaining soon."

"Can't." Knowing more discussion would embarrass Alani further, but seeing no help for it, Jackson rolled a shoulder. "All I remember is finding Alani in my bed. I was wasted, she walked out on me, and that's all I know. You're going to have to grill her for the nitty-gritty." And maybe in the bargain, he'd find out a few things, too.

Her elbow came back sharp and hard into his ribs. *So much for her concern.*

Trace's face went red. Jackson knew he wanted to curse, but he tried hard to curb his language around his sister.

"Then it's up to you, hon," Dare said to Alani. "Did you notice anything off, anything different, when you went to his place?"

Alani licked her lips. "Actually, I did." She cast a furtive glance at Jackson.

"He acted different? Drugged?" Trace asked. "And you still slept with him?"

She glared at her brother. "No. That is, other than seeming somehow . . . more sincere —"

"I was ever insincere?" Jackson asked her.

"Will you all stop interrupting?"

Dare encouraged her, saying, "Go on, Alani."

With an effort, she gathered herself. "Jackson mostly seemed the same as always. Cocky, flirting, trying to charm the pants off every woman."

Trace said, "I don't need to hear this."

"I don't mean *me*." But then she added, a little abashed, "Well, yes — me, too — I guess."

Jackson gave her another squeeze.

"But I was talking about his neighbor."

Everyone spoke at once, with Dare asking, "What neighbor? A woman?" and Trace saying, "You saw him flirting with her and still you stayed?"

Jackson announced, "I don't flirt with my neighbors."

Still on his lap, Alani raised a hand to quiet them all and then twisted to face Jackson. "I was going to tell you about this, but I wanted you to eat first."

"He doesn't need to be babied," Trace grumbled.

"You be quiet!"

Her outburst left Trace bemused — and silent.

Hoping to calm her, to be a contrast to Trace's animosity, which wasn't winning him any points with Alani, Jackson bit back his automatic rebellion against her concern. "He's right, honey. I keep telling you I'm fine."

She turned back to Jackson. "You were really sick."

"Yeah." He pulled her closer to whisper, "Otherwise we'd still be in bed right now."

Though he couldn't have heard, Dare said, "Knock it off, Jackson. You're wasting valuable time."

Grim, Jackson said, "The only female neighbor I talk with much is Mrs. Guthrie, but she has to be sixty."

Alani shook her head. "I assumed she was a neighbor because she was barefoot."

The men all shared a look. If she'd been barefoot, maybe it was for the sake of stealth.

"But I didn't watch her leave," Alani explained, "so I don't know where she went after she walked out your door. Maybe she wasn't a neighbor. Maybe she was a . . . a date."

Unable to think of any woman he'd have invited to his apartment, Jackson said, "Describe her."

Alani shrugged. "I'd say in her early thirties."

"No."

She frowned. "Being thirty removes her from your radar?"

Not since meeting Alani had he gotten overly involved with anyone. He took care of business and ended it there. Period.

He did not invite any woman into his home.

No way in hell would he admit that to Alani, though, much less in front of Trace and Dare. "I'm just saying I'm not seeing any women in their thirties."

"Short brown hair."

"How short?"

Her face pinched with annoyance. "Pixie cut."

He shook his head — and lifted a long

hank of Alani's silky fair hair to admire it. It was straighter and paler and a whole lot softer than his own. "Nope."

Alani refused to be diverted. "Dresses like a hooker?"

"In her thirties? No." There had been that one broad . . . No. That was ages ago and couldn't even be called a one-night stand. Maybe an hour-long stand . . . He snorted. "Doesn't ring a bell."

"And I suppose you know every woman who lives near enough to drop in?"

"Didn't say that." But, like any other red-blooded male, he'd noted the more attractive ladies. "Hell, if any of my neighbors were good-looking, and if I wasn't expending all my energy chasing you, I still wouldn't go that route."

Dare nodded. "Too close for comfort."

"Exactly."

Alani frowned. "I don't understand."

"Complications," Trace explained as he paced.

Suspicion narrowed her eyes. "What kind of complications?"

"The kind where, after the sex is done and the interest gone, you're stuck with an annoyed woman in close proximity to where you live."

Slowly, taut with judgment, Alani swiveled

around with a dark frown aimed at Jackson.

He said, "Uh . . ." Trace wasn't wrong, but he didn't have to spell it out to her like that.

"Doesn't matter now." Trace saved him by slashing his hand through the air. "Does she sound like anyone you've been with?"

Jackson shook his head. "Nope."

To Alani, Trace asked, "Did you speak to her?"

"Well . . . yes." With renewed annoyance, Alani glared at Jackson again. "She answered your door for you."

Jackson's brows shot up. "Where the hell was I?"

"On the couch." She poked him in the chest. "You were all lounged back, comfortable, your feet up on the coffee table. I was ready to leave since you appeared otherwise involved, but then you got up when you saw it was me at the door, and the woman said she had to go anyway, and . . ."

"Jesus, Alani."

"Don't use that tone with me." She turned her cannon on her brother again. "Did Jackson do anything you haven't done?"

"He was with another woman!"

She started to bolt off Jackson's lap, but when he held on to her hips, she subsided, too anxious to fight her brother to quibble over her position. "So? We didn't have any kind of understanding —"

"We do now," Jackson announced, just in case she'd missed that important fact.

"— and he said he was thrilled to see me."

Whoa. On a gut level, Jackson rejected that wording. "Thrilled?" Sure, he might have been thrilled, but would he really have been that obvious?

Dare grinned, shook his head and repeated, "Thrilled," with clear mockery.

"And that's all it took?" Trace asked.

She strangled on a deep inhale. "Are you calling me easy?"

"No!" Now Trace looked appalled. "Don't put words in my mouth."

"Jackson's sincerity was enough for me to stay. And then . . . well . . ."

They all waited.

"Oh, forget it!" And this time she got away from Jackson. "It happened, okay? Get over it so we can concentrate on the fact that he was *drugged.*"

"No one is forgetting that, hon."

She glared at Dare. "We need to know who she is."

"And if she worked alone," Jackson said.

"Doesn't seem likely." Silently fuming, Trace stepped up close to frown down at Alani. "What about your financier?"

Oh, hell. Jackson had forgotten all about Marc Tobin. Sitting forward, he stated, "That's over." Or at least it better be.

At the same time, Alani said, "I broke things off with him."

Tension washed out of Jackson's shoulders, leaving him with a certain sort of contentment. The persistent throbbing in his temples faded.

Trace looked from Alani to Jackson and back again. "Since when?"

"A little more than a week ago."

A whole week? And she hadn't come to him right away? Damn, had she been grieving over the breakup?

"Did you give him a reason?" Dare wanted to know.

"None of your business."

Trace brought her chin back around. "Sorry, sweetheart. Maybe you don't know how this works, but under the circumstances, we need to hear everything. It's the only way we can really analyze the potential danger."

"You actually think Marc could be involved?"

"He'd have reason to be furious with Jackson — or with you."

Surprise held her silent for a heartbeat before she scoffed. "You think *I'm* in danger?

That's absurd. Jackson is the one who was drugged."

Unable to hide his smirk, Trace said, "Getting all the facts is the only way we can protect Jackson, too."

Oh, now, that burned his ass. "I don't need —"

Before Jackson could finish protesting, Alani faltered. "But . . . Marc wouldn't have had anything to do with —"

"Jackson getting doped? Probably not, so don't get alarmed. But I want you to tell me everything anyway."

Jackson noticed so many things — the way her lips trembled, the new tautness in her shoulders, her pallor and shallow breaths.

"Trace," he said low. "Back off, will you?" Sure, she needed to be sheltered, but scaring her wouldn't accomplish anything.

Trace narrowed his eyes and cupped Alani's shoulder. "Nothing's going to happen to you, honey. This is just a precaution."

She swallowed hard and averted her gaze from one and all. "I told him I was thinking of seeing . . . someone else."

Dare put his elbows on his knees. "You mentioned Jackson to him?"

"No, of course not." She shook her head. "That would have been needlessly rude."

Since Alani was the epitome of graciousness, Trace accepted that explanation. "Did anyone know you were coming to see Jackson yesterday?"

"Jackson knew."

Doing a double take, Jackson asked, "I did?"

"I called you." Her sad smile came and went. "But I suppose you've forgotten that, too. I called you before leaving work."

"Anyone overhear that call?" Dare asked.

"I was in my office, so I doubt it." And then, head high and shoulders back, she turned to leave the room. "I'm going to put on coffee."

"Alani . . ." Knowing the idea of danger had shaken her, Jackson started to stand.

"No." She stopped him by raising an imperious hand. She pointed a finger at the food she'd brought him and gave a succinct order. *"Eat."*

No one gave him orders.

Jackson considered her. She'd left her rich boyfriend in the dust. She'd freely defended him to her brother.

She'd slept with him, whether he remembered it or not.

Overall, he was pretty damn happy with her, so he gave her a salute. "Yes, darlin'. Whatever you say."

Chapter Three

In the kitchen, Alani turned on the radio. Loud.

Accommodating them? Or tuning them out?

Didn't matter. Jackson sat forward. "Let me blow this up your skirt — I've met the bastard."

Dare raised a brow. "Her boyfriend?"

"Her *ex*-boyfriend. And yeah. He knows me, knows my face and first name."

"How the hell did that happen?"

Jackson flagged a hand. "I was chasing her, nothing new in that."

Trace snarled. "And you met him?"

"Yeah. Unless he's dumber than I think, he felt the chemistry between Alani and me." Jackson challenged Trace. "It's there and you know it."

Crossing his arms over his chest, Trace turned to Dare. "Jackson's been dogging her heels for a while now."

Dare looked between them. "You knew about this?"

"Yeah." Letting out a breath, Trace rubbed the back of his neck. "I knew."

"Wasn't a secret," Jackson said. "I told him. But shit's different now."

Deadpan, Dare asked, "You think so?"

Everyone kept their voices low.

"Hell, I was just hoping to get her to redo my place for me so I could get closer to her." Jackson ignored Dare's raised brows and Trace's annoyance. "But that didn't work out, and I figured I was back to square one, and now —"

Trace cut him off. "Jackson was keeping tabs on her, too."

That sounded bad, so Jackson explained. "With what she's been through, I didn't want the financier to do anything to make her uncomfortable."

"Like chase her?" Dare asked.

The taunt put Jackson on edge. "Like pressuring her. And you can bet he did." Could the financier have pressured her more than Jackson had just minutes ago? Shit.

"Why do you assume so?" Dare asked.

"Look at her!" This time Jackson thrust his hand toward the kitchen where, hopefully, Alani couldn't hear them. "She's so smokin' hot, most guys wouldn't be able to help themselves."

Dare choked. "She's the smaller, more female version of Trace."

What an appalling thought. "Not even close," Jackson denied. "You see her like a kid sister, same as Trace does." Sure, they had the same coloring of pale hair and bright hazel eyes. That combo might be noticeable on Trace, but on Alani it was outright striking, fascinating every guy who met her. "I see her differently."

Trace rolled his eyes. "But still you're noble enough to give her space?"

"Uh . . ." He'd thought so. When she'd hesitated to be alone with him, shying away from his interest, he'd walked away rather than torture himself. But this morning he *had* awakened with her naked. And since then, knowing she'd wanted him enough to sleep with him, he'd been on the make big-time.

Trace and Dare waited.

Disgust at his heavy-handed tactics hit Jackson like a ton of bricks. "Butt out, damn it."

"I should just kill you now and be done with it," Trace grumbled.

Jackson ran a hand over his face. "Yeah, maybe."

Dare coughed at that admission. "You trust him, Trace, and you know it."

"With my back," Trace snapped. "Not with my sister."

Shaking his head at them both, Dare said, "Tell me about the meeting you had with the financier."

"His name is Marc Tobin," Trace said.

Jackson curled his lip. Even the guy's name annoyed him. "I dropped in on her, but she was due for a date with the idiot, and I didn't bow out in time."

"Probably on purpose," Trace accused.

Jackson shrugged. So he'd lingered. So what? "He showed up, and you know Alani. Always so polite."

Dare choked. "She introduced the two of you?"

To Jackson's mind, Dare's humor was sadly misplaced. He gave one sharp nod. "Yeah."

"Did you act like an ass?" Trace asked.

"You mean did I pulverize him? Nah." But he'd wanted to. "I'm sure I mean-mugged him a little. He's just so . . . slick, it was hard not to, you know?"

It surprised Jackson when Trace agreed. "Slick, and too rich."

"You're rich," Jackson reminded him.

Dare reached over to slug him in the

shoulder. "Take what you can get, will you?"

He had planned to take Alani — again and again. But now . . . did she need extended time? Lots of space? God, he hoped not.

He peered into the kitchen and saw her stacking mugs on a tray. His guts twisted. Yeah, he had it bad. No other woman had ever made him feel this way. He didn't like it.

Having her would be the only cure. Or rather . . . having her again so he could commit the experience to memory.

"What now?" Ensuring Dare and Trace didn't misunderstand the situation, Jackson added, "She can't be alone."

"I agree." Dare rubbed his chin. "You did a background check on Tobin?"

"From the get-go." Trace leaned up against the wall. "Decent enough person, I guess. Privileged, but no criminal record beyond a few speeding tickets."

Jackson didn't like that assessment. "Every investment he makes turns to gold. I don't trust him."

"She left him," Dare reminded Jackson. And then, "But if he assumes he was dumped for you, then that could be motive enough for us to do a little more digging."

"It makes as much sense as anything." Besides, with nothing else to go on, Jackson wanted Tobin to be responsible. It'd be a quick and easy solution, and it'd permanently remove the competition.

"You think he sent a woman after Jackson, had her drug him . . . for what reason? To get him in bed so that Alani would walk away?" Trace gave Jackson a verbal kick, saying, "Hell, he always screws everything in sight, and still she went to him."

Jackson stewed. "Wrong." He was no more active than any other healthy adult. And since meeting Alani . . . well, he hadn't been all that *healthy*, no matter how a woman looked or how willing she might be.

He wanted Alani.

He'd had her, damn it, and from what she'd said, it was as mind-blowing as he'd always known it would be.

"You know how it is, Trace." Dare ignored Jackson's denial. "That just makes him more appealing to some women."

"Maybe." Trace gave Jackson an evil grin. "But not to Alani."

Knowing Trace might be right, Jackson picked up the sandwich and took a healthy bite. She wanted him to eat, so he'd eat.

Done tweaking him, Trace paced. "Doesn't matter now anyway. Whoever drugged him likely saw Alani at his place."

"So she's in the thick of it," Dare agreed,

"no matter how we look at it."

Around the mouthful of food, Jackson said, "I don't want to scare her, especially since odds are she's in the clear." He swallowed, a plan forming in his mind. "If she lets me stick close, then there's no reason her life has to be more disrupted than it already has been."

"You can watch her up close," Dare said, "while Trace and I start investigating things from the outside."

"And that being the case, you should have called us right away." Trace's temper shot up again. "Christ, was she left alone at any point today?"

Jackson winced. "All morning." Alone, saddened — and vulnerable. There really wasn't a good excuse for slipping up, not with Alani's safety on the line. "Thanks to the drugs, I wasn't thinking clearly at first. All I knew was that I'd missed out on —" he looked at Trace's set face and censored his words "— some important stuff. Soon as I could, I got ready and came here. Right about the time my head cleared enough for me to realize all the implications, she showed back up."

"And still you didn't get hold of us?"

"Yeah, about that . . ." Jackson hedged a little. "I was going to — right after I smoothed things out with Alani."

That got Trace's attention anew. "What's there to smooth out?"

Another peek in the kitchen showed Alani standing in front of the sink, her arms around her middle as she stared out the window.

As if she felt his stare, she glanced over her shoulder. Their gazes locked, and for him, it felt like a physical connection. Even from a distance, he saw her breathing deepen, her cheeks flush, the slight part of her lush lips, so maybe it felt the same for her.

Jackson's eyes narrowed — and Alani turned away to fetch the now full coffee carafe.

A deep breath didn't really help. She rattled him when nothing else did.

"Okay, look." Jackson squared off with both men. "Under normal circumstances, I would never discuss this with anyone, not even you two."

Discussing it with them now didn't feel right, either, but with Alani's safety potentially at risk, they had to know it all. Trace was right about that.

"I told you that I woke with a splitting headache, that I spent the first hour in the bathroom puking up my guts."

They waited.

"Yeah, well . . ." Never, not even if he lived to be a hundred, would Jackson forget that awesome moment when he found her curled comfortably in bed beside him, just as he'd never forget the devastation on her face right before she walked out. "You know as well as I do that Alani's been sheltered. Not sure what she was expecting, but it wasn't what she got. She . . . sort of misunderstood everything."

Confusion brought together Dare's brows. "You explained to her what happened?"

"Not then, no. Hell, I didn't know what had happened." Giving himself a second to organize his thoughts, Jackson took a big drink of the cola. He could use the caffeine kick. "The thing is, my head felt like it had cracked open, and Alani was there, naked." He filled his lungs again, but the tightness in his chest remained. "Those two things together threw me pretty hard. I didn't know which way was up, but I didn't need my brains intact to know I'd probably slept with her. I just didn't know what to do about it."

Trace stared up at the ceiling.

"Stop it, will you?" Dare shoved him. "She's a grown woman."

Jackson nodded. Alani was young but still

mature. The perfect mix of naiveté and ripe sensuality. Independent and yet so incredibly sweet . . .

Problem was, Trace had been playing protector too long. His attention zeroed in on Jackson. "I don't know if I want you seeing her."

In clear warning, Jackson said, "Stay out of it, Trace." No way in hell would he let him get in his way on this.

Trace took a stance and smiled silkily. "Or what?"

"Or you'll deal with me." Alani marched back into the room with a tray of coffee that she set on the table. She appeared resolute and too contained.

Jackson started to stand, but with one hand on his chest, Alani shoved him back to his seat. Surprise kept him from reacting.

Hands on her hips, she faced her brother. "I'll see him if I want to."

Jackson met Trace's furious gaze — and shrugged. Guess that was settled. Her attitude would make protecting her a lot easier, and it would afford him a lot more opportunities to work through the morass of his feelings.

Dare shook his head. "Stop looking so satisfied, Jackson, or he just might kill you."

"No," Alani said as she sat beside Jackson.

"He won't."

Though Trace's left eye twitched again, he didn't lurch toward Jackson. Trace was far too controlled for any lurching. If he wanted to attack Jackson, he would do so swiftly, without warning.

But Jackson wasn't worried about it. Trace might bluster, but he wanted the best for Alani, and right now, that meant having someone capable watching over her 24/7 until they sorted out what had happened.

It couldn't be Trace or Dare. Not only were they both now married, but their constant presence would only alarm Alani more. There'd be no explaining it to her without telling her how risky the situation could be.

So Jackson got dibs, and that suited him just fine.

Trace ran a hand through his hair. "Alani, seriously . . . Are you sure about this?"

Far too solemn, she eyed her brother and Dare. "I'd appreciate it if you two would drink your coffee and then go so that Jackson and I can talk."

Her announcement hit them each in a different way.

Not about to budge, Trace snorted.

Dare merely said, "No can do, hon."

And Jackson put his arm around her. "We

gotta make plans first."

"I have a plan." Spine straight, shoulders stiff, she shrugged off his touch. "I'm going to finish discussing this with you, then you will leave so that I can take a long shower and go to bed early."

Jackson opened his mouth, and she said with emphasis, *"Alone."*

Damn. She sounded cold and distant. Had she overheard them talking? They'd kept their voices low, but in her small house, even with the radio blaring from the kitchen, she might have picked up a word or two. Well, she'd just have to deal with it. But to be sure, Jackson asked, "What's wrong?"

Not only did Alani give him an incredulous look, so did Dare and Trace.

At the end of his rope, Jackson stood and took her hand. "Be right back." He started tugging Alani toward the kitchen.

She held back. "Jackson."

On the ragged edge, he leaned down to nearly touch his nose to hers. "Here or in private, woman. Make up your mind."

Trace took a step forward — and that decided her. She said to her brother and Dare, "Drink your coffee! We won't be long."

And then it was Alani leading the way.

Once in the kitchen, Jackson stepped

around the wall with her for a smidge of privacy. He caged her in with his forearms on the wall at either side of her head.

Staring up at him, she looked small and fragile and very appealing.

He had to taste her.

Murmuring, "I missed you," he kissed her bottom lip, her upper lip, and then he settled in for a soft but deep mating of their mouths.

Her breasts pressed to his ribs, her hands flattening on his chest before sliding up to his shoulders. With a small sound of hunger, she curled her fingers, holding on to him.

Yeah, he liked that. A lot.

He felt her racing breath, her trembling. . . .

"God, woman." With an effort, he freed her mouth but had to return for several more soft, quick pecks. "I don't want to rush you."

She dropped her forehead to his chest with a small, dubious laugh. "Funny, because all you do is rush me."

"Yeah, I know. Sorry." He nudged up her face. "What's wrong? Besides all that confusion from this morning, I mean. You went into the kitchen one way and came back another. What did you think about in here?"

"Everything."

That didn't sound promising. "Start with one thing, and we'll get to the others."

"Okay." She smoothed a hand over his chest, inadvertently inciting his lust; when Alani touched him, he felt it everywhere. "You want to go on like yesterday happened."

No woman had ever left him this confused. And horny. At the moment mostly confused. No, mostly . . . it didn't matter. "Yesterday *did* happen."

"But you don't remember it." Her eyes full of entreaty with an edge of uncertainty, she gazed up at him. "I want to be honest with you."

"Honesty is good." Because he honestly knew that she wanted him, too.

"It's disturbing that I can't think of anything else, but you can't even remember it." She looked down at his sternum, and her voice dropped to a husky whisper. "I still feel you, Jackson."

A bombardment of emotions took his breath. "Yeah?"

"I'm tender in places that I've never noticed before."

Ah, hell. Hearing that stirred him anew. He nuzzled her ear. "Like where?"

"You know where."

His muscles clenched. In a near growl, he

insisted, "Tell me anyway."

She hesitated, then nodded. "My thighs are shaky."

"I was rough with you?"

"No. You . . . you were exuberant."

Heat rose inside him. "Where else?"

Voice lower, filled with shyness, she admitted, "My breasts still feel full, and my . . ."

He bent to see her face. "Nipples?" Just talking to her was more exciting than sex with other women. He badly wanted to cover her breasts with his hands, to touch her, to draw her into his mouth and test how tender she might be.

Tilting back from her, he looked at the soft white swells above the top of her sundress. Putting a tight leash on his need, he trailed one fingertip over the top of each breast.

With her accelerated breaths, her flesh shimmered.

Slowly, with hot intent, he drifted his open hand over the front of the dress, cupped her right breast and gently circled the taut nipple with his thumb.

She gasped; her hands clutched at him.

His gaze sought hers. "They're sensitive?"

Long lashes fluttered as she closed her eyes and drew a shuddering breath through parted lips. "Very."

It'd be so easy to take her. Hell, even with her brother and Dare in the other room, she melted for him. He could put his hand up the skirt of her dress, inside her panties. He could cup that warm, wet peach, and she'd be coming in minutes.

Jackson fought himself. She trusted him. And she'd been through enough.

He couldn't stop himself from catching her nipple, giving one small tug that made her tremble and bite her bottom lip. *"Jackson . . ."*

"I know." He slipped his arms around her, easing her closer so that her head fit to his shoulder and her breasts pressed to his chest. He was so turned on, his dick threatened to rip apart the zipper of his jeans. "Better?"

The sound she made affected him like a hot lick. "I've never been this way. Last night was a revelation for me." Her hands knotted in his shirt. "And you don't even know what happened."

"I know I'm going to have you again. I know I'm going to be inside you, feeling you all nice and wet, slick and hot, and you're going to hold on to me while you come —"

To silence him, she touched his mouth, then took a few seconds to collect herself.

"For you, what we did, what happened between us, might not even be real."

Oh, it was real all right. He took her wrist, kissed her palm and carried her hand back to his chest. "You can't deny what's between us."

"No, I won't. But we both know that sometimes sex talk doesn't mean anything." She pushed back to look at him. "Men say things in the moment just because they want to sleep with a woman."

Waiting for a response to that death-trap statement, she watched him.

What the hell had he said to her last night?

He chewed the side of his mouth but gave up with a shrug. "Sometimes, yeah, maybe."

She looked down at her hands. "When they think sex is of utmost importance."

"That covers every minute that I'm around you, because when I see you, I want to be inside you."

"Jackson . . ."

"I'm obsessed," he admitted and meant it. If he just wanted sex, he could have it. He hadn't lacked for female attention since his late teens. Hell, if he wanted an orgy he could have it.

But he wanted Alani.

"Don't you see?" Not giving him a chance to muck it up with more drama, she went on. "Maybe if you knew the things you'd said, if you . . . remembered everything we'd done, you wouldn't even care about . . ."

"Having you again?" He tunneled his fingers into her baby fine hair, curving his hands around her head, lifting her face so he could see into her eyes. "Not a chance in hell, honey. Having you a dozen times wouldn't put a dent in my appetite. Not for *you.*"

The corners of her mouth quivered into an uncertain show of amusement. "Well, you sound confident enough about that, but I'm not." She licked the smile away from her lips. "So . . . I think we should start over."

The groan was there, fighting to come out, but Jackson swallowed it back and tried not to look predatory. "Start over . . . where?" If she meant all the way back to square one, he'd get her alone ASAP and show her that once wasn't enough, not for either of them, and to hell with what her brother and Dare thought about it.

She toyed with the front of his shirt, smoothing it and stroking him again in the bargain. His muscles twitched.

So did his cock.

His heart followed suit when she looked up at him with her big golden eyes. "I'm sorry, Jackson, but I can't jump back into bed with you."

That did it. He groaned.

"I *can't*." In a rush, she explained, "Not when you don't remember how we got there."

But he wanted to know. He wanted the memory of how she looked, the sounds she made at every small surrender, he wanted to watch her get hotter and hotter until she lost it, until she screamed out a climax. So . . . "We have to get there again? That's what you're saying?"

"Yes."

Huh. Well, that might be fun. He loved a challenge, and knowing he'd already won her over would make it easier. As long as she gave him an opportunity, as long as Tobin remained out of the picture, he didn't mind charming her anew.

Needing clarification, he held her face tipped up to his. "I need to make up one day, not the past months, right?"

Nodding, she looked at his throat, his chin, and her other hand lifted to touch him, too. "I woke up this morning already wanting you, and I haven't stopped wanting you since."

A full-blown boner made idle conversation tough. Trying to relieve the pressure in his jeans, he shifted, but nothing short of touching her would help. He leaned into her, letting her feel his erection and affording himself a modicum of relief against her soft body.

He growled low and kissed her throat. "I can work with that."

"It's not too much to ask?"

"Nah." To stay on course, he'd have to take the edge off, and soon. Tricky, given that he had no intentions of leaving her side. But he'd figure it out. "Be warned, woman, I'm going to enjoy getting you there again."

From the other room, Trace said, "Jackson, I will kill you."

Alani flushed. "Ohmigod." And in a panicked whisper, "Has he been listening to us?"

By the minute, Jackson felt more like himself, so he couldn't help but grin, especially with Alani turning so pink. "He can't hear anything." He smoothed her hair, touched her warm cheek. "He's just guessing at what's going on."

She groaned. "That's worse."

Maybe. Since Trace knew Jackson, he probably had a good idea of things. A little louder, so Trace was sure to hear, he said, "It's none of his damned business."

She surprised Jackson by smothering a

laugh. "Surely you don't think that will stop him?"

"Probably not." He knew what he was in for. But what she apparently didn't know was that, because Trace was overprotective, he would never be satisfied seeing his sister with a man who wasn't his equal.

Jackson fit the bill.

And despite all the bluster, Trace wasn't blind; he knew Alani was a grown woman, able to make her own decisions.

Right now, she was safer with Jackson than without him.

"Now that we've got that settled, what else?"

She bit her lip, and shook her head.

"You said there were other things bothering you."

"I know." She slipped her arms around him in a brief hug that he felt clean to his soul. "But we've been in here too long already. We'll talk about the rest later, when we don't have an interested audience waiting on us."

As if on cue, Trace said, "I'm counting to ten."

Enjoying the contact of their mingling heartbeats, how right and natural it seemed, Jackson said, "Ignore him."

"You're not worried about his reaction to

all this?"

He snorted. "Nah. Why would I be?"

After giving him a squeeze, she leaned away with a smile. "God, Jackson. What am I going to do with you?"

"That's the fun part, honey. As long as you're not pushing me away, you can do anything you want."

Chapter Four

Walking back in to face her brother and Dare was nearly painful. They weren't exactly condemning her, but Dare watched her with that quiet scrutiny that was so much a part of him, now sharpened with curiosity, too.

Had Dare ever seen her as a sexual being? Probably not. She hadn't even seen herself that way, especially not since the kidnapping to Tijuana. That, more than any other reason, had accounted for her problems with Marc. He wanted what she couldn't give . . . or rather, what she couldn't give until Jackson, until last night, until she'd discovered her own carnal nature.

Her brother . . . well, in any other circumstance, she would find Trace's behavior amusing. It wasn't often that she got to see him disconcerted. Even before their parents had died, he'd been an Alpha male in every way, taking charge of everything and everyone, always cool, always a rock.

But now, with the realization that her nightmare could be starting all over again, humor remained well out of Alani's reach.

As Jackson sat down, he brought her with him, ensuring she stayed close to his side. His hold was comforting but also intrinsically possessive.

Did it mean anything?

Giving him a subtle nudge with her elbow, she complained in an aside, "I'd prefer a little more discretion, please."

He kissed her ear. "Sorry." He loosened his hold, but didn't let her go completely.

And she was glad.

Dare and Trace watched their every move. Never had she envisioned her private life being made so public. Jackson didn't seem to mind, but she couldn't bear it.

"This is ridiculous." She wanted them both to leave so she could put Jackson back to bed — to *sleep.* He needed to recoup after his ordeal, and she wanted to be the one to take care of him. Usually he was so capable, so strong. This might be her only chance, her only excuse for keeping him close.

With all three men underfoot, she couldn't get her emotions in check. The dual assault of wanting Jackson again so badly, juxtaposed against the thrumming fear of danger, left her more flustered than usual.

She tried a direct look that came off weak at best. "If you two have finished your coffee . . . ?"

Dare half smiled at her obvious hint and lifted his cup for another sip.

Trace hadn't bothered with coffee. He crossed his arms over his chest. "Are you kicking out all of us, or just Dare and me?"

Short of admitting that she wanted to take advantage of Jackson's predicament, what could she do other than protest? "You're overstepping, Trace."

"Not the first time."

She stared at him, and he relented enough to say, "Until we sort this out, I don't think it's a good idea for you to be alone."

Jackson ran his fingertips down her spine. "Put your brother's mind at ease, honey. Tell him I can stick around for the night."

For the night? Oh, for pity's sake. Sure, she realized that she might have stumbled into things, but they were stretching it. Rather than admit that she wanted Jackson to stay, she said, "I promise I will be extra careful."

"Not good enough." Dare set aside his coffee. "You don't have the right skills to recognize a possible problem."

Her smile hurt. "Believe me, being kidnapped more than drove home that point for me." At her self-deprecating tone, each of them froze with uncertainty. It was almost amusing, given how big and skilled and dangerous they could be.

Knowing the way they thought, she continued, "It makes no sense that anyone would want to hurt me. Jackson was the one drugged." She held up a hand. "But yes, I realize that if that woman had anything to do with him being drugged, then she saw my face and she heard Jackson call me by name."

"It's a long shot," Jackson told her. "But why take any chances?"

Trace moved to stand over her. "It's also possible someone knew you would be at his place, and that's why Jackson got drugged in the first place."

Dear God. She hadn't even considered that. Had he been drugged so that someone could get to her? Had she inadvertently put Jackson in danger? Thinking aloud, she said, "I called him from my cell —"

Trace asked, "Not your office phone?"

"No."

Dare stood. "Where is it?"

"My purse." She nodded toward the kitchen. "In there."

Dare left the room to get it.

Jackson had been too quiet. She glanced at him, and got caught in his intent stare.

Overly gentle, he reached out to tuck her hair behind her ear. "I don't want you to worry, Alani. No one is going to hurt you."

Because people had already hurt her, an invisible fist squeezed her lungs. It took so little to alarm her.

Nothing really new in that. Since escaping Tijuana, she hadn't really stopped being afraid. Sometimes she hid it well, and sometimes . . . sometimes it woke her in the middle of the night, a scream burning her throat, her face wet with tears.

Swallowing down the shame of cowardice, she nodded. "I know." And then, hopefully with more strength, "So what now?"

Trace and Jackson shared a look. Jackson took her hand. "For about a dozen or more reasons, I'm hoping you'll let me hang around. If Trace wasn't leg-shackled —"

"Leg-shackled?" Sidetracked, Alani gave a laugh that sounded far too forced. "Priss would get you for that."

Jackson showed his teeth in a wicked grin. "Yeah, she'd probably try." He quickly held up a hand toward her brother. "Don't hit me, Trace. I'm not a hundred percent, so it wouldn't be fair. Besides, you know Priss is always on the fence about whether or not she likes me."

Trace sawed his teeth together. "Shut up about it."

Under most situations, her brother was the personification of icy calm.

When it came to his wife, Priscilla . . . not so much.

But then, given that Jackson, in the course of a rescue from intruders, had taken Priss naked from the shower, Alani understood why it nettled Trace.

After a tense silence, her brother reined in his anger to address her. "Do you have any appointments you need to cancel?"

Avoiding a direct answer, she said, "I usually work every day." She couldn't help but resist the idea of having her life turned upside down again.

Jackson turned her toward him. "You can still keep your appointments, but how about I tag along? Just as an extra precaution."

"But . . ." Okay, she got the need for vigilance. But would it never end?

Dare strode back in, still holding Alani's phone. "Do you need to jot down any of your saved numbers before I turn it off?"

"Why would you —"

"Cells can be traced. For now, Jackson can set you up with a prepay. Use it if you

have to make a call. Otherwise, just use your landline."

"For now," Trace reiterated. "Just till we rule out a few things."

Alani wilted. Surely they were overreacting. But the last thing she wanted was for any of them to know how cowardly she felt about it all. "I know the numbers I call often, and customer numbers are in my files."

Trace walked over to stand in front of her, then held out a hand. "My turn."

Ripe with mistrust, Jackson caught her arm to detain her. "Your turn for what?"

Good Lord, Jackson sounded confrontational. He might not worry about Trace's temper, and she trusted that he could fend for himself, but a physical confrontation between the two of them would be too ugly to contemplate.

She slipped away from Jackson and stood by her brother. "Be right back," she started to say, but Trace was already tugging her away.

He urged her all the way across the floor and out the back door to the patio. Through the kitchen window she could see Jackson craning his neck to look after them, his expression dark, dangerous.

Did he think Trace would steal her away?

From her own home? He was every bit as protective as her brother, and, unsure how she felt about that, she sighed.

"I think I'm going to puke," Trace said.

Alani slugged Trace in the shoulder — and probably hurt her hand a lot more than she hurt him. "You like Jackson, so stop it."

"I like his work. I don't like this situation, and I sure as hell don't like seeing you so lovesick."

Her knees locked. "Lovesick?"

Trace stared at her, then turned away to grouse before facing her again. "You are in love with him, aren't you?"

Well, shoot. She dampened dry lips. "I never said —"

"You don't have to. I know you, Alani. I can see it." His expression softened. "Dare probably sees it, too."

That thought horrified her. "Do you think —"

"That Jackson knows?" He shook his head. "Not unless you told him. Women always screw up a guy's intuition. You've got him spinning on his ass right now. If he hadn't been drugged, I might actually find it funny."

"I don't know what you're talking about." Jackson seemed as in control as ever.

"Trust me, figuring out women is more of

a challenge than facing off with a lunatic murderer."

Lovely. With false sweetness, Alani asked, "I suppose sisters are excluded from that analogy?"

"It's not at all the same." He cupped a hand over her shoulder and only hesitated a second before getting serious. "It's not going to be easy, you know."

She gave another long sigh. "I know."

"Jackson is . . ."

"Too much like you?" At his surprise, Alani shook her head. "And Dare, too. But I mean that in the nicest way possible."

He gave a fleeting smile before tousling her hair. "Brat." He quickly sobered. "Our line of work complicates relationships in a big way."

"There is that."

"He could be gone long stretches of time when he's on a case."

So Jackson was right — Trace was more accepting of their involvement than she'd realized. "I know."

"And you know you'll worry."

She nodded. "But you're my brother, Trace, so I'm already used to that." There were times when Trace would be gone for weeks — but during those times, he left Dare available to her for emergencies. And always, Alani knew he'd give up a mission if she needed him.

"It'll be different, honey. Believe me."

"Probably." She'd often wondered how Priss and Molly handled it. It was tough enough fretting over a brother, but the added intimacy of a romantic relationship would sharpen everything. That is . . . "I don't even know yet if it'll be an issue." Because she didn't know how Jackson really felt about her. "Everything is pretty up in the air right now."

The confessions he'd made last night no longer counted.

"You'll give him a chance to clear up the problems?"

"If you mean will I let him stick around, yes." She'd wanted to do that anyway, and this was as good an excuse as any.

Trace took in her expression with dark concern. "Do you know what you're doing?"

"Not really, no." She flashed him a smile. "Do you think Priss knew?"

At the mention of his wife, Trace scowled and rubbed his ear. "Probably." He dropped his hand and laughed. "At least, more than I did, because she always seemed to be a step ahead of me."

Alani had probably gotten the censored

version of their story, but she knew they'd both gone undercover at the same time, after the same person, and each had a specific agenda that didn't always mesh with the other's. Along the way, Priss had turned her control-freak brother upside down.

Spinning on his ass?

Yes, that aptly described it. "And what about Molly?"

His humor faded. "No. After all she'd been through, Molly was badly shaken. She was always practical, but at a loss how to get on with her life."

Alani remembered it well; she and Molly were both taken by the same people. They'd shared the same small, cramped confinement with other women. Stuffy air, chains, filth, fear and desolation . . .

Whereas she'd been too terrified to breathe, Molly had been brazen, arguing with their captors, defying them at every turn. To this day, it made Alani shudder to think of it. "She was so brave."

Probably knowing she drew unfavorable comparisons, Trace pulled her into a tight hug. "Molly handled it differently from you, that's all. And Dare always knows what he's doing, so he helped her work it out."

Alani didn't want to think about the awful kidnapping or the new danger presenting itself, so instead she concentrated on Jackson. "I don't know where things will go from here, but I'm not dumb." Not anymore. Last night . . . temporary insanity? That excuse worked for her. "I don't want you to worry about me. Jackson would never hurt me physically, and I'm the only one responsible for my emotions."

Trace kissed the top of her head. "All right. But if at any point you want me to stomp him, let me know."

He said that with relish, helping to lighten her mood. "He's not a slouch, you know. He might surprise you."

"Nope. I already know Jackson can handle himself. If not, he wouldn't be working with Dare and me, and no way in hell would I rely on him to keep you safe."

She skipped over the issue of her safety to say, "So you admit he's a lot like you?"

Slinging an arm around her shoulders, Trace said, "Why do you think I'm so worried?" Without giving her a chance to reply, he led her back into the house.

Alani hoped the discussions were now at an end so she could see to Jackson.

With the others out of the room, Dare spent his time eyeballing Jackson, irking him until Jackson stopped watching for Alani and instead barked, *"What?"*

Dare nodded at his crotch. "You really ought to get that under control."

Jackson looked down, saw he still had an obvious jones, and cursed. "It's a unique situation." Alani was a unique woman. He dropped a throw pillow over his lap. "Can't you drag Trace out of here?"

"Doubtful, but I'm not even going to try. At least, not until we have things settled."

Through his teeth, Jackson said, "You guys are making her more nervous than she needs to be. I can handle it."

Dare gave him a long, sober look. "Why do I doubt that you're thinking straight?"

"My brains aren't in my dick, damn it." Sure, lust left him tense. But Alani's safety would always be his number one priority. "I wouldn't let anything happen to her."

Unfazed, Dare shrugged. "Trace is her brother. I'm a pseudo-brother. Until we know what's happening, no one is budging." And then, as Trace and Alani walked back in, Dare stood, too. "All done?"

Alani said, "Yes," and started to sit by Jackson again.

He was just reaching for her when Dare caught her elbow. "Great. Now it's my turn."

Frustration pushed Jackson over the edge.

He shot to his feet. "This is bullshit!" He did not want Dare and Trace filling her head with reasons to run from him. "Let's roll credits on the drama already."

At his raised voice, Trace's muscles bunched up. "Watch your mouth in front of my sister."

"She's not a damn china doll."

Alani started to speak, but Trace didn't give her a chance. "You'll treat her with respect."

Jackson stiffened. He wasn't going to explain himself to her brother. What was between them was private — and he wanted to get back to it, damn it. But he wouldn't keep putting up with Trace's animosity, either. "You think I don't?"

Dare tugged Alani along. "Let's leave them to it, hon, okay?"

And Alani, left with little choice in the matter, again walked away.

"This is insane." Jackson dropped back down on the couch and glared at Trace. "You two will wear her out with all this covert chitchat, back-and-forth nonsense."

"You'll both survive."

Jackson wasn't at all sure about that. If they talked Alani into keeping her distance from him, he'd detonate. Trying to hide his tension, Jackson said more calmly, "What the hell did you say to her, anyway? And why couldn't you say it right here in the comfort of her living room?"

Pensive, silent, Trace leaned against the wall.

Jackson stewed until he couldn't hold it in. "And what the hell does Dare have to do with anything? He's not even her damn brother."

Eyes narrowing, Trace suffered him in silence.

With nothing more to do, and Trace being a bore, Jackson poured himself another cup of coffee.

He had just taken a sip when Trace said, "I assume you haven't told her everything."

What the hell could he tell her when he didn't remember even a smidge of the night? "What's that?"

Pushing away from the wall, Trace stood beside the chair Dare had vacated. "There are things about you, Jackson, added responsibilities that Alani's unaware of. Or have you told her about Arizona?"

Oh. That. *Shit.* "Not yet, no."

"I didn't think so."

As always when discussing Arizona, heat crawled up his neck. Half under his breath, Jackson said, "Haven't really had much chance for talking, not with you two hanging around, making her think the world is coming to an end." And besides, what woman would understand about Arizona? He sure as hell didn't want to shoot himself in the foot this early.

"If that's your way of saying I'm overreacting, Alani is used to my idea of caution. She'd think something more was wrong if I acted any other way."

Maybe he had a point. "If you say so."

"Tell her about Arizona, or I will."

That challenge couldn't go unanswered. Jackson set the cup down with a clatter. "It's my business, Trace." And besides, Trace might think he knew everything about it, but he didn't. Not by a long shot.

"When you're sleeping with my sister, it becomes my business."

Jackson locked his back teeth, but he'd never taken well to ultimatums. "Arizona has nothing to do with her."

"If you care about her, then Arizona has plenty to do with her." Trace crossed his arms over his chest and widened his stance. "And if you don't care, then I'm telling you right now, leave her the hell alone."

Hearing raised voices in the living room left Alani uneasy. She tried to rush back in, but Dare didn't let her.

He caught one of her hands in both of his. “Relax, honey. They’re fine.”

Didn’t sound fine to her. She chewed her bottom lip. “I think they’re arguing.”

Dare shrugged. “So? They’re both reasonable enough. They won’t come to blows.”

If only she had his confidence. She knew that when it came to her, Trace could be more than unreasonable. “All right, but let’s make this quick.” She tried to give Dare her attention, when truthfully, she strained to hear what her brother and Jackson were saying.

“You know I think of you as a little sister.”

“Yes.” And she thought of him as another brother. Dare and Trace had known each other for a very long time. After the death of their parents, Dare had been there, helping them both to cope. He’d been there through all the most important steps in their lives.

She flinched at a particularly loud curse from Jackson.

Insistent on getting her attention, Dare brought her face around to his. “I’m sorry to do this, but Jackson is slammed, and Trace just isn’t himself, so it looks like it’s up to me.”

Given the seriousness of his tone, Alani

almost groaned. "Do I really want to hear this?"

"I brought you out here because I didn't want to embarrass you."

"Too late for that, isn't it?" Already her faux pas — sleeping with a drugged man unaware of his own actions — had been aired to the people closest to her. "All things considered, I don't know how I could be any more embarrassed."

Apologetic, Dare asked, "Did you guys use protection?"

Shock took her back a step. Obviously she hadn't even seen the start of embarrassment yet.

Protection? She wanted to groan. "I . . ." Had they? That first time, yes. Her face heated as she remembered watching Jackson intently roll on a condom. But after that?

Dropping his head forward, Dare muttered to himself. "Don't tell me. It's none of my damn business. But with Jackson drugged, he might not have been thinking right." His probing gaze held hers. "That's the point of a roofie, you know. Complete lack of inhibition."

"I see." Putting a hand over her mouth, Alani racked her brain. Even after that first time, Jackson had remained insatiable, and they'd both been frenzied . . . She couldn't specifically recall the use of condoms.

"I don't suppose you're on the pill?"

She shook her head. "No need." And then she slapped a hand over her mouth, but it was too late. Dare had already absorbed that telling confession.

"Okay then." Dare rubbed her shoulder. "Without asking for details, I'm guessing — under the right circumstances — you might have been a little too inexperienced to pay attention."

"The right circumstances?"

He rubbed her shoulder some more. "Getting carried away and all that."

Her cheeks burned. How could he so easily discuss things so private? Much more of this and she'd be permanently singed. "Things did happen sort of . . . fast."

Dare's mouth quirked. "Not something Jackson would want you to share, hon."

"I don't mean . . . !" More heat flooded into her face, almost making her lightheaded. "That is, the decision to . . . and then again . . . I sort of forgot. . . ."

"I do understand." Dare fought off a grin. "But just in case, it's something the two of you should discuss, don't you think?"

She covered her face with both hands. "This just keeps going from bad to worse."

"Don't jump the gun, okay? Odds are, Jackson took care of it and even if he didn't, it might not be an issue."

She hoped not, because after that first time, she'd simply accepted anything and everything he wanted to do, no questions asked.

"But for future reference . . ." Watching her, Dare said, "I don't suppose you have any condoms here?"

Why would she? Sure, she'd recently turned twenty-four, and most women that age were sexually active. But after her kidnapping . . . No. She'd had no real interest.

Until Jackson.

"No. No, I don't." Even if she'd wanted to jump back in bed with Jackson, it didn't sound plausible. What could she do? Suggest he make a drugstore run first? She already knew he wasn't going to budge from her side, and she definitely wasn't shopping with him.

Putting her shoulders back, she faced Dare. "Is that it, then?" She wasn't sure she could handle any more.

He studied her face. "Jackson knows about you being kidnapped." It was a statement, not a question.

"Yes." She'd first met him when both

Trace and Dare were busy, and they'd put Jackson to the task of watching over her — an unnecessary precaution that neither of them seemed inclined to let go anytime soon. But then, they watched over everyone they cared about.

"Does he know details? Because it occurs to me he might be the right one for you to confide in."

Just the thought of detailing her imprisonment . . . no. She couldn't. It left her stomach queasy and her breathing shallow, her heart tripping and her skin cold.

More than anything, she prayed to just forget about it.

Wrapping her arms around herself, Alani sought to stifle her reaction. She drummed up a pathetic smile. "It's old news, Dare. No reason to rehash it."

"You know, hon, Molly has told me everything." He bent to meet her averted eyes. "It's important to talk about it. I know you're doing okay now, and I know you've moved on. Trace and I are both proud of you."

Absurd. She'd given neither of them reason to be proud.

"But it stays in here." With one finger he touched the center of her chest above her breasts. "And here." He brushed that same fingertip to her temple. "Until you share it."

"I have shared," she tried to say with a straight face. "With you and Trace."

Too astute for his own good, Dare shook his head. "I got you out of there. I understand why talking to me would be too much. And with the way Trace reacted, I know you never wanted to burden him more."

And it would have been a burden. In some ways, though he hid it well, her abduction had been harder on Trace than on her. "He was so distressed that you had to come after me."

"He'd have had a hell of a time keeping me away." Dare cupped the back of her neck, waggling her head in a familiar, friendly way. "But I know what you mean. He wanted to be the one handling things, and if he hadn't already been known to the bastards who took you, he would have been."

But since they had known Trace, the odds of him reaching her had been diminished. Sending Dare had upped her chances of being rescued, but had been oh-so-much-more dangerous for Dare.

Alani swallowed. "If I'd been paying better attention that day at the beach —"

"Then you might not have been taken.

And God only knows what would have happened to Molly."

She jerked her head up to stare at him. Solemn, serious, gaze direct, Dare stared back at her.

"I hadn't thought about it that way."

He gave one small nod. "No way in hell did I ever want you to go through all that, hon. You know that. But sometimes things happen for a reason. I like to think I was there for you so I could get Molly out, too."

Her eyes burned. She threw her arms around Dare and squeezed him tight. "Thank you, Dare." In his simple, caring way, he'd just lightened her burden.

Hugging her right off her feet, Dare kissed the top of her head and said, "Anytime, sweetie." He levered her back, grinned suddenly and then actually laughed.

A little affronted, Alani frowned at him. "What's funny?"

"The look on Jackson's face."

Oh! She turned — and there Jackson stood, his reddened eyes burning with an excess of emotion, his shoulders bunched, his jaw taut.

Trace stood behind him, his mouth twisted with irony. "I told him to stay put, but he didn't listen."

Chapter Five

Jealousy sucked. He didn't like it worth a damn. He especially didn't like it now, with Alani rolling her eyes at him, and Dare and Trace both amused at his expense.

Seeing her in Dare's arms, even knowing they were practically siblings, burned his ass big-time. Next to Dare, she looked so small and fair, and he could see in her golden eyes how she trusted Dare.

With her feelings and with her life.

Jackson had no doubts about his abilities — but did Alani? Next to Dare and Trace, he stood out as different. They'd ribbed him plenty of times for his appearance, calling him a ladies' man, a beach bum, making jibes about his preference for comfort over style.

Even now, Dare wore an expensive pull-over with untattered jeans. More upper-class in his style, Trace wore a button-up shirt and khakis.

That morning, he'd dressed in haste, anxious to get to Alani. But even if he hadn't, Jackson knew he'd still have reached for the ancient jeans that, through the years, he'd worn in just right. The scuffed boots helped to hide his knife. And his array of T-shirts, some plain, some with raunchy sayings, always won out for being comfortable.

But next to the men Alani admired, did he fall short? She was a classy lady, always done up just right, from the tips of her toes to the top of her head. Even now, with the late sunshine warming her skin, leaving it dewy, she looked fresh and sweet. A breeze stirred the humid air, teasing her beautiful hair and carrying her unique scent to him. Jackson inhaled, filling his lungs with the aroma of woman.

His woman.

He wanted to drag her close, to stake a claim.

And the guys knew it. With their presence alone, they taunted him.

Jackson swallowed hard, tried to loosen up, and asked, "Everybody all talked out? We can drive a stake through the clandestine crap? Good. I'll show you to the door."

Not fooled at all, Dare snorted. "We still need to work out the setup."

Moving to Jackson's side, Alani took

charge. "You should be sitting down." She put her arm around him as if for support. Ignoring the fact that he outweighed her by more than a hundred pounds and stood damn near a foot taller, she tried to urge him back toward the couch.

Unmanned by her mollycoddling, he stiffened. "I don't need you to —"

Trace pushed past them. "If he can't walk on his own steam, then leave him outside."

"Wanna hold my hand?" Dare asked him.

"Ignore them," Alani told Jackson. "I plan to."

Provoked beyond reason, Jackson rubbed the back of his neck.

"Are you okay?" She cupped the side of his face gently. "Does your head hurt?"

This mothering tendency of hers made him really uncomfortable. He hadn't blushed since his early teens, but damned if he didn't feel his ears getting hot.

"You're warm," she fussed. "Do you think you have a fever?"

"Poor baby," Dare muttered, then snorted.

Jackson's restraint broke. He wanted to take care of her, not the other way around. To prove to her that he wasn't handicapped in any way, Jackson scooped her up into his arms.

"Jackson!"

He kissed her hard, and when she would have pulled away, he kept on kissing her, hugging her close, tilting his head for a better fit. He kissed her until she stopped fighting him.

Against her lips, he said, "Unless you want further proof that I'm fine, stop babying me." And then he headed inside.

Dare snorted again, but he closed the door behind them.

Back in the living room, Jackson stood her on her feet. "Now, we need — *oof.*"

Her pointy elbow landed with unerring precision. He hadn't braced for it because he hadn't expected it. After being so sick that morning, his innards still felt sore, and she'd gotten him good.

A hand to his midsection, he straightened and stared at her. Her angelic expression lacked remorse.

As he stared down at her, incredulous, she smiled like a sinner. "Unless you want further proof that I object to manhandling, stop pushing me."

By slow degrees, Jackson's frown faded into a grin. "You want to play, darlin'?" More than a little aware of Dare and Trace standing back, giving him the opportunity to spar with her, Jackson said, "Oh, I love to play. Just know that paybacks are hell."

Her eyes widened. "But you're the one who started it by —"

"Children, please," Trace said. "Recess is over."

Wanting them gone, Jackson announced without preamble, "I'm taking her to my place."

Dare rejected that idea. "Your place is where this all started."

"No, not my apartment. My house." To Alani, he said, "It's not done yet, but it's livable. It'll give you a chance to think about designs and stuff. The plumbing is operational, and the security is already in place."

Alani shook her head. "You're taking a lot for granted."

Ignoring that, Jackson added to the men, "It's plenty private, too. We won't have to worry about passersby or visitors."

Dare considered it. "You used a different name when hiring the builders?"

"Alternate identity down the line." In an aside to Alani, he explained, "I always use an alias. Safer that way."

"Get real, Jackson. Trace is my brother, so I'm already aware of the need for secrecy."

"Oh, yeah? That's why you didn't give old Marc my last name the day I met him?"

"Of course."

"Brains are so damn sexy." And while she

sputtered over that, he said to Dare, "Everything was paid for in cash. No one can track the location to me."

Trace chewed on the idea. "You're what? An hour or so from where I live?"

" 'Bout that." Close enough to appease Trace, but far enough away that he'd have plenty of alone time with Alani. It'd just be the two of them, sunshine, water, nature . . . a perfect setup for romance.

Alani shook her head again. "No."

"It's isolated enough," Dare said. "You have a boat?"

Jackson put a hand to the small of Alani's back. He wanted her aware of the necessities, but he also wanted her to trust him to take care of everything. "One obvious, one hidden."

"I'm not going." Alani crossed her arms.

Figuring he'd get her there one way or another, Jackson hugged her — while also guarding against another blow. So far she'd waffled between treating him like an invalid and inflicting pain upon his body. "Everything will be fine, honey, you'll see. This is just a preventative measure, so don't get worked up about it, okay?"

"I am not worked up."

"Great. Just give me another minute here, and then I'll help you get packed." He addressed Trace again. “No one can get on the property without me knowing. We can hang out while you two do a little digging.”

“I’m not —”

“I already have the basics on Tobin,” Trace mused aloud, speaking over Alani’s attempted protests. “Should be easy enough to see what he’s been up to lately. If he had anything to do with drugging you, I’ll know it by the end of the week.”

Alani gasped. “You were spying on him?”

Jackson gave her a “duh” look. “You thought Trace wouldn’t?” She thought *he* wouldn’t?

Slowly but surely, her ire gathered. “Have you spied on every guy I’ve dated?”

Trace and Jackson said together, almost as one, “Who else is there?”

She glared at them both, then deflated. “No one.”

Redirecting everyone’s attention again, Dare said, “I’ll go by your apartment to see if I can unearth anything. I know you said you did that, but it can’t hurt to have fresh eyes.”

“Especially since my brains were numbed,” Jackson agreed. Beneath the hand he had at Alani’s waist, her muscles tensed. He liked the feel of her, the supple strength, the dip of her waist and the slight flair of her hip, the warmth of her sweet little body.

The sight of her naked would be forever emblazoned on his brain, but he wanted to see her again. He wanted to visually explore her to his heart's content.

"Need us to grab anything for you while we're there?" Trace asked.

"I'll text you a list if I think of anything." He didn't want to drag out their visit any longer than necessary. By the second, Alani got more rigid. That wasn't what any of them wanted, so the sooner he got rid of the guys, the quicker they could settle down and she could relax. "Molly's more reasonable than Priss, so maybe Dare could talk to the single women in the apartment complex and see if any of them know anything."

"Any single women in particular?"

Jackson shrugged. "Any that are good looking, I reckon. You could start with the description Alani gave, but don't limit it to that. Maybe check in with Brigit next door. She's single, has her girlfriends over on occasion."

Dare said, "Got it," while Alani slowly turned her head to stare at him.

"And maybe Carly. She's offered to help me around the place. She got in the door once, so she knows the layout of the place.

And maybe —"

Alani shoved Jackson. Hard.

Rather than drag her off balance with him, he released her before stumbling back a step. Her shove had been hard enough that she had probably hoped to knock him on his ass.

Silly woman.

At the continued show of violence, all three of them stared at her.

Jackson spoke first. "What the hell was that for?"

"Language," Trace reminded him again.

Alani's stance gave away her frustration. "You're all three being impossible. Listen up — I am not going anywhere tonight!"

"Just calm down," Dare said.

"No, *you* calm down." She glared at Dare until he held up his hands in surrender. "Look, I get it that you guys want to protect me. Great. Thanks. Appreciate it."

"Then what's the problem?" Jackson asked her.

She turned to shove him again. He caught her hands and yanked her close so that she tumbled against his chest. Looking straight into her eyes, he said, "Settle down before you hurt yourself."

Staying against him, she stated, "I will not

be steamrolled. I will not be treated like an idiot."

Again, they all went mute.

Jackson wanted her to be his responsibility, not anyone else's, so he was the first to speak. "No one thinks you're an idiot. That's just dumb."

Her expression turned incredulous.

"God help us," Trace muttered.

Hoping to smooth things over, Jackson asked, "You can't get the time off work?"

"It has nothing to do with work."

"So you are free?"

She gave him a killing frown. "I'm not currently involved with any redesigns. I cleared my calendar to work on your house, as you requested."

Huh. "That's why you came to see me yesterday?" Satisfaction sank into his bones.

"Maybe." She glanced at Trace and Dare, and pushed away from Jackson. "In part."

So maybe the other part had been intimate interest? Hell, yeah. "Then this is perfect. I think you'll like my house."

"Yes, well . . ." Going all prim and proper, she smoothed the skirt of her dress. "I'm guessing it has to be better than your apartment. But that's not the —"

"You don't like my apartment?"

Her gaze slanted his way, extreme dislike

in her eyes. "There are naked women everywhere."

Imagining her reaction to his decor, Jackson smiled. "Yeah." He added with a shrug, "Women's bodies are beautiful."

She again looked at Dare and Trace. "Have you two seen —"

"It's entertaining," Dare told her.

Trace smiled.

"Well, I think it's absurd! Every picture, every knickknack, even a few statues, they're all naked women."

"I'm a connoisseur," Jackson told her.

"You're a . . ." She drew up short, probably remembering that she'd been intimate with him last night, all night from her telling, and that everyone in the room knew it.

Mulish, she crossed her arms. "If I decorate for you, there'll be none of that."

"You're the designer." Considering it settled, he turned back to Trace and Dare. "So we're all set?"

Trace nodded. "You can be out of here before dinnertime?"

"No problem on my end." Trying to be a gentleman, he asked Alani, "You need more time than that to get ready?"

"No." She smiled. "Because I'm not going anywhere tonight."

Stubborn. But he'd win her over. "Both

Dare and Trace just finished up jobs."

"Oh?" She didn't hide her confusion.

Jackson nodded. "No matter how small the threat might be, do you really want them distracted with their concerns for you, instead of enjoying their downtime?"

The confusion morphed into resentment. "Dirty pool, Jackson."

He shrugged. Whenever necessary, he fought dirty. "We're the experts, right?"

"Yes."

"And we'd prefer that you not be alone until we get a handle on what's going on — so make a choice."

"What choice?"

"Me." He nodded toward Dare and Trace. "Or them."

Her narrowed eyes made her look really mean. Finally she muttered, "Then I guess it's . . . you."

Such a grudging concession. Pleased with her, Jackson smoothed his thumb over her cheek. "I promise not to make it a hardship." He couldn't touch her without the sharpening of awareness, both carnal and emotional.

As they stared at each other, Alani's anger melted away, replaced with breathless understanding.

Dare gave a theatrical cough.

Trace said, "For God's sake, pump the brakes on that, will you, Jackson? We need to make some decisions here."

Jackson smiled at her and bent and kissed her before she could turn away. With his arm slung around her shoulders, he turned to both men.

That Dare and Trace had so far stayed out of convincing her, leaving it up to him, suited Jackson. Unless they were waiting for him to fail so they could take over. He frowned at that possibility.

"I'd just like to point out —" Alani encompassed them all in her sweeping gaze "— none of you are thinking clearly."

Instead of taking offense, Jackson said, "Everything is fine." He punctuated that with a comforting hug.

"Oh, please. Only an idiot wouldn't be worried at this point." Her pointed look at Jackson drove home that barb.

"So now I'm not only a wimp, but an idiot, too?"

"I never said you were a wimp."

"You think I need someone hovering over me, like I can't take care of myself."

"Well, forgive me for caring."

Jackson went on the alert. "You care?" What did she mean by that? Did he want her caring for him? Well, beyond the sexual, because he definitely wanted her to care about getting sexual with him again. Over and over —

"Oh, for the love of . . ." Unaware of his mental fumbling, Alani propped her hands on her hips. "You're the one who was drugged, so if anyone has reason to come unglued, it'd be you."

Trace whistled low.

Dare looked up at the ceiling.

Alani glared at them both. "Oh, stop it. If he can dish it out, he can take it, too."

Jackson clenched his molars. "I have never come *unglued.*"

She waved a hand, dismissing his outrage as negligible. "If I wasn't involved, if I wasn't part of the equation, what would the three of you be planning?"

"I don't know, because you are a part of it." Jackson would remember that, even if she didn't. Losing all sense of discretion, he tipped up her chin. "And I'm telling you right now, one way or another, you'll be removed from even the most remote possibility of danger."

Her outraged gasp nearly choked her. "You're *threatening* me?"

"To protect you?" He gave one sharp nod. "Damn right, darlin'. Whatever it takes. And don't bother pouring that long wounded look on your brother, because he feels the same."

Trace shrugged. "Told you it wouldn't be easy."

Damn it! He'd already known that Trace would try to talk her away from him, but now he had proof. "It'll be easy enough if you don't fight me."

Alani took a step back, but not in fear. It looked more as if she braced to attack. "You're all being . . . *idiotic!*"

Jackson eyed her militant stance, crossed his arms and sighed. "I guess I had to see your not-so-sweet side sooner or later, huh?"

She fumed in silence for only a moment. "If any of you would stop to think, you'd realize that Jackson needs to go back to his apartment so whoever was approaching him can find him again."

Astute as well as stubborn. Jackson chewed the side of his mouth. He put his hands on his hips and glared at her.

"You know I'm right."

He opened his mouth to set her straight and said, "Maybe."

His agreement stole some of her indignation. "Obviously you'll be more careful about what you drink now. And . . . well . . ." Her gaze avoided his. "You probably shouldn't sleep with any women since at this point, you don't know who to trust."

Ah, a little jealousy. He grinned. "I know I can trust you."

Turning to Trace, her voice a little high, a little shrill, she said, "If he hides away with me, then whoever is responsible might just disappear and we'll never know who was behind this, or what he wanted."

Jackson looked at Dare and Trace. They looked back. Jackson saw the same surprise on their faces that he felt.

Alani had nailed it. Remove her from the equation, and he definitely would have set himself up as a target to draw out the bastard.

"You know it's true," Alani said. "And even if Jackson's okay with not knowing, I refuse to live that way."

"Sorry." Trace crossed his arms over his chest. "Fact is, you are in the middle of this, so we'll adjust."

Stepping around Jackson, she appealed to her brother with a hand on his arm. "I'd rather know than wonder. Besides, you know the sooner we find out what's going on, the safer I'll be."

Jackson hated to admit she was right, but . . .

"I have a suggestion," Dare said, "if Alani will work with us a little on this."

"How so?"
"Let Jackson play watchdog for the night. That means the two of you staying here until Trace and I can scope out his place. If it's all good to go, then he can head there tomorrow or the next day."
Jackson studied her. As soon as possible, they'd settle a few things — like how the relationship would work . . . if they had a relationship. He still wasn't sure about that. "She can be reasonable."
Alani lifted her chin. "Certainly, I can. But that doesn't mean —"
"Yeah, it does." He would not give on this point.
Dare continued as if the interruption hadn't happened. "As to that, if folks see the two of you together and know that Alani isn't alone, it might discourage anyone from targeting her."
"Or make her a target," Jackson said, grim at the prospect.
Trace shook his head. "No one can get past you —"
Jackson appreciated the confidence, since Alani didn't seem to share it.
"— and since we don't want to alert anyone that we're on to them, the ruse of a relationship between the two of you will work as well as anything else."

Alani licked her lips. "Anyone paying attention will think Jackson is sticking close because we're involved, not because he's a protector."

"Exactly."

"When we go back to his place, you'll make sure he's kept safe?" Alani wanted to know.

Jackson said, *"Woman . . ."*

His tone didn't faze her. "You'll be the one under attack if any of this backfires."

"We'll be vigilant babysitters," Trace promised her, cutting short Jackson's retort.

Jackson knew they'd be needling him for a year over Alani's misplaced concern. "I can take care of myself, damn it."

Dare grinned. "I think she's more worried about a woman getting to you than anything else."

Alani looked like she might strangle Dare, but he just laughed at her.

Well now, that was different.

" 'S that right, sugar?" Jackson took in the telltale jealousy in her bright eyes. "You feeling possessive?"

This time he was ready for her when she shoved past him on her way to the door. He didn't stumble a single inch.

"Now that that's settled." Alani grasped the doorknob and looked back in expectation for Dare and Trace to follow. "Well?"

Trace turned to Dare, who let out a long sigh. "Yeah, sure, why not? I'll be a distraction." Dare went to Alani while Trace went to Jackson.

Alani tried to protest, but Dare still managed to catch her slapping hands. "Let's take a breath of fresh air. You look like you could use it."

Jackson watched as Dare practically carried her outside. She must've been used to the high-handed treatment, given that she allowed it to happen.

For some reason she glanced back at Jackson as if he was somehow responsible.

Expression hard, Trace leaned in close to Jackson. "No private visitors."

"I know." Already his heart thumped with anticipation. Very soon now he'd have her alone. "I'll play doorman in case anyone does come calling on her."

"No unmonitored phone calls, either."

"I know." It seemed he'd suffered a combustible cocktail of emotions all day — lust, need, curiosity and tenderness . . . "I'll vet any and all calls."

"If you two decide to go out for anything, make sure —"

"Damn, man." Jackson shifted his stance. "You think this is my first rodeo?"

"With my sister, it is." Trace's expression hardened. "And even you know that you're distracted."

True enough, not that it mattered. "I'd die for her, if it came to that."

"And then she'd be left unprotected." Trace put a finger to Jackson's chest. "So no dying."

Jackson laughed at that somber, direct order. "Right. Got it. Wouldn't be my first choice anyway." He clapped Trace on the shoulder. "Anything goes down, I'll be in touch."

"You armed?"

"Yeah." He had a Glock in a back-belt holster, a knife in his boot, and the skill and imagination to make a weapon out of about a dozen things in her kitchen.

"Enough?"

"It's covered, okay?"

Dare stuck his head back in. "We're good?"

"Yeah." Trace looked at Jackson again. He lowered his voice even more. "I can't believe I'm saying this, but . . . sleep near her, okay? Don't let her force you out to the couch. I can't put a finger on it, but something about this doesn't feel right to me."

"Right outside her door, if that's what it has to be." In their line of work, gut instincts were never ignored. But where he slept was up to Alani — and Trace knew it. "I'll be able to hear her breathing. You have my word."

Trace studied him a second, then nodded. "All right then."

As Trace strode away, Dare approached.

Jackson put his fists on his hips. "God, what now?"

"It wouldn't hurt you to let her pamper you a little."

He grunted. "Yeah, like you would?"

"If it kept her busy enough that she wasn't afraid, and close at hand, yeah. Damn right, I would."

Huh. He hadn't considered that.

"Besides," Dare said. "You might find you like it. Sometimes, a woman's touch is just what you need."

"Now that's something I already knew." Jackson grinned at Dare's reaction. Yeah, he saw Alani as a little sister, too.

For her part, Alani remained near the door, now more frazzled than ever.

Impatient, smoldering, Jackson stood back as the guys took their time telling her goodbye. They each embraced her, and they each gave him last-minute instructions.

All things he knew, all things he would see to.

But he understood their need to voice their thoughts. They were, by nature, take-charge men, and even when giving the responsibility to someone they trusted, it wasn't easy to let go. He got it.

When they were both gone, Alani closed and locked the door.

Jackson braced himself for the rush of feelings now that they were finally alone.

When she continued to stand there at the door, her back to him, Jackson smiled in predatory determination.

Oh, she claimed she couldn't jump back into bed with him — but she wanted to. The sexual chemistry arced between them like a live wire.

But he wanted her to know she could trust him. She said she wanted more time, so that's what he'd give her — no matter how difficult it might be. For both of them.

Chapter Six

Silkily, Jackson said, "Alani."

For only a moment she bowed her head and then, resolute, she turned to face him. Her hands were behind her on the door-knob, her gaze watchful, her pose purposely relaxed.

So many reactions flitted over her face, Jackson had a hard time deciphering them. But he understood what he felt, first and foremost.

The need to put her at ease, to take away the nervousness.

His breathing deepened. He held out a hand. "C'mere, honey."

She took one halting step and stopped again. She rubbed her palms against her thighs. "Why?"

Why did she think? "You expecting me to jump your bones?" He quirked a smile. "You think I'm going to go all hot and heavy on you?"

"Yes, sort of."

So honest. "Hate to disappoint you, but I won't, I promise. At least not yet." He continued to hold out his hand. "You said you wanted time, so I'm giving you time. For now I just want to talk."

"Talk?" Her tongue slipped out over her lips. "About what?"

Man, he couldn't wait to feel that small soft tongue on his body. "You said this morning that I'd ignored everything you had to say, right?"

"You remember that?"

He remembered every second of seeing her naked, seeing her anger, her upset.

How he'd unintentionally wounded her tender feelings.

"I remember. You said you had a lot of arguments about why we shouldn't have gotten between the sheets. I was drugged then, but now I'm not, so this will be your chance to tell me — and my chance to convince you otherwise."

"I . . ." Hesitantly, one timid step at a time, she closed the space between them.

Jackson enfolded her hand in his.

Her fingers were cold, giving away her fear. Primal instincts rose up, the need to console, comfort, the driving urge to defend and shelter. "I'm going to take very good care of you." In bed, and out.

Her lips parted. Her fingers curled against his. "What we talked about doesn't matter now." In a rush, she started into the kitchen, towing him along with her. "We did already sleep together."

Once in the kitchen, Jackson pulled her around to him. Trying for casualness he didn't feel, he looped his arms around her. "But you want me to start over, so that's what I'm going to do." With her telling him what happened, how could he miss? She'd be his guide. "I know you want me, darlin'. I know you enjoyed yourself."

He waited, and she nodded.

Contentment settled over him. "So what's the problem then? What objections did you give me?"

Alani hesitated. She looked at her packages, now stacked on the table, at the half-empty coffee carafe, everywhere except at him. "I can't do this in the middle of the kitchen."

Imagination on hyperdrive, Jackson nudged her closer. "This?"

"Talk. About this stuff." She eyed the kitchen table. "Not *that.* Not what you're thinking."

She knew what he thought? Why was she thinking it? Had they made use of the table at his place?

Fun.

"Oh, I dunno." He bent to kiss her throat. "I think you'd make a real tasty treat."

She bolted away from him. "I need a drink."

Left empty-armed, Jackson propped a shoulder against the wall. "You think that's a good idea?" Did alcohol loosen her up? God help him.

"I mean something cold." She opened the refrigerator. "Tea or something."

"Nothing that's been opened already." He wouldn't risk the grim possibility that whoever had drugged his drink, had managed to tamper with anything at her place, too.

Frowning, she stepped back from the refrigerator, moved to her sink and picked up an empty container. "Dare must've dumped everything."

Course he had. "Why don't you drink a cola? Or better yet, take a seat and I'll mix up a new pitcher of tea for you." He pulled out a chair from the table.

"Oh." Realization brought her around to him again, the empty tea pitcher in her hand. She ignored the chair. "That's why you asked about the can of cola?"

"Gotta be careful."

Slowly, she put the container in the sink. She took a deep breath, then searched his face. "You think someone might have been in my house."

A statement, not a question. "Doubtful." It would be tricky, keeping alert while downplaying the possible danger. "But you know how it is. Why take a chance?" As a rule, he never did. With Alani, he'd use extra care.

Something passed over her features, something she tried hard to hide. She nodded. "You're all so cautious."

In their line of work, they had to be. "I have an idea. Instead of you showering and settling in for the night, why don't we go grab something for dinner, maybe rent a movie." It'd give her a chance to shake off the unease, and him a chance to lighten the sexual tension.

Her eyes flared. "But I thought . . ."

That they'd be in bed together within minutes? Wondering if she'd say it, Jackson waited, his smile banked, his lust churning.

Tucking her hair behind her ear, she shrugged. "All right. Sure." She rinsed the pitcher with unnecessary verve. "If you don't mind, maybe I could stop by the office, too."

Jackson approached her, and when he

asked, "Why?" from right behind her, she jumped.

Not turning to face him, she dried her hands on a dish towel. "If I can't take calls on my cell, I need to set up the phone there to forward calls to my landline."

"Sure, we can do that." Drawing her back against his chest, he rested his crossed hands over her stomach. "We can do anything you want, long as you don't try to go off anywhere without me."

For only a moment, she rested her head against his shoulder and put her hands over his. "You don't mind?"

"You're not a prisoner, honey. In fact, why don't you just think of me as a hired escort? You call the shots."

She went still. "Interesting concept." Turning in his arms, she smiled like an imp. "Will it lacerate your male ego for me to ask if you're up to it?"

"I'm up."

Her mouth twitched. "You know, I might take advantage of all this willingness."

"A guy can hope."

She laughed softly. "All right, if you're sure you feel okay now."

"I'll enjoy getting out."

"Then just let me go freshen up and we can leave."

When she started away, Jackson followed her.

She stopped in the hallway. "What are you doing?"

"Which room is yours?"

"Last room on the left. Why?"

Jackson moved her aside and strode ahead of her into the room. He stopped short just inside the door, struck by how much the room looked like her — neat, organized, soft and fresh. Very female. But not *too* perfect.

Flowers sat on a dresser, and from one drawer a pair of pale blue panties peeked out. Jackson grinned.

Squawking in outrage, Alani rushed in behind him. "What are you doing?" She zipped around the room rearranging, tucking away, closing and covering.

"I wanted to get a lay of the house." Undisturbed by her fervor, he opened the closet and took a peek, went to the window and checked the lock.

"Get out."

"Sorry, no." He opened the door to her connecting bathroom. A slinky bra that couldn't possibly do more than decorate hung over the shower rod. Next to the sink, a toothbrush stood in a glass by a dispenser of scented hand soap.

Her tub was large enough for two, if they stuck close.

"Jackson . . ." she warned.

An oval, fringed rug of cream and pale blue decorated the floor and matched the curtain on the shower and window. He fingered the fine material of the curtain. "Pretty."

While she did more complaining, he checked the lock on the bathroom window, too. Making note of her red-faced anger, Jackson started out of the room. "Go ahead and do whatever it is you have to do while I check the other rooms."

He stepped out the bedroom door and rethought his exit just in the nick of time.

His flattened hand kept her from slamming it shut. "Understand, Alani. If you lock me out, and I need to get back in, your door will suffer." He shouldered his way back in past her discontent. "C'mon honey. Work with me here."

"You're bulldozing again."

Jackson thought about it. "Okay." He put his hands, palms out, in his back pockets and took up a comfortable stance. "Here's the deal. I need to check the other rooms. I need to know that the windows are secure. I have to be familiar with every egress, all the phones and computers. I need the layout of the house and each room. And no, it's not because I expect anything to happen. I'd do the same even if I hadn't been drugged last night."

Her golden eyes searched his, and her anger melted away. "You seriously live that way?"

"Cautious? You betcha." Always, but especially with her security at stake. "If it bothers you that much for me to see your place, then I'm sorry. You can come along with me if you like. I don't mind the company. But either way, I'm looking around."

Alani dropped back against the door frame. "There's a guest bedroom, guest bath and my office." She waved a hand. "Feel free. But please don't snoop."

"You think I would?"

"Ha!" She rolled her eyes at him. "I know you would."

Jackson smiled. "Yeah, maybe." If he had a reason or thought he'd find something interesting. "But I'll respect your privacy as much as I can."

Expression dubious, she warned, "Don't go fumbling through the records on my desk. I have them neatly organized."

"Fumble? You don't have a real high opinion of my skills, do you?" To take the sting out of that rebuke, he dragged her close for a kiss. "It's a wonder I've survived so long without you."

A little slack-jawed, Alani watched as Jackson meandered down the hall and disappeared into her office. His long-legged, rangy walk set her heart to tripping; the thought of him going through her personal files slowed it again.

She snapped her mouth shut.

Was that parting shot of his mockery over her criticism or a sincere statement reflecting what they'd shared, the bond they'd forged last night?

A bond that only she could remember.

Groaning, she put her hands over her face and slumped back into her bedroom. She quietly closed the door and dropped back against it.

Being honest with herself, she had to admit that deep inside, she'd been expecting — maybe even hoping — that he'd press the issue of intimacy. He wanted her again. He'd been more than open and upfront about that.

But instead, he chose to honor her wishes, the wishes she knew to be more responsible. More reasonable.

It would be a very long night.

Taking her time, Alani freshened up, tidying her hair, brushing her teeth, giving her makeup a boost. With nothing more to do, she girded herself for Jackson's impact, both emotional and physical, and went in search of him.

She opened her bedroom door and found him right there in the hallway, leaning against the wall, relaxed, waiting for her.

Before she could apologize for making him wait, he straightened. "Ready?"

"Yes."

She stepped out, and his warm palm curved to the small of her back.

Alani felt the touch everywhere. But then, even if he hadn't touched her, she'd have been acutely aware of him beside her. When Jackson was in a room, he occupied everything — the space, the air, the attention of those around him.

Knowing they were alone, with the bedrooms at their backs, quickened her breath.

"I parked down around the corner."

Surprise slowed her steps, but since Jackson kept walking, she did, too. It hadn't occurred to her that his car was missing. If she'd seen it on the street in front of her house or in her driveway, she'd have been forewarned of his visit.

And maybe she would have avoided him.

"You didn't want me to know you were here?"

"I didn't want anyone else to know." His hand slid to her hip and nudged her a little closer to him. "In case I was followed, no way did I want to lead anyone to you."

Another reminder of the danger. "Well, you should bring your car up to my driveway now."

"Maybe later." He stopped at the entrance to her small living room where so much drama had already gone down. "For now, how about we take your car?"

"All right." She didn't mind that. With all he'd been through, it'd probably be better if he wasn't driving. Sure, he had to be macho and swear he felt no side effects from being drugged, but how could that be? If she took cold medicine, it wiped her out, and he'd been given a drug so heavy-duty that it had obliterated his memory.

In the kitchen, she found her purse, keys and Jackson's hat. She rejoined him in the foyer.

He took the hat from her, slid it onto his head and then held out a hand.

One brow raised, Alani looked at him questioningly.

"Keys?" he prompted.

She slid her purse strap over her shoulder.

"That's okay. I'll drive."

A priceless expression fell over his face.

"Oh, please." Alani had to laugh. "It's not like I asked to carry your gun."

He tipped back his hat and scoffed. "I'd say no to that, too." He scrutinized her. "But you do know how to shoot, don't you?"

"I know enough. Trace insisted." And after her kidnapping, she'd done plenty of practicing to ensure she could handle a weapon.

He reached for her purse. "You carrying?"

"No!" Alani snatched the bag away. "Of course not."

Considering that, Jackson declared, "We'll get you a piece. You shouldn't be out and about without it." He gave her small designer purse a look of dislike. "You'll need to carry something bigger, though."

She did not want to be armed. "You're here, so what do I need with a gun? Aren't you protection enough?"

He went so still, it almost made her laugh again. Until he said, "You suggesting I should stick around 24/7?"

"What?" A rush of heat hit her cheeks. "*No,* of course I wasn't."

Keeping her caught in his gaze for far too long, he studied her, and finally smiled. "Yeah, I'm protection enough. I guess as long as you're with me, you don't need anything else." He snatched the keys out of her lax hand. "Come on. Let's get out of here."

Objecting was beyond her. Jackson held her back while he opened the door and searched the area with a mere sweep of his gaze that, if she wasn't familiar with Trace's habits, she might have missed.

Apparently he considered the coast clear, and they headed out.

The bright late-day sun sank a little lower in the sky, casting long tree shadows over her sidewalk but not quite reaching her car.

"You don't park in your garage?"

"Usually, yes." The car would be sweltering after baking in the sun. "But since I hadn't planned to be home long, it didn't seem worth the bother."

He opened the passenger door for her. "You came home only to turn around and leave again?"

Trying to stay busy so she wouldn't think of him. Not that he needed to know that much. "I'd only wanted to change my sandals, that's all."

Scowling, he closed her door and strode around the hood to the driver's side. He started the engine but then rested his hands on the steering wheel and hesitated.

Alani half turned in her seat. "Jackson?"

Was he feeling sick again? God knew, she shouldn't ask, he was so touchy about it.

Dark, almost foreboding, his gaze swung to her. In a voice gone low and gravelly, he said, "It's sort of eating me up, knowing I hurt you."

Oh. So that dark look was out of concern for her? Some strange, pervading contentment lightened her mood. "That's so sweet."

His expression became outright volatile.

Smiling, Alani touched his shoulder. "But you didn't." She was sore, yes, but the trade-off had been well worth it. "I told you, you were . . ."

"Gluttonous?"

"Tireless," she corrected. "Yes. But I liked it."

Showcasing his lightning-fast reflexes, Jackson caught the back of her neck and drew her close enough to steal her breath with a hot kiss.

He turned his head, fit his mouth over hers, licked over her bottom lip until she opened up, then stroked in. Deep, thorough.

As he eased away, his thumb teased the corner of her mouth. "Thank you. Glad to hear it. But I was talking about your feelings."

"My feelings?"

"You stayed out today because I made you

feel bad." His gaze searched hers. "You're not the type to sit home and cry, so you got busy. Right?"

She would not bare her soul to him. "It's all right, Jackson. I understand now."

"No, it's not all right." He kissed her again, light and quick, over her lips, her jaw, then treated her to a tingling love bite at the side of her neck. "I'll make it up to you, honey."

Eyes closed and breath hitching, Alani tipped her head back to make it easier for him. "All right."

"I want the memory of this morning long gone." He trailed warm, damp kisses along her skin, from her neck down to the hollow of her shoulder.

Every place his mouth touched, she tingled; his promise had her stomach flip-flopping. "Yes."

"I'll give you better memories, Alani." His teeth touched her skin.

Without realizing it, she sank her fingers into his hair, knocking aside his hat, holding him closer.

"Easy now." He kissed her chin, the tip of her nose, and lastly, in a tender and non-sexual way, he pressed a lingering kiss to her brow. "Don't get jumpy on me, but we might have company."

The words didn't register. She tried to find his mouth again.

Smiling, Jackson murmured, "Darlin', you are so damn sweet." He tipped up her face and waited until her heavy eyes opened to focus on his. "Thing is, we're in your car in the driveway, in broad daylight, and I think we might have some surveillance going on."

Alani dropped back to the here and now with a resounding *thud.* Jolted, she started to look around, but his hands continued to hold her.

"No, don't look. There's no danger right now. But I think we ought to get going."

"Where?" she asked in a nervous whisper. "I mean, where are the people watching us?"

"No one can hear you, honey." But then to answer her question, he said, "At the next cross street, down from the corner. Sleek silver sedan. Darkened windows. They pulled up, stopped, and haven't budged in all the time we've been out here."

Alani nodded. Pulling away from him, she tucked her hair behind her ear, and — oh so casually — glanced toward the car and away again. Hands on her thighs, muscles tensed, she struggled to sound as unconcerned as Jackson. "What if they follow us when we leave?"

Jackson set his hat back on his head.

"Then we'll lose them." He put the car in gear and backed out.

"Just like that?"

"Yup."

"You won't get their license plate number?"

"Sure I will. And Trace or Dare will check it out. But it could be nothing."

"You don't believe that." Already she felt she could read him, and while he might act all nonchalant, he was on alert. "Do you?"

"I believe it's all under control." After pulling out onto the street, he glanced in the rearview mirror and drove forward. "Now, about you and me and that lousy morning after."

He couldn't be serious. "Are they following?"

"Don't worry about that."

Dismayed, she looked back, not surprised to see them closing in.

"How many times did I have sex with you?"

Thrown a little, she did a double-take. "I don't know."

He groaned. "Way to wound me, woman. You're saying it was so forgettable, you couldn't keep track?"

Ready to clout him, Alani growled, "Five times."

"Five! No shit?" He grinned. "That's a personal best for me."

He could be so outrageous. "I told you, you were very enthusiastic."

"I think it's more that you're so irresistible."

"Not likely." As she watched him, Jackson glanced in the rearview mirror several times. "No one has ever thought so before, but from what I understand, you've always gone overboard when it comes to sex."

"Nah. Who you been talking to anyway?" He made a sound and repeated, "Overboard," as if such a thing didn't exist in relation to sexual indulgence. "I bet you've always been a hot little number, but with Trace's eagle eye, all the interested guys were probably afraid to come calling."

Hot little number? "You make me sound like a race car." When Jackson turned the corner, she checked her side-view mirror and saw the car continue going straight. Her relief was so great, she slumped in her seat. "They're not following anymore."

"Nope." Jackson removed the hat and tossed it to the backseat. She noted that he seemed no less alert, though. "We'll get back to your hotness in a minute."

She wouldn't hold her breath.

Fishing his cell phone from his pocket,

Jackson pushed one button and put it to his ear. After another glance at her, he said, "Just shed a silver BMW sedan. Ritzy. Four-door. Tinted windows. License plate Echo-Lima-four-six-Delta-Bravo." He listened a second, glanced at Alani again and said, "Doubtful." He nodded. "You betcha."

After closing the phone, he put it back in his pocket.

"Trace?"

"Yup." He continued to check the mirrors, the road, the area around them.

"What's doubtful?"

"That any guy who meets you doesn't want you. Even if he doesn't tell you so, believe me, if he's straight, he's thinking about getting you naked."

What he said was so far removed from what she'd asked, and so removed from her reality, that it threw her. "That's —"

"You have a really fine body. Did I tell you that last night?"

Not that exactly, but he'd given her comparable compliments all night long. She didn't get it any more now than she had then. "I'm not real curvy." She glanced down at her own mediocre chest. "And compared to Priss and Molly —"

"No, whoa, hey, don't go there." Discomfort had him shifting his shoulders. "Priss and Molly are married to friends, so discussing their boobs is over the line. Can't do it."

He appeared so horrified that Alani snickered. "Makes you uncomfortable, does it?"

"Bad protocol, that's all." He turned on the road that would lead to the commercial area nearby. "Let's just say you're all three lookers but in different ways, okay?"

"You have to admit they're both well-endowed."

"I guess." He shrugged. "Doesn't matter, though, because they aren't you."

Ahhh . . . Her heart tumbled over. That was about the nicest thing any man had ever said to her. She reached across the seat and put a hand on his thigh. "You're so curious about what you did to me."

He stilled with sensual awareness. "Yeah?"

Beneath her teasing fingers, his thigh tightened. "Don't you want to know what I did to you?"

"What you . . . ?" On an indrawn breath, he flashed her a hot look — and the silver BMW appeared again, this time coming toward them.

"How did they —"

"Hold on." Barreling straight through a red light, the car crossed lanes and sped toward them.

Alani gasped. Tires screeched. Other drivers blared their horns. To avoid a head-on collision, Jackson did some fast maneuvering, taking them up and over the curb, narrowly missing a telephone pole and a stopped car. He came back to the street again just shy of colliding with a van.

At the side of the road, he hit the brakes.

Slamming the car into Park, he jerked his door open and stepped out to look after the retreating car. Watching over her shoulder, Alani saw the car fishtail, then right itself and disappear around a corner.

A truck driver came jogging over. "Hey, you guys okay? Anyone hurt?"

Two younger men, cursing every other word, offered a similar query. One of them said to Jackson, "Who the fuck was that? Did you see how that dipshit ran the light?"

His buddy added, "I thought he was going to ram you!"

Alani heard Jackson replying, his tone matching that of the other men — heated, furious . . . like the average male.

He was such a good actor; there was nothing average about Jackson. As she watched, he reached back and tugged down the hem of his T-shirt — to cover a gun.

She shouldn't have been surprised. Of course he was armed. Like Trace and Dare, he probably went nowhere without a weapon or two on his person.

The tripping of her heart began to slow. Why hadn't she noticed that particular bulge before now? Maybe because she'd been so interested in the rest of his body.

She had to learn to pay better attention. Hadn't her kidnapping taught her anything?

Jackson stuck his head in the door. "You okay, honey?"

Behind him, the other males peered in at her, too.

She realized she had a death grip on the door handle and deliberately loosened her hold. One breath, two . . . She formed the semblance of a smile. "I'm fine."

His gaze looked diamond bright and full of determination, but his tone maintained that "typical male" quality. "You sure?"

"Just shaken, that's all." She opened her door and stepped out. No one had wrecked, thank God.

Warm air blew against her face. Fading sunlight reflected off the concrete. Traffic began moving again.

Looking around the area, she saw so many parked cars, poles, streetlamps and people, it was nothing short of a miracle that they hadn't wrecked.

And wrecking, she knew, had been the intent.

Someone wanted to hurt them. Was she the target, or was Jackson? Not that it mattered; neither was acceptable.

". . . couldn't see the driver," the older man was saying. "Not with those darkened windows."

"I got part of the license plate number," one of the younger men said. "I wrote it on the back of a receipt." Anxious to be of help, he handed it to Jackson. "That dude could've killed someone."

Dude. The assumption being that anyone driving so aggressively was probably male.

Jackson said, "Thanks." He tucked the tattered receipt into a back pocket.

Lifting a hand, Alani shielded her eyes from the setting sun. "Well, hopefully the driver will get home without endangering anyone else."

Jackson studied her.

"We should be going," she told him. He needed to do . . . whatever it was he did during times of emergency. To hurry things along, she said to the bystanders, "Thank you so much for stopping."

"Wanted to make sure you were okay." The truck driver took off his cap and replaced it again, settling it in the exact same way. "That was some fancy driving you did there. It's a wonder you didn't crash."

True.

Next time, would they be as lucky?

CHAPTER SEVEN

Unsure what to think of Alani's mood, Jackson tightened his hands on the steering wheel. "You sure you're okay?"

"Yes." She kept her face turned toward the window.

Wanting to comfort her, or reassure her, or do . . . whatever she might need him to, Jackson pressed her. "Not shook up a little?"

She glanced at him. "Are you?"

He snorted. "No." He didn't get *shook up.* "Course not."

She sized him up, nodded and looked away again. "Neither am I."

Damn it. He didn't want her drawing comparisons because he didn't expect her to have the same reaction as him. Hell, he was a professional and some yahoo in a car playing chicken wasn't even close to the nearest miss he'd ever had.

"You looked spooked right after it happened."

Her shoulder lifted. "I thought we were going to wreck." With nervous fingers, she tucked her hair behind her ear. "But we didn't."

"You know I won't let anything happen to you?"

A smile — sad, bemused — came and went so fast he almost missed it. "You're not invincible, Jackson."

He repeated, with more force, "I won't let anything happen to you."

Almost as if to comfort him, she glanced his way and said softly, "Okay."

Deciding he'd just have to prove it to her, he drove in silence the rest of the short distance to the strip-mall parking lot.

As he pulled off the main road, she turned those big golden eyes on him. "What are you doing?"

"We're doing dinner and a movie, right?"

"We are?" Confused, she looked around the lot. "I mean, still? Even after that near miss?"

"As close calls go, that didn't even rank in the top twenty." He parked the car and walked around the hood to open her door.

Alani gave him a hard stare. "What are we doing really?"

He held out a hand. "We're really going to pick up some groceries for dinner and rent a movie. No chick flicks, though. Anything but that."

Alani didn't take his hand.

"All right, fine, a chick flick it is. I can suffer through one if it matters that much to you."

Her long sigh expressed sarcasm, annoyance and a refusal to budge. "There's no way you're this cavalier about a direct attack — and that's what it was. The car wanted us to wreck. But then what? You have to have a theory, and I want to know what it is."

He'd told Trace she wasn't a china doll. Well, she wasn't obtuse, either. He glanced around the lot but didn't sense any spying eyes. "Remember what you said about keeping our routine, to draw them out?"

Now that he'd given in, she accepted his hand and stepped out. "Yes."

"That's what we're doing." He put his arm around her and headed for the video rental first. "I don't feel anyone watching us, but in case anyone does, they'll think we wrote off that incident as a bad or irresponsible driver."

"Because you don't want to tip your hand."

"Better to keep the bastards guessing."

"Thank you for telling me."

They stepped into the air-conditioned video store. Making his preference known, Jackson steered her around toward the action movies. "I don't want to freak you out. That's why I didn't tell you."

Solemn, she asked, "You expect me to freak out?"

He thought about it, studied her earnest face and shook his head. "Not really, no. You're a little bitty thing, and there's this air of innocence around you." He leaned down to speak closer to her ear. "It's sexy as hell, let me tell you."

At his whispered words, she came to a dead stop in the aisle.

Jackson straightened and got her moving again. "But I think you've got a hell of a lot more guts and backbone than you let on."

This time, her "thank you" held more real gratitude.

"Trace will have my ass, but if you really want the blow-by-blow, then I'll give it to you."

"So you haven't been giving me the . . . blow-by-blow?"

"Nah." Stopping in front of his favorite movie section, he chose a new release with Bruce Willis in it. "Look, this one is on sale. We can buy it instead of rent it."

She took the movie from him. "So what

else have you kept from me?"

Uh-oh. She sounded pissed again. Jackson rubbed his ear. "You know when the car stopped following us?"

"It turned down a different street and I thought that was the end of it."

"Yeah, I know you did." He never, ever, wanted her robbed of that innocence. "Thing is, I knew it'd be back."

Comprehension dawned. "When you were talking to Trace, you said something was doubtful."

Off to their side, two women stared at him over a rack of movies. Jackson ignored them. He and Alani spoke low enough that no one could hear them, and the women, beyond gawking, weren't a threat in any way. "He asked if I'd lost them. But I figured the car was trying to get around ahead of us to cut us off."

"How could you know that?"

"Instinct." Jackson cupped her face, and he didn't give a damn who saw him kiss her. He kept the contact brief, but sometimes, around Alani, *not* kissing her wasn't an option. "He also told me to keep you clear of danger, and I said I would."

Alani stared at him through several heartbeats before she glanced over at the nosy women. She glared at them. "Those women are looking at you."

He shrugged. "I'm not looking back, now, am I?" With one finger under her chin, he brought her face around. "Pretend they're not there."

"You were still aware of them."

"I'm aware of everything, sugar. Including your jealousy."

"My . . . ? Ha!" Fuming, his movie choice in her hand, she headed for the checkout.

He kept pace with her. "Whoa. Hold up, will ya?" A few more people glanced their way, but most were busy making their own movie choices. "What's the matter now?"

She looked hot under the collar, her expression tight, her face flushed with annoyance. He waited for her to deny any jealousy, and instead she said, "You knew that car would come back around again and you didn't tell me."

"I suspected," he clarified. "And you're causing a scene, blowing our hoax big-time."

Her expression pinched even more.

He had to bite back a smile. She was so darned cute when riled. He started to tuck her hair behind her ear, but she jerked her head away, and he dropped his hand. "If you don't lighten up, we may as well shout to the whole parking lot that we have nefarious types tailing us and we know it. And let me tell you, that's going to open up a whole can of worms from the local police on up the chain of command."

Miraculously, as Jackson watched, her features smoothed out. Though her eyes still glittered with annoyance, she laughed, swatted at him, then went on tiptoe to kiss him right on the mouth.

Almost like they'd had a spat and then made up.

Leaving one hand on his chest, she settled back on her own two feet and asked innocently, "Better?"

"Oh, yeah." Her agility in handling that, in maintaining the cover, flattened him. And turned him on. The woman had untapped skills. "If you want, you can kiss me again for good measure."

Instead, smiling at him, she trailed one fingertip down his chest all the way to his belt buckle. She looked back at the women — who were still staring after him — and dropped her hand with a satisfied smile. "Let's go."

Yeah, Jackson thought. Let's. He couldn't wait to get her alone so they could really talk.

And so he could really kiss her.

And maybe get her hand back on his belt buckle.

But fifteen minutes later, after buying the movie, they were halfway through the grocery shopping when he realized she was more pissed than he'd first thought. By rote, she dropped items into the grocery cart, staying a few steps ahead of him, constantly keeping him at her back.

Giving him the cold shoulder.

She'd withdrawn from him. Again.

He didn't like it. He much preferred her teasing, or even her anger, because at least then, she opened up to him. But this, the silent treatment, sucked.

He waited until they were in front of the produce, away from most prying ears, before he asked, "So what'd you do to me?"

A nearly imperceptible stiffening of her shoulders gave her away. She remained silent as she placed a fat tomato in with the other groceries.

Undaunted, Jackson leaned on the cart handle, his arms crossed. "Remember, you said I should stop asking what I did to you, and instead ask what you did to me. So I'm asking. And my imagination is running wild."

She didn't acknowledge him when she put a five-pound bag of potatoes in the cart.

Did that mean she expected to feed him more than once — or did she always buy five pounds?

"C'mon, Alani," he prompted her, hoping to draw her out of her mood. "If I got a hummer, I'd really like to know —"

She slammed a bag of carrots into the cart, so close to him that he had to duck back.

Fascinated with her temper, he waited, watching her closely, anticipating what she might do.

She stopped, drew a breath. Her eyes narrowed meanly. "Yes."

A tidal wave of heat snapped Jackson's spine straight. "Yes, *what?*"

"Yes." She smiled with smug satisfaction. "You got a . . . a hummer." Saying it brought a blush to her fair skin, but it didn't stop her from looking boldly toward his crotch. "And while I'm not real practiced, you definitely liked it."

Oh, hell. She knew how to fight dirty, too.

As she sauntered past him, secure that she led in the score, he turned the cart and rushed to catch up. "So . . ."

All kinds of images ripped through his mind, some of them achingly sweet, most of them scorching, a few even raunchy.

Strangling on his lust, he cleared his

throat. "Did I . . . you know, coerce you into doing that?" He hated that thought as much as he loved the other thought — that she'd wanted to taste him, that she'd maybe initiated that particular form of intimate pleasure loved by all men. "Or did you —" he searched for the right word "— volunteer?"

Over her shoulder, she said, "I can't be coerced." And she smiled that taunting smile again. "I was curious. You were accommodating." She shrugged as if that explained everything.

Yeah, he could just imagine how accommodating he'd been. He wouldn't mind accommodating her again, real soon.

Jackson moved up alongside her. It wasn't easy since he had to push the cart through the crowded aisles. "So . . ." Damn, but he'd never been hesitant with sex talk before. He had to clear his throat again. "Did you like it?"

"Sure." She didn't even take a second to think about it. "Actually, I loved it."

His knees went weak. His heartbeat galloped. No way in hell could he shake the visual of Alani's mouth on him, her tongue moving over him, her cheeks hollowed as she . . .

Oh, God. In a croak, he asked, "Interested

in doing it again?"

"That depends."

Oh, no. No, no, *no.* He would not bargain with her. He wouldn't let any woman, not even Alani, manipulate him with sex. Hands tight on the cart handle, his abdomen in knots, he asked, "Depends on what?"

"How our relationship progresses, of course." This time her laugh was legitimate as she stopped and turned to him. "Did you expect me to negotiate? To offer you favors in exchange for . . . what? Less cloak-and-dagger? More openness?"

"I dunno." He would never understand her, but by God, he would keep trying. "Maybe."

Gently, as if explaining to a child, she said, "You do what you do, Jackson. Within your specialized field of expertise, I mean." She flapped a hand. "If you're anywhere near as good as my brother or Dare, then most everything you do has a motive, I'm sure. I might not always like the method, but I do understand the intent."

His molars clenched. "I'm every bit as good as them, damn it."

"And so incredibly modest, too." Turning her attention to the shelves, she examined a few spices. "But none of that has anything to do with our private relationship, now does it? And I'm afraid the two are going to clash."

He grabbed some peppercorns and tossed them in with the steaks. "Clash how?"

"I'm not in your field, remember? I don't thrive on danger. I don't think in terms of targets and threats and countermeasures. I'm just your average, run-of-the-mill interior designer."

He let his gaze drift over her. "Nothing average about you, woman."

For only a second, she looked moved by the compliment — before she shored up her resistance again. "Unless you explain your motives on occasion, how am I to decipher when I'm being kept in the dark for my own good, versus when you just plain don't want to share something with me?"

He rubbed his ear. "I dunno."

"I don't know, either. But it makes it impossible for me to gauge things." She touched his jaw. "And that's a conundrum."

A woman brushed by in her cart. Though she had what looked to be a two-year-old facing her, she gave him the once over and smiled.

As if to shield him with her body, Alani stepped in front of him and glowered at the poor shopper.

"Down, killer."

"I suppose you just love all the attention, don't you?"

"I —"

"Forget it, Jackson." Refusing to let him reply one way or the other, she indicated their collected groceries, the thick steaks, makings for salad and potatoes. "Do we have everything?"

"Looks like."

"Great. Let's get out of here." She forged forward, expecting him to follow.

"Yes, dear," he said, mostly to himself because he didn't want her any more worked up over something as silly as unsolicited attention. He watched the sway of her hips as he trailed her to the front of the store.

"I suppose you can't help it."

His attention lifted to her cold shoulder, and he asked with false sweetness, "You talking to me?"

"Yes." She spared him a look. "I'm being unfair and I know it." And then even more grudgingly, "Sorry."

" 'S okay." Actually, it was kind of nice to see her jealous. After all her indifference, this felt like a balm to his pride.

A hand to her forehead, she muttered, "You can't help it that you're so good-looking." She glanced at him again. "And tall."

Jackson shrugged.

"And . . . sexy."

The smile came slow and easy, but his mind remained in turmoil. "Since you're talking to me again, can I ask for clarification?"

"On what?"

"This whole conundrum thing you mentioned." To keep making headway with her, he needed to understand. "Are you saying that when it's better for you not to know something, I should tell you that there's something I'm not telling you?" He shook his head. Damn it, that even confused him.

But she nodded. "If I know you're being evasive to guard the end goal — protection-wise — then I won't think you're just shutting me out."

"Wouldn't do that anyway." Hell, he wanted to be closer to her. At least for now.

Until he shed the sharp need for her. And that should take . . . oh, a couple dozen sexual encounters at the very least.

"Oh, please." They sidled up in line behind an older couple. Lowering her voice, Alani asked, "So you're willing to open up and tell me anything I want to know?"

Cautious now, afraid of a trap, Jackson

said, "Yes?"

"You don't know if it's yes or no?"

"Actually, I don't know what type of corner you're backing me into."

"No corner. I'm just trying to establish the parameters of our . . . association."

"Relationship, damn it."

The fiftysomething lady in line ahead of Alani glanced back, then did a double take, and this time she didn't look away.

Jackson lowered his voice more. "We've slept together, and we'll sleep together again —" at least he hoped so "— so we're in a *relationship*." How far things would go . . . he didn't know yet. But he wouldn't let her deny what they had, just because he didn't remember it.

Shit.

Alani smiled. "Let's test this theory."

Even more cautious, Jackson braced himself. "Okay." And then, "How?"

"I have so many questions about you."

God, he hated the old introspection stuff. If she was any other woman, he'd just tease her, bed her again and then put a whole lot of space between himself and her curiosity.

But he couldn't do that now. Not only did he need to stay close to Alani to keep her safe, but he wanted her. Again and again.

"Maybe we could put that off for a bit?"

Demure, Alani said, "Sure, Jackson. There's nothing I really need to know."

"Damn it, I didn't say that."

"Yet you're dodging me already."

He gave a pointed look at the older woman, whose husband more or less dragged her off, and the young cashier who kept sneaking peeks at him. "Dodging eavesdroppers, actually."

She followed his gaze and scowled. "Unbelievable."

It was their turn at the register, and while Alani alternately slapped their purchases onto the belt and mean-mugged onlookers, he scanned the parking lot through the massive front windows of the store. Cars rearranged themselves in a continually shifting tide, some leaving, some parking, with pedestrians milling about.

He didn't see the silver sedan, but then, someone would have to be either a special kind of stupid, or incredibly arrogant, to continue using the same car, especially with it being so identifiable. Not many could afford a hundred-thousand-dollar vehicle.

Ostentatious. Whoever dogged them had a need to flaunt their wealth.

Or else the car was stolen and would be abandoned soon in favor of a different vehicle.

When Alani started to open her purse to pay the clerk, he caught her wrist and frowned at her. "Don't even think it." While the young cashier popped gum and looked between them, Jackson pulled a credit card from his own wallet.

Alani leaned over his hands to read the name on the card, and her right eyebrow lifted.

Trusting her not to question the alias listed on all his IDs, he ran the card, got the receipt and lifted the bags into the cart. Voice low, he said, "Stay to my left and slightly behind me."

"You're expecting trouble?"

"Nah. But I always prepare for it anyway." Luckily, they got to her car without a glitch and with no sense of being watched. Hazy waves of heat emanated from the blacktop lot. He felt his T-shirt stick to his spine and noticed that enticing glow on Alani's face again.

"Go ahead and get settled while I load the bags into the back."

She went one further and opened the driver's door to let out some of the accumulated heat.

"Thanks." After kicking up the air-conditioning, he put the car in Drive and continued to scan the area even as he drove from the lot.

Alani watched him. “Do you need me to be quiet so you can concentrate?”

Cute. And thoughtful. “Nah, it’s fine, but thanks.” He looked over at her just long enough to smile at the sincerity on her face.

“You’re sure? I don’t want to be the cause of distracting you.”

“I can multitask.” And good thing, since she’d been distracting him from the day he met her. There were times when he *almost* couldn’t think of anything else. “Luckily, my instincts take over when necessary.”

“So can I ask you something?”

Too late, Jackson realized that he might have avoided the inquisition if he’d let her believe he had to concentrate. Warily, he said, “Uh . . . sure,” as he pulled back onto the main road.

Passing back the same way they’d come, he noted the recent tire burns where, thanks to the silver BMW, others had been forced to brake hard to avoid colliding. He saw the gouge in the grassy area, left by his tires when he’d gone off the road. He saw gravel spit everywhere across the roadway.

At no point had he felt out of control with the car, but it pissed him off that anyone had put Alani in harm’s way. When he found the one responsible, there’d be hell to pay.

"How did you hook up with Dare and Trace?"

Uh-oh. Not exactly the type of question he'd been expecting. To buy himself a moment to think, Jackson pulled up behind a red light and said, "What's that?"

Her look said she recognized his ploy. "I know Trace doesn't recruit. That'd require advertising, and naturally, as a very private mercenary for hire, he can't do that. You guys had to meet somehow, but I've never heard how it came about. So tell me —"

"Did you swallow?"

They stared at each other, Jackson with an inner wince, Alani with incomprehension at that dropped-in, out-of-the-blue question.

Jesus. He'd been desperate to derail her line of questioning, but he hadn't meant to toss that out there like that. Course, it was something uppermost on his mind, eating at him, making it difficult to keep desire stomped down.

Only problem, she didn't seem to understand. She shook her head in confusion. "Swallow what?"

So he had to spell it out? Well, at least he'd gotten her on another topic. He cleared his throat. "You know . . . me."

Her brows rose, her lips parted.

The traffic light turned green. Jackson divided his attention between driving, surveying the area and studying Alani's dawning awareness.

His breathing deepened. His voice thickened. "Did you?"

She licked her lips. "You didn't give me a chance."

He reached for her hand and brought it to his thigh, holding it there with his own. The contrast maddened him, how small and delicate her hand felt under his, how it affected him for her to touch him at all, even on top of his thigh through his jeans. "Tell me how that all came about, will ya?"

Her fingers curled, biting into his muscle. "I was . . . kissing you. There." She nodded at his lap.

And damned but he felt it. "With you so far."

"You . . . you had a hand on my . . ." To show him, she reached up with her free hand to the back of her neck. "You were sort of guiding me, I guess."

"Yeah?" His dick twitched with the visual. "Like this?" He reached out for her nape, closing his big hand around her, kneading her, his fingers tangled in her silky hair.

"Yes."

"We were in the bed?"

"No. That is, you were. You sat on the side of the mattress, but I was . . . on the floor. In front of you."

Hell, yeah. Semi-erect now, he couldn't stop tormenting himself. "On your knees?"

Nodding, she licked her lips again. "You were making these rough, sexy sounds, like . . . I don't know. Low groans. Almost like you were in pain, but liked it."

"Yeah." A delicious pain. He was back there again, hurting for her.

Her hand on his thigh slid higher, the edge of her fingers nudging against his testicles. He hadn't come in his pants since middle school, but if he didn't cool things down, it could be a possibility.

Releasing her neck, Jackson closed her slender fingers in his and moved her hand to safer ground — on the seat between them.

One-handed, he turned a corner, not directly toward Alani's house, but rather to where he'd left his car in a private garage.

She didn't notice.

He knew she'd wanted to go by her workplace, too, but he didn't think he could handle it. Not now. Not with the way she twisted him inside out.

"Go on," he prompted.

"Suddenly, you sort of . . . broke." She

rushed her words between hastened breaths, as if the retelling affected her as much as it did him. "You pulled me away and came down on the floor with me and then . . ."

"Then?"

"You were inside me and it was hard and wild and . . ." She let out a sigh. "Pretty wonderful."

Chapter Eight

Okay, time to refocus.

Jackson adjusted his jeans and shifted in his seat. Knowing Alani watched his every move, her expression anxious, he again reached for her hand and brought it to his mouth.

Against her soft skin, he growled, "I'm going to love getting inside you again." God willing, that'd be tonight. Or better yet, before dinner. "But to keep from embarrassing myself, we gotta change the subject, pronto."

She clutched at his hand — until he pulled into the private garage. "What are you doing?"

"Fetching other transportation." He rolled down the window and pushed in a code on the security entrance. A gate rolled up, and he drove into the darkened garage.

Looking around in surprise, Alani realized they weren't exactly "down around the corner," as he'd claimed.

Her accusing gaze swung back to his. "Okay, Jackson *Davidson,* so now would be a good time for you to start explaining."

She deliberately stressed his fictitious name, so he addressed that first. "Settle down, woman. You knew I used an alias."

All her soft, heated sensuality of a minute before coalesced into temper. "Jackson Davidson," she repeated with derision. "How did you come up with that?"

"What does it matter?"

"It matters because now I'm wondering if I even know your real name." She sat back in her seat, arms crossed, expression stark. "Now I'm wondering if I know anything about you that's real."

His own black mood crowded in. "You know I want you." He leaned into her anger. "And you know I'll protect you. Doesn't that count for something?"

"Is there a woman you *don't* want?" She poked at his chest. "And as to protection, Dare or my own brother could see to that."

She just had to keep pushing him, infuriating him with unfamiliar feelings — like possessiveness. His voice lowered to match his frustration. "Damn it, woman, I haven't wanted anyone else since meeting you."

The harsh words echoed in the cavernous garage.

Alani blinked big eyes at him. "Really?"

God help him, she made him nuts. "Dare and Trace don't need to hover over you, because I'm on it. Me and only me. Get used to it." And with that forceful command, he kissed her harder than he meant to — and was surprised when she kissed him back.

Nothing could have gentled him quicker, smothered him with more emotion, than a reminder of how much she wanted him, too.

With a soft sound of acceptance, she gave in to him, and Jackson again had to fight himself to regroup. "Easy, love." He kissed her bottom lip, the corner of her mouth. "Let's get to your place and then we can pick up from here."

Caught between relief that Jackson hadn't noted the lack of a condom in her retelling of their lovemaking, and annoyance that he'd outright lied to her over where he'd parked, Alani hadn't been prepared for the impact of his kiss.

But he had an astounding effect on her. Like it or not, she had to accept that where Jackson Savor was concerned, she had no willpower.

He said that he hadn't wanted anyone else since meeting her. She pushed her hair from her face and dragged in a deep breath.

"Is your last name really Savor? Or is that a deception, too?"

Taken aback, he gazed at her, irate, turned on, maybe even a little lost.

No, what was she thinking? A man of Jackson's caliber, a mercenary with his skill set, did not feel lost over romantic conflicts.

"Yeah, that's my name. Don't spread it around, okay?" On a wave of irritability, he snatched his hat from the backseat, opened the car door and got out. After slamming the hat onto his head, he did more adjusting to his jeans, making it impossible for her not to notice his erection.

He leaned back into the car.

Dark green eyes direct, voice sharp, he said, "For your information, this was one of those precautionary measures that, at the time, I figured you didn't need to know."

"And now?"

"Hell, woman, the way you've kept me twisted, the location of my car was not uppermost in my mind."

Alani considered that and understood. "Okay."

He started to relax.

"You'll tell me how you and Trace met?"

He didn't even try to hide his groan. He even managed to look long-suffering.

She didn't need to be hit over the head. "Forget I asked. God forbid I dig out a state secret, or push you past your comfort zone over something so —"

"Fine." One hand on the car roof, one on the open door, he dropped his head forward in a hangdog pose. "I'll tell you when we get to your place, okay?"

He made her feel guilty, and she didn't like it. "Not necessary."

"Yeah, I think it is." His gaze sought hers. "I won't apologize for being set in my ways. I've always been private, and working with your brother has made me more so."

"I didn't ask you to apologize." She wanted honesty, not contrition.

"Thing is, the how and why of the way we met isn't something I like to talk about. But you might as well hear it from me, instead of your brother. He'd probably distort it just to make me look bad."

Back to square one. "If you really don't want —"

"Doesn't matter." He shook his head. "It was bound to come up sooner or later."

Sooner or later, meaning he intended to be involved with her beyond the immediate future? She just didn't know. "Okay."

"Good. Then scuttle your sexy little ass over here behind the steering wheel so we can get a move on."

Grabbing up her purse, Alani chose not to scuttle in favor of getting out and walking around the car. The garage wasn't that big, and she counted twelve cars inside. "What is this place?"

"Private parking garage. We make use of them in areas we visit often. Soon as you set up house, Trace secured this place."

She slid in behind the wheel. "Who parks here?"

"We do." He went about fastening her seat belt for her.

She was intrigued enough that she let him. "But who do the cars belong to?"

"Why?" He surveyed the colorful array of vehicles in various price ranges, from brand-new to barely roadworthy. "One of them appeals to you?"

"It's not that." She'd never been car-crazy. She wanted reliable transportation, period.

"Long as you don't have a preference, I think I'll grab that black SUV. It looks like it has some muscle."

Knowing she was about to learn yet another secret, Alani asked, "What do you mean, you're going to grab it? Surely you don't steal cars as a regular habit."

"Course not. These are all ours, here in a pinch in case we have to lose a tail." He closed her door and then rapped on the roof of the car. "Head straight home. I'm not expecting any trouble, but know that I'll be right behind you."

In openmouthed surprise, Alani watched him go to a truck and open the passenger door. He lifted out two duffel bags, then got something from the glove box. He closed and locked the truck and went to the shiny new SUV, opened it and got inside. Through the door window, he waved her around him.

Amazing.

Apparently there was a lot more to her brother's enterprise than she'd ever imagined.

She had a feeling there was more to Jackson Savor, too. Everything about him enthralled her.

She couldn't wait to learn even more.

While Jackson prepped the steaks, Alani put potatoes in the microwave and got the salad together. By silent agreement, they chose to get the food ready before weighing in on what was sure to be a lengthy conversation.

Jackson had left his duffel bags just inside the front door. Alani figured he didn't yet want to store them in the guest room, in hopes that he could share her room.

She sort of hoped that, too.

On her patio, the grill heated. They planned to eat outside, so she'd already loaded a tray with place settings and napkins. Though they were both busy, she couldn't stop stealing glances at Jackson. Even watching him wash his hands in the sink, the slide of his long fingers, now soap slick, left her fascinated.

She loved his hands. They were big and capable, twice the size of hers. They'd touched her gently, and when she wanted it most, not so gently. Somehow he'd known how to touch her, where, when, to get the most effect.

The cowboy hat, now gone, had further rumpled his hair. Alani had a vivid recollection of his head between her legs, her hand in his sun-streaked hair as his beard-rough jaw teased her tender inner thighs in direct contrast to the soft play of his tongue on her, in her.

Letting out a shuddering breath, she drew his attention. Keeping his back to her as he stood at the counter with the steaks, he glanced at her, then came back for a longer, knowing perusal.

His gaze roamed over her — her breasts, her belly. "You okay, sugar?"

"Yes." Here in the kitchen, alone with Jackson while preparing dinner together, she felt better than she had since her kidnapping.

The corner of his mouth lifted. He turned with the steaks on a platter. "Penny for your thoughts."

Never before had she taken part in sexual banter, but if he wanted to play, she'd give it her best shot. "I was thinking how much I like your body." But that didn't quite cover it, so she shook her head. "Not just how strong you are, but everything else, too."

He leaned back on the counter. "Like?"

"Your hands. Your feet. The way your shoulders move under your T-shirt. The slide of your Adam's apple when you swallow. Even your ears are nice."

He made a sound that was half humor, half chagrin. "I think you and I have unfinished business and it's tainting your brain." Gesturing with a nod of his head, he said, "Come on. Keep me company outside while I grill these bad boys."

"Okay." She stuck the salad in the fridge, pulled the potatoes from the microwave onto a plate, and followed him out. "At least the porch is shadowed this time of day."

"You have a nice place. I like it." The sizzle of beef wafted into the air as he put the steaks on the hot grill. After taking the potatoes from her, he said, "Take a seat. Talk to me."

"About what?" She smoothed the skirt of her sundress and sat on the bench to the picnic table. The flowers planted in and around her landscaping drew bees. Chickadees flitted in and out of the birdbath. A light breeze kept the hot, muggy air moving.

"In the car, when the BMW ran us off the road . . ." He seasoned the steaks with salt and cracked pepper. "You were shaken up for only a few seconds."

The evening had turned sultry and ultra comfortable. Alani didn't mind making admissions of her weakness, not to Jackson. She slipped her feet from her sandals and wiggled her toes. "Actually, it almost stopped my heart."

"No way." Letting the steaks sizzle, he stepped to the side and crossed his arms over his chest. "You looked cool as a cucumber."

The things he said waffled between outrageous and hilarious. "Not me." Wrinkling her nose, she confessed, "I'm a terrible coward."

He pointed a big fork at her. "If you'd ever

dealt with a real coward, you'd know better."

"I suppose you have?" She'd envisioned him going up against the cruelest villains, facing off with practiced criminals, trading fists with killers — and walking away triumphant. But she'd never thought about him engaged with a coward.

"Plenty of them. Deep down, most of the people I encounter on jobs are chickenshit. They love to bully and abuse because it makes them feel more powerful. But when they know they're busted, they resort to pleading real quick."

"That makes them cowards?"

"The worst kind. And I can tell you, you don't fit the bill. You kept your head, and our cover, today. After the crazy way that car came after us, a lot of women would've been rattled and blubbering." He rolled a shoulder. "Some men, too. But you hid your reaction and smiled at me."

"I didn't want the others to see me upset."

He shook his head. "Bet they were as impressed as me."

When he turned back to the grill to check the steaks, Alani thought about what Dare had told her.

Should she confide in Jackson? She didn't want him to have a false impression of her.

She'd done her fair share of blubbering. Sometimes, when the darkness closed in around her, she cried still.

"I . . . I sometimes go into panic mode."

Alert to her changed tone and the gravity of what she said, Jackson set aside the fork and gave her his undivided attention. "You mean, since the kidnapping?"

She nodded. "For the longest time, my life seemed charmed. Nothing bad could happen to me." She'd been so naive. So *dumb.*

"You lost your parents." Jackson sounded too solemn. "Nothing charmed in that."

"I know." Her smile fell flat, but she still mourned the loss of her mother and father, and talking about them always left her wistful at what could never be recovered. "After they died, Trace seemed determined to insulate me from anything negative. Not just sad feelings, but . . . life in general. He never wanted me to be gloomy or insulted or disappointed about anything."

"I know he's protective."

"Somehow, that word doesn't quite cover it." This smile was more genuine. "Trace has always watched me so closely, probably more so than our parents would have."

"Because he was afraid of losing you, too."

Alani nodded.

"That had to be tough on a young woman." He teased her, saying, "How could you cut loose with Trace's eagle eye on you?"

"Exactly." For her, there'd been no acting out, no cutting loose. Not until she'd gone to the beach — and then she'd been taken . . . She squeezed her eyes shut.

"Hey." Jackson put the steaks on a plate and closed the grill. Straddling the bench beside her, he enclosed her in his arms.

Softly, Alani said, "I let Trace take responsibility for me. It was so much easier than being responsible for myself."

"And because he was all you had, too."

"I didn't want to disappoint him."

Using just his baby finger, he eased a few strands of hair away from her cheek. "I don't think you could."

She half laughed at that. If she hadn't disappointed Trace, she'd more than disappointed herself. "But you know Trace. You know that he excels at everything he does. For the longest time, he was the biggest, strongest, smartest, most capable guy I knew."

"A regular superhero, huh?" Jackson glanced down, then back into her eyes. "I guess no other guys measured up?"

"They seemed wimpy in comparison, and

just plain uninteresting."

"Shit."

Restraining her smile, Alani leaned into him. He felt good, and smelled even better with the way the humidity had warmed his skin and hair. She loved the softness of his cotton T-shirt over firm, pronounced muscles. "But then I got taken. . . ."

"And retrieved." He kissed her temple.

"And then I met you."

His hand moved over her back, stroking, caressing. "So I measure up?"

Anxious for a lighter tone, Alani stood. "I'll let you know after I taste my steak."

Jackson waited until her eyes closed in pleasure and she made a purring sound of contentment. Damn. She even made dining sexy. "Good?"

"Delicious."

That she wasn't a picky, rabbit-food-only kind of gal was a huge bonus for him. "It's the cracked pepper." He wolfed down his own big bite of juicy steak.

"Could be the company, too." Her lashes lifted, and she gave him the warm look of a woman romantically involved.

It should have set off alarm bells, but instead, Jackson basked in her acceptance. "So I pass muster?"

She paused with a big bite of salad halfway to her mouth. "I'd say you excel."

"At more than grilling?"

She lowered the fork. "Yes." She sighed. "Last night . . . you were amazing."

He'd be amazing again, soon as she was ready.

"Before the kidnapping, I never dated much. With Trace on guard duty and most guys naturally wary of him, it always seemed like too much trouble."

He wanted to know everything about her, the good, the bad and the shit that never should have happened. "After the kidnapping?"

"I was afraid." She said it in an offhand tone, complete with a shrug.

"Afraid of men?" Jackson waited, and after a few more bites, she looked at him again.

"Afraid of everything, really. Guys asked me out, and I kept wondering if all they wanted was a date, or if they were luring me away again."

Luring her away . . . He'd dealt with enough victims to get a full visual, and God, the knowledge of what she'd gone through ate at him. "That's what happened on the beach?"

Introspective, she picked at her potato with fork and knife. "I thought I was being so daring." Her laugh sounded self-deprecating. "I was twenty-two, and finally on my first real vacation, on my own for a change. I had friends there with me, but they were already involved and their boy-friends were there and I felt weird, being the only single woman."

At that age, especially with her sheltered life, she'd been a girl rather than a woman. But so much had changed since then. "Guys flirted with you."

"Some."

"You in a bikini?" He took another bite to encourage her to do the same. "Come on, Alani. I bet they all flirted."

Modesty kept her grin at bay. "It was so fun, having that attention, teasing back." She peeked at him. "Even sneaking a few kisses here and there."

Unwarranted jealousy burned through his veins, but he kept his tone mild, wanting her to confide in him. "And more?"

"No. Not . . . not then." Disgusted, she set down her utensils and dropped her face into her hands.

The first sound she made set off alarm bells. Crying?

Usually, a weepy woman brought out all his macho instincts. He considered tears to be the womanliest a woman could be, and that made him feel indulgent, like a big protector. While coddling a woman, he often got . . . turned on.

But with Alani, his stomach bottomed out, and his chest constricted. He reached for her hand. "Babe, what is it?"

She made the sound again, a dry laugh that pained him as much as tears would have. That she could so easily jerk around his feelings bugged him big-time.

"Think about it, Jackson." She lowered her hands. "When Trace is around, he sees everything."

"And he was always around."

"I barely got asked out, rarely got kissed. I didn't have much success at anything else."

"So . . ." She'd been a virgin before being kidnapped?

"Bet I was even more naive than you imagined, huh?"

An invisible vise clenched around his heart. "The assholes who took you . . . ?"

"No." She shook her head. "They didn't rape me. Not . . . like you mean."

Fury stole his voice. He watched her.

"They . . . well, they were saving me." She tightened her lips; her breath trembled. "I was too afraid to understand much of what they said, but they got their point across all the same."

He couldn't move. Hell, he could barely breathe.

"I'm sorry." She rolled her eyes. "Here I am, spoiling our dinner."

Needing to touch her, Jackson reached for her hands. "How long did they have you, honey?"

As if the damn broke, she started talking fast. "Time runs together and drags out when you're terrorized. I couldn't tell day from night. It felt like weeks, but I know it wasn't. I didn't sleep, and I didn't want to eat, but they insisted. I was so dirty, I could smell myself." She squeezed his fingers, holding on tight. "We were all dirty. The room was so hot and there wasn't any fresh air, and they didn't really give us the means to clean up."

He knew from talking with other victims how the loss of dignity hurt as much as the physical abuse.

"They do that on purpose. To break you down." Jackson wasn't sure she heard him. "But you didn't let them."

"I felt so sick from whatever they'd given me. When they'd get near me again, I'd do this awful dry heaving, and they laughed about it. I was so ashamed. Especially with how they treated Molly."

Molly, now Dare's wife, had been in an

altogether different situation. They hadn't planned to sell her. "Did she talk to you?"

Alani nodded. "One of the men kept pinching me. Not hard enough to leave a mark, just enough to get me hysterical again." She chewed her bottom lip. "Molly would yell at them, call them names." Her eyes sank shut, and she whispered, "They weren't as concerned about bruising her."

Jackson swallowed hard. He knew Dare still had to suffer his own torment over what Molly had gone through.

"I wanted to beg her to be quiet." Alani stared at him, her expression desperate. "But I was afraid to say anything."

He drew her hand to his mouth and kissed her white knuckles. "I'm glad Dare killed them."

"Yes." By small degrees, she composed herself. She stared at her half-empty plate before searching his face. "You'd have killed them, too?"

"With pleasure."

"You . . . have killed people?"

Jackson went still inside, wondering what she needed to hear, how much he should tell her. He tried to weigh the ugliness of truth against the morality of justice.

Alani's smile came and went. "It's okay. I know you can't say much." She started to pull her hands away.

He didn't let her. "When it's warranted, I have no problem at all putting someone out of commission."

"Meaning . . ." She had a problem with the word, saying tentatively, "Dead?"

He had no problems. "Definitely dead."

Unfazed by his answer, she asked, "Have you saved any women from human traffickers?" She rushed on to explain. "I'm not being nosy. Well, I mean, I guess I am. But I know most of what Trace and Dare do these days centers around that."

"Yeah." Seeing that she was back to herself again, he let her hands go and pressed her plate toward her. "How about you finish eating while we talk?"

He waited for her to say she wasn't hungry. He waited for her to give in to the upset of old memories, to maybe have lost her appetite.

Instead, she agreed and cut into her steak again.

In so many ways, she pleased him. "From what I understand, Dare and Trace started out doing anything and everything they considered righteous. Like saving a senator's kidnapped son, rescuing a businessman held hostage in another country, busting up a cult —" he raised a brow "— or busting up a government conspiracy. That kind of stuff."

"Seriously? Wow. I knew he did dangerous work. And I knew he had some major contacts. But I hadn't realized . . ."

"He's shielded you." Jackson couldn't fault Trace for that. "Some of the shit they've dealt with isn't fit for sharing with a baby sister."

"How do you know? Do you have a sister?"

"Nope. No brothers, either." Now wasn't the time to talk about Arizona, and he really didn't want to go into family comparisons. "They'd tangled plenty of times with human traffickers, sometimes out of the country, sometimes in. Then you were taken, and that made it more personal for Trace."

"But it's not personal for you?"

Since meeting her, it'd gotten real personal, but he only shrugged. "I'm good at what I do. It suits me better than anything else could."

She finished off her iced tea and pushed back her near-empty plate. "You really are confident, aren't you?"

"If you're worried about me keeping you safe, don't be."

"It's not that." Going all sweet and shy on him, she ducked her face. "After those men took me, I couldn't seem to get very interested in any man. I tried, though."

"With Marc Tobin." Saying the bastard's name left a foul taste in his mouth.

"That's just it. The reason we split up, I mean. I wanted to like him. I did like him as a person." She shrugged. "Not so much as a man."

Was she saying what he hoped she was saying? "You didn't sleep with him?"

Hesitation held her, and then she shook her head. "No."

Damn. Bet that burned Tobin's ass. Jackson knew firsthand how it was to want her but not have her. Venturing a guess, he said, "You got tired of him pressing the issue?"

"Yes."

The last rays of the setting sun blazed across the sky in fiery shades of red, casting mysterious shadows over Alani's face. "But you slept with me?"

Her deep breath drew his attention to her breasts. "You." She took two more breaths. "And only you."

His gaze shot to hers. He croaked, "You were a virgin?" *And he'd missed it?* Not that he'd ever before considered a woman's virginity to be a prized asset, but with Alani . . . yeah. He loved the idea that no one else had touched her.

"And you were incredible." She tipped her head, timid but determined. "I've thought about this ever since, and if you don't mind showing me everything there is, everything I've missed —"

"Hell, yeah," he rushed to say.

But she hadn't finished. "If you don't mind a no-strings-attached type of relationship . . ." She let that trail off, something stark in her expression as she watched him, waiting.

What the hell? He pokered up in affront, unsure what to say to that.

Softly sighing, she braced her shoulders and stared at him. "Well then, I'd like to . . . you know."

Damn it, that "no strings" comment stung. He wasn't ready to dissect his own feelings, but he *did* feel something. Lots of things, actually, not all of them physical. It burned his ass that she might not be as involved as him.

"You want to experiment with me? Is that what you're saying?" He made it sound like a sneer, expecting her to correct him, hoping she'd say that she wanted more — from him and with him.

Instead, she nodded. "Yes." And almost as an afterthought, "Please."

God, she wanted to use him. For sexual

pleasure. *Her* pleasure.

She'd just flat-out admitted it.

He felt like a lab rat — a really, *really* turned-on lab rat. Anticipating everything she might want to try, the explorations that came to mind had him sweltering with need.

Jackson pushed everything to the side of the table and reached across it for her.

He'd always known he had a breaking point — and Alani, bless her innocent little heart, had just found it.

Chapter Nine

One minute Jackson had her half over the table, his hands clamped onto her upper arms as he devoured her mouth with enough intensity to press back her head, leaving her helpless in his embrace.

In the next instant, he was on her side of the picnic table, stationed in front of her as if to shield her with his now tensed body.

But from what?

In his right hand, he held a steak knife. She recognized the lethal way he gripped it from demonstrations given to her by her brother.

Alani tried to adjust to the new circumstance. She didn't even know how he'd gotten to her side of the table so quickly. She definitely didn't know why he wielded a knife. "What the —"

"Go inside."

The hard command brooked no arguments, but she couldn't seem to budge without knowing why he wanted her gone. She tried to see over his shoulder, but got a glimpse of only her yard — no threats. "Jackson, what in the world is —"

Her ex-boyfriend, Marc Tobin, poked his head around the side of the house.

When he saw them, he drew up short, startled.

They stared at each other. Marc's gaze went from Alani to all over Jackson, and no way could he miss Jackson's aggressive mood.

"Marc." Alani had to speak from behind Jackson, since he wouldn't let her move around in front of him. "What are you doing here?"

Not since telling him, indisputably, that they were done had she heard from Marc. Their relationship hadn't ended well, not that there'd ever been much of a relationship to begin with. But she couldn't see Marc as dangerous. Annoying, yes, but he wouldn't hurt her.

"I knocked." His dark eyes went from Jackson to what little he could see of Alani on tiptoe looking over Jackson's shoulder, and back again.

Already, Jackson had relaxed his stance, flipping the knife around so that instead of it being gripped as a weapon, he held it as a utensil.

But his other hand continued to keep Alani at his back.

Indignant, disapproving, Marc took another step toward them. "What's going on here? Alani, are you all right?"

She peeked again — and saw that Marc looked ready to jump to her unnecessary defense. If she let that happen, Jackson would annihilate him. She didn't have a single doubt.

"I'm fine." She pinched Jackson hard on the rump and said with insistence, "Excuse me," as she stepped around him.

Jackson, who was focused on Marc with burning intensity, jumped from the goose. "Ow, woman." Blindly he reached for and found her wrist to keep her at his side. To Marc, he said, "You're interrupting our dinner."

The rudeness appalled her. Once again, Alani made use of her elbow; this time, it had no discernable effect on Jackson. He stood there, a large immovable object, his gaze a laser of dislike aimed at Marc.

"Oh, for the love of —" She didn't want to cause more of a scene, so she pasted on a smile. "Marc, I'm sorry, but obviously you've caught me at a bad time."

"It was a great time," Jackson drawled, "until he showed up."

"I see now." Marc put his hands on his hips, his aggression pulsing off him in waves. "You left me for him."

"I was never *with* you," Alani reminded him. "We dated a few times, that's all."

"I wanted more."

Yes, he'd wanted sex. When he wouldn't take no for an answer, she'd ended things. "That was never going to happen, and you know it."

"Because you were fucking him, is that it?"

The crude insult stunned her. "You're way out of line."

That Jackson remained silent was nothing short of a miracle. But then, maybe he didn't mind letting Marc make an ass of himself.

Dressed in a pullover and black slacks that showed off his trim, muscular build, Marc looked as impeccable as always. He also looked petulant.

Somehow he ran a hand over his styled, dark hair without mussing it at all. "I need to talk to you, honey. Alone."

Jackson said, "Ain't happening," and when Alani tried to step forward, he amended that to, "She has nothing to say to you, pal.

Tough breaks, but that's how it goes."

God, she would kill Jackson. Later. Glaring up at him, she said, "Let me go."

His eyes narrowed, but his shrug looked casual enough as he opened his hand and released her.

Apologetic, Alani took a few steps toward Marc. "You remember Jackson Davidson?"

"We met," Marc agreed, not looking away from her. He wore a deliberately tortured expression. "Couldn't we find a little privacy?"

Knowing that wouldn't happen, not with Marc being a potential suspect, no matter how ridiculous she found that to be, Alani made her excuses. Voice low, she said, "Marc, it's over between us. There's nothing more to say."

He breathed harder. "So I was right. You're with him now?" He jerked his head toward Jackson.

To her relief, Jackson again said nothing. When she glanced back at him, Alani found him searching the distant area beyond her backyard. She frowned and turned back to Marc. "We're dating," she fibbed, because that sounded better than saying they were in lust.

"If it's the same type of dating we did, does that mean you haven't slept with him?"

Enough already. Alani put back her shoulders. "That is none of your business. I meant it when I said it was over."

Marc took a fast, forceful step toward her.

Alani flinched, waiting for Jackson to attack.

She glanced back again in time to see him seat himself at the table, his expression bored. Odd. And almost insulting.

"I want it to be my business." Marc paid Jackson no mind. "That's what I need to talk about with you. I know I . . . I screwed up."

She did not want to have this conversation in front of Jackson. "It really had nothing to do with you, Marc." He wasn't Jackson, so no matter what he did or didn't do, it never would have worked out.

Marc denied that with a shake of his head. "I rushed you, and I'm sorry for that. I should have shown more patience."

Jackson cracked his knuckles and yawned loudly.

Knowing Jackson to be unpredictable, Alani concentrated on ending the conversation, and fast. She took Marc's hands. "It wouldn't have mattered, Marc. I'm sorry, but it just wasn't there for me."

"I don't buy that." He tugged her closer, his voice now intimate. "We had fun. You were warming up to me, you just needed more time."

Jackson made a sound of impatience.

And his tone generous, superior, Marc added, "I didn't realize at the time that you had sexual hang-ups."

Alani's eyes flared at hearing Marc say such a thing.

"But we'll work around that." He lowered his voice, sounding more intimate. "I have some ideas."

"Tobin," Jackson said with disbelief, "you are seriously whack-a-doodle, you know that?"

Whack-a-doodle? That was his reaction? Bemused, Alani stared at Jackson.

He shrugged. "Well, he is." And then with insistence: "You do not have hang-ups."

True enough. With Jackson, she had no inhibitions, sexual or otherwise.

Marc's mouth touched her neck. "Give me another chance, Alani."

A wave of revulsion landed her firmly back in the here and now. *"No."*

He resisted her efforts to put space between them. "If you give me another chance, I can help you."

Help her? "You *are* whack-a-doodle!" Oh God, now she sounded like Jackson.

"When you want me to intervene," Jackson told her lazily, "just lemme know."

"Fuck you!" Marc said.

Jackson raised a brow. "What do you say, honey? Couldn't I muss him up just a little?"

Alani groaned. For whatever reason that suited him, Jackson had allowed her to handle this situation when she knew it went against the grain for him to do so. Like Trace and Dare, he was a man who would intervene for any woman facing a pushy suitor, but for a woman under his protection, it had to be doubly tough to stand aside.

Marc, being an astute man, should have realized his precarious position. Apparently, he did not.

Time to take charge. "I do not need —"

"We'll go slow, babe, I promise." He put his mouth to her temple even as she strained away from him. "I'll ease you into things. You'll love it."

"You will *shut up.*" She gasped. "Right now." Her face burned. Her stomach jolted — in disgust. Marc had never appealed to her sexually. No man had until Jackson. "I do not have hang-ups."

"She doesn't," Jackson confirmed.

"And," Alani said loudly, before Marc could react to Jackson's jibe, "I don't need

your help."

He caressed her upper arms. "But you were so squeamish about everything."

If being utterly disinterested counted as squeamish. She slapped his hands away. "What is wrong with you? How dare you talk about this here, now?"

"With me listening in, she means," Jackson offered helpfully. "Crass, man. Really crass."

"You're not helping, Jackson." God save her from the male species.

"You won't let me help."

"Can't you go inside?"

He snorted. "I can take him apart, that's what I can do." At his leisure, Jackson unfolded himself from the table and stood — tall, broad-shouldered, oh-so-imposing, in front of them. Sporting a hilarious, pleading face, he implored, "C'mon, Alani. Let me hurt him. He's begging for it."

Marc bunched up like a junkyard dog. He snarled and set her aside. "Why don't you try?"

Alani felt she had to be fair. She stepped in front of Marc. "Just so you know, he *will* destroy you. And given how you're behaving, I might let him."

"I'm not a slouch." He flexed his hands. "I can handle myself."

"I never said you couldn't. But don't let Jackson's laid-back attitude deceive you. He would love to fight right now, and you truly wouldn't be a match." Not in any way. "You should trust me on this."

"Spoilsport," Jackson muttered. And that set off Marc anew.

On the balls of his feet, he bounced to the side of her, then to the left, then the right.

Jackson tucked in his chin. "What the hell?"

Marc lunged forward with a wild swing. Jackson actually laughed as he easily dodged the fist.

Enraged, Marc swung again . . . and again he missed.

Grinning, Jackson said, "Is there a punch line to this routine?"

When Marc charged forward, Jackson landed a short, effortless jab square on his chin. Eyes rolling up, Marc went stiff, then fell back hard, his legs buckled awkwardly, his arms out at his sides.

Alani gasped. "Jackson!"

"What?" Unrepentant, he peered down at Marc. "He started doing crazy hops and shit. It was just reflex."

"You didn't have to knock him out."

"What'd you want me to do? Hug him?" He made a face. "I barely tapped him. How was I supposed to know he had a glass jaw?"

Dropping to her knees, Alani patted Marc's slack face. The last thing she needed right now was a fool knocked out in her yard. "Marc?"

Bleary-eyed, Marc came around and stared at her in confusion. A purpling bruise swelled on his jaw.

"I didn't hit you that hard, you pussy." Jackson nudged him with his boot. "Get up, for God's sake."

He groaned. "What happened?"

"You got knocked out, that's what happened!" Sitting back, Alani blasted him with her annoyance. "I told you not to harass him, didn't I? I *told* you this would happen."

Hands on his knees, Jackson peered down at Marc. "She did tell you."

Marc looked beyond her, contemplated Jackson, who now smiled evilly, and met her gaze again. He half sat up with a wince. "I don't want to distress you."

"You already have." She took pity on him. "Things are over between us, Marc. For good."

He worked his jaw and winced some more. "Because of *him.*"

"Oh, for the love of . . ." She pushed back to her feet. "He has nothing to do with it. Why not admit that you were never all that involved in the first place? No, you don't have to say anything, Marc. I'm not stupid. I know I wounded your male ego, and I'm sorry for that. Really, I am. But I was nothing more than a challenge for you. You don't want me, not really."

Jackson snorted. "If that's true, he's a total dumbass on top of being a loudmouth wuss."

She whipped around to confront him, and he held up both hands in concession.

Silently daring him to make another sound, Alani waited, but other than a slight tilt of his mouth, he did nothing more. She gave a nod of satisfaction.

Lord. For the longest time she hadn't dated anyone, and no one had seemed to care much about that. Guys didn't chase after her. Guys definitely didn't fight over her.

Now she had two of them being possessive.

"You should go, Marc." The day felt never ending.

Casting a cautious glance at Jackson, he lumbered to his feet. "I don't want to leave you alone with him. He's violent."

That had her rolling her eyes. "Actually, he showed great restraint."

In his sexy drawl, Jackson said, "Thanks,

darlin'."

She would not look at him again. "Now, no more drama, Marc. I want you to leave."

Marc hesitated, then unwisely drew her close for a big hug. In her ear, he whispered, "If you need me, for anything at all, call. Somehow I'll figure it out. Okay?"

Right. What could he do? Jackson had put him down with a negligent tap. No, she was much safer sticking close to Jackson, but saying so to Marc would serve no purpose. "Sure, thanks." She would *not* be calling him.

Jackson stirred behind her. "He's got two seconds, Alani, before he finds himself on his ass again, and I don't care what you think about that."

Alani wiggled out of Marc's embrace. She showed her teeth in what she hoped looked more like a smile than anticipation of strangling Jackson. "Goodbye."

His hands fisted, his gait a little unsteady, Marc finally turned and left.

When Alani started to speak, Jackson held up a finger. In the past five minutes, he'd had more mood swings than a menopausal woman. First turned-on, then territorial, bored, aggressive and now on alert. If she let him, he'd make her dizzy with his ever-changing disposition.

In stealth mode, Jackson caught her hand to draw her into the house. Sensing that something had him on edge, she went along willingly. He led her through the house to the front window where, with one finger, he lifted aside a curtain to peek out.

Standing back, Alani folded her arms. "What, exactly, are you doing?"

"Making sure the bastard leaves."

She knew he meant Marc. "Why wouldn't he?"

"Why wouldn't he have called to tell you he was coming by?" Jackson's profile went taut at whatever he saw through the window. "Why would he have crept around to the back of the house?"

Before she could question that, he said, "He *was* sneaking, hon. Otherwise I'd have heard him sooner."

So . . . unlike her, Jackson hadn't been so involved in that devastating kiss that he'd lost sense of time and place?

Great. She'd been smart to ask for a commitment-free affair. No reason to advertise to him that she was already half in love.

She wanted him, no two ways about that. But she had her pride. Not knowing what Jackson felt kept her from being obvious about her own feelings. "He's been here before, Jackson. He had no reason to be sneaky."

"Yeah? Then why did he park down the street so far from your house?"

No way. Alani squeezed in front of Jackson's broad chest to look for herself.

With his nose in her hair, he said, "That's his car, right? Metallic gray Mercedes?"

"Yes," Alani murmured, "that's his car."

Jackson nuzzled against her neck. "Not as rich as the BMW, but still pretty costly."

Sure enough, Marc had parked several houses down, when usually he would have parked in the driveway. What was he up to? "Maybe he saw your car and . . . I don't know. He guessed I was with another guy so he wanted to just . . . take a peek?"

That sounded lame even to her.

"You think he wanted to spy on you?" Slipping an arm around her, Jackson opened his hand over her belly. "I can buy that."

Now that Marc was in his car ready to leave, she stepped back from the curtain. "What do you really think he was doing?"

"Besides being an ass?"

She couldn't defend Marc; he had behaved horribly. "He wasn't usually like that."

"I don't care what he was like, he still had his hands on you." Jackson caught her wrists and turned her so that her back was to the wall beside the front window. With sensual intent — and a firm press of his hips — he pinned her there. "And he insulted you. Even though the dipshit didn't make any real headway, I've got the urge to remove every thought of him from your memory."

Not necessary. With Jackson around, how could she think of another man? But she had a feeling she'd appreciate his efforts all the same. Their banter throughout the day, all the kissing and touching, and especially Jackson's outspoken desire, had worked against her.

Alive with need, Alani squirmed beneath his hold. "What do you suggest?"

His gaze brightened. He bent to kiss her, but the kiss didn't last. "Soon, honey."

Soon? But her brain — and her body — had already jumped ahead to what they would do. Now.

The setting sun sent streaks of pink, purple and orange across the graying sky. The temperature had cooled, but not enough. Mosquitoes feasted relentlessly.

So Jackson had a new girlfriend? Huh. Or maybe, given that most of the women didn't last any longer than it took for him to bed them, this was his first real girlfriend.

The frail little blonde not only had him at her place, she had him facing off with another guy.

Interesting.

The binoculars were a great investment. They'd made it easy to see everything, even from a good distance away. It was a novel thing to see Jackson playing house, sitting down to a picnic table to eat. Of course, that hadn't lasted long before he had the poor woman half dragged over the table so he could have at her mouth.

Jackson Savor had no sense of moderation.

Luckily the other guy had shown up, interrupting things just as they got nauseating.

Voices didn't carry so far, but it didn't take a genius to read the body language. Though he tried to hide it, Jackson didn't like the other guy talking to her, touching her.

He wasn't just protecting the woman. Nope, he'd staked a claim, guarding her like a prized possession.

Was he in love?

Love could be used against a person. Love was a most powerful weapon.

Plenty of trouble would be heading Jackson's way.

Soon everyone would know just how equipped he was to deal with it.

■ ■ ■ ■

Damn, but it wasn't easy to turn his back on Alani, especially with her looking so . . . *ready.*

Finally.

If the delays had happened to anyone else, he'd find the situation hilarious.

Not so funny when he was the one suffering a perpetual boner.

But as much as he wanted to accommodate them both, he felt a menace — maybe Tobin, but maybe not. And damn it, he couldn't chance her security.

He dug out his cell phone.

Breathless, all warmed up, Alani asked, "Who are you calling?"

He had to close his eyes against the urge to put off responsibility. "Your brother."

She threw up her hands. "Great. By all means. Keep Trace apprised. I'll just go put up our dinner mess."

Jackson swung her around, kissed her hard and said against her mouth, "There's nothing I want more than to get busy with you. You gotta know that." He searched her gaze, willing her to understand. When she nodded, he kissed her again. "I'll make it worth the wait, I promise."

She curled her fingers over the front of his belt and gave a small tug. "I'm going to hold you to that."

He stood there, horny as hell, as she walked away. When she went through the back door, he shook himself and trailed after her. Until he figured out what was going on, he wouldn't let her out of his sight.

With the push of one button, he called Trace. Her brother answered on the first ring.

"Yeah?"

Alani carried a filled tray back into the house, and he followed. "You at my apartment?"

"Yup." Trace sounded distracted. "Not finding too much, though."

Damn. "I was afraid of that, but it was worth a shot."

"That why you called?"

"No." He tracked Alani's movements as she began rinsing plates and sticking them in the dishwasher. "I know you've got your hands full, so is there any chance Chris can look into the whereabouts of Tobin?" As Dare's friend and superassistant in all things, Chris had access to all kinds of information.

"Already done. Supposedly he's off on a leave of absence. His staff thinks he's out of the country, and according to them, he's been gone since about the time Alani broke things off. I find it hard to believe he's taking the breakup that hard, but who knows? I can dig some more, but —"

Jackson finally found his voice. "He was just here."

A pause, and then, "Interesting."

"Yeah." Jackson saw Alani smile, a shy, curious, anticipatory smile. Heat roiled through him, and he said absently, "I knocked him out."

"You want to tell me why?"

"Yeah, he —" Alani stepped up to him, so Jackson said, "Hang on a sec." He covered the phone.

She folded her hands together and cleared her throat. "I'm going to take a shower."

He started to offer to shower with her, but she cut him off.

"And I'm going to lock the door." She tried to look stern, but instead she looked flushed and maybe a little nervous. "A smart man would know not to intrude."

Explicit visuals blasted his brain: Alani naked, wet, soap-slick . . . He swallowed and managed a nod. "If you linger too long, I'm a goner. Just so you know."

Heat colored her cheeks and parted her lips. "When I'm done, we're going to clear the air."

Clear the air how? Of sexual tension? That worked for him. "You mean . . . ?"

"We'll talk. That is, if you still don't mind answering some questions?"

He could think of a dozen different things he'd rather do, and they all involved Alani naked, but he shrugged. "Sure thing, if that's what it takes."

Her gaze went to his mouth; her hand touched his chest. "And then you promised to help me make up for lost time."

Oh, yeah. That promise he would keep, and then some. "After your shower, don't bother getting dressed."

"Jackson," she warned, "I do want to talk first."

"And we will. In bed. Naked." He cupped her cheek. "Deal?"

Excitement darkened the gold of her eyes and made them look slumberous — the same way he imagined she'd look right after a climax. She took two deep breaths, then nodded and hurried away.

Jackson watched the gentle sway of her hips, how her long blond hair shimmered down her back.

Damn, he needed to get off the phone, and fast.

He put the cell back to his ear and rushed

through the rest of his explanations. "Tobin had it coming. He was being an ass, insulting her, even challenging me —"

"No way."

"Yeah." Jackson still couldn't credit how the idiot had tried to punch him. He shook his head. "I let him take two wild swings before I decked him. The big baby went out cold, and when he came to, Alani sent him packing."

Trace laughed. "Figures. So what did he really want? "

"I don't know. Yet." Jackson went on to explain about how Marc had parked up the street. "He was too far away for me to see the license plate number, but I got it the first time I met him."

"I already have it."

Jackson had figured as much.

"I'll take care of unraveling Tobin. But have you told Alani about Arizona yet?"

Hell, there hadn't been much opportunity for full disclosure. Though he didn't want to admit it, even to himself, he dreaded that particular conversation. It could be a deal-breaker, and he didn't want to risk it. Not yet.

Jackson looked toward the hall where Alani had gone. "I'll get to it."

"You better, because the school sent you

some mail."

Shit. He hadn't given Trace a key to his mailbox, but that wouldn't have stopped Trace. Knowing damn good and well that he'd already read it, Jackson asked, "All right, let's hear it."

"They're discreet. The letter informed you of a need to meet."

That was usually the message. What had happened now? Jackson let out a long breath. "I'll see to it." After he saw to Alani. But for now, he was more than ready to drop the topic of Arizona. "Keep me posted if you two find anything."

"The same." Trace disconnected the call.

Jackson looked around her house. He could hear the shower running, so he figured he had a few minutes yet. He went through the house, locking up, taking some extra security measures so that he could better see to Alani without concern that intruders could slip in unnoticed. Sure, he'd still be aware of anything that happened, but he could relax a little.

He heard the shower shut off, and his abdomen tightened. He was already getting hard just thinking about her.

Before she emerged, he went to his duffel and got out a box of rubbers. Detouring into her bedroom, he turned down the bed, set out the rubbers and cleared space for his weapons.

Wrapped in a towel, her hair twisted atop her head, Alani walked in. She froze in the doorway when she saw him.

God Almighty, she posed the greatest temptation he'd ever seen. The towel barely covered her from breasts to upper thighs. She had her knees squeezed together, her bare feet touching.

Clutching the towel for all she was worth, she licked her lips. "You were waiting for me?"

"Getting ready." He pulled off his shirt and tossed it to a chair. Next he sat on the bed and unlaced his boots. As he pulled off the boots and his socks, he said, "I'm going to take a quick shower, too. You'll stay here in the bed until I'm done?"

She nodded. "Yes." But she didn't move.

Jackson smiled at her — and stood. Keeping her gaze locked in his, he unbuckled his thick, heavy belt.

Her eyes flared wide.

Reaching to the small of his back, he held the holster and slid the black leather belt from the loops on his jeans. He took the Beretta from the holster so he could keep it with him, but put the holster and belt, along with the knife from his boot, on her nightstand.

Her gaze traveled all over his body, but she asked, "What are you going to do with the gun?"

"Nothing, I hope. But where I go, the gun goes." Bare-chested and barefoot, he closed the space between them. This near to her, he could smell the lotion she'd used, and the subtler, sexier scent of her skin and hair, and her growing arousal. He let his gaze wander over her, from her smooth, narrow shoulders, over her upper chest, still dewy from the shower, down to her cleavage, enhanced by her white-knuckled grip on the towel.

He'd had a lot of wants in his lifetime, some basic, some frivolous, many carnal. But nothing compared to how he wanted her.

Keeping the gun away from her, he reached up with his free hand and, with the backs of his knuckles, brushed a few escaped tendrils of hair away from her temple. His hand shook. With her hair up, he could see the wild thrumming of her pulse in her throat.

With one finger, he touched her knuckles. "You okay, darlin'? You look like you might faint on me." He trailed that teasing finger up and over the exposed swells of her breasts. "I'd sooner you be wide awake and participating, you know? Maybe giving me a nice moan or two."

"I was just . . . I forgot to bring a robe with me into the bathroom, so I didn't . . ."

Little by little, he pried her fingers loose. He imagined those soft, graceful fingers circling around his cock, holding him tight, and his stomach took a free fall while his muscles contracted.

Locking down his iron control, he lifted her hand to his mouth and kissed her knuckles. "Let's lose the towel, okay?" He put her hand on his upper arm and, going slow, unwrapped the towel, holding it out at her sides, drinking in the sight of her nudity. "Damn, woman, you make me salivate."

She swayed toward him, but he stepped back, keeping enough space between them that he could look his fill. "Not yet." She wanted to protect her heart against him, she wanted "no strings." Fine. He'd manage it. Somehow.

But it wouldn't be easy when he had the overwhelming urge to gather her close and promise insane things, when he wanted so much in return. Lust surged through his veins, but it wasn't at the forefront of what he felt.

Instead a mishmash of sensations threatened to lay him low.

She shivered, so he asked, "You cold?"

Face downcast, she shook her head.

"Your nipples are tight." He wanted to feel them against his chest; he wanted them in his mouth so he could draw on her, tugging and sucking . . . He dropped the towel and put both hands on her breasts, closing his eyes a moment as he absorbed the silken feel of her, her shuddering response and his own.

He thumbed both puckered nipples, lightly pressed them between finger and thumb, gently pulled — and heard her gasp. Holding her like that, with her nipples caught, he murmured, "Still sore?"

Again she shook her head and, if anything, turned her face farther away.

He forced his attention up from her breasts to her averted face. "Alani?"

Her fingertips bit into his biceps. She said nothing.

Jackson cuddled her breasts one last time and released them. That caused her to gasp, too, and again she swayed.

The easy way she fired up could burn him alive.

Using the edge of his fist, he raised her face so she had no choice but to look at him, to let him see her thoughts and her reservations.

Her eyes were velvety soft, heavy. "I need to know, honey. Is it bad memories, or are you just feeling shy?"

"No bad memories. It's just that I'm not . . ." Her tongue slipped over her upper lip and she took several breaths. "I'm not used to being naked in front of anyone."

"So shy, but not uncomfortable?"

"No."

"Good." He smiled with determination. "You'll get used to me looking at you, because you're going to be naked in front of me a lot." And because he felt bitter over her stipulation that they keep things impersonal, he added, "It's part of experimenting."

She looked distressed for only a heartbeat.

"I'll push you." Hell, he pushed himself with this insane sensual torture. "But I'll make certain that you love every second of it, and that's a promise I can keep."

Nodding in acceptance of that, she pressed in close to him, her arms going around his bare back, those stiffened nipples teasing him. Knowing she couldn't see him or his over-the-top reaction to holding her like this, Jackson closed his eyes and folded his arms protectively around her.

Possessiveness rode him hard. He couldn't see the future, he didn't know how she'd deal with Arizona once he got around to telling her, but for now, for this moment, she was his and his alone.

"If at any point you get uncertain about things, I want you to tell me." After what she'd been through, after living a nightmare, bad feelings and memories were bound to surface, triggered by God knew what. "This is for pleasure. *Your* pleasure, Alani. Understand?"

"Yes." She kissed his chest. "But you're so different from those men, when I'm with you I don't even think of them."

Jesus. He dropped his hands to her ass, stroked her, lifted her to tiptoes while pressing his face to the top of her head.

Sure, he wanted to fuck her. He wasn't dead.

But he wanted to cherish her, too, to make love to her fast and hard. Slow and sweet. He wanted things raunchy, and he wanted things special.

Because she was special.

Separating the carnal from the emotional wasn't easy, but she'd laid the ground rules, so he pressed her back and forced a smile. "Wait for me in the bed."

She looked at his chest, lower to his abdomen. Her breathing quickened, and she nodded.

Thinking of her there, between the sheets, naked and anxious, would be more incentive than he needed to rush through the shower. "Be right back." He left before he changed his mind and didn't go at all. She needed to talk, and he needed to get a handle on things.

That meant getting a handle on himself, first and foremost.

No matter what it took, he would make this good for her.

Chapter Ten

Huddled under the quilt, her back propped against a pillow on the headboard, Alani felt her anticipation expand with every second that passed. How Jackson had bared her, looked at her and touched her, both detached and hungry, left her thoughts and her feelings in turmoil.

Last night, everything had unfolded naturally, stemming from his claims of wanting her, needing her. Today, he was so different, like another man.

But he was still undeniably sexy.

Unable to help herself, she listened to every sound he made. She was so familiar with her house, with living alone, that she could track his every movement by sound alone.

Water running, water shutting off, the silence while he toweled dry, the opening of the bathroom door, footsteps in the hall leading to her bedroom . . .

Her heart threatened to explode with urgency, need, uncertainty.

That he was so different heightened everything; it'd almost be like making love for the first time.

How would it be, now that Jackson was back to normal? Last night, he'd been overflowing with words of love, caring, commitment.

Today, he'd accepted her offer to keep things noncommittal.

Her thoughts scattered when he stepped through the doorway. Naked. Already erect.

She couldn't swallow, could barely breathe. She refused to look away.

He had the most amazing body she'd ever seen, with the attitude and capability to go along with it.

"Relax, babe." He strode to the nightstand, a man uncaring of his nudity, without a shred of modesty — not that he needed it.

She suffered insecurities. But with good reason, he did not.

"All things considered," she whispered, "relaxing isn't easy."

His mouth quirked. He put the black Beretta on the nightstand with that awesomely lethal-looking knife, his belt and the holster. "You wanted to talk, right? So we'll talk."

What in the world had she been thinking? She looked him over, wondering if she could wait, if she could prioritize the way she knew she should.

He planted his big feet apart. "You want me to stand here a little longer? I don't mind you looking, you know. Hell, I like it."

Did she want him to? She could spend all day soaking up the sight of him, but just looking wouldn't be enough.

"Before you make up your mind, you should know that your wide-eyed, fascinated gaze makes me edgy, so the longer we do this, the shorter our conversation is going to be."

She still said nothing. How could he blather on with so much nonsense when she could barely blink?

"Cat got your tongue? I guess I better take control of things, huh?" He lifted the quilt and slid into the bed beside her, facing her propped on a forearm. "First thing we need to do . . ." He tugged the quilt from her fisted hands and drew it down below her breasts. "That's better."

For what felt like the longest time, he studied her, his gaze burning, his jaw twitching.

She didn't know where to put her hands, what to do, what to say. Last night, he'd swept her away with romance.

Today, he scorched her with his raw sexual hunger.

It was a toss-up which she liked more.

"First question, woman." Body relaxed, voice more so, Jackson said, "I'm doing my best, but this isn't easy on me. So make it quick before my control snaps and I jump on you."

Her gaze skittered over to the weapons and back again. Mouth dry, stomach taut, she gathered herself. "The way you handled things with Marc, how easy it was for you to level him . . ."

"That was nothing. He's a sissy."

Yeah, right. Maybe to Jackson, but to the average man, Marc was fit, capable and arrogant enough to give pause. His wealth made him powerful, yet Jackson had treated him like nothing more than a playground bully. "Will you tell me about yourself?"

"What do you need to know?"

Odd, that he'd put it that way: what she *needed* to know, versus what she *wanted* to know. Was that how he saw it? Did he see her questions as a requirement he had to fulfill? Would he tell her only enough to appease her curiosity?

He was as private as her brother and Dare, and God knew, those two sidestepped even the most mundane queries. "I don't mean to push —"

" 'S okay." His legs shifted, and one hairy thigh slid over her knee, pinning her leg. "I have some questions for you, too."

He did? Well then . . . "I want to know all about your background. Your life." With him staring so intently at her breasts, her nipples ached. "I want to know what influences in life made you the type of person who can do what you do."

"Meaning?"

"You face off with danger as if it's a joke. In a group of Alphas, you'd take charge and no one would question it. You can be deadly, but you're so laid-back that many people might be deceived."

He shrugged, and with the quilt only to his waist, she got an up close view of how any movement at all sent muscles flexing over his shoulders and chest.

"I've been on my own a long time, that's all. I either had to take charge or get left behind." His hand settled on her midriff, below her breasts, over the quilt, but still *there,* sending her nerve endings into overdrive. "I'm not the type who likes to follow others."

Because most weren't as capable as him. But he worked fine with Dare and Trace, and he had their respect. "I want to know what carved that personality. You said you don't have any brothers or sisters, right? But what about your parents? Are they supportive? Do they approve of what you do? Do you see them often?"

He went still, so still that he didn't even seem to be breathing.

"Jackson?"

"That was a shit-ton of questions."

She frowned. "So pick a few to answer."

As if it didn't matter, he shrugged again. "No siblings, thank God. I had a drunk for a dad, and Mom split when I was a teenager, so it's better that there weren't other kids caught in their web."

Sympathy squeezed her heart. He said that so dispassionately, but he couldn't possibly be that removed. "What do you mean, she split?"

"She had a boyfriend, several boyfriends, in fact. She hated how Dad drank, and she hated being saddled with me. So she took off." He lowered the quilt more so that he could touch her bare skin.

Alani drank in a deep breath and covered his hand with her own. "That had to be awful."

"Guess so. I never really looked like my dad, so I always wondered if Mom had been cheating even when she got pregnant with me." His gaze lifted to hers. "Dad always wondered the same."

Anger replaced some of her pity. "He actually told you that?"

On a humorless laugh, he said, "Many times. Not that it matters that much. There was no love lost between us, believe me."

How sad. "He was the only father you knew?"

"Yeah." Jackson leaned over her and kissed her belly. "Damn, woman, you smell good."

Her heart broke for the little boy he'd once been. She put her hand in his damp hair, understanding his need to dilute the conversation. She often did the same when talking about her kidnapping. "Is he still alive?"

"Nope. He came home drunk one night, passed out in the driveway and must have hit his head. He'd been out there in the rain all night." Jackson's mouth curled with disdain. "After he died, I wasn't anxious to go find another dad, ya know? If he hadn't fathered me, oh well. I was better off without parents."

Such an ugly, hurtful story. She stroked his hair, her voice softening. "What about your mom? Have you had any contact with her at all?"

"No. I've never had a burning desire to look her up, either." He wrapped an arm around her hip and looked up at her, his attention wavering between her breasts and her face. "Is that enough?"

Dare had told her it'd be good for her to talk, so wouldn't the same be true for Jackson? Had he ever told anyone the whole story? Probably Trace and Dare knew, because they wouldn't work with him without having every detail. But that wouldn't be the same as a sympathetic, caring ear.

"You don't ever think of them?"

He dropped his head forward with a laugh. "Why would I? Long ago I decided I'd be different from them, and then I closed that door for good."

"Different how?"

He gave her a long-suffering smile, but cynicism narrowed his eyes. "No drinking, no whining and no miserable marriage." He half hugged her. "Your criteria of staying commitment-free fits right in."

But she'd never meant that, and she hated that he'd taken her comments that way. "What if you fall in love?"

His expression said loud and clear that he didn't consider it likely. "You know, Dad claimed he drank because Mom never loved him. And during arguments, Mom told him she cheated because he never loved her." He shook his head. "Neither one of them seemed much capable of love, if you ask me. But either way, their excuses were pretty damned thin. A drunk is a drunk because he has no willpower, and he wallows in his own weakness. A cheater cheats because she lacks morals and cares more about herself than anyone else."

Such an awful way to view human error. "How old were you when your mom left?"

"I don't know. Fourteen, fifteen maybe."

Caught between being a boy and a man. "It must have been really tough coping."

"I slept around a lot." He dragged the quilt a little lower and tried to kiss her again, this time on her hip bone.

Alani's hand clenched in his hair.

"Ow, damn."

She loosened her hold and gave him an apologetic caress. "What do you mean, you slept around a lot?"

Laughing, he bent to lightly bite her waist and then pushed the quilt completely off her.

Being suddenly exposed curled her toes, especially with the appreciative way he sat up to study her body.

"I learned early that great sex makes everything easier. And just so we can wrap this up, let me tell you the condensed version of the rest." He wedged a hand between her legs, cupping his palm over her sex. His fingers were still, firm against her, and it left her breathless.

Jackson stared into her eyes as he finished the telling. "I blew off the idea of college. The school atmosphere isn't for me and I wanted to get on with my life. So I got a job working for a concrete company."

Alani wanted to ask him about that, but coherent questions weren't easy, not with his hand there, possessive, just holding her.

"I did the heavier labor, and loved it. I really got into feeling stronger, more fit."

"A man, instead of a kid."

"Yeah. I enjoyed the physical stuff enough that I took some training, to get stronger, faster, to fight better — not that I wanted to fight professionally or anything. I just enjoyed it. And I have a knack for it, too." He grinned at her. "I'm a natural."

That intrigued her enough that she managed to ask, "But that's not what you wanted to do?"

He shook his head. "I always figured one day I'd open up my own construction company."

She believed he would have, if that's what he wanted. Jackson was a man who would make things happen.

"Instead I got in with Trace and Dare."

"How —"

Watching her, he shifted his hand, and his middle finger searched, prodded, sank into her.

Her whole body stiffened; she felt herself getting wetter and didn't know if she should be embarrassed or not. She caught his wrist; their gazes clashed. "How did you meet them?"

Again his eyes narrowed, this time with satisfaction. "It was a dark night. Raining like crazy. My truck broke down, so I had to walk the last few miles to a gas station."

Alani watched him look off at nothing in particular, as if remembering something unpleasant. She was acutely aware of many things: his awesomely nude, buff body; the tension in the air and in his shoulders; the feel of his finger pressed inside her, motionless, big, intimate.

Her lungs labored for breath, and she had to struggle to concentrate instead of sinking under the spell of sensuality. Hard as she tried, she couldn't stop her muscles from tightening around his finger.

Jackson, damn him, seemed unaffected.

"On my way back to my truck, I had to cross over a bridge, and there were three guys there, trying to throw something over."

Oh, God. Instinctively, Alani knew what that something was. "A woman?" she whispered.

"An eighteen-year-old girl, though I didn't realize it at the time. I just knew something was wrong, and I reacted."

As Dare and Trace always did. "What happened?"

"They didn't notice me when I crept up on them. Their car was idling, making some noise, and it was storming hard. When they tossed their bundle, I heard a scream, and then . . . I knew." A deep breath expanded his chest, tightened his jaw. "I think I snapped, but in a cold way. Not panicked. I'd fought before, plenty of times. But never like that. Never with a life in the balance."

"You knew you had to take them down so you could get to her."

"That's about it. So I leveled them."

"All three of them?" She pictured it in her mind.

"No choice. I didn't exactly fight fair. I figured if they died, who gave a shit? In less than . . . I dunno, a minute maybe, two of them were out and the third was disabled. So I dove in after the girl."

Awe, respect, affection and . . . gratitude all swamped Alani, making her voice rough.

"In a storm, off a bridge?"

"Yeah, hell of a thing, huh? They had tied her hands, so the odds of her surviving were zilch if I didn't get to her, and quick. Luckily, she was kicking like crazy, just managing to keep her head above water, and I could hear her splashing. I got her, and she fought me like a wildcat." He smiled, gave a short, soft laugh. "I got more bruises from her than I did from the bozos on the bridge."

Horrified, Alani covered her mouth. "She must have been so panicked."

"You know, she was, but not like you'd expect. She wasn't hysterical, wasn't crying. Even with her hands tied at her wrists, she fought. After I dragged her up to the shore, I had a bitch of a time pinning her legs so I could explain that I wanted to help. And even then, she didn't quite believe me. I got out my knife, cut her hands free and then jumped back from her so she wouldn't feel cornered. We sort of stared at each other for the longest time."

"How badly was she hurt?"

"Banged up." He opened his mouth to say more, then shook his head hard and pressed his finger deeper into her. "Dare and Trace were on the scene. It was this big clusterfuck, with me not knowing who to trust, and her scared stiff, and them both calm and, I don't know, just to the point, maybe. They took over, said they'd get rid of the men and the car."

If Alani were a different person, if she hadn't experienced her own trauma, she might not have understood. "So you had killed them?"

"I never asked. They were part of a ring that dabbled in human trafficking. They sold girls, sometimes exchanged them for drugs or weapons, and if anyone dared try to escape . . ."

"She'd get dumped over a bridge."

"After being . . . abused." He seemed to have trouble getting the words out. "If they weren't dead when I finished with them, Dare or Trace would have taken care of that."

"Good."

He looked at her. "When the guys showed up, she sided with me. I guess she already knew I'd pulled her from the river, but she didn't know what they would do."

"She sensed that you'd protect her, with your life if necessary."

His mouth twitched. "Yeah, I would have, but I doubt either of us was thinking anything that dramatic. I figured I could take them both if I had to, and she'd have a chance to get away. Turned out I didn't need to fight them and probably wouldn't have fared as well as I thought I would anyway."

"You don't meet many men like them. Like you."

"True enough." He pressed his finger deeper again and smiled at her soft sound of growing excitement. "Later, when Trace told me he wanted me to work with them, he said that my way with women was as valuable as my other skills."

"Yes." Her eyes sank shut; her willpower waned.

Jackson turned his hand, worked his finger in as deep as he could. "I don't think Trace meant you when he said it."

Alani knew he was being evasive about the details of how he got started working with Trace, leaving out as much as he told, but with the way he touched her, she let him slide.

Her back arched a little. "Probably not."

"And now," he whispered, "I'm done talking about the past, because I want to concentrate on the here and now. On you. On *this.*"

Moaning, Alani closed her eyes and gave in. Not that Jackson afforded her much choice in the matter. His mouth covered hers, and their conversation officially ended.

■ ■ ■ ■

Talking about the past stirred feelings that, when mixed with the need bombarding Jackson now, conspired to do him in. He hated rehashing his family history; it left him almost as angry as thinking about that awful night when he'd seen a young lady thrown into a cold, churning river, her hands tied, her face and body bruised . . .

As the perfect foil to his dark mood, Alani's fingers sank into his hair. She curved her slim thigh up and over his wrist, trapping his hand there.

She kissed him deep as her inner muscles clamped around his finger.

So wet. So hot. Her mouth, her sex.

He couldn't get enough air, and he couldn't get enough of her. But he wanted to go slow, to make it last.

To torment her in the most heated, sexual ways possible.

In the shower, he'd gotten off, knowing he had to blunt everything he felt when touching her, looking at her.

Tasting her.

"I need more," he whispered, taking his hand from her, putting his finger in his mouth to suck away her excitement.

She moaned in response, the sound achingly real and honest.

Moving up and over her, Jackson straddled her thighs and looked at her body, so delicate and so damned sexy. He cupped both breasts. “You’re about the prettiest thing I’ve ever seen,” he said, circling her darkly flushed, stiffened nipples before leaning down to draw one into his mouth.

She arched again, her head back, her hands kneading his thighs.

He kissed his way to her other breast, caught that nipple with his teeth, tugged, licked. Sucked hard.

“Jackson,” she whispered.

He loved hearing her say his name. He loved hearing her moan, too. He continued drawing on her for a long time, switching from one nipple to the other, occasionally just petting her, barely touching, then taking her into his mouth again.

She rocked her hips up against him, seeking a different touch now.

“Easy.” Sitting up, Jackson ran his thumbs over her wet nipples while watching her expressions. She twisted, turning her face to the side, but he didn’t mind. She wouldn’t be able to hide from him for long.

He took his time, pulling gently, rolling, playing with her until she trembled all over, and still it wasn't enough.

He didn't know if he'd ever get enough. Not of her. Of this. Of feeling the way she made him feel, things he'd never imagined before.

He moved off her, put his hands on her soft, pale thighs and opened her legs.

She bit into her bottom lip, waiting, taut with anticipation. Already he could see the moisture, smell her heated scent.

Before he finished, she'd be as addicted as he felt.

"Let me look at you, Alani." He eased her leg up, bending her knee, and sat between her sprawled thighs. His heartbeat hammered in his chest. His voice dropped to a gravelly timbre. "Damn, so pretty."

"I'm not used to this, Jackson."

"I know." With one fingertip, he traced her swollen lips, pink and shiny, further spreading her wetness but avoiding her distended clitoris.

She gave a humming groan and shifted.

On a growl, watching intently, he sank two fingers into her. The fit was snug enough to rob him of composure.

God, she squeezed his fingers, so how would she feel on his cock? How would she feel with him filling her up?

He pressed in, pulled back while turning

his hand, and slowly slid back in again. Deeper this time, thrusting into her, pulling almost all the way out, in again.

Over and over.

Alani squirmed against him, her thighs tensing, her little clit there, needing his touch. He could put her over the edge and he knew it.

But not yet.

Breathing harder, determined to prove something to her, to himself, he continued to build the sensations. Her modesty shot, her legs opened wider, her hips lifting up to him, her every breath a ragged moan.

With his other hand, he cupped each of her breasts in turn. "I like that you're small. It makes it easy for me to reach all of you at once."

She made some incoherent reply that sounded like a plea.

"You want to come, Alani?"

"Yes."

"From my hand?" He pressed deeper again. "Or my mouth?"

Her eyes squeezed tight and reserve held her back for a long moment before she gasped out, "Your mouth."

"Yeah, that's what I was thinking, too." He pushed back in the bed, resting on his stomach between her pale slender thighs.

Intoxicated, he inhaled her scent, so hard he hurt. "Put your legs over my shoulders."

Awkwardly, hampered by arousal, she did as told. Mmmm, nice. He liked having her warm thighs against his jaw. He cupped her hips and snuggled her a little closer. He blew softly on her, making her shudder.

With his fingertips he parted her, then leaned in to trace with his tongue.

"Jackson . . ."

Licking deep, he stabbed into her with his tongue until her hands knotted in his hair, and she tried to direct him.

Smiling against her, he flicked her most sensitive flesh with the very tip of his tongue — and she damn near came.

Groaning, her hips lifting off the bed, she dragged him close again. "Oh, please . . . Jackson, no more."

"You wanted to experiment." Even as he said it, he knew he was done. He couldn't play it out any longer. If he even tried, he'd embarrass himself. Jerking off in the shower hadn't even come close to relieving his need.

"No," she cried. "I want you. That's all." And again she said, *"Please."*

"Shh." He pressed his face against her, licking, seeking her clitoris, and finally drawing her in.

Her ragged moan was loud and unrestrained, further exciting him. She bucked up against him, her rhythm frantic. It wasn't easy, but Jackson got two fingers in her again — and she cried out, harsh, deep, her whole body bowed taut as her orgasm crashed through her.

He loved it. He loved . . . Huh-uh. Nooo. He wasn't going there. No way. Not right now.

As soon as the wild quivering left her, he jolted up to the bedside table to grab a rubber. Neither of them said anything. Alani didn't look capable. She laid there, her legs sprawled, her breasts heaving, eyes closed and lips parted. Tears dampened her temples, ripping at his heart. Her breathing remained uneven, strained.

He settled between her legs, kissed her swollen lips. "Baby, look at me."

It took her three breaths to get her eyes open.

Jackson held her face, their heartbeats aligned — and he thrust into her.

Her head went back.

His head dropped forward.

She groaned anew.

He locked his teeth.

"Damn, you're tight." He rocked into her, each stroke easing more than the one before it. "Ah, God, so fucking tight."

Her arms went around his neck, her fingers into his hair.

"Wrap those pretty legs around me. Hold me."

She stared up at him, her eyes dazed with an expression of awe. Slowly, she hooked first one leg around his waist, then the other — and he sank deeper.

"I'm not going to last," he admitted through his teeth, and he knew it had as much to do with how she looked at him as anything else.

Alani swallowed. She pulled him down for a kiss and whispered, "Then harder, please."

He shattered. He reared up on stiffened arms and hammered into her as the pressure built unbearably.

The second he felt her squeezing him and heard her vibrating cry of release, he let himself go.

It was perfect.

It was mind-blowing.

Because it was Alani.

He didn't know if he ever wanted to let her go. He liked her company. He loved having sex with her. She set him off in ways he hadn't known were possible.

Was that enough?

It hit Jackson that he didn't have to decide anything right now. He'd have a while to figure out what he wanted for the long haul, and if Alani fit into that plan, he'd find a way to keep her in his life.

For right now, he only needed to keep her in his bed. And given the way she clutched him so tightly, that wouldn't be too difficult at all.

Chapter Eleven

He should have been sleeping. He should have been dead to the world. Instead, Jackson lay on his back, one arm behind his head, the other keeping Alani curled close to his side. He stared at the shifting moon shadows on the ceiling, his body drained of tension but his thoughts clamoring.

Alani had one thigh over his lap, one lax hand resting over his abdomen, her nose pressed to his ribs. He could feel her deep, even breaths, smell the sultry scent of her skin and hair.

They'd destroyed the bed.

She'd destroyed his peace of mind.

If Marc Tobin was the one who'd drugged him, Trace would have him, and soon. The threat would be gone. Alani wouldn't need him for protection — and then what?

He had time, but how much? Days? Weeks?

How long would be enough?

Without thinking about it he tightened his hold on Alani. She stirred, so he kissed the top of her head and soothed her until she settled again.

The steadily shifting hands on the bedside clock taunted him as they registered a little after two in the morning. He needed to get some sleep, but his mind wouldn't rest. Annoyed at himself, Jackson closed his eyes and tried to clear his mind.

He was about to give up on that pointless undertaking when suddenly the house went still. Where before he could hear the thrum of the air conditioner and kitchen appliances, now an obsidian blackness closed in, and he heard nothing.

The complete, utter lack of sound was more deafening than a gunshot. Automatically Jackson listened, knowing something was wrong. He heard nothing beyond the silence.

Sliding his arm out from under Alani, he said in a breath of sound, "Babe, wake up."

"Mmm?" She cuddled closer. "What —"

"Shh." He put a finger to her mouth. "Someone is here. Probably still outside, because I'd have heard him come in. I have to go check it out." *And maybe kill someone.*

She had the sense, the wherewithal, to speak in near silence. "Wait." She grabbed him while levering up in the bed, struggling to orient herself. "The electricity is out?"

"Yes."

"Maybe it's just —"

"It's not." The threat was real; he sensed the intrusion. Prying her hands loose, he said, "Stay put," and with every fiber of his being, he believed she would do as she was told.

She said nothing else, and he appreciated that. Grabbing up his gun and his knife, Jackson left the room without making a sound.

In the hallway he stopped to listen again. Letting his senses take over, he absorbed every shadow, the creak of the house and the breeze outside. He peeked into the other rooms, but his gut told him they were empty and secure, so he went down the hall to the living area. On the way, he glanced everywhere, through each window, each nook and cranny, into the kitchen — he stepped back again for a second, more cautious, looked into that room.

Through the kitchen window he saw a shadow that didn't belong. How he knew it didn't belong was one of the mysteries of instincts. He *always* trusted his instincts.

His chest swelled. His muscles relaxed.

In seconds, at his stealthiest best, he

removed the barriers to the sliding doors, slipped out of the house and across the back porch. Jackson had the sense to stick to the shadows, but thanks to the bright moon, he saw the intruder moving up close to the house, near Alani's bedroom window.

Though it had to be in the mid-eighties still, the guy wore a knit mask and dark clothes.

Jackson, on the other hand, was buck-ass naked.

He grinned.

On the prowl, more than ready to engage physically, he slunk closer. As he passed the meter box, he saw that it was disconnected — thus the lack of electricity. Some of Alani's landscaping had been trampled so that the bastard could cut the seal and remove the retention ring to pull out the electric meter.

Not real smooth. Holding back, he studied the form again — and recognized Tobin by the way he moved, his body type.

Son of a bitch. *Ballsy move, asshole.*

Jackson flipped the knife around in his hand so that he held it hilt first — perfect for gutting someone. He could handle Tobin with one hand tied behind his back — or, as the case may be, while naked as a baby.

No reason to blast a gun and alert the neighborhood.

He moved so close to Tobin that he could touch him — and the obtuse moron didn't even know it.

When Tobin went on tiptoe to look in Alani's bedroom window, Jackson tapped him on the shoulder.

Tobin screamed. Loudly.

Sleeping birds took flight in screeching excitement, adding to the impact of the moment.

When Tobin continued to scream, Jackson silenced him in the most expedient way by thumping his face into the bricks. Tobin slumped, but Jackson kept him upright with an arm locked ruthlessly tight around his neck and his chest shoved into the shorter man's shoulders. The knife pressed tight beneath his chin.

"Disturb her further," Jackson snarled, "and I'll kill you right now." Far as Jackson was concerned, Alani had been through enough. She didn't need Tobin harassing her now, too.

"Jackson?" Tobin slumped further in what seemed to be relief. "Get off of me!"

"Shut the hell up." Using his gun hand, Jackson jerked off the ski mask, then smashed Tobin's bare face into the bricks again. He leaned into him more, making it hard for Tobin to breathe. "What the fuck are you up to?"

"Nothing!"

For the love of . . . "Bullshit." As incentive to talk, Jackson thumped his face into the bricks again. "Let's hear it."

Tobin's struggles caused a thin slice to the skin of his throat.

"Keep jerking around," Jackson said. "You'll cut your own damn throat and save me the trouble."

Realizing he couldn't get away, Tobin froze again. "I was just . . ."

"Just what?" Without pockets, Jackson had no place to put the gun. He tucked it under his arm and patted down Tobin, checking for weapons.

Oddly enough, unless stupidity could be a weapon, he didn't have any. Not even a pocketknife.

Jackson spun him around and, with a hand on Tobin's shoulder, slammed him up against the wall again. He held the knife to his ribs. "Talk."

After darting wildly around the yard, Tobin's gaze zeroed in on Jackson — and widened. "Good God. You're naked!"

"You expected me to sleep in a suit?"

His mouth flapped open, then smashed

shut. "So you are sleeping with her? I was right about that?"

"Given I'm armed and pissed, that should concern you a whole lot more than where I slept."

Breathing hard, again searching the yard, Tobin shook his head. "You're insane."

"Says the guy slinking around in the dark in a ski mask mid-July." Jackson took a step back and hefted the knife. "I have better things to do, Tobin, so stop straining my patience."

"Right." Eyes narrowed, Tobin turned his face away.

So pathetic. Jackson drove his fist into Tobin's gut. He doubled over, wheezing, one hand reaching out for support against the wall. "Next one will break your nose."

Tobin gasped, "I wanted to impress her, that's all."

"Yeah, squashing her flowers ought to do it."

Stupidly, Tobin looked at the crushed landscaping. "I'll buy her new flowers."

"The hell you will." No way would Jackson let Marc Tobin anywhere near Alani. He grabbed Tobin's hair and pulled his face up for emphasis. "You'll never see her again, you moron. You're going to be rotting in jail."

"I only wanted to scare her, okay? That's all."

Jackson released him with a shove. "No, it's not okay."

Marc rubbed his face, eyeing Jackson warily.

"Should I kill you now, or beat the answers out of you?"

He must've sounded convincing, because Tobin rushed to say, "I disabled the meter, and then I was going to heft a rock through the window. I figured you were in bed, but I was looking in to make sure. I assumed if you were asleep, and with the house dark, it'd take you a few minutes to even think to check the meter." And with accusation, "Why the hell didn't you check the fuse box first?"

"Because I'm not a numb-nuts like you." Jackson studied him. "How was this going to help you any?"

Like a rat, Tobin's gaze searched everywhere. "Shouldn't we talk inside?"

The fine hairs on Jackson's nape tingled. Trouble. Trouble beyond what Tobin brought.

No way in hell would he bring danger into Alani's home.

Grabbing Tobin by the shoulder, Jackson turned so that Tobin's back faced the blackness beyond the yard, and shielded his body. That afforded him a little protection, and an opportunity to grill Tobin.

Alarmed, Tobin said, "I know what happened to Alani."

Jackson said nothing; he found it very hard to believe that Alani might have confided in him.

Tobin nodded frantically. "She told me. I know that's why she couldn't — wouldn't — get physical with me. But I figured if bad shit followed you, she'd get tired of you and your redneck manner, and come back to me, where it's safer."

A red haze filled Jackson's vision. Alani had been through enough. "So you were going to do more of this shit?"

Pained, squirming in nervousness, Tobin nodded. "Yes, sure. That was the plan, yes."

Slowly, Jackson put the gun back in his hand, his finger on the trigger. Low, mean, he asked, "That's the best you could come up with?"

"What?"

"Not buying it, Tobin."

"It's true!"

"Part of it, maybe." There was a rock on the ground by Tobin's feet, and he had no weapons on him. But he was rich enough that if he'd wanted to terrorize Alani he'd have hired some grunt to do it for him.

Jackson pressed the tip of the knife to Tobin's windpipe and leaned down to growl right into his face, "I should have done more to you earlier today. I should have broken your damn nose at the very least."

"No." Tobin flinched back, ready to run if it came to that, though even he knew he wouldn't get far. "What will you do?"

Knowing he needed more answers, Jackson tamped down his rage. "Undecided." He sawed his teeth together. "The least you deserve is for me to beat the shit out of you."

Tobin quickened with regained dignity. "A fight, *mano a mano?* No police, and without the knife or . . ." He flicked his gaze to the Beretta. "The gun?"

"We'll see." Shooting Marc, just once, would feel real good. Course, using his fists on him would be nice, too.

"I'll accept a fight." Urgent, Tobin straightened to his full height, which was a few inches shorter than Jackson.

"You'll do as you're told." Jackson lowered the knife. "First, plug the meter back in." He needed the yard lit, to help ward off any other threat.

Tobin tried to put distance between himself and Jackson, but he wasn't successful. Jackson stuck close, dividing his attention between Tobin and the wide-open yard.

"This is partly your fault." Annihilating more flowers, Tobin stomped over to the meter box, his attitude defiant but wary. "She cares about me, you know. If it weren't for you, she wouldn't have left me."

"Yeah, yeah, whatever." Jackson prickled under the growing sense of menace. Not from Tobin — but then, who? *Come out, you cowardly bastard,* Jackson thought. *Come out and show yourself.*

"It was only because of what she went through, the kidnapping and everything, that she didn't want to pursue our relationship."

"You're history, end of story."

Marc jammed in the meter. "You're probably the reason she got kidnapped." As the house hummed back to life, Tobin continued to prattle and turned to Jackson. "Anyone can see that you're dangerous. Look at your weapons! Do you even have permits for that —" Suddenly sidetracked, Tobin went mute and froze.

Ready to engage any threat, Jackson followed Tobin's line of vision and saw Alani standing in the open sliders. His mouth went dry.

Rather than stay in the bedroom — in the bed — as he'd ordered, she'd pulled on a sleeveless white nightgown and followed him. She'd also flipped on the kitchen ceiling switch, leaving her slim, shapely form backlit, rendering her gown all but transparent.

Alani, oblivious to why they stared, said, "Jackson!" Scandalized, she took one step out. "What in the world's going on? You're *naked,* for crying out loud." Her gaze went to Marc. "What are you doing here?"

Not only was Alani now out in the open — in the line of danger — but Marc was seeing her in the sheer gown.

Jackson clubbed Tobin in the head with his fist. "Turn around, damn you!"

His shout was loud enough to rattle the leaves in the trees, but it got Marc's attention off Alani. His expression dazed, his lips parted, Tobin stumbled as he jerked around.

"Get her inside," Tobin whispered.

Jackson felt his fear, damn him. "You!" He pointed the knife at Alani. "Get back inside. *Now.*"

Instead of obeying, she got her back up. Mouth pinched, she took another step toward him. "Be quiet before you alert the neighbors."

Since she'd moved away from the light, she looked a little more decent — but that did nothing for her safety. Jackson wrapped an arm around Tobin's neck in an unbreakable choke hold and, dragging him along backward, approached Alani. He'd put her inside if necessary, and deal with the consequences later.

Tobin fought him — not that it did him any good. At the moment, Jackson was so furious, he could have snapped Tobin's neck with ease.

He stomped up to Alani. Through his teeth, he said, "Get in the house. Right now."

Bristling indignation had her leaning into his anger. "You are not my boss."

He caught her arm, more than ready to force the issue.

A projectile zipped through the air and struck the house with enough force to splinter a piece of brick. Confused, Alani turned to look, but Jackson knew that sound and reacted without thought.

He shoved Marc away from him and in the same movement drove Alani down. They hit the ground together with bone-jarring force. Keeping her head covered, Jackson rolled and came up with her on the porch, near the picnic table. He upended it so that it shielded her.

"What in the —"

"Bullet." Gun in hand, on high alert, Jackson waited, but all he could hear was Tobin's loud, thundering escape. *Shit, shit, shit.* "C'mon."

Keeping her shielded with his body, he half crouched, half ran with Alani into the dubious safety of her house. He tucked her into a corner away from the windows and hit the light switch, sending the kitchen into darkness again.

"Jackson?"

"I'm right here, babe." Rarely did he have to engage in polite conversation in these situations. "Stay down, okay? Someone's shooting at us."

"I didn't hear anything!"

Her panicked tone pulled his gaze like a lodestone. "It's okay. But you *will* stay put, understand?"

Nodding, she brought her legs up to her chest. "Are you positive it was a shot?"

"Shush." Finger on the trigger of the Beretta, Jackson sat near the patio doors, his back to the wall, and waited. He kept his gaze on the door opening, his ears prickling.

Nothing.

And then, too close for comfort, he heard another shot, this one lacking the benefit of a silencer. The resonating "pop pop" of gunfire echoed over the quiet night, followed by a curse before everything went silent again.

Dropping back against the wall, Jackson worked his jaw. Maybe Tobin hadn't gotten away after all, but what did he have to do with anything?

"It went wide," Jackson said aloud, as much to himself as to Alani. Tobin had been fearful. Of what? Who? "Either the shooter sucks, or someone interfered with his aim."

"Interfered?" she whispered. "I don't understand."

No, he didn't, either. Yet. Jackson chewed on his thoughts. Why use a silencer one second, then not the next? "Two guns," he concluded. "Two people?"

"You're not making any sense."

"I know." He got to his feet but stayed hunkered down. "Woman, don't you dare move, do you understand me?"

Eyes wide in the darkness, her pale face reflecting the moonlight through the window over the sink, Alani nodded. "I get it. You don't have to beat it into the ground."

Prickly to the bitter end. Unable to appreciate her moxie at that particular moment, Jackson said only, "Good. 'Bout damn time."

He lunged to the other side of the patio doors and shoved them shut, then secured them. Finding the drawstring for the vertical blinds, he closed them. If no one could see them, then they wouldn't be such easy targets. He darted over to Alani. "Come on."

She took his hand and, following his lead, hurried around the doorway of the kitchen and into the hallway.

Once there, away from windows, he led her down the hall toward the bedrooms, but again held back. "Stay right here while I check things."

"Okay." Her hand squeezed his. "Be careful."

"Yeah." She released him, and he went into each room but found nothing. After snagging his jeans and stepping into them, he grabbed up his socks and boots and came back to her with a blanket. "Get comfortable."

"Here in the hall?"

"Shit just got real, babe, so yeah, for now you wait in the hallway." When her shoulders slumped, Jackson put one hand to her nape and tugged her into his side. She shivered, as much from nerves as anything, he knew. Holding her close, lending her his heat, he helped her wrap in the blanket. "Better?"

"Yes, thank you."

Adrenaline pumping, he kissed her mouth, quick but thorough. "Trust me, okay?" He dug out his cell and hit a button.

Trace answered on the first ring.

"We're fine," Jackson told him without preamble, "but someone — two people, actually — shot at the house. One silencer, one not. Tobin was here, somehow involved —"

He heard Alani gasp.

"— skittish as hell, and when the shots came, he high-tailed it out of here. We're safe for right now, but I wanted you to know."

"Stay put," Trace said. "I'll be right there."

"Not necessary." Jackson rubbed Alani's shoulder. "I'm taking her out of here."

"Do not move with my sister, Jackson."

Impatience gnawed on him. "Waiting for you will just hold us up." And he wanted Alani tucked away somewhere safe. "I know how to evacuate. I know how to watch for —"

"Yeah, you do. And if it was anyone but Alani, I'd be fine leaving it up to you. But she's my sister, and I'm already on my way."

Jackson drew a breath, glanced at Alani's upturned face and wide-eyed uncertainty, and nodded. She didn't need to witness a pissing contest between him and her pushy brother. "Yeah, all right. But make it fast."

He disconnected the call and tucked the phone back into his pocket. Wrapping both arms around her, he hugged her into his chest. With his chin on top of her head, feeling very much the macho protector, he asked, "You all right, honey?"

Seconds ticked by — and she pushed him away. "Don't you *ever* speak to me like that again."

Confused, Jackson glared at her. "What the hell?" If this was her idea of hysterics, it made no sense. "All I did was ask if you're okay. You're shaking all over and your face is whiter than my ass, and you —"

She threw up her hands. "You shouted at me in front of Marc. You *ordered* me into the house. You —"

"We could both see through your nightgown."

"You were nasty and — what?"

"Could see you." Jackson leaned closer, his lip curled as he fingered the fine material of the nightie. "Everything," he stressed. "This damned fetish-inspired, virginal sacrifice gown didn't hide a single detail."

"Virginal sacrifice? *Fetish* inspired?"

"Might as well be." He shrugged. "I know that's where my mind went."

Her mouth opened twice, but she said nothing. She looked down at herself. "It's opaque."

"Yeah, well, not so much when you've got

the light behind you." He brought up her chin. "I had my hands full dealing with your boyfriend. I didn't need you flaunting yourself on top of everything else."

"He's not my boyfriend," she snapped. "And *you* were naked! Right out there in the yard!"

Jackson shrugged again. "I don't give a shit who sees me."

"That was obvious!"

"But I don't want anyone ogling you."

Irritation brought color back into her cheeks, and she thrust up her chin. "I don't care."

"About?" It sort of tickled him that she'd forgotten her fear in favor of bitching at him. He'd take her angry over terrified anytime.

"Whatever the circumstances, I don't want you to use that tone with me."

"I'd already figured someone else was lurking out there besides Tobin." He put his hands on her and, mindful of the remaining threat, savored the narrowness of her waist contrasted to the gentle flare of her hips. So sexy. "My *tone* was meant to get you to safety."

She flipped back the silky fall of her hair. "It failed, now didn't it?"

"Yeah." He drew her hips closer to his.

"So next time someone has cut your electricity and someone else is shooting at us, I'll try to politely ask you to keep your sweet little ass inside — as I nicely instructed before I left the room — so that my attention won't be splintered."

Her whole face tightened . . . and then suddenly she grinned.

More hysterics? Wary now, he said, "Alani?"

She fell into him, her face against his chest. "You were *naked,* Jackson."

She did seem hung up on that. "Clothes weren't a priority at that moment." Protecting her would always be his top consideration.

"What if you'd had to fight Marc?" Her voice sounded high and quick. "With your . . . your . . ."

"Family jewels?"

She gasped. ". . . exposed, and your . . ." She gestured at his lap.

"Dick?"

Her mirth expanded until she choked on her humor. "Yes, that. It was just sort of . . . out there." She snickered. "Vulnerable."

"Yeah." He pressed *it* against her warm, soft body. "Not my preferred way to fight, but I wouldn't let it slow me down."

"Thank God I don't have neighbors living

close." Her shoulders shook as she fought off more nervous giggles.

He didn't mind. Because her hair fascinated him even at the worst of times, he smoothed it back, tangled his fingers in it and smiled. "That damned Tobin almost pissed himself when I busted him. You sure know how to pick 'em, don't you?"

That snuffed her humor real quick. Suspicious, she asked, "What did you do to him?"

"Not enough. And now he's gone, even though he's somehow got a role in this whole shit storm tonight."

"Your language is deteriorating." She put her arms around him and rested her face on his bare chest. "In the future, I will try to concede to your expertise and do as you ask — but only if you ask. No more orders."

"I'll do my best on that." He couldn't make any promises. "Don't crucify me if I slip up now and then in the heat of the moment, okay?"

She nodded. "Actually, if I hadn't heard Marc, I would have stayed tucked away. I'm not stupid. But I peeked out and you two were chatting so . . . amicably, I thought it was all a big misunderstanding or something."

"Nothing amicable about it." Apparently she hadn't seen him punch Tobin. "The bastard said he had some half-ass plan to scare you back to him, but I'm not buying it." Jackson related the conversation to her, then said, "You actually told him what happened to you?"

"No. Not all of it. Just that I'd been briefly kidnapped. He thinks it was for my brother's money, not so I could be —"

Jackson didn't need her to say that she would have been sold for sex. "He knows about Trace?"

"Marc never met him, but since Trace backed me when I started up my design business, most everyone knows I have a wealthy brother. Trace drops in at my office sometimes, and we're out to lunch together a lot." Her fingers moved up and over his pec muscles. "Of course, he doesn't know what Trace does for a living, or anything like that. When he kept pressing for us to get . . . closer —"

"When he wanted in your pants."

"— I felt like I had to tell him something, so I said I'd been held for ransom."

Jackson mulled that over. "And he thinks Trace paid?"

"Yes." Her eyes closed and she kissed him, just above his right nipple.

The brush of her lips on his skin drove him to distraction.

"None of that, woman. I'm working."

"I know. I'm sorry." She smoothed his chest. "You're just so . . . edible."

God. He cupped her nape and turned up her face. "Trace is on his way. We have to move out of here tonight, soon as he gets here."

"I thought you insisted on being with me because we weren't supposed to bother my brother."

"Unnecessarily." Her safety was very necessary. "You'll be able to grab a few things, but not a lot, so start thinking about what you'll need."

She nodded, licked her bottom lip, then bit it. "Where will I go?"

Jackson had an easy answer for that, and despite the circumstances, it filled him with satisfaction. He kissed her, quick and to the point. "You go with me."

If not always, at least for now.

Chapter Twelve

It had taken no more than a perfectly aimed kick to throw off the shooter's aim, sending the shot wide of the mark. Firing a bullet near his head had kept him from attempting retaliation.

That shot had missed on purpose; who wanted to deal with splattered brains and lengthy justifications? It'd be tough to stay anonymous if there were dead bodies to explain.

The shooter was gone. But for how long?

The scant light of stars and moon weren't sufficient for using the binoculars. Jackson had wisely killed the lights in the house and yard, and the neighbors were far enough away that their lights didn't reach. The only activity visible was the arrival of headlights from a car.

So Jackson had backup. Figured. There was no reason to stay out in the humid, bug-happy night.

Before packing it in, the spot was cleared so that few would know what had transpired. Only someone highly trained would detect any evidence of surveillance — and Jackson more than qualified as highly trained.

Would he put the puzzle pieces together? Not yet. Not completely.

But he would know he had a shooter on his tail.

Time to go. For now. When the time was right . . . then they would start this all over again.

Trace arrived without Dare, which was one small blessing. When the three of them got together, their machismo was enough to choke a body.

Dealing with Jackson on his own was enough to tax her wits. She didn't need the testosterone in triplicate.

Trace came because he loved her, she knew that. Yet when he arrived, he was all business and barely spared her a glance once he saw her unharmed.

Unlike Jackson, who kept a gun in a holster at the small of his back, Trace wore a shoulder harness over his T-shirt. It bisected his body and emphasized pronounced muscles. Around his waist he wore a heavy utility belt laden with . . . stuff — nylon cuffs, a deadly knife, a stun baton, extra ammunition . . .

She'd never before seen him like this. It unnerved her a little. Jackson took it in stride, as if he'd seen Trace so heavily armed plenty of times.

"We'll get Tobin," Trace said to Jackson. "I already have someone on it."

"Not Dare?"

Trace shook his head. "He was driving straight home to Molly after leaving your apartment."

Fascinated, Alani said, "So you guys have other people working with you?"

Both men stared at her as if she'd grown an extra head. Trace had an arrested look on his face. Alani thought he might have been weighing the odds of telling her the truth versus covering up with a fabrication.

But Jackson took her question in stride. "The less you know, the better."

"Another of those situations, huh?"

" 'Fraid so." Jackson rolled a shoulder. "Just know that your brother has contacts everywhere. When necessary, he can call in a favor or two."

Assuming the favor wasn't illegal? Or did a request from Trace supersede even that consideration? Alani knew he had cultivated associations in all facets of law enforcement and many within the political arena.

In so many ways, her brother was a most astounding man.

"But you didn't just hear that," Trace said. He scowled at Jackson for the disclosure, then entered the kitchen. With the house still unlit, he went to the kitchen window. Booted feet planted apart, he leaned to look out at the yard. "Could you place the shooter?"

"Yeah." Jackson kept her behind him. "Voices carry across these big yards, so taking that into account, I'd say about a hundred yards." He nodded at her farthest neighbor to the back. "Somewhere behind that house."

"It's for sale," Alani told them. "It's been empty for a few months now."

"Perfect place for a shooter to dig in." Trace headed for the door. "Get her packed. I'll be right back." He went out the door in a low sprint.

Over Jackson's shoulder, she watched Trace blend into the thickest shadows. "He'll be safe out there alone?"

Jackson grunted. "Worry for anyone he runs into, not for Trace."

Her hand fisted in the waistband of his jeans. "The shooters?"

"Shh. Relax. They're long gone."

Tiredly, she leaned against Jackson. Her life had been so much simpler before the cloak-and-dagger drama. "So what's the point then?"

"He's gonna check out the area around that house, see if he can pick up any clues, that's all. It's what I would have done if . . ." His voice trailed off, and he fell silent.

Guilt weighed on her. Her uncomplicated, mundane life was so at odds with what Jackson did for a living. "That's what you'd have done if you hadn't been babysitting me, right?"

Keeping watch out the window, Jackson reached back for a hug. "If there wasn't an innocent to be protected."

"You wish you were out there now, don't you?"

Her morose tone brought him away from the window. His expression probing, he brushed the backs of his knuckles along her cheek. "I'm exactly where I want to be."

"Stranded on the sidelines with me?" Trying to be realistic, Alani accepted that the contrasts of their lives could be a deterrent to a lasting relationship. "I'm sure you love that."

His big hand cupped around her head. "Your safety is of particular interest to me, babe, no two ways about it. So, yeah, I love being here with you."

That "L" word left her thunderstruck and tongue-tied.

"But truth is," he continued, "I wouldn't have left anyone behind unprotected."

So . . . was she special to him or not? She couldn't tell by what he'd said.

To lighten the mood, she asked, "Not even Marc?"

He snorted. "Yeah, right. That fuck-up can fend for himself."

Since he'd tossed Marc away the second the firing started, she'd figured as much. Still taken aback over the idea that she might truly be special to him, Alani said, "Trace wanted me to get packed."

"Yeah. We'll get to that in a sec." There in the shadowy kitchen, appearing far too introspective, Jackson bent to kiss her, lingering, sweet, attentive and so gentle. "You're holding up okay?"

"I'm fine."

His half smile did funny things to her stomach. "You bet you are." His gaze slid down her body. "Better than fine."

All things considered, she did feel all right. A little shaken, exhausted, but not really scared. "I can't believe Marc is a part of this."

"He's a part of something." Jackson turned back to the window. "But I don't know what." He straightened. "Here comes Trace."

Alani looked over his shoulder and saw nothing, yet seconds later, Trace came through the door.

Amazing. Putting aside the danger, she rather enjoyed seeing the men at work.

Grim-faced and larger than life, Trace glanced at her. "You packed yet?"

She didn't bother saying that Jackson had held her back. "I'll only need a minute."

"Get dressed, too, okay?"

Both of them watched her again, their expressions almost identical. "Meaning the menfolk need to talk?" She rolled her eyes. "You could just say that."

"Yeah," Jackson told Trace. "She's being really reasonable about classified stuff."

But Trace's determination didn't change. "Feel free to turn the light on in your room now. I'll help you carry out your stuff in a minute."

"And with that dismissal . . ." Alani headed out of the kitchen, but before she'd gotten too far down the hall, she heard Trace and Jackson speaking quietly, so, without remorse, she paused to listen in.

After all, this concerned her very much,

and no matter how helpless they thought her to be, she wanted — needed — to be informed.

"There were two shooters," Trace confirmed. "One at the front, left side of the house, and one at the back near the patio. I'd say there was a scuffle out back, too, but someone tried to cover it up."

"Huh. So one shooter went after the other? That explains why one had a silencer, and one didn't."

"Yeah. And it's anyone's guess why they were both scoping out Alani's house."

"Competition maybe. Is there a bounty on my head that I don't know about?"

"Who the hell knows? Low-life creeps seem to gravitate to one another. All I care about is disabling them, fatally if necessary."

"That plan works for me."

Alani stood there frozen, her mind cramping, her heart picking up speed. Hearing them talk about "fatally disabling" people made it so damn real. Not that she'd waste a moment feeling bad for anyone involved in human trafficking. She knew firsthand just how traumatic the enterprise could be.

When the men fell silent, she hurried into her room and started throwing together her most necessary items. She didn't want to take too much because she didn't want

Jackson to think she was moving in on him.

The temporary relocation was only a necessary part of keeping both her and Jackson safe. Nothing more.

Even after the men joined her in the bedroom, she continued to think about what she'd overheard. Their assumptions nagged at her until finally she couldn't stand it anymore.

With her suitcase packed, she found a change of clothes but paused before going into her bathroom.

Trace fixated on the box of condoms on her nightstand.

Defiantly, Jackson gathered up the box and dropped it into her suitcase.

Both men looked at her, Jackson with tempered heat, Trace with irascible discomfort.

Awwwwk-ward. Determined to get their thoughts on something less personal, Alani announced, "I listened in."

Trace's brows climbed up.

Jackson asked, "To what?"

"You two talking. About the shooters, I mean."

The men shared a look. At least they seemed to have forgotten about the condoms.

"Two shooters, right? And you assume

they were both out to get Jackson. Or me. Whatever." She flapped a hand. "But I was thinking . . . What if one of them was trying to help?"

"Then why be lurking around in the dark in the first place?" Jackson asked.

Trace agreed.

But Alani wasn't put off. She hugged her clothes to her chest, looked at each of them in turn, and stated the obvious. "You guys sometimes lurk in the dark, but you wouldn't be out to hurt an innocent person. Think about that, okay?" And on that parting shot, with both of their faces registering surprise, she went into the bathroom to change.

Slumped in the passenger seat beside Jackson, Alani slept on the drive to his home. That suited him, because it gave him time to think.

To come to grips with what she'd done to him.

He used to be an easygoing guy. He knew what he wanted, he went after it, he had a lot of fun.

He had a lot of sex.

He had plenty of women.

Now . . . he glanced her way. As always, her pale hair, falling forward to hide half her face, made him think sexual thoughts. Like how it felt in his hands, against his shoulder.

How it'd feel on his abdomen, his thighs.

She'd dressed in slim jeans and a loose casual tee. Before falling asleep, she'd kicked off her sandals.

Her hand, palm up, rested beside her sweet little tush on the seat.

She looked open, trusting. Delectable.

Even sleeping, her breathing steady and deep, she turned him on like no other woman could. He shifted, his gaze constantly scanning the horizon. They'd finally left the more congested suburban area and were on the rougher back roads leading to his property. There'd been no trouble, no sign of the ritzy silver BMW. No one following at all.

But he wouldn't relax, not until he had her safe in his home.

In many ways, the land he'd bought was similar to Dare's. Wooded, near a lake, private and overrun with nature. He was so secluded, he could drink his coffee outside buck naked, and no one would see him.

Again he glanced at Alani. Maybe he could talk her into that. He'd love to see her bare under the morning sun.

He enjoyed seeing her naked, period.

Actually, more than enjoyed.

He looked at her, and it was beyond lust. Beyond mere attraction. Beyond anything familiar.

Beyond anything comfortable.

In the past twenty-four hours, he'd run the gamut of emotions, from tormented and furious, to hot and possessive, to demonstrative and . . . needy.

Shit.

Uncertainty burned over him, and he didn't like it. He flexed his hands on the wheel and tried to concentrate on the rising sun. It broke over the land in a great crimson tide, so breathtaking that he wanted Alani to see it, too.

He reached for her hand, twined his fingers in hers. "Hey, babe."

She shifted, wincing at what appeared to be a kink in her neck.

"C'mon, sleepyhead. Open those mesmerizing eyes for me."

Blinking, she yawned, stretched her back and turned heavy eyes on him. "Jackson."

She sounded and looked like a woman fresh from an orgasm. "Yeah, still me." How he could remain so fired up, he didn't know. He'd always had stamina and a strong sex drive, but this was getting ridiculous.

"Hi, you."

He smiled, lifted her hand and kissed her palm before returning both hands to the wheel. "You're a heavy sleeper."

She rubbed at her eyes. "I guess." She yawned again. "God, I need coffee."

"We'll be at my place in a few more minutes. But I wanted you to see the sunrise."

She sat up to look, and the sunlight reflected in her eyes, burnishing the gold, showing off her long lashes, the perfection of her skin.

God, he had it bad when he started waxing on like a drunken poet.

"It's beautiful, Jackson. Thank you for waking me."

The reverence in her voice matched his mood. "From my back porch, I see that every morning." And every time he'd seen it, he'd found himself wondering if Alani would like the view, too. "When it comes up over the lake, it's even more impressive because the colors sort of play over the surface of the water."

"Sounds amazing." She tucked one leg up under her. "I've seen the setting sun at Dare's, but not the sunrise."

"You like being near the water?"

"I love it. Everything smells better, and there's this peace that just settles over everything and everyone."

That was exactly how he felt. "Maybe we can take a boat ride later. One side of the lake butts up to a steep rise, but there are a few homes down toward the south cove. Mostly farmland. In the early morning, you can see the cows along the shoreline."

"Definitely a boat ride." She smoothed her hair and leaned her head against the seat back. "I'm sorry I fell asleep on you."

"You needed the rest." And he'd enjoyed watching her, just being near her, knowing that finally she was his.

"You do, too." She half turned toward him and put her hand on his biceps. The touch felt affectionate and interested in equal measure. "With all you've been through, you have to be running on lost reserves."

She made him sound like a wuss. "I'm okay." More than anything else, he wanted her again.

When would he not want her?

A smile slipped over her face. "You don't have to be macho for me, you know."

That burned his ass. "I'm not." That she thought he might be playing a tough guy sounded even more insulting. "I'm just . . . me."

"You're pretending that nothing happened."

He snorted. Nothing all that much had, at least not to him. "The drugs have worn off. That bullet didn't hit me. We're both safe. What'd you want me to do? Whimper? Curl up in the backseat while you drove?"

"Maybe just admit you're tired."

"I'm horny," he told her with succinct honesty. "If you were up for it, I'd take you straight to bed for another couple of rounds."

"Wow." She drew a deep breath. "Enticing as that sounds . . ."

Knowing he'd lost all finesse, he laughed.

"I need food, and sleep and a shower. And I want to see your home, your land."

His lust deflated. "I should have left you alone until things were settled."

"No." She smacked his arm. "I wanted you, too, remember? But I'm not used to sex, period, much less sexual excess."

And even though he didn't remember their first time together, she said he had been excessive. Add in what he did remember, and of course she wanted to pull back a little.

He glanced at her, and memories crashed in. "You are so small." His abdomen knotted. "I'll have to be more careful with you."

Talking sex always left her flustered.

"I don't want you to do a single thing differently." She ducked her face. "Just remember that while you might be invincible, I'm happy to admit I'm all too human."

He blew out a breath and reminded himself to be patient. As he'd told her, his place was livable but sparse on furnishings.

There was only one bed, so if she thought to put too much space between them, she'd just have to think again. For every night together, he planned to sleep with her, whether or not they had sex.

"Okay, so it's still early. Once we're at my place, we'll catch up on our zees. When you're feeling more bushy-tailed, you can soak in the Jacuzzi tub. That ought to help revive you."

Through half-lowered lashes, she studied him, then asked tentatively, "You plan to go back to bed with me?"

"Yeah." He rolled a shoulder. "I wouldn't mind sleeping. And until someone tracks down dumbass —"

"You mean Marc?"

"— there's not a whole lot that can be done from my end."

She fell silent for a heavy beat of time, then asked quietly, "And after they do locate him?"

A surge of determination flexed his hands on the wheel. "I want to talk to him." For

Alani's benefit, he kept his tone void of menace. "He knows something. I'll find out what."

"It wasn't him in the silver BMW."

"You don't know that, but so what? Guys like him have cronies who do most of their dirty work."

"A crony who has a car costing more than a hundred grand?"

Yeah, okay, so that sounded off in many ways. "I don't know, babe. But I'll find out." He pulled down the gravel drive to his home.

Alani sat up straighter. "This is it?"

He liked her tempered excitement. "Yeah. I'm pretty much hidden by trees, but this whole area is monitored."

Oaks, elms and sycamores grew so thick at either side of the road that, with the branches spread out, they formed a sort of canopy. It was as if they were driving through a green cave but with dappled sunlight everywhere. Jackson slowed for a rabbit that looked at the car, twitched its whiskers and finally hopped away.

Farther down, he pointed out some deer to her. Birds darted in and around the trees, occasionally doing a kamikaze dive in front of his car. Alani gasped each time, even though the birds avoided colliding with his windshield or tires.

Finally the front gates came into view and, beyond that, the house.

Aware of Alani's silence beside him, Jackson pulled off his sunglasses to enter the gate code. "Like Dare's, it's run by a keypad, but you can use a remote when leaving the property. There's an intercom and sensor device so that I always know when someone approaches."

She nodded, looking beyond the gate to his home.

Uneasy, Jackson waited for the gates to open and then drove over the long paved driveway to the house. "It's a ranch, but set up like separate quarters all connected. I liked the architecture of it."

"It's amazing." Her gaze went all over the house, from the garage attached by a utility room, to the main entrance and to the jutting master suite.

"Not a whole lot is done yet, but eventually the basement will be finished. There'll be a fourth bedroom down there, an exercise room and a recreation room."

He pulled into one of the three attached garages and turned off the car. Alani immediately slipped on her sandals, opened her door and stepped back out of the garage to look around.

Shielding her eyes, she looked up at the tallest trees with awe.

"I deliberately built around the trees," Jackson said as he joined her.

"I'm glad. It's perfect." She headed up the walkway to his massive front door.

"We could have gone in through the garage."

"I want to see the outside first." She circled around to the side of the house, picking her way along the wildflowers and weeds.

"I haven't even touched the yard yet." He wished she'd slow down and say something, maybe tell him her thoughts. She didn't know it, but through the process of choosing the house plans, the location, he'd been thinking of her. Considering her reaction.

She stopped on the back porch and looked down at the lake. Ducks swam by. Off in the distance, a fish jumped.

Alani brushed away a fly, then tipped her head back and breathed deeply.

He liked seeing her here, like this.

On his property.

"It's going to be a scorcher today." But the July morning had nothing on his internal heat. "In a few more hours, the humidity will make you sweat as soon as you step outside."

"I don't mind a little sweat."

No, she wouldn't. Slipping his hands around her, Jackson brushed aside her hair, nuzzled the side of her throat and kissed the softest part of her neck. "When you're up for it," he said suggestively, "I'd like to lay you out here on a blanket and make you scream with pleasure."

She quickened. "In the open?"

"Yeah." He lifted one hand to rest just under her breast, and felt her heartbeat thumping. "It's private enough. But I'd be able to see every inch of you."

Her hands settled over his. "You already did." Her voice quavered. "Before, I mean."

"But it wasn't enough." He was starting to feel like a masochist. "Until then . . ." He stepped back from her, wrestled with and conquered his control. "What's first? A tour, coffee or sleep?"

She turned to face him. "If I drink coffee, I won't be able to sleep."

"Then let's go back to bed for now."

Her palm settled over his chest. "Won't that be . . . hard on you?"

"Yeah." He grinned crookedly. "But it'd be harder knowing you were alone in my bed, all sleepy and warm and sweet." He took her hand and led her back around to the front. "I'll show you the master suite, and you can get settled while I unload our stuff."

As she looked everywhere, he took her in through the garage, through the vaulted kitchen and entryway, and down a connecting hall into the bedroom. Once there, he turned her and cupped her face. "I'm still working on things, so this is one of the few finished rooms — and the only bed." Did she understand?

She eyed the spacious room and the big bed, made up with a few pillows, sheets and a quilt. "It's big enough for a whole family."

She said that tentatively, almost like a question.

The thought threw him. Sure, the house was spacious, with enough rooms to accommodate most family units. But as a rule, family was never one of his considerations. He didn't think of his folks since they'd never really been a stereotypical family, and while he'd enjoyed the women he'd been with, he sure as hell hadn't looked at them as the start of a future. Sex was for relief only, and he was careful when it came to protection, so kids of his own had never been a concern.

Briefly, he thought of Arizona — but no. He didn't want to go down that path right now. He'd told Alani what she needed to know, and the rest would wait.

Hell, he'd just gotten her to admit there was something between them. For now, he wanted to enjoy her — and only her.

Guilt prodded him, but still he joked, "Your brother has no interest in being here, babe."

Something shone in her eyes, something elusive and female and wary. Her fleeting smile lacked genuine warmth. "Maybe for a visit."

Relieved that she didn't push it, Jackson nodded. "Maybe." Much, much later, if he had his way. "For now, there's just the two of us, and we'll be sleeping close." He wouldn't mind having her right on top of him — or better still, under him. He kissed her mouth. "Okay by you?"

She reached up to run her fingertips over his jaw, down his throat. "All my life I've slept alone, but I wouldn't have if I'd known how nice it is to sleep with someone."

"With *me,*" he clarified, in case she had thoughts of trying it with anyone else.

"Yes." She touched his bottom lip. "I do like sleeping with you, Jackson."

"Good." She could so easily twist him into knots. When she touched him, even in such a sweet way, maybe especially in a sweet way, he wanted to get inside her. "I need to secure the house, do a quick check of things." And that'd give him a chance to bank the fires a little. "I'll be right back."

"Take your time."

Like hell. He wanted to hold her as she fell asleep. It was important to him that she get used to being with him in all ways, that she enjoy it as much as he did. In less than fifteen minutes he ran through a check of the alarms, locks and monitors.

When he came back into the bedroom, he found Alani in nothing more than the T-shirt and panties, looking out the private patio doors from his bedroom to the back of the house.

He knew she could see the lake, the hills, nature and privacy.

His attention narrowed on her, on her beautiful legs and the way her blond hair hung down her slim back, how the T-shirt barely covered her ass, captivating him. He'd known more beautiful women. He'd known sexier women — and more sexual women.

He'd known women who concentrated on making him wild in bed.

But none of them were Alani.

Lost in thought, she looked very reflective and a little withdrawn. Did she resent being stuck here with him? Was she worried about that ass Tobin, or fearful of the threat?

Was she already wishing she could get back to her job, her home, her routine?

Jackson realized he was fretting, second-guessing himself, and that annoyed him. He'd gone hand to hand with murderers, been in shoot-outs with human traffickers, traveled over borders to retrieve kidnapped victims and dealt justice to the ones who'd taken them, all without fretting. He knew what to do, he did it, end of story.

Frustrated, he dropped her suitcase and his duffel bag. Alani looked up.

Even as they watched each other, her uncertainty, her nervousness beat at him in waves . . . until a yawn overtook her.

Full of mumbled apologies, she covered her mouth with a hand.

Jackson relaxed again. While she was here, he'd take care of her, pamper her; he was good at making women feel special. Usually in bed, but so what? He'd handle the "out of bed" stuff, too.

After turning back the covers, he patted the mattress. "C'mon, sleepyhead. In you go."

Barefoot, she padded over the thick carpet and climbed in. "I'm sorry I'm so tired. I didn't get much sleep last night, or the night before."

"Because of me." He didn't want her worn out, but he enjoyed knowing he was responsible for her exhaustion.

"Because of *us.*"

"True." Liking the sound of that even more, he drew the drapes to shut out much of the morning sunlight. Gray shadows now filled the room.

"I can't believe you're not more tired. After being so sick, you've gotten as little sleep as I did."

"But I'm a man."

"And that makes you impervious to weakness?"

No, but as a man he wanted her enough that he barely noticed other discomforts. She probably wouldn't appreciate hearing that, so instead he said, "I've done without sleep plenty of times. Guess I've adjusted to it."

With Alani watching his every move, he sat on the end of the bed to remove his boots and socks, then peeled off his T-shirt. He stood and disarmed himself, putting the weapons on the nightstand at his side of the bed.

"It's odd, you know." By the second she sounded sleepier, a little mysterious. "You treat weapons with the same comfort as your car keys."

He glanced at her. "In a pinch, I'd rather have my gun than my keys any day."

Turning on her side and tucking a hand beneath her cheek, she stared at his chest. "I don't regret it, you know."

"What's that, babe?" He eased the zipper down over his boner, and shucked off his jeans but left on his boxers. Better not tempt his control at this point. Now that he'd had sex with Alani, he wanted her even more. Knowing she was here, in his home where he'd so often envisioned her, only heightened every combustible feeling.

"Doing without sleep to be with you."

Hearing so much more than the simple words, Jackson went still.

Alani stared at his body. "Before that, before *you,* when I thought of going without sleep, it was to remember that airless little trailer where the traffickers took me."

Ah, hell. His heart in his throat, Jackson sat on the bed by her and put a hand on her hip.

She turned her gaze up to him. "I was too afraid to sleep, then, too afraid to even close my eyes. I didn't know what they'd do to me. Not that I could have stopped them just by staying awake. But I at least wanted to see it coming."

He lay down beside her and pulled her

into his arms. He'd always boasted an overactive libido. Many times he'd gone without sleep in favor of a sexual marathon.

Right now, Alani needed different things. He wouldn't be walking away from her tomorrow or even the next day, so he didn't have to get his fill up front. "You can sleep now. I won't let anyone hurt you."

Her tone soft, her voice low, she whispered, "But I hate wasting our time together. It's so nice seeing you like this, at ease, being yourself, letting me see you for who you really are. I'd rather be awake." She licked her bottom lip. "I'd rather be soaking up more experiences."

"Tease." It amazed him how she could take his dark and dangerous mood and fracture it with tenderness and humor. "Now that we have an agreement, I'll try harder to balance things, okay? Sleep with sex."

She smiled. "And food, and sightseeing and more talking?"

"Sure, if that's what you want." With one arm under and around her, Jackson held her hip, keeping her close. The other hand he cupped over her shoulder. In stark contrast to him, she was small-boned, her features so fine and feminine. "Food, then sex. Sightseeing, then sex."

She laughed. "Talking and sex?"

It wasn't a combination he usually enjoyed, but what the hell? "As long as you're not running away from me, I reckon we can fit all that in."

"I can't really go anywhere, now can I?"

He mulled over that sentiment, resenting it, wanting her to *want* to stay. "You shouldn't feel like a prisoner."

Curled into his side, she murmured, "Believe me, I know the difference."

Shit. "I'm a dumbass. I didn't mean —"

"I know." She fell silent for a moment, then said, "We talked about that the first time, you know."

"The first time we had sex?" *The time he couldn't recall.* When she nodded, he asked, "About what?"

"How long this would last."

His heart stuttered. What the hell had he told her? It was damned awkward not knowing.

She levered up on one elbow to look at him.

For only a flash of a second, he thought he saw culpability in her big innocent eyes, and he wondered at it. "Alani?"

"We agreed that as long as it stays fun and exciting, and we're both enjoying ourselves, sexually I mean, we would keep . . . experimenting."

What the hell? Had he really spelled it out so bluntly? Sure, he sometimes did that with other women because he didn't want them to get ideas. He wanted them to know up front not to have expectations. But that was *other* women.

Had he been that insensitive with Alani, too?

He wasn't sure he wanted to know, so instead he said, "Why wouldn't it be fun?"

"I don't know." She didn't quite meet his gaze. "You promised me great sex, and you've more than delivered. But neither of us wanted to get locked down."

"We didn't, huh?" That didn't sound like her. He knew better than most that Alani had never slept around. She was an all-or-nothing kind of woman — or so he'd always assumed. But her sheltered life might have kept her from sowing any wild oats.

Was he her damned oats?

Great sex, that's what she wanted — what she expected? How much pressure was *that?* Sure, he had every intention of delivering, but all guys had an off time now and then. If he didn't leave her limp and smiling, did that mean she'd go off to a different guy with newfound sensuality and confidence?

Over his dead body. Before he let that

happen, he'd —

"Jackson?" Gentle fingertips touched his brow. "You're frowning."

Because she turned him upside down. He was just disgruntled enough to mutter darkly, "You're already expecting me to fall short!"

Her eyes widened . . . and then her mouth twitched. "Not really."

"But if I do, you'll use that as an excuse to book, won't you?"

"We already agreed that I couldn't book, remember?"

That provocation brought a feral growl from deep in his throat.

His attitude left her playfully puzzled. "Do you expect to be a bad lover?"

"No!"

Then . . .

"You shouldn't use that as an excuse to cut things short."

Searching his austere gaze, she bit her bottom lip and ventured cautiously, "Just how long do you expect this to last?"

"Uh . . ." Damn it. He'd talked himself into a corner. He wasn't the insecure sort, but he didn't really want to fumble through a confession of his indecisive feelings without knowing exactly how she felt first.

And a plan came to mind. She'd just made

it clear that she expected mind-blowing sex. Fine. He'd blow her mind. Big-time. He'd yet to meet a woman who didn't eventually spout her feelings during release. Vows of affection went hand in hand with orgasms.

Give 'em an O, and they got lovey-dovey in return.

Most of the time he was indulgent about professions of love, sympathetic to the attitude if not the actual significance.

"Do we have to decide right this second?" Once he had her blindly moaning out her darkest secrets, then he'd figure out what he wanted, and how much.

As her shoulders slumped a little, Alani let out a breath. "No, of course not. I wasn't pressuring you." And then, defensively, "You're the one who brought it up."

Jackson knew he'd both confused and embarrassed her. He cuddled her closer. "Why don't we talk about all this later?" Much, much later. He kissed her forehead. "For now, let's get some sleep."

Her drowsy eyes studied him, but in the end she shrugged and settled back down again. She got comfortable with her thigh over his, her hand resting over his heart. "One thing, Jackson."

He swallowed back a groan and waited.

"I might not have a lot to compare with,

but I'm sure you do, so you have to know that the sex, at least for me, has been nothing short of amazing."

A fair start. "You can thank me later — when you're better rested." With Alani, he wanted to be more than amazing.

Now, tomorrow . . . and for the foreseeable future, he wanted to be the only one.

Chapter Thirteen

Marc Tobin got one eye open. The other eye . . . he didn't know. He hurt so bad, in places he'd never thought of, muscles he'd never used. He tasted old blood in his mouth, smelled new blood on his clothes.

Pinpricks of pain ran up and down his arms. They'd been tied behind him for what felt like days, but he really had no concept of the time that had passed. All he knew with certainty was that he had to get away, or they'd kill him.

He'd told them all he knew, but it was never enough.

Jesus, when it came down to it, he didn't know Alani all that well, and he barely knew Jackson at all.

His tormentors didn't buy it — or else they didn't care.

He wanted his old life back, the security of money, social connections, the power of prestige and respect from peers. He thought of the fists that had hit him. Black leather gloves. Cruel eyes staring through a mask. Guttural questions and more questions, coming rapidfire whether he had answers or not.

He'd dated Alani on a casual basis. He'd met Jackson twice, not counting that last time when the shots were fired, when he'd thought to escape, when someone had clubbed him in the back of the head and later awakened him with a punch to the gut.

It hurt to breathe, but he had to. If he ever wanted to get away, this might be his only chance.

Once, when they'd opened the door to his small cell, he'd seen trees. Sky. Outdoors.

He wasn't in a room in a bigger building, but rather a small, isolated structure. Maybe a shed. Or a garage of sorts.

No windows, but filtered sunlight crept in around a crack between the wall and floor, beneath the old door and in a vent in the ceiling.

He couldn't lock his broken jaw, but he did his utmost to stifle grunts of misery as he struggled to pull his arms free. Blood and sweat wet the binding around his wrists, now loosened from his involuntary jerking of pain during the last "questioning."

For now, the room was empty. Dark.

Smelling of his fear and pain.

Agony ripped through him, but he pulled at his right hand, leaning forward, praying he didn't do more damage to his abused body — and finally his hand came free.

It so surprised Marc that he slumped forward for a second, panting, fighting the blackness that closed in around him, before he finally realized what had happened.

He studied his hand. Blood covered his skin, looking obscene in and around his swollen fingers. He was certain a few were broken, given they were black, blue, oddly bent.

His stomach recoiled. Puking would only hurt more, and it'd definitely slow him down, so he swallowed convulsively until the nausea abated.

He was a strong man, capable of fighting for what he wanted, insisting when necessary. He'd faced off with more than one confrontation, dealt with more than one conflict. He was fit, athletic, more physical than most.

But he'd never been through anything like this. Not even close.

Given the abuse he'd suffered, it took him long, agonizing minutes to free his other hand and his feet. When he stood, his right knee wanted to give out. But by God, he'd crawl if he had to. Using the chair, he steadied himself.

He was leaving here. Now.

Praying he would find the door unlocked, he hobbled over to it, turned the doorknob — and inhaled in relief as it slid open.

He peeked outside, but he saw no one standing guard. A drizzling, miserable summer rain soaked everything in sight, leaving the muddy ground sodden, the sky dark gray. Off in the distance, through sparse woods, sat an old stone building. It looked dilapidated and abandoned.

But then he heard . . . sounds. Awful sounds. Moans, cries.

Begging.

Oh, God. Frantic for escape, he looked around, but everywhere he saw woods and more woods. He didn't know which way to go, so he started walking away from that stone house, from the shed that had imprisoned him. Praying more, he put as much distance between him and the suffering as he could.

As he made his way along, he remembered their exchanges. Early on he'd tried to bargain with them, but they cared nothing about his financial offers. When he'd threatened legal repercussions, they'd laughed. *Stop fighting it. There's nothing you can do.*

Nowhere you can go. No one to help you. Even if you made it away from here and got to the police, they'd never find us.

But we'd find you. Never doubt it.

And he didn't. Oh, he'd go to the police. Eventually. But God willing, if he made it out of the woods alive, he'd find a hospital first, and then he'd call the only person he could think of who might actually be able to keep him safe.

He'd call that crazy fucker Jackson.

It rained for three days.

All his plans to take Alani out on the lake, to skinny-dip with her, to explore his property together, were pushed aside . . . for endless sex.

As per his plan, he'd taken advantage of the close confines.

Just that morning he'd awakened to thunderstorms that shook his house. It made him horny. But then, as irregular as it seemed, a stiff breeze could make him urgent with lust when he had Alani within reach.

As crackling lightning split the dark sky, he'd kissed Alani awake, then kept on kissing her — everywhere — until she'd cried out in a rush of pleasure.

Only after she'd insisted had he rolled on

a condom and slid inside her. She'd moaned with verve, clung to him, bit his shoulder.

But other than saying she couldn't get enough, other than praising him and doing a little sexual praying — *Oh God, oh God* — she hadn't confessed a damn thing.

That was hours ago.

Midday, rays of sunshine finally cut through the gray skies. His third day with her.

And yet, nothing had changed. Or it hadn't changed enough.

Wearing only jeans, his chest and feet bare, Jackson stood on the covered patio and let the humid breeze drift over his body. Thanks to the rain, the air was fresh but thick. He filled his lungs and watched the waves on the shore.

He should have felt peaceful. Since arriving at his house, he'd been sating himself on Alani's body, soaking up her smiles, her sighs, and at the height of pleasure, her lusty groans of release.

He loved the raw, real sounds she made, her naturalness during sex. Physically, she never held back from him.

She gave him her body. But her heart? Her mind?

Damn it, he didn't know. As an astute man in all things, and especially a man who knew women well, Jackson could tell something wasn't one-hundred percent right.

Around making love to Alani, he'd kept to a schedule of sorts. He made use of his gym to burn off excess energy when Alani fell asleep on him. He worked on his house whenever she wanted time on his computer to search out interior designs — usually for decorating one of his rooms.

He loved it that she took an interest, and so far, her suggestions had been perfect. Soon as they could, he'd take her with him to hit up a store. Together they'd pick out more furnishings for him.

They took turns cooking, with her mostly doing breakfast, and him grilling their dinner on the back porch under the overhang. They often soaked in the Jacuzzi tub together, and each night they slept entwined.

But it wasn't enough. Jackson had the burning need for more.

A lot more.

As usual, he felt Alani's presence the moment she joined him. He turned to find her at the patio doors, her face clean of makeup, her hair in a loose braid.

She wore a bikini, and like him, her feet were bare.

"God Almighty, woman." His mouth went dry. "That's some sexy icing on the cake."

"I'm glad I thought to include it when I packed." Her shy smile didn't fool him; she knew the effect she'd have.

The slinky white material, edged by black lace, clung to her body. It showed off the outline of her nipples and every plump seam of her sex.

Jackson reached for her, but she darted back and held a beach towel in front of her body.

"I'm going swimming."

"No, you're not." He was already hard and getting harder by the second.

As if he hadn't spoken, she said, "If you want to join me, that'd be great. But this is the first clear day we've had —"

"It's not clear." He started toward her, and she backed up, circling away from the doors. "More clouds are rolling in."

Giggling like a schoolgirl, she stayed just out of reach.

And he continued to stalk her.

"Then I'd better hurry." She back-stepped off the patio.

"Careful." The land sloped gently down to the lake, and the wet grass could be treacherous to slippery feet.

She held up a hand, palm out, still giddy and teasing. "I want to swim, Jackson."

"We'll swim after."

"You said it yourself, the sunshine might not last."

"If you really wanted to swim," he told her, keeping her in his sights as she took another step back, "then you shouldn't have put on that boner-inspiring getup."

He finally got close enough, and Alani stunned him by cupping her hand over him, kneading him, stroking a little. His eyes closed, his breath quickened.

"How about," she teased, "we count the swimming as foreplay?"

"I won't last."

"We had sex this morning."

"So?" He caught her wrist and held her hand in place while he stripped the towel away from her. Man, she was a feast for the eyes. Staring at her belly, he muttered, "Around you, I stay hard and ready."

"I noticed, and I'm flattered."

Flattered? His gaze shot back to hers. "What the fuck does that mean?" *Flattered.* He snorted. She should be a damn sight more than flattered. "What do you think? That all guys are sexual machines? 'Cuz I can tell you, they aren't."

"Sexual machine . . . yes, that describes you." She snickered, but quickly sobered. "Do you know you always get fractious when you're aroused?"

His brows shot up. Fractious? Is that what she thought? More like he was desperate, lost, frantic with need.

"One insult after another." He burned for her, and every day just seemed worse than the day before. And yet, she wanted to swim. "I ought to hold out on you."

The smile played over her mouth. "Maybe you should." And then, playfully pleading, "At least until after I've had a swim?"

Jackson measured her mood and slowly nodded. "I'll make you a deal."

"I'm listening."

"We'll swim — but you lose the suit."

"Lose . . ." She blinked fast. "But I thought you liked it."

Watching her, keeping her gaze locked in his, he slipped a hand inside her bra top, over her breast, rasping her nipple with his palm. "Yeah. I do. It's a turn-on."

Her lips parted, and her eyes grew heavy.

"But you naked is better. Always."

Undecided, she turned to look down at the lake.

"No one will see you. There's a reason I chose to build here. The cove is private. But even if someone did come by, you'll be in the water. Hidden." He teased his thumb over her. "To everyone but me."

Filled with resolve, her gaze came back to

his. "Fine."

Oh, man. He started to growl out a few alternate suggestions to swimming, but she didn't give him a chance.

"You have to be naked, too."

"Not a problem." He grinned at her. "I don't even own trunks."

"You don't . . ." Nettled, she slipped away from him. "For heaven's sake, Jackson. So you always swim naked with women?"

"Keep up, will you?" He took her arm and started them both down the hill. "I haven't brought any other women here." And to make sure she got the significance of that, he tacked on, "Just you."

Bees flitted across the clover in front of them, and Jackson steered her around to a path of sorts. Eventually he'd put in a stone walkway, but it wasn't high on his list of priorities.

"So." Alani stepped with him onto the dock, then curled her toes on the sun-warmed boards. "I know I'm here because of a threat."

"There's that." Mindful of a full erection, he unzipped his jeans.

"What if another woman was threatened?"

"I'd do what I could." He pushed down his jeans and stepped free of them. Naked, the sun hot on his back, he stood before her. "But I wouldn't bring her here."

Her attention darted from his body, to the entrance of the cove and back again. Making him more than a little nuts, she licked her bottom lip — and focused on his dick.

Man, oh man. "Dangerous territory, babe, if you know what I mean."

She shook her head. "You're incredible."

He choked back a laugh. "With you staring, I'm sure to get more incredible by the second." Jackson turned her. His fingers on the band holding her braid, he said as casually as he could, "This is my home, honey. My getaway." The band slid free of her silky hair, and he smoothed it, running his fingers through the ripples left behind, before pushing it over her shoulder.

He trailed his knuckles down her spine. "Your brother and Dare have been here. Their women are welcome."

"You are such a caveman," she muttered, but gooseflesh rose in the wake of his touch. "They're wives."

"And women." He knew better than Alani just how possessive a man in love could be. Blocking that disturbing thought, he caught her hips. "Point is, I would never bring my work here. That'd defeat the purpose of having a private place."

Did she understand that, for him, she was

more than work? More than sex. More than . . . he didn't know.

More than anything he'd had before, or ever expected to have.

Drawing her back against him, he kissed the side of her throat, opened his mouth over the sensitive spot where her shoulder met her neck.

Tipping her head to the side, she whispered, "I feel on display."

"Yeah." He found the back tie to her top and lightly tugged it apart. The cups over her breasts loosened enough for him to get his hands underneath. "If I could, I'd lay you out right here on the dock."

Breathless, she whispered, "I couldn't," almost like she were considering it.

He played with her nipples, making her — and himself — nuts. "We'll see." In a rush, taking her by surprise, he opened the tie around her neck, and the top fell to the dock.

Going to one knee behind her, Jackson tugged down her bottoms.

Her knees locked, and on a gasp, she covered herself with a hand. Putting his hand over hers, he pressed her fingers in, turned on by the idea of her touching herself.

He kissed her lower spine, down, over one

cheek — and she jumped away. Staring at him wide-eyed, she opened her mouth, said nothing, then turned and in two quick steps reached the end of the dock. She dove in.

Left sitting there holding air, it took Jackson a second before he grinned and stood to follow her. Just as she'd done, he dove in, dousing his lust in the chilly water.

He surfaced right in front of her. Water spiked her lashes; her slicked-back hair looked darker, her cheekbones more pronounced, her lips moist.

They tread water together. "You do realize that the cold has a negative effect on men."

"Really?" One hand on his shoulder to help keep her afloat, she held his gaze, and with the other hand under the water, she found him, wrapping her small fingers around his shaft, squeezing. "I don't think so."

"I've created a monster." Being a strong swimmer, Jackson easily moved them both to the ladder. He held on with one hand, and she held on to him with both. "You wanna try some water play, is that it?"

"Yes." And then, "Is it possible?"

He didn't have a condom with him, but that didn't mean she had to wait. "I'll show you." While kissing her, he coasted a hand over her waist, down over her hip, back and over her rounded ass. "Open up for me, Alani. Put your legs around me."

Buoyed by the water, she did so easily, and damn, it felt good, the contrast of her heat with the cold water.

From behind he explored her, making her gasp so that she arched closer — but couldn't retreat from his touch. He opened her, pressed a finger in. Two fingers.

He was ravaging her mouth, pressing her back into the ladder, working her with his fingers when he heard the intrusion.

Already knowing what had happened, he lifted his head, muttered, "Damn it," and tried to figure out how best to handle the situation.

"Jackson?"

He groaned, his face against Alani's neck. An interruption was not welcome.

Still mired in need, Alani whispered, "What is it?" Writhing against him, she touched her lips to his jaw, his ear.

He felt her tighten around his fingers and said, "Sorry, darlin'."

"For what? What's wrong?"

No easy way to tell her. "Your brother is here."

"My brother . . . *what?*" Frantic, splashing, she tried to look around, but Jackson had her pretty much pinned in place. "Where?"

And then, from somewhere midway down the hill between the house and dock, Trace called out, "Jackson?"

"Ohmigod." Face coloring hotly, eyes flared, Alani froze. "Not again."

"He has the rottenest damn timing." Jackson shifted his fingers inside her, and she went berserk.

"Off!" She shoved at him, splashing more, nearly making him lose hold of the ladder. "Get off of me. Now. Hurry."

"Shh." He couldn't help but groan as he eased his fingers away from her. "Calm down. I'll handle it."

"Jackson?" Trace sounded closer.

Alani squeaked.

He kissed her forehead. "Just stay put."

Shrill, she asked, "How did he get in? I thought your place was secure!"

"From Trace?" He snorted. "Get real. If he wants in, he gets in. But as it happens, he also has the codes for entry, just as I do for his place and Dare's." Moving Alani to the side of the ladder, Jackson took two deep breaths and pulled himself up to the edge of the dock. He glanced down, saw Alani staring at his junk up close and personal, now at eye level with her, and wanted to groan again.

Seeing him, Trace paused, but not for long. "Why didn't you answer?" His footfalls rocked the dock.

"Go back up to the house, Trace."

Taking in Jackson's face, Trace stopped, then cursed.

"Yeah, I know."

Expression tight with annoyance, Trace said, "Where's Alani?"

"She's here." *Breathing on my dick.* "Go back up to the house. We'll be there in a minute."

Trace noticed Alani's bathing suit on the dock, and a feral sound came from his throat. He dropped his head, paced a circle, then stopped and pointed at Jackson. "Three minutes, got me? Three fucking minutes."

"Yeah, sure." What — did Trace think they'd try to finish up first? Didn't he know Alani any better than that? She was damn near ready to drown herself already. The mood had fled her the moment her brother came calling.

When Trace marched away, Jackson dropped back down in the water to submerge his head. He surfaced in time to see Alani half up the ladder, peeking over the edge of the dock.

What a body — understated in the curve department, but so sexy the water should have been steaming around her.

Better still, her adorable, soft bottom was right *there,* in front of him. He hesitated, but what the hell? He rose up and kissed her cheek, making her squawk and fall back onto him.

He went under again, this time with Alani on his head, thrashing so hard she damn near drowned him.

Catching her to him, Jackson held her still and surfaced, gasping for air. She sputtered in his face, so he waited for her to catch her breath, too.

"All right?"

"No." She pushed hair out of her face. "I don't believe this."

"You're telling me." Burying the moment to get down to business, Jackson moved her to the ladder once more. "But Trace is here for a reason, so we gotta get a move on."

She stared at him. "You think something is wrong?"

"I know it is." Trace had had that killing look about him, and only part of that had been due to finding his sister making whoopee in the lake. "Up and out."

Tucking in her chin, Alani said, "Ha! Not on your life." She gestured for him to precede her. “Be my guest.”

“You want the peep show, huh?”

“More than I want you to have it.”

“Spoilsport.” Hauling himself out, Jackson tried not to think of what she saw, or what he could have seen if she’d gone ahead of him. He turned and offered her a hand. “Get a move on.”

“Get my towel first.”

Now that her modesty had returned in force, it was an ordeal getting her out of the lake. He held the towel for her as she stepped back into her bottoms, but she didn’t bother with the top, choosing instead to wrap tightly in the towel.

When they started up, Trace stepped out to the patio to watch. Jackson knew him well enough that he read the signs of feral rage. Most of the time, Trace was the most urbane, sophisticated man you’d ever meet. When necessary, he bore the innate cunning and deadly reflexes of a wild animal.

This was one of those times.

At the door, in front of Trace, Jackson gave Alani a quick kiss. “I’ll entertain your brother while you go get dried off.”

Trace stood at the edge of the patio, a file folder held loosely in one hand, his gaze focused on the lake.

Jackson wasn't fooled. Trace never missed a thing.

After Alani put up her chin in defiance and marched in, Jackson went to sit on the lounge chair. "Okay, let's hear it. Make it quick, though, because I can guarantee that your sister won't hide for long."

"It's not in her nature," Trace agreed, still looking at the lake. Then lower, maybe even with a little humor: "I can't believe she was skinny-dipping."

Not about to comment on that, Jackson sat forward, his forearms on his knees, and waited.

Trace surprised him by saying, "You're good for her." He turned to look at Jackson. "The animals who took her did damage, but they didn't break her. She's coming into her own — more so with you than ever before."

Jackson didn't know what to say to that, so he said nothing. Alani would be fine. She *was* fine.

Despite her naturally reserved personality and circumspect manners, she was stronger than her brother knew.

"I hope you realize the predicament you're in."

Course he did, but still Jackson said, "Meaning?"

Trace shrugged. "If you do anything to hurt her, it's not going to sit well. With Dare or me."

"Yeah." Jackson stared down at his slack hands. "Thing is, I couldn't stay away from her."

"I know." Trace went steely again. "Marc Tobin knows it, too, as does someone else. And that's why I'm here."

His worst suspicions confirmed, Jackson closed his eyes. "Shit."

"You'll have to handle Alani."

That got his eyes open again. "What the hell does that mean?"

"It means she's going to be in the middle of this —"

"No way."

"— and it looks like you're the one who'll have to ensure she does as told."

"You're kidding, right?"

"You started this, Jackson. You changed the dynamics of the relationship. Sooner or later she has to accept what you do and how you do it." As if it hurt him to say it, Trace ground out the words. "You're the one she'll listen to now, not me. So it's up to you to make sure she toes the line, and that she stays safe."

Jackson had a very bad feeling. "Spit it out, damn it."

"You're going on a shit mission."
"To see Tobin?"
Trace nodded. "And Alani has to go with you."

Chapter Fourteen

Stunned, Alani paused in the doorway.

Unwilling to be left in the dark, she'd hastily thrown on an oversize T-shirt over her suit bottoms. Her wet hair hung in tangles down her back. Grass clung to her still-damp feet.

She'd rushed back out, ready to force her way into the conversation.

But what was that about her going on a mission?

Without really giving it much thought, she decided to listen in again.

But it didn't work.

Coiled with tension, Jackson looked toward where she hid. "Come on out, Alani."

Trace seconded that, saying, "This concerns you, too, honey."

Knowing her face bloomed with guilty color, Alani stepped into the bright sunshine. "Trace." When all else failed, she resorted to impeccable manners. "We weren't expecting you."

Unlike Jackson, Trace hid his aggression with a crooked smile. "Obviously." He nodded toward Jackson. "Take a seat, okay?"

"Could I get you something to drink first?"

"No." He strode to her and took her arm, urging her to the seat.

Next to Jackson.

She could feel the urgency in the air, the charge of hostility. It wasn't directed at her, but it left her uneasy all the same.

Tapping a big file folder against his thigh, Trace said, "I wanted to talk to both of you about this."

Jackson didn't touch her, and she felt the loss of his attention like freezer burn. She looked from Jackson's set profile back to Trace's face. "What's going on?"

"A lot, actually." Trace pulled up a chair in front of them. "Tobin called for you, but he got me instead."

"The son of a bitch called her?" Cold, detached, Jackson said softly, "I told him to stay the hell away from her."

"And if he hadn't been so desperate, he might have listened to your warning."

"Desperate?" Alani didn't know what to think. "Those people who fired at Jackson? Were they aiming for Marc? Has he been injured? Shot?"

"At this point, it's anyone's guess who was the target that night. Tobin says someone wants him dead. Wants the two of you dead, too." Trace watched her. "I went to see him, but he'll only talk to Jackson."

A drumbeat of silence made her ears ring and compressed her lungs so that it was hard to breathe.

Trace inhaled. "And only if you're there, too."

"Fuck that." Alive with fury, Jackson sat forward. "I'll make him talk."

"Sorry, but someone already tried that."

Alani covered her mouth with a hand. "You?"

"No. He was already in the hospital when I saw him. But someone hurt him. Damn near killed him, actually." Trace studied her. "He's in a bad way."

"Jesus," Jackson muttered, more in disgust than out of sympathy.

Trace handed over a hospital report. "Given what he survived, I'd say he's tougher than I thought."

After perusing it, Jackson closed the file without a word. He worked his jaw.

Trace didn't look too happy, either. "Somehow he got away, and he's saving all the details for you."

"I don't understand this," Alani said. "Why Jackson?"

Jackson answered her. "He knows I can protect him."

"That's about it," Trace agreed. "He wants Alani there because he figures she can keep him safe from more of the same, at least from you."

While Alani struggled to sort it out, Jackson nodded in comprehension. "He wants protection, figures I can give it, but he doesn't trust me not to finish what someone else started."

Trace reached for Alani's hand. "I'm sorry, honey, but he does trust you. And much as I hate it, we need to find out what we can from him."

Before Alani could assimilate that, Jackson pushed from his seat. "He's still in a hospital?"

"And will be for a few more days at least."

Pacing the length of the porch, Jackson said, "He wants us to come there?"

"Yes."

"Could be a trap."

"I know."

The rapid-fire back and forth made Alani's head spin. "Whoa. You're making plans around me!"

"Necessary plans," Jackson told her. And

then to Trace, "You and Dare will cover us?"

"Me inside, Dare outside."

"When?"

"Sooner the better. There's a chance that when he escaped, if he truly escaped, they weren't able to follow and haven't yet located him."

None of this made any sense to her. "What do you mean, if he escaped?"

Trace shrugged. "It's possible someone let him go, guessing he'd contact Jackson."

"Hoping to draw us out," Jackson said.

The trap he'd mentioned. Feeling a little queasy, she put a hand to her stomach.

Finally Jackson looked at her. "Go get dressed."

The terse order pushed her past her limit. She slowly rose to her feet. "I beg your pardon?"

Trace collected the files and turned for the patio doors. "I'll be inside."

That her brother walked off now told her plenty. He wanted her to get ready, too.

"If you don't want to go," Jackson told her, practically jumping on the possibility, all but heaving in anger, "say the word. I'll figure out something else."

"Trace said I needed to."

"Fuck that. Fuck him." He grabbed her upper arms. "I can work it another way."

He was concerned for her, but Alani would not let him dictate to her. "How?"

"I don't know yet. It's not for you to worry about it."

How could she help but worry? With his demands, Marc put her right in the middle of danger. But to be honest with herself, scared as it might make her, she preferred to be with Jackson.

The idea of him being hurt scared her most of all.

She knew she was in love with him, and keeping the words to herself the last few days hadn't been easy. But if she couldn't say it, she could at least show it.

She stepped closer and stared up at him. "I will get dressed." Her bottom lip quivered, and she swallowed hard. "I will do what needs to be done. But I will not —"

He kissed her hard, stealing her breath, shocking her. His tongue came into her mouth as he lifted her to her tiptoes, forcing her head back, devouring her.

She made a sound of alarm, and he lifted his mouth away.

Breathing hard and deep, he said, "Not how it works, babe. Not now."

Alani flattened her hands against his chest, but he was as immovable as cold steel.

He let that settle in, let her feel her own

helplessness, then said, "You want to play along? Fine. But you'll have to put aside what's between us. *I'll* have to put it aside."

She wanted to ask what that could be, because he'd never said, but she didn't. Now was definitely not the time to press him on his feelings.

"You do what I say, when I say. You breathe when I tell you to breathe." He inhaled. "And you run when I tell you to run. No matter what, no questions asked."

"You're crossing a line, Jackson."

"It's already crossed." He released her to rub the back of his neck. "It's been crossed since the day I met you."

Her heart broke a little. "I don't know what that means."

Cupping her face, he looked down at her. "It means you need to be away from danger, not surrounded by it."

Was he counting himself in the group with danger? "You would use this as an excuse to . . . to . . ."

"No." He drew her forward for another kiss, this one softer, almost an apology. "It means I care enough that I can't stomach the thought of you hurt."

Relief nearly took out her knees. It wasn't exactly a declaration of love, and she knew Jackson cared for a lot of people; he couldn't do his job if he didn't care. But at least he wasn't forcing her away.

"I don't like the idea of you hurt, either."

His expression hardened. "That's what I'm talking about right there. You can't think that way."

Was he nuts?

"You will not, under any circumstances, second-guess an order from me."

"No, I won't." She exhaled a deep breath, then another, before finding her grit. "But we already discussed this, if you'll recall. Nasty orders aren't necessary. I can follow directions just fine."

His brow went up. "And yet, you still haven't gone to change your clothes."

She ignored that. "I can be ready in fifteen minutes if you and Trace want to finalize your plans."

His mouth flattened — until she went on tiptoe to kiss him. "I trust you, Jackson. It'll be fine."

And with that parting shot, she walked away from him.

Inside, she shook in fear. For Jackson to be so over-the-top outrageous in his attitude, the situation had to be treacherous.

But she wanted, needed, for him to know that she could handle it. She could handle him and what he did for a living. Dare's wife, Molly, was strong. Trace's wife, Priss, was even more so.

She needed to measure up, or give up — on herself, on Jackson, on a future together. But she loved him, so giving up was not an option.

That meant she had to make this work, and one way or another, she would.

The trip to the hospital, made in terse silence, left Alani strained. She wished Jackson would reassure her, but in full-defense mode, he spent his time scanning the area . . . and thinking.

She didn't want to interrupt his vigilance, but the silence left her so edgy, she couldn't relax.

"Dare is already at the hospital?"

"Stationed somewhere outside at a vantage point, to ensure we get in and out safely. He hasn't spotted anything or anyone yet, or he'd have told me."

The silence droned on again. Alani cleared her throat. "And Trace is inside?"

"Doing surveillance on the area, making sure Tobin's room isn't being watched by anyone but him." Jackson glanced at her. "Do as I say and you'll be fine."

"I wasn't worrying," she lied. "Just . . . curious."

"If you say so." He flexed his hands on the wheel. "We'll be there in a few minutes. As we go in, stay to my left, a step behind me. Don't look around. It gives away too much."

"Will you be armed?"

"Yeah, but not the way you think. Don't worry about it."

His insistence that she was worried bugged her. "I've never done this before. I want to know what to expect."

"You don't need to know. Just do —"

"As you say. I know." She sat back in her seat, wanting to ask more questions but deciding against it. The last thing he needed was for her to distract him. "Am I going into the room with you, or waiting in the hall?"

"In the room." He pushed the file toward her. "And now that you mention it, you ought to take a look at Tobin's photo beforehand. He's a mess, and I don't want you to be . . . surprised."

She stared at the file with uneasy curiosity. She wasn't one to faint at the sight of blood, but she'd never seen anyone really hurt, especially not someone she used to care about.

"The photo is held on the folder with a paperclip. Right there in the front." Since she hesitated, Jackson flipped it open himself. "I can tell you from experience that it always looks worse than it is, especially with head wounds."

Dear God. Among notes and printouts, the snapshot of Marc jumped out at her. If Jackson hadn't told her it was Marc, she'd never have recognized him. One eye was swollen, black and purple and red. The other had a bandage over it. His entire face sported bruises and stitches, with his nose, jaw and chin grotesquely misshapen.

At her horrified silence, Jackson reached for her hand, gave her a squeeze, then released her again. "Trace says he can talk, but it's not easy with a broken jaw and nose. His eye is bandaged for a fractured eye socket. Nothing that won't heal, if he can steer clear of more trouble."

"And that's where you come in?"

"That's his plan."

"What's your plan?"

"Depends on what he has to tell me." Jackson brooked no argument when he said, "If he set you up, if he had anything to do with your kidnapping, he's a dead man."

That thought hadn't even occurred to her! "What if he was just after you?"

He gave her a sideways glance. "There's no telling how he's involved, so let's not borrow trouble."

"Or anticipate murder?"

"I'm prepared for anything. Get used to it."

Another order?

He pulled into the hospital lot and parked a good distance from the main entrance. She started to look around, but he caught her chin. "Don't. If anyone is watching, I don't want to tip our hand."

The idea that anyone could see them now made her skin crawl. *How did he do this job?* "You want them to think you're unaware of the possible danger?"

Derision showed in a crooked smile. "I don't want them to think I'm stupid." He opened his seat belt and then hers. "But thinking I'm cocky, that I trust Tobin, that'd be a plus. It'd give me the upper hand." He opened his door. "Stay put until I come around."

With reflective sunglasses in place, Jackson circled the hood to open her door. Alani stepped out — and moved to his left as he'd instructed. She wanted to ensure that she didn't slow, hinder, or in any other way interfere with his work. He probably expected her to be a liability, one more person he had to protect, but she badly wanted to prove him wrong.

She wanted his attention only as a woman, not as a potential victim.

Parked so far out, they had to pass scraggly landscaping, disreputable cars and a few loiterers. Each time panic tried to come alive inside her, she did her best to conceal it with bravado; if Jackson wasn't concerned, why should she be?

"Deep breaths, honey. Remember, no one is going to take you again."

Because Jackson wouldn't let them. "Of course not." Her smile fell flat. "I'm sure it's fine."

He gave her a telling look, but said nothing.

Wishing she could see Dare or Trace instead of just trusting that they were where they should be, she walked fast to keep up with Jackson's long stride.

They had almost reached a walkway that circled around the hospital when something moved in the bushes. A deep-throated, raspy, growling snarl emerged.

She jumped — but Jackson didn't.

"It's okay. Just an animal."

"Here?" That seemed unlikely to her, given the congested area.

Frowning, Jackson stared a moment, and then moved closer to the bushes and went down on one knee.

The urge to scan the area almost overwhelmed Alani. “Jackson.” She tried to remove the shrill note from her voice. “What are you doing?”

“Wait.” He made a sound, gentle and persuasive — and a furry-faced cat poked out its head. Giant emerald-green eyes shone through long gray and cream-colored fur.

“Ohhhhh.” Alani’s heart dropped. The poor thing looked half starved, skittish and a little wounded with his long fur all fuzzy and matted. “A kitten.”

“He’s full grown,” Jackson said, “just scrawny.” He continued to hold out his hand, and the cat got close enough to sniff him before darting back into hiding.

“I bet he’s hungry.” Alani could never bear to see any animal in need. One of her favorite charities was a no-kill animal shelter local to her home. When she could, she volunteered to walk the dogs and brush the cats. “I know this is bad timing, but I hate to just leave him here.”

“It’s important to you?” Jackson didn’t sound judgmental as much as curious.

Again, she glanced around the area, but other than a few cars finding parking spots, she saw nothing. Still, better not to drag out this conversation. “I know in the scheme of things, with human lives on the line, one stray cat doesn't seem like a big deal."

"It's a big deal to me." He turned back to watch the cat. "I don't like to see anything suffer."

Such an amazing man. Alani put a hand on his shoulder. "Maybe once we're on the road and it's safe, we could make a call to a shelter or something."

Jackson came back to his feet and took her hand again. As they walked, he said, "Let's see what we can figure out when we come back this way. Maybe I can catch him or something."

"You're serious?"

He rolled one shoulder. "Why not? If he's still hanging around later, then it won't hurt to try." He lifted her hand and kissed her knuckles in apology. "But right now, I can't."

Alani looked back over her shoulder and saw the cat staring after them, his big green eyes hopeful but wary.

So Jackson would kill Marc, but he wanted to coax out a mangy cat to care for it? "Amazing." She hugged herself to his arm. "I hope he hangs around."

"Me, too." He led her along to a service entrance probably used for deliveries.

She expected an alarm to go off when he

opened the door next to a loading dock, and when it didn't, her heart settled back into a normal rhythm.

Now that they were inside, she felt safer, and even let out a breath. "Thank goodness we —"

In the next second, Jackson stopped and put her behind him. "Footsteps, coming fast."

And that put him in combat mode? They were in a hospital, after all. A quiet branch of the hospital, but still . . . She peeked around him and saw a long, empty hallway with numerous closets. Matching her tone to his, she whispered, "Could it be a custodian, maybe?"

Right before her eyes, he seemed to get bigger, harder. "I don't think so." He opened one of the closet doors and pressed her inside. "Back wall. And not a word." Then he stepped into the room, too, but stayed near the open doorway.

Going numb with fear, Alani peered around and saw stacked boxes of supplies along with some mop buckets, bottles of cleaner, and various-size brooms and vacuums. Stepping over and around the clutter, she backed up until her shoulders touched the far wall, just as Jackson had requested.

With each footfall that sounded closer,

her windpipe seemed to constrict and her heartbeat accelerate. She didn't know what to expect, but in the back of her mind, she still thought it was probably a lot of worry for nothing.

Surely it was just someone visiting a patient.

Or a doctor. Or nurse.

She'd almost talked herself into breathing normally again, and then suddenly Jackson and another man were physically engaged.

It happened so fast that she had to slap a hand over her mouth to stifle a scream. Jackson moved away from the closet even as a large dark man lashed out toward his face with a knife.

On the balls of his feet, his limbs loose, his expression anticipatory, Jackson ducked the lethal blade, then, showing lightning-fast reflexes, punched the man in the throat.

He followed that with an elbow to the man's head, and a knee to his midsection.

Oh, wow.

The knife clattered to the linoleum floor, and the man, doubled over, grabbed at his throat. Already turning blue, his eyes bulged as he choked and gagged. The awful sound he made resembled a goose's honk before Jackson shoved him back into another man who tried to draw a gun.

Thrown off balance, the second guy stumbled, and Jackson moved in. His fist landed on the man's jaw with unerring force. Head snapping back, the man staggered, and when he righted himself, Alani had no doubt that he suffered a badly broken or dislocated jaw. The grotesque misalignment of lips and teeth made her stomach lurch.

Not giving the man an opportunity to recover from that first blow, Jackson hit him again, shattering his nose and sending blood to spray all over his shirt. One more punch, and the guy crumpled awkwardly, one leg twisted beneath him, his ankle unnaturally turned.

"Oh, my God." Alani knew that Jackson, Dare and her brother were capable, but she'd never seen, never expected . . .

After picking up the gun and knife, Jackson leaned into the closet and caught her wrist. "Out."

"Oh, my God," she said again as she began picking her way over the clutter, her thoughts rioting, her limbs quaking.

"Move your ass, babe. They won't stay out forever."

"I'm sorry." Remembering her determination to be an asset, not a liability, she blocked the gruesome sight of fallen bodies and hastened her step.

Besides, she did not want them coming to while she remained in the vicinity.

Once out of the way, she peered at the demolished men. Jackson had taken them out with very little effort. He wasn't even breathing hard. "Unbelievable."

"So little faith in my ability?" With practiced ease, Jackson shoved the first guy, who'd passed out from lack of air, onto his stomach. Using nylon restraints, he bound his hands behind his back, and then his feet. He dragged him into the closet and came back out to do the same to the second man.

The guy started to revive, and, casual as you please, Jackson slugged him again, putting him out once more.

Alani looked at his big fists, at how he wielded them so effectively, and at the same time she couldn't help but think of how gentle he could be when touching her.

Jackson was not an ordinary man with simple motivations and morals.

The amazing contradictions left her fascinated.

In efficient haste, he bound both men, and then, using the big knife, he cut strips from their shirts to gag them.

They were left so uncomfortably constrained that Alani almost felt sorry for them. Almost.

Lastly Jackson hobbled them by attaching their foot restraints and hand restraints together. If they came to — and Alani had no idea if they would — they'd be able to do no more than flop about like beat-up fish.

Feeling very ineffectual, she stood by in an agony of suspense, certain that someone would come down the long hall and bust them doing things so . . . illegal and scary and insane.

But with the men both secured, Jackson let out a breath, smiled at her and used both hands to finger-comb his hair back. "Ready?"

Speechless over his ability and negligent disregard of what had just happened, she stood there.

He said, "Shake it off, woman. I need you with me one-hundred percent."

"Of course." She nodded, swallowed and finally found her tongue. "What do you need me to do?"

He barked a laugh but said nothing else as he freed the cell phone from his jeans and, using his thumb, called Dare. After a brief hesitation, he said, "Disabled two, but there has to be a . . . you got him already? Great. Yeah, I'll let Trace know."

Alani said, "There was a third?"

He disconnected the phone and nodded. "Yeah. Someone had to tell them where we came in, right?"

Oh. She hadn't even thought about it. They'd entered, and the bad guys were just . . . there. "They wanted to kill us?"

He shrugged. "No worries, though. These two are through, and Dare took care of the other guy."

She had no idea how Dare had taken care of him, and didn't ask.

Using the phone again, Jackson hit a few keys, waited and the phone beeped back in return.

The complexities of their operation astounded her. "Code?"

"Yeah. Letting Trace know what happened." He tucked the phone away and looked at her in expectation.

Alani shook her head. "You're scary."

"Yeah. Scary, but with mad skills, right?" He smiled and slung an arm around her shoulders for a brief hug. "Damn, but I needed that."

"You . . ." She couldn't credit his manner. "Why in God's name would you need bloody violence?"

"Sexual frustration?"

Thinking of his excessive drive, her jaw

loosened. "I've left you frustrated?"

"Course not. But we keep getting cut short."

"Cut short?" She couldn't believe she was having this conversation now.

"That's right." He slewed a hot look her way. "I only had you alone for three days."

And they'd made love multiple times each day, sunup to sundown, and a few times he'd even awakened her halfway through the night. "Are you insane?"

"About sex? With you?" He gave her a lazy look. "Probably." He switched gears again. "I doubt there are any more of them here right now, but we'll find out soon enough. C'mon."

She said nothing else as they made their way through the hospital. Once they reached the elevator, they could see people in the lobby, which, to Alani's mind, diminished some of the danger.

But still she couldn't relax.

"Hey." Jackson drew her into his side. "Take a deep breath."

She tried, but it didn't help. And that frustrated her, too. He was so blasé that her edginess seemed amplified in comparison.

Jackson looked down at her. "You did good."

If only, but she knew the truth. "I did

nothing."

"You didn't get in my way. You didn't scream." He teased a lock of her hair. "You didn't faint. Or puke."

True. She put her hands behind her, not wanting him to know how she trembled. "There's no doubt they were bad guys?"

"Definitely bad. You saw the knife and gun, right?"

She pointed out the obvious. "I've seen yours before, too."

He snorted. "Not the same thing and you know it." The elevator doors opened, and Jackson drew her inside with him. "They weren't selling cookies, babe."

Odd, considering what had just happened, but Jackson no longer oozed menace. "You seem more relaxed now."

"Yeah, well, I knew that was coming but didn't know when, and I was a little . . . wary?" He liked that word and nodded. "About how you'd take to it, I mean. I didn't want to upset you."

That had been his uppermost concern?

"But like I said, you did good. Real professional."

She'd cowered in the closet as instructed. "You like how I follow orders, do you?"

"Is that what you were doing?" He bent and took her mouth in a warm kiss. "Maybe

I should try a few orders in bed. What do you think?"

It stunned Alani, but she sort of liked that idea. "Maybe."

His eyes flared — and then he kissed her again. "Dirty pool, woman. You're giving me a jones when I can't do anything about it."

Alani started to look to see if that was true, but he hugged her closer.

"No, don't stare. It'll make it worse."

When she laughed, he grinned at her. Amazing, amusing, macho Jackson. Surely no other man could be like him.

The second the elevator doors opened on the right floor, he caught her hand and stepped out. "Let's keep it together while we see your ex, and then I can get you out of here and maybe someplace more private."

Now knowing that Marc played a part in the recent tribulations, she didn't appreciate the teasing. "You don't have to refer to him that way."

"Why not? You dated the putz, remember?"

And that was his point? To make her remember? She wanted to elbow him, but decided against it when he stopped outside a door.

"Ready?"

Nervousness overtook her. She thought of the pictures he'd shown her, the way Marc had betrayed her. No, she wasn't ready at all, but she nodded anyway.

Jackson wasn't fooled. He cupped both hands around her neck under the fall of her hair. "You're a gutsy broad, Alani. You'll do fine, trust me."

Gutsy broad. Coming from someone of Jackson's caliber, it was the nicest compliment she'd had in a long while. "All right, then. Let's get this over with." She pushed the door open, stepped inside and drew up short at the sight of the bloodied, battered, unrecognizable man resting in the hospital bed.

Now she might faint.

Chapter Fifteen

Jackson didn't give Alani a chance to get too wobbly. That she put on such a brave front was admirable enough. He appreciated the effort, but he wanted her to know it wasn't necessary. He put an arm around her, as much to steady her as to reinforce his claim for Tobin's benefit.

Looking a lot like peeled, bruised fruit, Tobin peered toward them with one black-and-purple eye so swollen it was a miracle he could see out of it. A white bandage covered the other eye. Dark bruises spread out over the bridge of his misshapen nose. With bloody ears, fat lips and various other injuries — and that was just on his face — he made a pitiful sight.

Not that Jackson planned to show him any pity. Hell, no. "How's it hangin', Tobin?"

When the bastard groaned, Alani came alive. "Marc, oh God, are you all right?"

"I'll survive," he whispered in a pained

rasp. "I'm sorry . . . a drink. Please."

Jackson held Alani back. "I'll do it." He didn't want Alani anywhere near the prick. She was so bighearted that she'd be forgiving before they even knew how badly Tobin had compromised her security.

Circling to the other side of the bed, Jackson lifted the paper cup with the straw and put it to Tobin's cracked lips. Alani stared at him in wonder, as if he'd surprised her again.

She'd done that a lot today.

After several sips, Jackson set the cup back on the rolling bedside table. He pulled up a chair for Alani, making sure she kept a safe distance away, then crossed his arms and stared down at Tobin.

"So you got worked over, huh?"

"Yes."

Unwilling to hold back his disdain, Jackson grunted. "No more than you probably deserved."

Tobin surprised him by agreeing. "I fucked up."

"No shit? And you're smart enough to realize it?"

"You thought I got rich by accident?" He shifted, his face frozen in pain for several seconds as he caught his breath. Finally, moving slower, he got situated in a more upright position. "I'm not an idiot."

"Can't prove it by me."

Even one-eyed, Tobin managed a sour frown. "I took a pain pill a few minutes ago." With one wrapped hand, he held his ribs. "God willing, it'll kick in soon."

It blew Jackson away that Alani kept quiet through that display of pain. Expecting to see her near tears, he glanced at her, but instead, she frowned intently, and she had her hands locked together in her lap.

Upset but not falling apart.

Proud of her, he turned back to Tobin. "The meds don't put you to sleep?"

"No. No rest. No sleep. I don't dare. Not until I know . . ."

"That your ass is safe?" Jackson leaned against the bed. "I get it."

"Actually, I'm not the villain you want me to be." He looked beyond Jackson to Alani. "I know you can't forgive me. I can't forgive myself. But when you dumped me . . ." He labored for air, wheezing, struggling to suppress a cough. "It killed my ego, as you said."

Jackson's eyebrows shot up at the admission. "Not your heart, huh?"

"No one has rejected me in a long time." He lifted a hand but lowered it back carefully to the bed. "The perks of power and prestige."

Alani stood but didn't go near Tobin. Instead she sidled up next to Jackson. "What did you do, Marc?"

"After I left your place that first time, people approached me. They said he was dangerous to you. They said they were bounty hunters and he was wanted, that there would be a reward. They said . . ." Self-loathing filled his broken confession. "They said a lot of shit, and after the way he took me out, I wanted to believe it."

Did that saccharine admission work on Alani? Jackson curled his lip. "You want me to think you acted out of her best interest?"

"Not then, no. But now . . . I know you want to keep Alani safe. I realize now that's what you were doing. I didn't know . . . never suspected that people would be so . . ." He fell quiet. "Is that what you went through? When you were taken?"

Jackson worked his jaw. He prayed not. To keep Alani from answering, rehashing the past and giving Tobin too much info, he said, "Let's talk about you, Tobin, okay?"

Tiredly, the man nodded. "Yeah, let's. Here's the deal — guarantee my safety first, and then I'll tell you what I can so that you can keep Alani out of their reach."

A red haze clouded Jackson's vision.

"Yeah, you're an altruistic motherfucker, aren't you?"

"You can't make me feel worse than I already do, and it changes nothing. I want to live."

"What makes you think I can ensure that?"

"Because even though they wore masks, I saw their eyes." Tobin met his gaze unflinchingly. "And you have the same look."

"Fuck you."

Alani's hand moved up and down his arm. She leaned into him — and that was all he needed to regain his cool composure.

"I don't mean . . . mean cruel." Tobin swallowed, wincing in more pain. "I mean capable. You walk in the same stratum. You understand them."

True enough. Jackson narrowed his eyes as he considered things. "Tell me what happened without the bullshit. Straight-up facts, that's all I want. All of it. Start at the beginning."

Tobin nodded. "When I killed the electricity . . . it was to set you up." He paused for two heartbeats. "I wanted to hurt you and I wanted to hurt her. I just never suspected . . ."

Alani shifted. "That you were dealing with monsters?" Shaking, she took a step forward. "They could be the very people who kidnapped me. The people who would have *sold* me."

Jackson watched Tobin and saw no reaction to that disclosure. So he'd already known they were human traffickers?

"They could have *killed* Jackson."

"Or you," Tobin said. "But I didn't realize. I thought they'd take him, rough him up. I thought they had some personal beef with him. He'd be out of the picture, and I'd be the one there with you."

"And then what?" Alani demanded. "There was never anything substantial between us."

"Hell, I don't know. I figured you'd be upset, need a shoulder . . ." He swallowed. "I admit it's the dumbest move I ever pulled."

Trying to be subtle, Jackson tugged Alani closer again. He didn't want to make a big deal of her upset, especially with her trying to hide it.

He stated the obvious. "You know she was taken by human traffickers."

"I do now." Sad, apologetic, he looked toward her. "I was kept in a small structure. Like a shed maybe. When I got free, I saw there was an old stone building nearby, too.

I could hear . . ." He stopped, struggling for breath.

"Shit." Jackson put Alani back as he stepped forward. "You bastard. You left women behind, didn't you?"

Tobin nodded. "I couldn't help anyone. I could barely get myself out of there. But I heard . . . suffering." Again he glanced at Alani. "Several women."

Jackson already had his phone in his hand. "Tell me where, and make it fast."

"You'll keep them from killing me?"

"If I don't kill you myself."

Somehow his swollen, broken lips worked in the way of a smile. "That's what she's here for." But he wasted no more time. "I was off the highway, about a mile into the woods." He told what he could, then waited, his gaze locked on Alani, while Jackson relayed the message to Trace.

It wasn't easy to keep his cool, especially with Tobin eyeballing her like that. Jackson stepped in front of him to block his view. Holding the phone away, he asked, "When did this happen? How long since you've been away?"

Tobin gazed up at the clock, then flinched. "About twelve hours."

"So much time," Alani worried aloud. "They could be gone by now."

"Probably are," Jackson said, but he filled in Trace before disconnecting the call. He turned to Alani with an air that she didn't misinterpret: the less Tobin knew, the better.

She nodded in understanding.

Did she also understand that he would do everything he could to find the women, and so would her brother and Dare?

Subsiding, she back-stepped until her calves found the seat. She dropped into it again.

Jackson paced between her and Tobin. "How'd you get away? No way in hell did you walk the forty miles to this hospital. And there's another hospital that's closer anyway. How'd you end up here?"

"Two hospitals are closer, but they were too risky. I figured they'd look for me there first. After a trucker picked me up, I stayed with him for as long as I could stand to, until I . . . until I thought I'd die if I didn't lay down. Then he dropped me off in the emergency entrance, and here I am."

Not bad. At least Tobin had tried to think ahead and act a little smarter. "You'd have been better off skipping hospitals all together, but then, I guess you don't have a doctor who knows how to keep quiet?"

"Never necessary before."

"Think about it for the future, because they've already found you here. I took care of a few goons on my way in."

Panic lifted Tobin up despite his pain. "Where? How many? Why didn't you tell me —"

"Shh. It's all right." Suddenly Alani was there again, offering Tobin another drink of water. As he sipped, she said, "They can't hurt you right now. Jackson won't let them."

Jackson lifted a brow — but damn it, she was right.

"They weren't dead when I left them, so who knows how much time we have. If you've got information worth your life, you better start sharing it."

Alani set the water aside. "The trucker didn't call the police?"

"No." Groaning, Tobin settled back again. What little color had rushed into his face leeched out once more, thanks to aches and pains. "I gave him my watch to keep his mouth shut."

Jackson scoffed. "You're telling me they didn't take your watch?"

"Believe me, I offered it to them. Even begged them to take it. They laughed and hit me some more." One hand curled but not tightly; from the looks of his fat fingers, his tormentors had popped a few knuckles.

"They said I might as well understand that all they wanted were answers."

"What were the questions?" Alani asked.

Jackson curled his lip. "Apparently nothing that he could help them with, or he'd be dead right now."

"Exactly. I'm ashamed to admit it —"

Folding his arms, Jackson said, "Yeah, yeah, you're suffering shame. We get it."

"— but I told them what I knew."

"Which was squat." And thank God, because if Tobin had led the cretins back to Alani, Jackson would be finishing him off himself right now.

"I told them your name, where Alani worked, the hours she kept."

"Oh, Marc." On the verge of panic, Alani covered her mouth. "My employees, my office —"

"They'll be fine," Jackson assured her. "Already took care of it."

Without questioning that, proving her trust, Alani wilted. "Thank God."

"I'm so fucking sorry." Tobin swallowed and turned his face away. "They wanted to know where Jackson took you, but I had no idea. I tried telling them anything I could think of, but it wasn't enough."

"And so they continued to coerce you." Alani drew a slow breath and put back her shoulders. "You're not accustomed to those types of people. I understand. Few would hold up in the face of deliberate pain." Blindly she reached for Jackson's hand.

Surprised, he went one better, tugging her into his body, wrapping his arms around her from behind.

Surrounding her as much as he could.

He needed her to know that he would never, not under any circumstances, betray her. He'd happily die first.

As if she understood, she leaned back against him and folded her hands over his. "If you want to make some amends, Marc, you can answer Jackson's questions now."

"Of course." His one eye grew watery. "I'm grateful that you were with Jackson, and that you weren't hurt by what I did."

"Be grateful that Jackson wasn't hurt, either, or my attitude would be entirely different."

Huh. Nice sentiment. After Jackson gave her a small squeeze of appreciation, he reclaimed control of the topic. "The other night, who was the second shooter?"

Tobin looked at him in confusion.

Disgusted, Jackson shook his head. "Don't get cagey now. In for a penny and all that shit. You might as well tell me."

He stared at Jackson. "I don't understand."

"One person shot at us," Alani explained. "But someone else was there, too. A second shooter."

"I only know about one shooter. The same one who grabbed me when I ran off. The same one who had told me you were out to hurt Alani."

Deadpan, Jackson said, "Seems you're not much more help to us than you were to them."

"But . . . I swear. I don't know —"

The shrill ringing of the hospital phone made Alani jump and wrought a short screech from Tobin.

They all looked at the phone, there on the bedside table.

Horror filled Tobin's gaze as he said, "You told someone I was here? Who did you tell?" Voice higher, panicked, "What the hell have you done?"

"Not a damn thing." Jackson strode to the phone and picked it up. He put it to his ear and, not saying a thing, waited.

A digitally enhanced voice greeted him. "You son of a bitch, you took out two of my best men."

Tuning out Alani and Tobin, Jackson concentrated on the caller. "Three actually."

Surprised silence greeted him. “Guess you just can’t get good help these days, huh? But then, you should already know that crime doesn’t pay.”

“And you’re a smartass, too.” A demonic laugh came over the line. “I should have realized.”

Jackson lifted out his cell and thumbed in a code. There wasn’t much Trace could do about a caller on the line, but he needed to know everything, every step of the way.

“Nothing to say to that, I take it?”

“You were waiting for confirmation?” Jackson faked a yawn. “I didn’t realize.”

“Well, realize this, you smug bastard — I’m coming for you.”

“Yeah?” He got the code back from Trace. No one suspicious or obvious in the area, inside or out. But the caller knew of the men he’d disabled and left in a closet. Did that mean they had someone undercover in the hospital? “When should I expect you?”

“Soon enough.”

He cut to the chase. “How’d you know to call here?”

Another evil laugh. “I’d lie and say I found the dupe, but truth is, I had a lackey call every area hospital until he was finally connected to a room with Marc Tobin.”

Believable, but he wouldn’t swallow that

just yet. "And the goons I massacred?"

"I dispatched a few to each area hospital — just in case."

"No shit? You're that thorough?" And obviously part of a large operation.

"Always. Very. You might want to remember that."

Like he would forget? "So how did you know I walked through them?" Fishing for answers, Jackson asked, "One of them get loose?"

Another beat of silence. "You mean . . . you didn't kill them?"

It struck Jackson then: "Wait, I get it. You know they're done for, because I answered the phone, right? If they'd been successful —"

"You'd be on your way to me right now instead of hanging out in that fool's room."

Not dead himself? Interesting. "You know, since we're having this nice little chat, why don't you tell me what it is you want?"

"Initially . . . just you."

Relief coursed through his blood. So Alani was only a bystander to it all? Preferable.

But before he could relax, the caller said, "Now, since you've put me to so much trouble, I figure I'll take the girl, as well."

Jackson tamped down the gut-wrenching rage to keep his tone indifferent. "Yeah?"

Refusing to look at Alani, he asked, "What girl is that?"

A rusty laugh. Another and another, building in pleasure and anticipation. "Maybe," the voice whispered with abrupt malice, "I'll just take them both."

The call disconnected.

Jackson wanted to be calm. He wanted to be precise and methodical. In the past, no problem. His cold detachment from a fight was one of the first things to earn praise from Dare and Trace.

But that was before Alani.

Now, it seemed he shared a live connection with her that impacted every nuance of his being. Sometimes even his heartbeat fell into sync with hers, making him aware of every change in her demeanor, her excitement, her worry.

And right now, her distress.

She moved so close to him that he could feel her warmth and breathe in the sweet scent of her. Her presence made his life better — and more difficult.

He took a second to compose himself, to clear his head and open his mind to possibilities other than her being grabbed by a trafficker capable of beating a putz like Marc Tobin to the brink of death.

He'd get her out of here, he'd keep her safe.

No one would take her from him.

First things first.

Shooting for nonchalance, he turned back to the room. "Where were we?"

"Well," Alani said patiently, her gaze watchful, "I'm close to hyperventilating, and Marc passed out."

Bemused, Jackson scowled down at the other man — and saw it was true. "Oh, for the love of . . ." He stalked over to Tobin and clapped his hands over his head.

Loudly.

Tobin came to with a lurching cry.

"We'll move you today."

Gaze darting everywhere in unrelenting fear, Tobin asked, "To where?"

"Better if you don't know that yet." He went to the window to look out, then to the door to check out the hallway. He came back to the bedside to hit the nurse's buzzer. "Stay awake, and keep a nurse in here with you if you can. Tell her something is hurting. Shouldn't be a stretch, right?"

"For how long?"

"An hour or less. It's being arranged." Jackson pointed a finger at him. "In the meantime, don't talk to anyone. Don't contact anyone. Don't get a wild hair and check in with your office or notify family that you're fine. None of it. You got me?"

"Yes." He tried to shift up in the bed and grimaced.

"Stay put. People are on it. You won't see me again for a while, but you'll be fine."

Drawing a slow, deep, careful breath, Tobin asked desperately, "You're sure of that?"

"Positive."

As if given a vast reprieve, he closed his unbandaged eye and sank into the bedding. "Thank you."

"I'm not doing it for you."

"Jackson." Reproachful, Alani shook her head at him before addressing Tobin. "He's surly, but he wouldn't lie. If he says you'll be okay, then you will be."

Tobin gave one nod. "I know."

It was bad enough that Tobin had been a party to the bullshit, and still Jackson had to ensure his safety. He'd keep him alive. He didn't need Alani bolstering the guy, too.

Jackson took her hand. "Come on. You and I need to have a little talk, sooner rather than later."

Alani held his one hand with both of hers. "About what?"

As he exited the room, they passed the nurse. She did a double-take, smiled and watched as he kept walking.

Alani scowled back at her, but he reclaimed her attention by saying, "I've been putting it off, but it's past time now, so I have to tell you about Arizona."

"Arizona?"

The hall was clear except for the bustle of rubber-shoed nurses and doctors reading charts. He had a lot to do to wrap up the day, and he wanted to get to it. "The girl I told you I saved on that bridge?"

"Oh." Full of understanding and sympathy, she trotted beside him.

How long would that last? he wondered.

"You think that has something to do with Marc and the people who had him?"

"Probably." At the elevator, he held the door for an elderly couple. The woman, in her eighties, pushed a wheelchair with an equally aged gentleman seated inside. She struggled with the chair, so Jackson said, "Let me."

Aware of Alani smiling at him, he helped them inside the elevator, and then, because it was necessary, he also rearranged the older man's load of flowers, an overnight bag and paperwork.

"Thank you," the woman said. "Milton has picked up weight and that's the truth. It makes pushing his chair a little more difficult."

Jackson doubted old Milt could go over one-twenty, but he just nodded at the woman.

Looking at them with faded blue eyes, Milton grunted. "I told her it was too much for her." He patted his pointy knee and said to his wife, "You should come on up and we'll both ride along."

"Milton." She swatted his shoulder to hush him. "He's always outrageous when he has to visit the hospital."

"Uh-huh," Jackson said. "I'm betting he's outrageous all the time — and that you love it."

Milton grinned. "You got that right."

"Oh, you." The old woman swatted at Milton once more. "Behave."

When Milton reached up and covered her hand with his own, Jackson had the oddest feeling, almost like . . . melancholy. He looked from those aged clasped hands to Alani, but she was watching the couple, her expression ripe with tenderness.

"If you don't mind me asking," Alani said, "how long have you been married?"

"Fifty-seven years," the man told her. "Every day has been better than the day before."

The woman sighed her agreement. “We’re blessed.”

Jackson couldn’t stand it; he had to reach over and take Alani’s hand. She squeezed his fingers in understanding.

In the lobby area, he told her, “Stay right next to me,” and he assisted the man and woman to the front doors where a valet took over.

They each thanked him. Jackson waved them off, saying, “Have a good day.” He was still smiling as he turned away.

“What an amazing couple,” Alani whispered.

That particular tone from her had his heart skipping a beat. She was such a gentle person, and despite being impressed with how well she’d held up while facing Tobin, he never wanted her to lose her softness.

That someone had just threatened her suffused him with determination and protectiveness.

He put a hand to the small of her back, but rather than head for the doors where they’d entered, he detoured into the lounge. After digging change from his pocket, he loaded it into a vending machine.

“What are you doing?” Alani asked. And with disbelief: “You’re . . . *hungry?*”

Jackson shook his head. “You wanted me

to catch that cat, right? If I get him something to eat, it'll be easier."

"The cat!" She half laughed, half moaned, and her golden eyes went all misty. "I can't believe I forgot all about that poor little thing."

"You're allowed, honey." A few others in the lounge gave her glances of sympathy. They likely assumed a sick relative brought about her dismay. She'd gone from smiling at the seniors to near tearful over a stray cat.

Jackson pulled her around so others couldn't see her. His arms around her, he spoke close to her ear. "You okay?"

"Yes, of course I am. I just . . ." She leaned into him with a long sigh. "Seeing Marc like that was awful, especially knowing that the same people who did that to him are actually after us. And then you were so kind to that couple, and they were so adorable."

Did she expect him to be unkind? "Is this one of those confusing womanly reactions to stress?"

She laughed but continued to lean into him. "It has been like a roller-coaster ride."

For him, too. Now that he knew Alani was also a target, renewed determination cut through his veins. "I would never let anyone hurt you."

She turned her face up to his. "Please don't say that." Her small, cool hand touched his jaw. "I don't want to be hurt, you know that. But regardless of your machismo and orders to the contrary, it would devastate me if you got hurt because of me."

Flattened, Jackson frowned at her. He started to speak, couldn't quite manage it and finally hooked her arm to escort her back into the hall.

What would it take to make her understand his ability? As to that, what did her damned statement even mean? She didn't want him hurt? Hell, she hadn't wanted Tobin hurt, either.

But, he told himself, she hadn't looked at Tobin with her beautiful eyes all liquid and filled with . . . who knew?

Fear? Lust?

Love?

He growled out his frustration. "Swear to God, woman . . ."

Bustling beside him, she gave him a quick double-take that almost made her trip. "You're upset?"

"I don't get *upset,* damn it." No, what Alani did to him was too volatile for that namby-pamby word. Too red-hot and deep and disturbing.

He pulled her around the corner away from prying eyes, ready to give her a piece of his mind. But then she frowned up at him, and just that quickly, he lost it.

Chapter Sixteen

Putting his mouth over hers, Jackson prodded Alani's closed lips with his tongue until she opened, and then he sank in, tasting her, exploring the textures of her mouth and teeth, kissing her breathless.

There in the hallway, danger around them, her brother and Dare on lookout duty, a scraggly cat waiting to be rescued, he flattened a hand on the wall behind her and kissed her like a starving man.

Like a man who had already lost the fight but didn't want to admit it.

He groaned.

Alani didn't fight him. In fact, she kissed him back with wholehearted enthusiasm.

When he regained his wits and eased away, he realized her hand was knotted in the front of his shirt.

He kept his face close, her mesmerizing eyes gazing into his at close range. "Swear to God, Jackson."

Even knowing she mimicked him, that she poked fun, he had to fight off a grin. "What now?"

Using the fist in his shirt to thump his chest once, she said, "You confound me." Then she licked her lips. "But that well-timed kiss was just what I needed to get my mind off other things."

God, she was precious to him. He cupped her face and ran his thumb over her bottom lip. "Glad I could help."

She tilted her head to study him. "Want to tell me what that was about?"

"The kiss?" He shrugged. How could he explain all the ways she stirred him, his body, his mind, even his damn soul? Over and over, he felt obsessed with proving something to her, or maybe to himself. At the moment, they didn't have time to waste, so he settled for saying, "You're hot."

She rolled her eyes. "Jackson Savor, that is not an answer."

The stern, warning tone amused him. Giving in to the grin, he disengaged her fingers from his shirt and took her hand in his. Time to get them on their way once more. "You care about me." If she dared to deny it, he'd kiss her again.

"That's news to you?"

He missed a beat before saying, as offhand

as he could, "It shouldn't be?"

He got another eye roll. "Would I sleep with you if I didn't care?"

"I dunno." He'd slept only with women he liked, but he couldn't say he cared about them beyond the moment. They didn't plague his dreams or keep him in a fever of lust. He didn't think about them after they'd gone — and they all left, because he didn't allow them to stay. He didn't want them around just to be with them, the way he did with Alani. "Would you?"

"No."

The telling smile broke over his face, but he didn't give a damn. It was a start and better than thinking she only wanted him for sex. Though being wanted for that was pretty damned sweet, too. "Good to know."

In blatant exasperation, she threw up her hands. He heard her mutter, *"Good to know,"* in insulting mockery.

Ready to get off that particular uncomfortable topic, Jackson paused by a closet, looked around to ensure no one watched them, and opened it.

Arms folded, expression aggrieved, Alani asked, "Now what are we doing?"

Little by little, her nervousness had faded as she adjusted to the circumstances. "I need a box."

"For the cat?"

"That's right." He shoved a few things out of his way. "Keep watch for me."

"Oh." Startled, she forgot her grievances and snapped to attention. "Okay, sure." Taking the task far too seriously, she scanned the hallway several times.

Shaking his head and grinning again, Jackson found a box that was just about the right size but still filled with paper towels. "This'll work." A punch to the top of the box split the tape and he opened it to dump the contents on a shelf.

"Good. Let's go." Alani took his hand and tugged. "I'm not cut out for surveillance. It makes me too jumpy."

"You don't look jumpy. You look bossy." Toting the box, he let her lead him along until she slowed by the closet where he'd stowed the goons.

A little sick, she tightened her hand in his. "You think they're still in there?"

"If they weren't, we'd know it." He kept her close, and his voice low. "Either they'd have gone out back, where Dare would have seen them, or back the way we just came, and Trace would have seen them. It's under control, babe, so just keep walking."

"Believe me, I wasn't going to peek." Shuddering at the thought, she charged forward again.

When they reached the exit doors, Jackson pulled her up short. "Hold up a sec." He surveyed the yard while putting in a call to Dare. "All clear?"

Dare said, "I'd have let you know if it wasn't."

Right. Alani had *him* second-guessing things now. "We're on our way out. Just so you know, I'm going to nab a cat."

"That stray you noticed when going in?"

"If it's still hanging in the bushes, yeah."

"It is. I swear, I think it was watching for you."

"Smart."

"Most cats are. Be careful with him, though. He doesn't seem feral, but he's still skittish."

"Will do. Later."

Alani raised a brow. "What was that all about?"

"Dare says the cat is still there."

"That's it?" She dropped back against the wall. "He didn't question why you'd be catching a stray?"

By way of explanation, Jackson said, "He's an animal lover, too." As he pushed open the doors, he scanned the area. "Dare said we're good to go."

"But still you're on guard."

"Pure habit." Two sets of eyes were always better than one. Once outside, he paused to look for the cat. He didn't have a lot of time, not with the threat to *two* women, but if he could grab the cat quickly, then he would. As if it had indeed been waiting for him, it stepped out of the bushes, turned a high-stepping circle in pleasure, then sat down to stare at him in expectation.

"You're a pretty boy, aren't you?"

Alani agreed. "He really is. And once he's cleaned up and brushed, he'll be even prettier."

This time when Jackson crouched down with some lunch meat off the vending-machine sandwich, the cat edged closer. It had already started a throaty purr that sounded like a broken engine trying to start.

Voice soft, her mood more so, Alani said, "Poor thing is hungry." She knelt down next to Jackson.

"Yeah." He was just able to touch the cat's head with the tip of one finger. He stroked gently. "We'll let him eat a bit before grabbing him."

After a minute or so, the cat let Alani pet its head, too, and rubbed up against her. "Maybe we don't need to trap him. Try setting the box out with more of the food inside."

Jackson considered that and decided she might be right. "He'll need a bed, too, for the long ride back." Standing, Jackson stripped off his shirt and layered it in the bottom of the box, then set the food inside next to it.

Staring up at him, her lips parted in surprise, Alani swallowed. "Do you plan to drive home like that?"

"Why not?" He crouched next to the box and encouraged the cat. "We just want to help, Buddy. Come on. You'll be all cozy, I promise."

The cat investigated, sniffed the shirt, gave a deep crackling meow and sat down inside to eat the rest of the food.

"Huh." Amazed that it could be that easy, Jackson slowly closed the box flaps. For a second or two, the cat panicked, snarling and trying to get free. Jackson held the box closed and murmured to the animal while Alani looked upset.

"He's scared."

"He'll settle down." Jackson took half a minute more to talk to the cat, shushing, soothing. Finally it became still. "That's it. Easy now." He lifted the box carefully.

Alani whispered, "You know, Jackson, there are facets to your personality that I never noticed before today."

"Like?" He kept the box tight over the cat and tried not to jostle it too much.

"It's incredible how you take everything in stride. Disabling two men, talking to venal fiends, assisting the elderly and rescuing a stray. You act as if it means little to nothing, as if it slows you down no more than picking up a penny."

"We're not on a timetable, so how could any of it slow us down?" The cat started to fuss again, but he just murmured to it while heading to the car.

Alani rushed around to open the back door. "What will we do with him?"

He'd already thought about it, so he hoped Alani approved. "We need to head to Dare's anyway. He has a vet he trusts, so that's first on the list."

Her chin tucked in. "We're going to Dare's next?"

"Making a stop there, yeah." He didn't yet tell her that he planned to leave her there while he took care of other business. She'd be safe with Dare, and that's what mattered most to him.

Using a seat belt to ensure the box wouldn't open, he stowed the cat in the backseat. "Plans change. This one just did in a big way. All you can do is go with it."

"I'm going," she muttered, seeming confused by him, and then the rest of what he'd said sank in. "But wait! If you want Dare's vet to look at the cat . . . does that mean you're going to keep him?"

"Sure, why not? It needs a good home. I have a home." He opened her door. "And maybe you can help me out with him when I have to be away?"

Surprise stole her voice.

"You don't like that idea?"

"Actually . . . I'd love to." But she sounded subdued about it.

What was she thinking? Deciphering Alani's moods could keep him busy for a lifetime. That idea appealed to him in a big way, but would he get the chance? Knowing his time was up, Jackson walked around, folded himself behind the wheel and started the car.

Left mired in his own deceptions, he squeezed the steering wheel. "And now we talk."

Proving she hadn't forgotten, Alani said, "About the girl on the bridge?"

"Yeah." Cold dread raced through his veins every time he thought of her being hurt again. She hadn't called, so he had to trust that she was okay. Still, he wanted to check on her and soon.

But he also needed to know that Alani was

away from harm.

Whenever Alani thought he needed comfort, she touched him, his arm, his shoulder.

She did so again, reaching over and curling her fingers around his biceps. "You said this all happened in Arizona?"

"No." With his thoughts jumping ahead to what had to be done, how Alani might react when she heard the whole truth, Jackson drove out of the lot. "Arizona is her name. And she could be in more trouble than we are."

Lounged back in her seat, her legs out in front of her, she halfheartedly watched the fight unfolding in the middle of the barroom floor between two barmaids. The scrap amused her, mostly because the women didn't have a clue how to actually brawl. They just screeched and pulled hair.

Absurd.

In the casual sprawl, she could study each patron in the sleazy establishment without anyone noticing. So far, she hadn't found the one she wanted — but she would. Sooner or later, she would.

Attuned to everyone and everything around her, she felt it the second a man approached.

She pretended she didn't.

She pretended not to care. About anything.

If only that were true.

He sat down at the table beside her. "So what's happening here?"

Without looking at him, keeping her attention on the catfight, Arizona leaned to the side and said, "Blondie started pissing on Red's good mood. Red didn't like it and shoved her onto her ass. Blondie didn't like that, so she slapped her and called her a bitch." Arizona shrugged. "Now they're girl fighting — which somehow equates with losing clothes, boobs showing and lots of hair pulling."

The guy was quiet a second. "You've got a mouth on you, little girl."

"Yeah." She'd been told that before, many times, by many men. "Brain, too. Basically all the same shit you have — without the gonads or pipe."

He snorted. "Nasty, too."

Slowly she turned to face him — and got flattened by incredible good looks. He was big. Really big. Like six feet, five inches big. Broad shoulders, bulging biceps, no fat and a to-die-for face.

His silky brown hair was almost as dark as his heavily lashed bedroom eyes. Without thought, she breathed, “Yeah, when I need to be.”

Doing his own fair share of staring, the guy said, “What’s that?”

“Nasty.”

“Oh, right.” The intensity of his sinner’s eyes scrutinized her. “So you can be, huh?”

Arizona shrugged. Her definition of nasty probably differed from his.

She’d never seen a guy so gorgeous, which only meant he’d gotten used to getting his way with women. When he didn’t, what would he do? Resort to force? To brutality?

Would he, like so many, try to use his size and strength against her?

She sorta hoped so. Then she’d annihilate him.

And then she’d forget about him.

But for now, she continued to stare, going over his high cheekbones and once-broken nose, down to solid shoulders shown off by the dark fitted T-shirt, flat abs and longer-than-long jeans-covered legs.

He wore the T-shirt outside his jeans. To cover a weapon?

His right eyebrow lifted high. “Like what you see?”

Conceited dick. She curled her lip. “You don’t look like you belong here.”

“No? What look would that be?”

"Dirty. Poor." She leaned out of the way of an elbow when a drunk staggered by. "Coarse."

"Then you wouldn't fit here, either, right?"

A squeal sounded, and they both looked back to the brawling women. Arizona leaned back in the seat and crossed her arms. "My money's on Blondie."

"An actual bet or a figure of speech?"

She considered it, then thought, *what the hell.* "Fifty bucks?"

Slowly, he shook his head. "I don't think so." His gaze went to her mouth. "How about a drink instead?"

"I don't drink."

He eyed her near-empty glass of cola. "I'll replace that. But what I meant was company with the drink anyway."

"Forget it. Not interested."

"Liar."

Never did she let anyone goad her, but damn it, she swiveled to face him. Annoyance didn't lessen his impact on her senses.

And he didn't shy away from her direct stare.

"So." Propping her elbows on the table, Arizona studied him. "What are you really doing here?"

Lifting one of those impressive shoulders,

he smiled, making no pretense of the lie. "Looking for companionship."

"Bullshit. What are you hiding?"

Bold as you pleased, he reached out to finger a long lock of her hair. "You use that language as a front? Tell me, little girl, what are *you* hiding?"

Alarm slammed into Arizona. She slapped his hand away and lurched to her feet. Not being a dummy, she decided to put a whole lot of gone between her and a guy like him.

She was halfway across the crowded bar before she realized that he'd followed, that he was, in fact, right on her heels. She glanced back — and found him watching her ass.

Great. Just freaking great.

Instead of heading out as she'd intended, she detoured to the bouncer. He lounged at the end of the bar, massive tattooed arms crossed, bald head shiny with sweat, enormous feet planted apart. He had the air of a dunce just itching for a little violence.

She knew his type. Most seedy little bars had a bully just like him. Foul-tempered, a few screws short. Dirty fighters who liked to think their badass attitudes impressed others.

Morons.

The guy behind her said something, but

she didn't slow down to find out what. She marched right up to the bouncer. He noticed her coming and straightened in interest.

Nothing new to Arizona. Most guys eyed her with lust. She'd learned to live with it.

Only one man had treated her differently, but he wasn't here right now. God willing, he'd never again have to put himself out for her.

The bouncer started to speak. Arizona cut him off as she turned to point at the man following her. "He's bugging me."

Tall and Good-Looking let out a sigh.

Squat and Muscle-Bound cracked his knuckles.

The plan was to engage them in a real brawl, then she'd make her escape.

Unfortunately, it didn't quite go that way.

The bouncer swung one meaty fist, missed, and Tall and Good-Looking knocked him clean out with a straight jab right to the chin.

Arizona watched the bouncer go down, his fists still raised, his eyes crossing, his back stiff. His substantial weight jarred the floor beneath her feet. Someone jumped out of the way, and in the process a table overturned. Drinks spilled. Men cursed. Chairs shoved back.

Chaos exploded.

Shaking her head, she slowly looked back up at her pursuer and got caught in those dark bedroom eyes.

Without looking particularly pissed or even annoyed, he held out a hand to her.

Well, shit. So she'd have to do this herself. Wouldn't be the first time, probably not the last.

Faking a sweet smile, she took his hand, and she took the lead. Dragging him out the front door, only stomping a little, she resolved to settle things quickly.

Down the front steps she marched, across the gravel lot, moving toward the empty section where security lights didn't quite reach.

Timing herself and him, Arizona waited for exactly the right opportunity, then she jerked around, her knee aiming for his crotch.

Spencer followed along behind the girl. She was tall and slender, with ebony hair, honey-colored skin and the palest blue eyes he'd ever seen. Exotic. Sexy. Restless.

Up to something.

Equal parts concern, curiosity and interest sparked inside him. First time in a long time.

Wrong time.

Really bad timing, actually.

The humid night air carried back her scent to him, cleansing away the rank smells of alcohol, old sweat and desperation. He detested bars.

But he relished the info he got from them.

She didn't carry a purse, but in her back pocket he saw the outline of a slim wallet, and in the other pocket, maybe a cell phone.

If she thought he'd speak first, she'd be surprised. He'd found he got more from people with silence than through questioning. His fingers swallowed up her smaller, slender hand. Fine-boned, she looked delicate but spoke like a seasoned hooker with a raspy, deep voice that mesmerized almost as fast as her eyes.

It didn't hurt that she had an impressive rack, too.

It did hurt that she looked incredibly young, too young to be in the dive they'd just exited.

Even as her bold stare screamed experience, an aura of vulnerability surrounded her.

Once they walked into the shadows, he felt the difference in her intent. Anticipation ran up his spine, prepped his muscles and sharpened his wits.

What would she do? He could barely wait

to find out.

When she twisted around, he was ready for her, and instead of her knee crushing his balls, it landed on his thigh — and she landed in his arms.

Careful not to hurt her, he wrapped her up tight.

Shock rendered her mute and stiff, utterly still. He could almost feel her thinking, weighing her options — not that she had any.

Why had she attacked him anyway?

Keeping her on her tiptoes to maintain the advantage, he pinned her arms to her sides. Her hips smashed up against his thighs, and her head only reached his chest, so she couldn't head butt him.

But she could still bite, so he said softly, very matter-of-factly, "Put those teeth to me and I will turn you over my knee."

Defiant, she tipped her head back and stared up at him. "Now what?"

Not for a very long time had he been so aware of a woman in his arms, the softness of her skin and hair, her curving shape, the aroma and warmth of her body. The need to end his long stretch of celibacy knotted his guts, but he wasn't here for that, and she didn't look real receptive anyway. "Let's start with your name."

Her incredible mouth formed a smile. "Arizona. Yours?"

Now she wanted to be cordial? No reason not to play along, especially if it meant he'd get to hold her longer. "Spencer."

"Nice to meet you, Spence."

"Spencer," he corrected. But the grin tugged at his mouth. He had to ask. "How old are you?"

"Old enough." She relaxed in his arms, unconcerned, arrogant. "You?"

"Too old." At least for her. At least . . . he thought so. He did not relax his hold to match her more casual pose; that was one of the oldest tricks in the book. "Define old enough."

"Twenty, actually." She let one beat pass, and then, "Define too old."

Not even legal yet, so what was she doing in the bar? "Thirty-two."

"Oh yeah, that's ancient." She shifted, tipping her head to the side. "So Spence —"

"Spencer."

"Anything else you want to know about me?"

He wanted to know all kinds of things. "Is Arizona your real name? It's unusual."

"Yeah, I know. Jackson gave it to me."

"Jackson?" A husband? A cohort? A pimp? He didn't like any of those possibilities.

"This white-knight dude I know. My own name was used up, so . . . he came up with Arizona."

"Used up?" At only twenty, how could that be? But he knew, and it both sickened and saddened him.

She wrinkled her nose, looked down at his chest. "Forget that."

He shook his head. "I know what it means, Arizona." The urge to open his hands over her back, to stroke her, comfort her, made him twitchy. "So you're in hiding?" He put his nose closer to her temple and breathed in the scent of her. "From what?"

She clammed up tight.

Spencer sorted through all she'd said — and damn it, he believed her, even though most of it didn't make any sense. There was something about her, some sense of defiance that bespoke great hardship. "Okay, forget the name thing." He'd work that one out later, when she didn't fill his arms. "Define white knight for me."

"You know, a do-gooder. Out to save a world that can't be saved."

"It can't?" He often felt the same, but hearing that bleak acceptance in her voice cut into his soul. No one so young should be so cynical.

"The best you can hope for is to chip away

at the . . ." She stopped, drew a deep breath. "Look, Spence, I'm kind of tired of hanging here in your grasp. Now that I answered your questions, you wanna loosen it up a little?"

"Not really, no." But he knew he had to, or he'd be crossing the line . . . more than he'd already crossed it. He spun her around so her back was to his chest. She had a great ass to go with the great rack, perky and firm and rounded just right. It stirred long dormant carnality, prompting him to his senses. "But I will."

He released her so fast, she stumbled. When she turned, he was already out of her reach.

"Afraid of me?" she taunted.

"I like the family jewels just as they are, without them being rearranged by your knee."

Disgust had her looking away from him. "I missed anyway."

"Doesn't mean you'd miss a second time." It wouldn't hurt to throw her a bone. "You almost got me. It's just that I'm —" he shrugged "— fast."

"And strong," she agreed. "You know, I expected you and the bouncer brute to do some battle."

Gently, he told her, "No."

"Yeah, I realize that now." She moved over to lean against a fence post. "So, what are you doing here?"

Why not tell her? She seemed as curious about him as he was about her. "Ferreting out info, actually." He took a step closer, not relaxing his guard but hoping she might. "You?"

"Until you interfered, I was doing the same."

His blood ran cold. The indifferent way she said that, as if it were the norm for a breathtakingly gorgeous twenty-year-old girl to snoop around in a lowlife bar that catered to the criminal element left him scared for her. "No."

"Why not?" Disdain dripped from her words. "You think you're more capable than me?"

"Yes." Breathing faster, he edged toward her. "I know I am."

In a whisper, she said, "Sorry, Spence, but you are oh so wrong."

With no other warning, she lunged forward, locking her hands together and swinging her doubled fists up and around to pop him in the chin.

For such a dainty girl, she knew how to pack a wallop.

Since he hadn't seen it coming, he didn't

brace for it. His head snapped back, throwing him off balance. His feet slid on the gravel before he found purchase again and righted himself.

Blindly he reached out; his fingertips brushed the ends of her long hair as she sprinted away.

Damn it. He tried to give chase — why, he didn't know — but the darkness swallowed her.

He stopped to listen and wasn't surprised that she made very little noise.

She had skills, and that, as much as anything, left him throbbing with curiosity.

He turned at the sound of a car door opening and closing again. Headlights came on, lighting the distant reaches well beyond the parking lot. A car engine started. Gravel spit as she revved the engine, and then she sped away.

Breathing hard, infuriated at himself, Spencer watched her taillights fade away. He was considering chasing after her when he got diverted by the familiar voice of a man exiting from the bar.

The man spoke hurriedly into a cell phone; a cohort kept pace with him.

Thankful that Arizona had left him in the concealing shadows, Spencer watched the men with burning hatred. He felt the weight of the gun at the small of his back, the press of a switchblade in his boot. His muscles knotted, and his hands flexed.

Doors opened, highlighting hated features for an instant as the men got into a silver BMW.

Already on his way to his truck, Spencer kept track of the BMW as it skidded over the gravel lot in a hasty exit.

Was it coincidence that they rushed out directly after Arizona? Had someone notified them of her departure?

If so, then that would have to mean that someone had been watching them —

The thought barely formed before he was attacked. Reacting by instinct alone, Spencer caught the momentum of the lunging body and fell to his back. Using his feet, he tossed the man over his head, then jumped onto him, gaining the upper hand. He landed two sharp blows before taking one on the jaw himself.

The meaty fist sported brass knuckles, and for an instant he saw stars.

Before the second punch could land, he rolled again and came to his feet — with his knife in his hand. He grinned at the other man, ready, anxious even. "Come on then. I don't have all night."

Then the real bloodshed began.

A minute later, with senses peeled and rage honed to a lethal edge, Spencer drove away with the intent of catching up to the BMW.

For a minute there he'd felt bad about how things had gone with Arizona. But the scuffle with her had given him the opportunity to lift her wallet. All he'd needed was a reason, any reason at all, to track her down.

It's what he did.

And he was better than good.

Thanks to the silver BMW, he had all the reason he needed. He'd be seeing her again. Odd as it seemed, and despite the personal pursuit of justice, he already looked forward to it.

Chapter Seventeen

Concerned, Alani waited as Jackson again made a call. He'd done that several times, without much success.

"Still no answer?"

He shook his head. "We'll be at Dare's in a few more minutes. I'll get you and the cat settled, and then figure out something."

With the reflective sunglasses shielding his eyes, she couldn't gauge his intent, but she didn't like the sound of that. Since telling her about Arizona, he'd been distant from her.

And it hurt. "What exactly do you mean, get us settled?"

Evasive, he tightened his mouth and glanced at his mirrors.

Even knowing that Dare and Trace trailed them, he'd been especially watchful. "Jackson?"

"You have to be getting hungry." He reached over and patted her thigh.

Trying to pacify her? She studied his handsome profile, saw the strain in his shoulders and opted not to press him. "I could eat."

"And the cat needs out of that box."

Alani looked over the seat. The cat had settled down and currently seemed okay with the ride. He'd worked around until he got his head poked out of the box, and now, except for the occasional raspy meow, he stared out the window as if mesmerized. "He's doing okay." She reached back and scratched under his chin.

Jackson glanced at the clock. "Thanks to the traffic, this trip has taken longer than it should have."

"Only by a little." His concern for Arizona left him cold and distracted. Alani knew he had a plan, she just didn't think she'd like it. Now that the girl had a name, Alani wanted to know more about her.

But he'd become evasive, defensive and increasingly detached.

"You've got to be getting hungry, too."

"Maybe." He didn't look at her. "But I've got some other stuff to take care of first."

Meaning Arizona? Did he think she wouldn't understand? More than most, she knew how difficult it could be for a woman to overcome the trauma of such an experience. She wanted to talk to him about it, but doubted, in his current mood, that he'd be receptive. "Is there a work number where you can call her?"

He hesitated, his frustration clear, then shook his head. "I tried the school already."

"The school?"

"Yeah, it's . . ." Furious with himself, he rubbed the back of his neck. "Forget that."

Not likely. As she continued to stare at him, he glanced at her and flattened his mouth as if she'd just coerced him into some great admission.

"I had her in school, all right? But swear to God, that girl runs off more than she stays put. Seems every couple of months, the school has to get in touch. I thought that was what had happened again, but now . . ."

Stymied, Alani asked, "How old is she?"

Again he glanced at her, then away. "She's only twenty."

Twenty was a woman, not a girl.

Grudgingly, he added, "She needed an education."

Hmm. Okay. Feeling her way, Alani asked, "College?"

"Yeaaaah." He dragged out the word. "Well, sort of like an all-girl school."

Alert to what he didn't say, Alani propped

herself into the corner of the seat. "An all-girl school, you say?"

"Yeah." He rubbed his neck again. "More like . . . a small women's college. You know, where you get an education and also learn all that crap about society functions and stuff."

Without realizing it, she sat forward again. Surely he didn't mean finishing school. "You're kidding, right?"

"She wanted to go!" Color climbed up his neck. "Or at least, I thought she did."

Fascinated, Alani took in the signs of his discomfort. Why would all of this bother him so much, and if it did bother him, then why had he done it? "Exclusive schools like that cost a fortune."

He snorted. "Don't I know it."

But then, if it was so expensive . . . It occurred to her that she really knew little about Jackson's finances. "You can afford it?"

"It's absurd what I make working with Dare and Trace. I thought I had a good job in construction, but this?" He shook his head. "I have a house, land, decent transportation. What else am I going to spend it on?"

Alani couldn't take it in. Absently, buying herself a little time to think, she reached back again to stroke the cat. "So, you rescued this young lady, and then . . . what? You felt obligated to help her get her life together? I can understand that." *Sort of.* But financing college stretched the definition of generous, especially a costly, exclusive college, no matter how lucrative his work with her brother.

But beyond the monetary consideration, such generosity suggested a more involved association with Arizona.

"She's a good kid," Jackson said, but he looked wary.

"Mmm-hmm." Something didn't add up. "So you're paying for her to have a specialized education, with the end goal being . . . ?"

"You don't have to make it sound so messed up."

"Did I?" Eyebrows lifting at his abrupt tone, she pondered his mood. Just how much did Arizona mean to him, and in what way? "Is she pretty?"

"Very." He paused, shook his head. "No, that doesn't cover it. Arizona is more than pretty. She's drop-dead gorgeous. An exotic bombshell. Beautiful face and built like a . . ." He shifted, took a breath and amended, "She's built nice."

Back stiffening, Alani stared at him. Even though she felt for Arizona, she couldn't help being peeved by his description. "Do tell."

"Now don't sound like that. She's a kid."

"You said she's twenty."

Cautious, he stole a quick look at her. "Right."

Her stare didn't change. "I'm twenty-four."

"I know how old you are, darlin'." He flexed his fingers as if trying to ease tension. "It might only be four years, but believe me, there's plenty of difference in Arizona at twenty, and you at twenty-four."

Something kept him on edge. "Really?"

"A *world* of difference."

If he wasn't concerned with discussing Arizona's physical appeal, then why did he still look so . . . suspicious? "What kind of differences?"

"You're sophisticated. And mature." Something dark, something wolfish, filled his gaze. "And you make me insane with lust."

And Arizona . . . didn't? Biting her lip, Alani thought about it, knew she shouldn't press, but she couldn't hold back. "So you and Arizona never . . . ?"

"No!" He steered down the long drive to Dare's property. "God, no. Nothing like that."

Did he have to make the idea sound so far-fetched? "If she's that attractive —"

"You have to understand, honey. When I first met Arizona, she was so injured, in so many ways, that no way in hell could I think things like that. She didn't want to trust me, but she didn't have — *doesn't* have — anyone else."

Hearing him say it broke Alani's heart. From what Jackson had told her, Arizona had been held captive a lot longer than she had. And after Dare rescued her, she'd been cocooned in love, surrounded by understanding. Dare and Trace had seen to that.

But Arizona had no one. "That's indescribably sad."

Jolted, he glanced at her and nodded. "Yeah."

Did he expect her to react badly? To make broad assumptions despite what he'd just told her?

Or was he just that uncertain about doing such a wonderful thing for someone in need?

At her continued contemplation, Jackson chewed the side of his mouth. "The same people who kidnapped Arizona also killed her folks. But even before that, she'd had a shit life."

Guilt had Alani sinking a little in her seat.

She'd spent very little time with traffickers, and still she had nightmares.

How must it be for Arizona? "I'm glad she has you then." And maybe, if things worked out, she'd get to meet Arizona, too. She would love the opportunity to talk with her.

Jackson didn't seem to hear her. "She was so damned terrified and aggressive and suspicious, even after I told her the bastards were gone. She didn't want to share her name, or any part of her past."

Leave it to Jackson to show so much patience, to win her over. "I'm glad you were able to talk her around."

He snorted. "Not likely. We decided she needed a new name anyway. You know, for a new life. And since I found her in Arizona . . ." He shrugged.

Dear God. Her thoughts swam. "You *named* her?"

"Got her false IDs, the whole shebang. To the world, she's officially Arizona Storm."

Because he'd found her in a storm? That would border on laughable if not for the tragic circumstances. "She lives by an alias?"

"Yeah. The school thought we were siblings." He smiled at some memory. "Not that anyone would ever think we're related."

"You gave them a different alias for yourself?"

"Course."

Curiosity gnawed on her. "Do you have a photo of Arizona?"

He shook his head. "Too dangerous. If anything ever happened to me, I didn't want anyone to be able to track her. She and I came up with a backup plan. If she's in trouble, then I hope like hell she remembers it."

Head reeling, Alani said, "Okay, let's go back a step. The women's college?"

"With just a little help, she got her GED. I knew she wanted to continue her education, but she didn't want me spending my own money, and she had none of her own. I insisted on her taking a car, and a gun —"

"Dear God."

"— but when it came to the school, she said she was so socially inept that she'd stand out like a turkey among hens, or something dumb like that. She's usually . . ." He glanced at her again, cleared his throat. "She's ballsy. But I know she's also insecure about some things. Stuff most would take for granted. Like eating in a restaurant, even one that's not fancy."

Alani tried to imagine a young girl so wounded, and how she might have felt in

Jackson's shadow. She'd been raised with Trace and had known Dare forever, and still their take-charge confidence could intimidate her.

"Thanks to working with your brother and Dare, more than one influential person owed me, so I pulled some strings and arranged for her to attend the exclusive school. It's this upscale little college on the East coast. For the right price, they go out of their way to make her feel like a queen. And being there kept her secure, occupied and, I thought, for a little while anyway, that she was finally happy."

No matter how well intentioned, that sort of atmosphere would be daunting to anyone. "I take it she wasn't?"

"I dunno." He pulled up to the security monitor at Dare's home. He sat there a moment. Finally he took off his sunglasses and looked at Alani. "Thing is, I didn't know what else to do with her. It wasn't safe for her to be on her own, but keeping her in the same house with me wasn't . . . right."

It hit her like a tsunami. "She wanted more with you, didn't she?"

As if expecting recriminations, he dropped his head back. "I've never talked with anyone about this."

Alani scooted closer. "Why not?"

"It's . . . personal. For her, I mean. Well, me, too." He eyed her. "Not many people would understand."

Oh, she understood all right. It was unfair that one man could be so incredibly gorgeous, so sexy and so bighearted, too. She sympathized with Arizona because, really, who could possibly resist him?

She couldn't.

"I'm glad that you're telling me." She wanted his trust as much as he demanded hers. "You know that I understand her feelings. You were more than kind, and you're not exactly an ogre." He'd stolen her heart so easily. "It's not your fault Arizona looked for more."

Pinching the bridge of his nose, Jackson said, "God, it was awkward." He swiveled his head to face her. "No one had ever really done anything for her, so she mistook my motives. Or maybe she wanted to do something to repay me." He scrubbed his hands over his face, and his voice dropped low. "Arizona's not always easy to understand."

He said that as if it were a great understatement, making her wonder.

"She broke my heart. I wanted to protect her and make her happy, you know? But that idea was so foreign to her that she couldn't accept it at face value."

Alani couldn't imagine a man more sexual than Jackson. And by his own admission, Arizona was a beauty. Yet he hadn't taken advantage of her. It sounded as if he hadn't even been tempted.

She realized something very important then: Jackson didn't pity her. He didn't see her strictly as a victim because if he had, he'd treat her the same way he treated Arizona.

But Jackson wanted her. Often. He was so open about his sexuality that she knew, while he empathized with what she'd gone through, he truly accepted that she'd survived intact.

He trusted in her strength, and that made him almost too irresistible for words.

Opening her seat belt, Alani crawled over the center console to him. His brows shot up, but he hurriedly opened his belt, too.

When she went to straddle his lap, he helped but asked, "What are we doing here, babe?"

"You're being wonderful, and I'm showing you how incredible you are."

"Incredible?" He didn't take the compliment well. "What the hell brought that on?"

Cupping his face, Alani smiled at him, then sighed. "You do so much."

"No." His brows scrunched down and his

mouth flattened. “Hell, no.” He tried to lever her away, but she held on, and with the steering wheel and console in his way, he couldn’t pry her loose. “Damn it, Alani, don’t make me into a saint, for Christ’s sake. It wasn’t like that.”

“It was exactly like that.” Despite the terrible upbringing he’d had, or maybe because of it, Jackson showed such empathy to others. He put himself out there to help everyone — from abused women to the elderly to stray cats. More than his sex appeal, more than his alluring charm, *that* stole her heart and sealed her fate. “It’s still like that.”

“No, I just —”

To shut him up, she kissed him. A deep, thorough kiss that, if only he realized it, showed the love she felt for him. It was the first time she’d initiated things, and it made her feel powerful. She’d been wanting that kiss ever since they captured the cat.

Right now, with her heart full and her eyes misty, seemed like as good a time as any. It fed her soul and hopefully would help to ease Jackson’s tension.

He continued to resist her, until she licked over his bottom lip.

On a hungry groan, he dragged her closer and turned her a little so he could take over the kiss. One big hand sank into her hair to hold her head still, and the other went down to her bottom so he could snug her up tight against his body.

He ate at her mouth, consuming her, bruising her lips and raising her temperature . . .

Until someone tapped on the window.

So fast that Alani didn't get a chance to protest, he had her in her seat and his gun drawn.

Outside the window, his arms in the air in comical surrender, Chris sneered at him. "If you shoot me, Dare won't like it."

Today Chris wore ragged khaki shorts with a faded T-shirt sporting a musical logo that looked as if they'd been worn swimming in the lake. And they probably had.

At six-two, lean and athletic, Chris was gorgeous in his own right. His feet were bare, his black hair disheveled by wind and water, his blue eyes as irreverent as always. Beside him, Dare's dogs — Sargie and Tai — wagged their tails in excitement over company.

Hand to her heart, Alani groaned, but the sound turned into an embarrassed giggle. Good grief, poor Chris. Not only had he found them making out at the gate, but Jackson *still* had the gun pointed at him.

Unlike Dare, Chris didn't cook, and he

had no fashion sense beyond comfortably sloppy, but as Dare's good friend, personal assistant, manager, computer whiz and housekeeper, Chris was used to guns and the edgy defense of Alpha men. In most cases, his sharp wit matched Dare's overwhelming protectiveness.

When Chris leaned down to see her better, Alani mouthed, "Sorry," to him and got a wink in return.

Ignoring the gun, he said, "There's an empty room inside if you two would like to move this little lovefest from the driveway to the house."

She waited for Jackson to give some retort, but he sat there, chagrined, bemused, comically hostile, as Chris moved away.

"I didn't even hear the gate open."

"It's kept well oiled." The priceless look that remained on his face had Alani choking back a laugh. "It's all right, Jackson. I'll tell Chris it was all my fault."

"The hell you will."

The cat came out of the box to stand with his front paws against Jackson's seat back. His emerald gaze went back and forth between them, and, after one deep gravelly meow, he leaped up and over into Jackson's lap.

A horn beeped, and Alani turned to see

that Dare had pulled in behind them. Trace wouldn't be far behind.

Still breathing hard, Jackson stowed the gun while giving her a glowering look that promised retribution. As if he handled a longtime favorite pet, he pulled the cat up to his chest and, ignoring Chris, drove through the gate.

The silence lasted for a few seconds more before he said, "I hope you plan to finish what you started."

"Absolutely." She could hardly wait. Now that she'd made up her mind on what she wanted, she intended to go after it full force.

"Sex," he stated. "Without all that mushy bullshit thrown in."

"Mushy bullshit?"

"Yeah." He scowled at her. "That nonsense about me being wonderful."

Their first night together, Jackson had claimed to love her. She knew now that it had likely been the drugs talking, the same drugs that muddled his senses so much he hadn't thought to use protection. The reality was that she could be pregnant. If that was the case, she wanted Jackson to return her love *before* she told him.

She wanted Jackson. Now, always. If he didn't feel the same, then pregnancy wouldn't change that. But he was honorable enough that he'd probably want to marry her.

She didn't want him trapped. She wanted him willing.

She wanted to hear him make another declaration of love but this time, without the influence of drugs.

Careful not to block the entrance Dare would use, he parked outside the garage. She knew he'd been stewing, waiting for her to argue with him, but she had no intention of doing so.

"It'll have to be a quickie."

"Okay." Alani smiled toward him.

He scowled some more. "Not that I don't want to make it last, but I'll be heading back out soon as possible."

He'd be leaving — but she wouldn't? "Heading back out where?"

"When I return," he told her, "I promise to be more thorough." He left the car without answering her question.

Not giving him a chance to open her door, Alani hurried to follow him. She wanted Jackson to know that she understood the work he did and was strong enough to deal with it.

She wouldn't get in his way, but she would share it with him.

If he didn't accept that, they couldn't

share a future together. What he did was too much a part of him for him to cut her out of it.

"You're going after Arizona, aren't you?"

He gave one abrupt nod while petting the cat on his way through the garage. "Too much has happened, and now she's not answering the phone. I have to know that she's okay."

"I understand." The others would join them soon, so she didn't waste time. "It'll be dangerous?"

"I don't think so. If she remembers the backup plan — and she's spontaneous but not dumb, so she should — then I could be back by tomorrow in time for dinner." He turned heated green eyes on her. "This is something I have to do."

To settle her suddenly fluttering stomach, Alani drew a deep breath. "Of course it is." And for the sake of their future, she'd do what she had to do, too.

An hour later, everyone had gathered at Dare's. Alani hadn't yet had a chance to "finish what she'd started" with Jackson because she'd barely seen him once they were all in the house.

She wondered at his lack of attention. With getting Marc settled elsewhere and being unable to reach Arizona, he had his hands full, she understood that.

But he *always* had his hands full, and still he'd chased her and been so amazingly attentive . . . that she felt spoiled.

The last thing Jackson needed right now was a clinging woman. She would be supportive of him, and when time permitted, they'd talk privately.

The men hung out for a long time in the kitchen. "Boy talk," Priss explained with an air of indulgence. She and Molly, kind as always, visited with Alani while she set up the guest room and got refreshed. They were very curious about her new relationship with Jackson.

As much as she could, without giving away her own insecurities, Alani shared what had transpired.

"If he's anything like your brother," Priss said, "I'm amazed he let you out of the bed."

That made her blush and Molly laugh.

"Sometimes," Molly confided, "Dare doesn't. Let me out of the bed, I mean. Luckily Chris makes himself scarce on those days, or I'd be forced to embarrassment."

They laughed.

The women were very different and loads of fun. Alani liked them a lot.

"Before Jackson," Alani admitted, "I

wasn't all that interested. Now . . . well, thanks to him, I have a hard time thinking of anything else."

Molly grinned at her. "Morning, noon and night, I know."

Priss agreed. "And the guys are so macho, they're sometimes up for three times a day."

"And occasionally four times," Alani said. She laughed — until she realized that both of the women were staring at her. "What?"

"That was a joke, right?" Priss lifted her brows. "Four times?"

"Uh . . . no." Was that so unusual? Alani felt her face getting hot. Jackson had claimed to be a sex machine. Had he been serious? "No joke."

"That's happened?" Molly gaped at her. "Seriously?"

"More than once or twice?" Priss clarified.

Since it had happened quite a bit with Jackson — and in fact, felt more like the norm when circumstances allowed — she cleared her throat. "Often."

Priss dropped back with widened eyes. "That stud."

"Wait." Molly cocked a brow with suspicion. "Is this when he was drugged?"

"The first time, yes." Seeing them as great confidantes, Alani shook off her shyness and leaned in. "But since then, too, he's been . . . insatiable."

Priss and Molly sat silent for a moment, then burst out laughing. "That dawg," one said, and "Such a hedonist," said the other.

Alani found herself grinning, too. "It's pretty wonderful, I have to say."

Molly hugged her. "Glad to hear it."

"All this sex talk has me wanting to see Trace." Priss stood. "Let's go find the guys."

"Yeah," Molly said. "I need to let Dare know he's been a slacker."

They fell into fits of laughter again. Alani shook her head at them, but she kept grinning, too.

Hopeful that she and Jackson could finish their conversation, she decided to wait behind. "You go on. I'll be there shortly."

Lingering in the bedroom, she waited for Jackson for what felt like forever. When he finally came to her, it was just to tell her that everyone had convened in the family room for casual conversation and food.

He carried the cat, giving it more attention than he did her.

Deflated, but not quite outspoken enough to keep him alone with her in the room when he showed no real interest and everyone else waited for them, Alani went along to join the others.

Dare sat in a big chair with Molly in his lap. He gave Alani a long look when she walked in, until Molly elbowed him.

Her brother and Priss stood by the fireplace. Priss cupped his face and whispered something in his ear. He drew back, shook his head.

She gave a slow smile and murmured something again.

He turned a dark glower on Jackson, but when Priss started snickering, he gave up and squeezed her.

While Alani fought a blush, Jackson looked at each varying expression. Finally he said, "What?"

"Show-off," Dare said. "But now I feel challenged."

Molly pretended to swoon, making Dare laugh again.

Still confused, Jackson looked at Trace, but he said, "Forget it. If you want to know, talk to my sister."

So he transferred his baffled gaze to Alani.

She cleared her throat and shrugged.

"We'll discuss this later," he told her in a stern tone.

And everyone cracked up again, even her brother.

Despite her embarrassment, a sense of contentment settled over Alani. Dare and

Trace had each found someone very special to them.

Jackson deserved someone special, too. She wanted to be that person.

If her brother and Dare could make it work despite the dangers of their jobs, then surely she could, too.

Chapter Eighteen

Very attuned to his present mood, Alani continued to watch Jackson. When his expression remained impassive and somehow distant, she gave up. As much as she loved him, she wouldn't chase after him. But at the first opportunity, she'd demand he explain his bad humor.

After she took a seat — alone — in the remaining chair, Jackson sat at one end of the couch.

If anyone noted the significance of that, they kept it to themselves.

With Molly curled against his chest, Dare said, "Chris can keep the stray with him until after the vet has given him a clean bill of health."

Both of Dare's dogs, Sargie and Tai, sat at attention near Jackson's feet, very alert to a new pet in the house. But Liger, Priss's enormous cat, who always came with her when she visited, made a beeline for Trace.

Though Liger weighed a hefty twenty-three pounds, he made an agile leap up into Trace's arms.

Trace held the cat on one side and Priss on the other. "Once the vet clears him, we'll introduce him to the other animals."

"I hate to leave him." Jackson scratched under the cat's chin. "He doesn't have his front claws, but if he did, they'd be in my hide right now."

He was so gentle with the cat that Alani wondered how he'd be with a baby. Her heart swelled. Jackson had shied away from talk of family or commitment, but if it turned out she was pregnant, what would he think? How would he feel?

"He'll adjust fine. My girls won't hurt him." As Dare spoke, he stroked his fingertips up and down Molly's bare arm. "They love everyone and everything."

"Do you know what you're going to name him?" Priss asked.

Jackson looked to Alani. "What do you think?"

That he'd include her in the decision while being so contrary only confused her more. "I don't know." She studied the cat. Thanks to the placement of fur on his wide face, he wore a perpetual frown. "He's awfully grim about everything."

A fleeting smile played over Jackson's mouth. "And he sort of looks like a gremlin, doesn't he?" He leaned around to see the cat's enormous eyes. "Grim for short. I like it. What do you think?"

Everyone admired the name.

While Jackson continued to talk to the cat, Chris carried in a tray of coffee, colas and sandwiches. He set it on the coffee table and dropped down next to Jackson. He scratched the cat's ear. "Want me to take him while you eat?"

Jackson hesitated — earning more points with Alani's heart. In such a short time he'd already bonded with the cat and, as appeared to be customary for him, he already felt protective.

More than a little famished, she stood up to get some food, hoping that would prompt Jackson to do the same. He'd been running all day without letting up. "You know Chris is good with animals."

Molly said, "Chris is good with *everything.*"

Dare snorted, but he didn't disagree. He and Chris had been the best of friends forever, and now Chris ran his house for him. He did everything from organizing the landscapers and repairmen, to the grocery shopping and laundry, to computer work and errands. Dare trusted him completely, and luckily, Chris and Molly got along great.

"I suppose." Reluctantly, Jackson transferred Grim into Chris's arms. Unconcerned with cat hairs or a possible scratch, Chris drew the cat in close and started stroking him.

Instead of eating, Jackson paced to the patio doors to look out at the lake.

Chris lounged back with Grim and within seconds had him purring loudly. "I already called the vet, by the way. She'll be here soon to look him over. After a checkup, she can recommend what shots he might need. For tonight, I made him up a bed and litter box in my laundry room. Tomorrow, after I make sure the animals all get along, I can run into town to get a collar and whatever else he needs."

"You see," Molly said. "Isn't he amazing?"

"Yeah." His back to the room, Jackson said, "I need a Chris."

Because Chris was gay, Dare choked and Trace laughed.

Chris, one dark brow lifted, said, "Yeah . . . not."

"I didn't mean for that." Secure in his masculinity, Jackson didn't take offense at the ribbing as he turned to survey the room. "I mean now that I have a house, I need someone I can trust to keep it together, too."

Alani made a point of not looking at him, but her heart thumped and her pulse raced. She tried to be blasé, but she felt Jackson's rapt attention on her.

"When I have to be away for a week or more, it'd be nice to know someone was looking after things."

Was that a hint? A suggestion? Or just an observation based on the way Dare and Trace ran their own households?

"Tough to have plants — or pets — without someone around on a daily basis," Molly agreed.

"I'm one of a kind," Chris told them. "They broke the mold after me."

Dare snorted. "Thank God."

Trace gave Jackson a telling look. "Priss keeps our place running smooth, and she keeps my life pretty damned organized, too."

"He agreed to my assistance under duress," Priss told them.

"Not really." Trace kissed her temple. "I don't want you involved in anything dangerous —"

"Hear, hear," Dare said, lifting his cola in a toast and earning a hug from Molly.

"— but you're great on the computer at tracking down records. And you've got a diabolical mind when it comes to deciphering the motives and probabilities of maniacs."

"Meaning I make a good sounding board." Priss grinned.

Shell-shocked over that disclosure, Jackson said, "You tell her things about . . ." He caught Priss's challenging stare and rethought his words. "You know, business?"

"Sometimes, sure." Trace shrugged. "I trust her, and she's good at helping me fit the puzzle pieces together."

"But you know there's still a lot you don't tell me."

"I'll take the fifth on that." Trace kissed her before she could protest.

"I have to be careful what I say," Dare mentioned.

Molly grinned. "He worries that I'll borrow trade secrets for one of my suspense books." She smacked his shoulder. "But of course I wouldn't."

They all laughed.

Growing antsy under Jackson's unrelenting stare, Alani looked up. She felt the touch of his gaze clear down to her soul. She tried a smile, but he was so contained, he didn't return the gesture.

Determined to be proactive, she picked up a sandwich and a cola and joined him at the other end of the room. Even while suffering great misgivings, she held on to his gaze and her smile.

"You should eat." She offered him the food.

He took everything from her and set it on the table behind him. Lifting a long lock of her hair, he brought it up to his face, his eyes closed, expression pained. "You have the most amazing hair. So damn soft."

"Jackson?"

He drew her into his arms, his nose at her temple, his hand sliding into her hair, around her skull. "It's almost as pretty as your eyes."

He seemed somewhat . . . desolate.

"What is it?" she whispered. The others were talking, pretending to pay them no attention.

She and Jackson both knew better; nothing got past Trace and Dare.

He pressed a lingering kiss to her forehead, then kissed the bridge of her nose, her cheekbone. "Don't make me out to be something I'm not, okay?"

"You're worrying me, Jackson."

"Mmm." He turned her so that her back rested against the patio door, and he shielded her from the gazes of others with his body. "That's something I never want to do."

She drew a fortifying breath. “Caring and worrying go hand in hand. Even if you didn’t have such a dangerous job, there would be times of concern.” She rested a hand over his strong heartbeat. “I can’t help that. I’m female.”

“Very female,” he murmured.

Now *that* sounded more like Jackson. “So you’re finally noticing that again?”

“Did I ever stop noticing?” Not giving her an opportunity to reply, he said, “There’s a lot to decide, a lot to be done.”

She didn’t like the sound of that, either. “Like what?”

He looked down at her mouth, then up into her eyes — and his cell phone rang. For one heartbeat of time, he froze. Everyone turned to them.

Alani saw the change in his demeanor and posture as he went hard and resolute, dark and dangerous in a nanosecond.

He stepped away from her while digging the phone from his jeans pocket.

He looked at the caller ID, and a calculated smile of satisfaction sent chills up her spine. “It’s Arizona.”

Both Dare and Trace came to attention. Their wives, too.

Alani reached out to touch Jackson, but as he opened the phone to answer, he stepped out of her reach — and then, to her disbelief, he turned his back on her.

Instinctively needing Alani distanced from any possible threat, Jackson separated himself from her before answering the phone. She already had some messed up, skewed perception of him, thinking him all noble and honorable.

He wasn't a damn saint. Far from it, and he didn't want his worry for Arizona to add to her confusion.

Her quick acceptance of things had left him reeling. It wasn't what he'd expected. Jealousy, sure. A snit, maybe. He'd deliberately kept things from her — still kept things from her — but she accepted it with ease.

She was so goddamned understanding that it made his brain spin.

Would she as easily accept that Arizona was a part of his life now? He couldn't abandon her.

But he wouldn't give up Alani, either.

Done speculating, Jackson put the phone to his ear and, following protocol, said nothing. He just waited.

"It's Arizona."

Relief stiffened his spine even more. He went right to the point: "You're okay?"

"Yeah, sure."

He wasn't buying that, not until he saw her himself. "Where are you?"

"Weeeellll . . . That's the thing. I'm sort of . . . on the road."

He paced away from the door, wishing he had real privacy — or more to the point, that the women weren't in the room. But damn Dare and Trace, neither of them made a move to make that happen, and he felt the intrusion of the wives, of Alani, as a keen imposition. "I called."

"You did?" She sounded surprised, but with a lack of apology, said, "Couldn't answer."

"Why not?" Then it occurred to him that if she wasn't returning his earlier calls, she had to have another reason. "What's wrong?"

"The thing is, I don't want you freaking out."

Insulted, he paced to the window to stare down at the lake. "I do not freak out."

"Yeah, right. Well then, I don't want you going off on a killing rampage. How's that?"

Determined to get to the truth, he asked softly, "Why would I want to do that?" Her sarcastic attitude always hid fear. As elusive as she remained, he knew that much about her. "Tell me what's going on, Arizona. Now."

She gave a long, dramatic sigh. "Okay, fine, don't get your boxers in a bunch."

"Arizona."

"I lost the cell. That is, I lost the one you were probably calling on. I still have this one."

Just as he, Dare and Trace each carried two cells, he'd given Arizona two, as well — one for true emergencies, and one for just talking. It was her "around town" phone — and to keep their relationship secret, she wasn't supposed to use it to call him. "How?"

"Some guy I met in a bar —"

"Where are you?" She *had* used the phone to call him, so something had to be seriously wrong. Ready to go after her, he took a few steps, but he didn't know where to go and it left him incensed.

"I'm *fine,* Jackson. Honest. Geez, take a breath already, will you?"

He did, damn her. "You're sure you're all right?"

"I'm awesome, cross my heart. I'm not calling for backup. Now if you'll let me finish —"

"You said you were in a *bar?*" He didn't know any reputable bars that'd willingly serve an underage girl. But he knew plenty that would let in a girl who looked like

Arizona.

She laughed. “Yeah, you’ve heard of them. Local drinking hole? Place for shitheads to get plastered and bimbos to get laid.”

“God help me,” he muttered mostly to himself, and then, “What bar? When? Where exactly are you now?”

“Doesn’t matter what bar, because I’m nowhere near there now. Happened last night and I’ve been on the road ever since. As for where I am now, I’m just crossing over from Ohio into Kentucky.”

“Highway?”

“Yep.”

So for now, she should be clear. Enough traffic remained on the main roads that it’d be tough for anyone to get to her without being exposed.

“What about the guy at the bar?” He studied the sky. It remained light ’til late, so he had plenty of time yet to get to her. He wanted to be moving, doing, but he needed facts first.

And getting facts from Arizona was enough to make him grind his teeth.

“Well, don’t blow a gasket, but I sort of tussled with this big dude who was there to . . . See, at first I mistook what he wanted. But, I dunno, maybe he was just there to scope out the scumbags, same as me."

His hair nearly stood on end. Scope out scumbags? *Tussle.* His back to the room and voice low, he said, "Been playing vigilante again?"

"Call it whatever you like. Thing is, I don't know why he was rousing the rabble, but I figured him to be different, ya know? Well, not *that* different."

Fist on his hip, phone to his ear, Jackson dropped his head forward and groaned. "What happened?"

"He lusted, I laid him low, end of story."

Of course he'd lusted. Arizona had that effect on most guys, which was probably why she had expected him to be the same. "If it was the end, why are you calling?"

"That's the thing . . . he followed me. And the sticky-fingered SOB must've taken my wallet, too, when we . . . well . . ."

Squeezing his eyes shut, Jackson supplied her word back to her. "Tussled?"

"Yeah. That's probably when I lost the phone, too." A grin sounded in her tone. "But I can handle him, so that's not why I called." She paused, his anticipation built, and then she said, "It's the silver BMW."

Going rigid, Jackson snarled, "Silver BMW?"

That got Dare and Trace coming to attention, too.

"Yeah — the same one that tried to run you off the road. Different plates now, though."

"The same . . ." How the hell did she know about that?

"Crying out loud, are you going to keep repeating what I say, or can you let me finish?"

Pissed off but with no recourse, Jackson stared at Dare and Trace. They stared back. Yeah, they couldn't help him. Hell, when it came to Arizona, he couldn't help himself.

He avoided looking at Alani and shook his head. "Is the BMW following you?"

"Not anymore. I lost them about an hour ago."

Fingers of alarm clamped around his heart. "But it was tailing you? You're sure?"

Another pause, and then, "Actually, know what? It'd be better if we talked about all this in person."

Finally. "Hell of an idea. Tell me where you are and I'll come get you."

"No need. I'll come to you."

"Arizona . . ." He couldn't give her Dare's address. The trust issues went both ways. "It'll be better if we meet."

"Yeah, I know. I wasn't planning to come

see you tonight. I meant that I'll figure out a good place for us to meet closer to where you are. But tomorrow, okay? I'm beat."

God, but he wanted to go to her. Now. This instant.

As long as she insisted on doing her own thing, running wild and looking for trouble, he had to assume she found it.

No way in hell would he let her lead that back to Dare's home where it could endanger Molly or anyone else.

"Tonight works better for me."

"Yeah, because you're freaking Superman. I remember. But as you keep telling me, I'm just a girl, and I need rest." She gave a loud, effective yawn. "It's been a long day."

Tension knotted his muscles. "Listen to me, Arizona. Whoever is in that BMW means business. There's been a lot going on. A lot you don't know —"

"I'm betting you'd be surprised what I know. Like . . . two shooters?"

He went mute. No. No way. But . . . probably. Back teeth locked, he said, "That was you?"

"Gotta look out for my number one guy, right?" She made a kissing sound into the phone.

"No."

She ignored his whispered denial. "But,

hey, don't worry about any of that right now. I can explain everything better in the morning, after I've gotten some shut-eye. For tonight, I'm just gonna find a hole in the wall —"

Jackson heard her winding down, and it left him sick with urgency. "Don't you *dare* hang up!"

"— and I'll be in touch sometime tomorrow morning."

"Goddammit, Arizona, I mean it."

Voice going very soft, she whispered, "If I need you, Jackson, I really will call. Thanks to you, I've gotten used to living." He heard the smile, and the truth she seldom admitted. "I even sort of like it."

She ended the call.

Primed, his vision clouded with a red haze, it took all Jackson had not to crush the phone in his fist. But if he broke the damn thing, how would she reach him when she needed him? And he knew that she would.

She played some dangerous game. A game that, despite her wishes to the contrary, didn't suit her.

Everyone watched him, waiting, and it was too damn much. "She hung up on me."

"She's okay?" Trace asked.

"Says she is." But Jackson wasn't buying

it. Not really. It took everything he had to sound calm, to maintain a posture of control. "I don't know where she is. Not at school." He shook his head. "On the road, she says. Coming into Kentucky."

Alani stood close behind him. "She wanted to meet you?"

"Tomorrow. She said she'll call back and arrange something after she gets some sleep."

Dare sat forward. "The silver BMW?"

"It was following her." He heard Alani gasp. "She says she lost it."

"You believe her?"

He didn't know what to believe. "The second shooter at the house? Well, Alani was right."

"I was?"

"We assumed it was two adversaries, but Arizona claims that it was her."

Silence sounded louder than a gun blast, assaulting his ears. There was so much he'd never told them about Arizona.

"She was at my house," Alani said, "but she had no way of knowing me or where I lived." She touched his arm. "So the question now is whether or not she followed *you* there, or did she follow the shooter?"

"Yeah." Whichever the case, she'd come armed. If only to follow him, then did she do it as protection? But why? What did she know that he didn't, to make her think he needed protection?

The woman at the house, the one who'd drugged him . . . No. He felt sick for even thinking it. Alani had described the woman to him, and at mid-thirties with short hair, she sounded nothing like Arizona.

But then who?

So many unanswered questions.

Every muscle in his body strained with the need for exertion. He wanted to run. Or swim.

Or fuck.

He glanced back at Alani.

As if she read him like a book, her golden brown eyes darkened. "You should eat," she said softly. "You'll need your strength."

A promise? His heart started tripping.

With Grim in his arms, Chris stood and walked to a wall monitor. "Vet's here." He glanced back to eye first Jackson, then Alani. "Yeah, why don't I just take care of it?"

Jackson worked his jaw, tried to find something logical to say, but he couldn't.

Alani spoke up. "Thank you, Chris."

Priss and Molly bounced their gazes between them. He didn't know what had the wives looking so tantalized, and he wasn't sure he wanted to know.

He pulled himself together, but it wasn't easy. "I can do it."

Dare said, "No." He took his wife's hand and tugged her from the chair. "Let Chris and the ladies take care of it. And yes, Alani, that includes you."

Alani started to protest, but Dare overrode her on it. "It's always better to go over everything while it's fresh in the mind to get another perspective."

Knowing Dare was right, that he needed to look at this logically when logic hovered right out of reach, Jackson nodded. "I might have missed something."

Hands on her hips, Alani turned to him.

He expected her to be hurt. Maybe angry.

Of course, she forever gave him the unexpected.

Stepping forward, she wrapped her arms around him for a big hug. When he resisted, she hugged him tighter, staying close until her warmth seeped in, and her scent filled his head.

Finally she levered back and smiled at him. "Somehow, it's all going to be okay." And with that, she walked out.

Dazed, he stood there a minute before he realized Trace dissected him with an analytical stare, and Dare looked impatient to get on with it.

Out of the blue, Dare said, "It's not a competition, you know."

"What?"

Trace made a sound. "You're always a show-off. But with my sister?"

Jackson stared at them. His muscles clenched, and even knowing he was defensive for no reason, he growled, "What the hell does that mean? Stop being so cryptic."

"Four times in a day?"

He shook his head.

"Sex," Dare supplied. "Seems the women have been gossiping."

"Oh." He sorted through all that, and then it dawned on him what they meant. *"Oh."* Alani had talked with Priss and Molly? About *them,* in the sack?

If it was anyone else, under any other circumstances, he'd grin, brag a little, even exaggerate some. But not now, not with Trace wearing such a black frown.

Jackson shrugged. What else could he do? "I'll have a talk with her."

Grinning, Dare shoved Trace. "Since Alani wasn't complaining, you might as well get used to it."

Knowing how new things were to her, Jackson didn't begrudge Alani a little girl talk — except that he wanted to be more to her than a good lay. A hell of a lot more.

"I guess so." Not so severe now, Trace shook his head. "Excessive bastard."

"Yeah, well . . ." Jackson knew he had been excessive, but then, he didn't know how long it'd last with Alani, and that pushed him to take as much as he could, for as long as he could. "This is a damned awkward conversation."

Trace went for a cola. "I expect there'll be more of them to follow."

"I guess." *He hoped.* Cracking a grin, he said, "She keeps me on my toes."

"They all do." Dare watched him. "Kind of nice, isn't it?"

Jackson didn't bother to pretend confusion. "It's scary as shit, actually."

Trace relented enough to say, "It gets better."

Not sure that he wanted it to, Jackson grabbed up his food and dug in. Around a big bite, he said, "There's stuff I haven't really told you about Arizona."

Crossing his arms over his chest, Dare said, "Now would be a good time then, don't you think?"

"Yeah." He swigged back half a cola. It wasn't like he had much choice at this point. They had to know. Better to get it out of the way while the women were otherwise occupied. "You guys might want to take a seat."

Chapter Nineteen

When the men remained standing and impatient, Jackson saw no hope for it; he went right to the point. "Arizona has skills."

"That could mean a lot of different things." Carrying his drink, Trace took up his position against the fireplace again. "What are we talking about here?"

"When she got caught by the traffickers . . . It was because they busted her stalking them." Sandwich in hand, he gestured between them. "Much like we do. She'd uncover them, make a few calls, and if things didn't go the way she wanted, she took matters into her own hands."

Disbelief destroyed Trace's casual pose. Appalled and incensed, he took two steps forward. "She hunts traffickers?"

"Something like that." The story was so sad, Jackson hated to repeat it. And he wouldn't, not all of it. It was her story to tell. But he could share the bare bones.

"When she was seventeen, her dad traded her in a drug deal. When her mom tried to stop it, they killed her."

"Jesus." Dare inhaled sharply. "They probably killed the dad, too, then."

"Yeah."

Trace didn't say a word; he was too furious to speak.

"They had her for a few months before she escaped." They all knew that under those conditions, a month would feel like a lifetime in hell. "She says it took her a year to realize she needed revenge. From then, until she got nabbed again and I found her, she'd been tracking them. She knows what to look for, how to recognize the signs. She's one hell of a driver, good with weapons and a more than adequate thief."

"Still?"

"I don't know." He finished his sandwich. "I gave her money, but she hated that. She'd rather steal from a dealer or take it gambling, than let me help her. It's been an uphill battle all the way with that girl."

"You trust her?"

"Completely. At least, her motives." Though he spoke calmly enough, inside Jackson raged. "Her methods . . . I have no fucking idea what she's done or what she's up to now." He didn't want to betray Arizona's trust by telling the others that she'd called him her number one guy. He knew she said it as an affectionate joke, that in some unreasonable way she felt beholden to him.

Just as he knew that in other ways, she resented him for doing things she couldn't.

"It bugs her that I saved her."

"She wanted . . ." Unable to say it, Dare shook his head.

"To die? No. At least, I don't think so." He prayed not. And if she had, well, that was over. She enjoyed living now — she'd said so herself. "She wanted to be the one to kill them all."

Trace worked his jaw. "Does she have what it takes to do that? Is she capable of following through?"

"Says she is." By the second, Jackson got edgier. Another minute and he'd implode. He needed physical release.

He needed Alani.

"All I have to go on is what she tells me." And how she looked while telling it. "She hates traffickers enough. Could she pull the trigger? *Has* she pulled the trigger? No fucking idea."

Trace came over and took a seat. "That's what the school was about?"

"Yeah." Jackson had to laugh at himself.

"She told me all she knew how to do was hunt scumbags and defend herself. The idea of any legit job, according to her, gave her the willies. But now . . . You know, I think she accepted the idea of going to the school because it took her off my radar."

Dare nodded. "She knew you disapproved."

The reality of that sounded harsh and judgmental, when he hoped he hadn't been. "Any sane man would disapprove of a twenty-year-old girl dabbling in bloodthirsty revenge against criminal maniacs." With one hunger satisfied, Jackson sprawled back on the couch and concentrated on cooling his burning emotions. "You know the really strange part? She breezed through getting her GED. And even with her skipping out on the school for long stretches, the instructors had nothing but good things to say about her. Somehow, around all the crap she pulled, she was still on track with her credits to graduate with an associate degree. She even carried a 3.7."

"Smart and brazen — it's a dangerous combo."

Jackson snorted. "Since that describes Priss —"

"Don't," Trace warned. He shoved out of his seat again and paced away.

Jackson knew Trace still suffered a few moments of panic whenever he remembered how close Priss had come to real harm. He was especially prickly about discussing her with Jackson, since Jackson got to see "the goods" before Trace when he swiped Priss out of the shower — all with altruistic motives.

"If I hadn't let her get involved with the work," Trace said with his back to them, "God only knows what she would have gotten into on her own."

"She's like an adrenaline junkie," Dare said. "You have to admit, it's addictive." He stretched. "That is, it was addictive until I found a better way to expend my energy."

That brought Trace back around, and he even smiled. "Wives do come in handy for working out the tension, don't they?"

Given that he wanted to work off some tension with Alani, Jackson agreed. But since Alani wasn't his wife, he wisely kept his mouth shut. Still, their discussion had given him a few ideas.

Could he bring Arizona around by giving her a lesser role to play? She'd be contributing, she'd be involved, but only to the point that he could maintain control of all situations. It was something to think about.

"Until Arizona calls me in the morning,

there's not much I can do."

"You'll stay here tonight?" Dare asked.

He nodded. "I don't want Alani alone when I go to meet with Arizona, so it'll be best if she stays here."

Dare gave him a look he didn't understand. "Meet her where?"

"My guess is she'll head to a prearranged location. It's what we talked about in case of an emergency." But Arizona was so unpredictable, he couldn't swear to anything — and that made him most nervous of all.

"Is the location close to your apartment?"

"Less than ten minutes away."

Trace mulled that over. "Now that you know there's a problem, can you make your place secure enough?"

"To protect myself?" He didn't like that insinuation at all. "It's secure."

"Actually, I was thinking about Alani."

Jackson did a double-take. "At my apartment?"

Aggrieved, Trace shook his head in a pitying way. "You do realize that she's not going to stay behind willingly?"

Unconcerned with that, Jackson stood. "She's been reasonable about it all." And bottom line, he'd do whatever necessary to keep her safe.

"That was before you were going off to

meet another woman." Dare came to his feet, too. "Word of warning — if you don't handle it right, Alani's going to be pissed, hurt or both."

Jackson wondered if he'd be getting unsolicited advice from Dare and Trace from now on. He wouldn't mind so much, if it meant Alani stayed his a little longer.

Course, nothing yet guaranteed he'd be involved with her beyond sating her curiosity. He knew plenty about keeping a woman happy in bed.

Out of bed? He'd never really tried before.

Given Dare and Trace were both in long-term relationships, maybe getting a few tips from them wouldn't be a bad thing. "So what's your idea of handling it right?"

The look they shared screamed conspiracy, and Jackson didn't like it worth a damn. "What?" Under the microscope, he bristled. "You got something to say, let's hear it. I'm all ears."

Dare made up his mind, then got Trace's nod of approval. "This could be the perfect opportunity."

"For what?"

"It's chancy," Trace agreed. "But if we're all there . . ."

"All *who?*" Jackson didn't like the sudden tension in the room, as if they both expected trouble. "If you mean Alani, forget it."

"Look at it this way," Trace told him. "If we're all going, we can't leave her behind."

"We who?"

"The three of us . . ." Dare said. "*And* Alani."

None of that made sense to Jackson. "Why the hell would she be going?"

"Because we need to find who's behind this. And whoever is following Arizona already knows about Alani — and now they want her, too."

His stomach bottomed out, then burned with acid. "You want to use the women for bait."

Trace took an aggressive step toward him. "Even you can't be that stupid."

Dare inserted himself in Trace's path. "You're not thinking this through, Jackson. Take out your . . . association with Arizona and Alani. Take an unbiased look at things. A cold perspective."

He didn't want to. He couldn't. *Association?* What a bland, dispassionate word. That's what they thought he had with Alani? Did she still think that, too?

Sure as hell felt like more to him.

A lot more.

No way could he ever be cold about anything that concerned her. But he caught their drift anyway — and knew they were right.

Temper shooting up another notch, Jackson accepted the truth and ground out the obvious. "This might be our best chance to trap the bastards."

Dare nodded. "Whoever is following Arizona won't hurt her, because they need her to lead them to you, and to Alani."

Trace picked up on the explanations. "Unfortunately, if they know Alani isn't with you —"

"Then Arizona could become collateral damage." Shit, shit, shit.

"But thanks to her call, we're on to them," Trace said, "and that gives us the upper hand. We'd all three be watching over her, but from different vantage points."

"Which means we can keep both women safe." Dare clasped Jackson's shoulder. "But Alani can't know."

"And neither can Arizona." Trace reined in his anger. "They'll be easier to control if they don't suspect danger."

"Women tend to get protective." Dare blew out a slow breath. "Complicates the shit out of things."

That was a mighty big secret to keep from Alani. She wouldn't like it. And he wasn't convinced it was necessary. A history of treating her like a kid blinded Trace and Dare, but Alani was a smart, responsible woman with good instincts. At the hospital, she'd put her own nerves aside to handle the situation with intelligence, savvy and dignity.

"I don't know." He'd prefer to carry Alani off to his home and keep her there until he'd unraveled the mystery of who'd drugged him and who was after them.

Trace snapped, "And I don't like it that some whack-job wants to get to my sister. I want this shit resolved, and if we see him coming after her, we *can* resolve it."

"In a controlled environment," Dare reasoned. "This is our best-case scenario and you know it."

"Don't worry," Trace said, prodding his anger. "She's my sister. I'll make sure she doesn't get hurt."

Dare groaned at that well-placed dig.

But Jackson didn't take the bait; he was too busy sorting out all the scenarios in his mind. "You know I won't let anything happen to her."

"Is that right?"

"It is." If it was anyone but Alani, he wouldn't have to think about it, but with her, everything was different. Knowing he really had no choice, that in the end this would be in Alani's best interest, Jackson agreed with one short nod. "All right, I'll do it."

Dare made a rude sound. "Was there any question about that?"

"No." He frowned. "So what's the plan?"

Together, they sorted out all the possible circumstances, how they could change, how the men could be affected and what to do in case they were.

It seemed like a sound plan to Jackson, but he knew Alani would be pissed. Trust was important to her — and she'd earned his trust.

"Soon as Arizona calls you," Trace said, "let us know. In the meantime, you might want to make sure my sister is on board for another trip, but unsuspecting of —" Trace's cell rang, cutting off the rest of what he would have said.

After glancing at the caller ID he opened it without concern. "Got it done?"

Jackson and Dare both listened in, saw Trace's satisfaction and relaxed.

"Great. Keep an eye on him. If he thinks of anything else, let me know, but otherwise, I don't want him contacting anyone for any reason. Right. Hell, lock him in a closet if he gives you any problems." Trace grinned. "Yeah, I'll deal with it later if it comes to that. Thanks."

After he disconnected the call, Trace stowed the phone. "Marc Tobin is relocated. I left two men to babysit him."

"Is he making things difficult?" Dare asked.

"Actually . . . no. They said he's mostly limping around the room, unsettled, antsy." Trace gave a grudging shrug. "He wants to be clearheaded in case he thinks of anything that might help, so he's refusing pain meds."

"He's still a prick, but at least that takes care of one problem." Making up his mind, Jackson snagged up one more sandwich and devoured half in a single bite. "Guess I might as well get on with tackling the other."

Trace folded his arms over his chest. "You're saying my sister is a problem?"

"Biggest one I've ever faced." He slapped Trace on the shoulder before leaving the room. "But don't worry about it. It's nothing I can't handle."

Sitting under a tree out front, Alani allowed Grim to do his business while keeping a close eye on him. The vet had done a few cursory tests, and overall had given the cat a clean bill of health. But he needed to be brushed — something Alani had just been working on — and he'd need to be brought in for more vaccines once the tests were finished. Chris had promised to see to it, since no one wanted her going out.

Danger lurked.

It seemed so surreal. Prior to being kidnapped, her life had been so secure, so happy and so . . . surface-level. Sure, she'd loved — her brother, Dare, the parents she still missed.

And she'd enjoyed — her studies, her work, her friends.

But everything she felt now was enhanced by the knowledge of how easily it could be taken away. Fear honed her senses. Simple joys, like planning the decorating of Jackson's house, meant so much more to her.

Loving him meant everything.

She wanted to tell him how she felt, but he had so much going on right now, how could she add to his burden? What if he didn't feel the same? Jackson thought himself invincible, but she knew the truth.

In a heartbeat, everything could change. She didn't want to waste a single second of her time with him.

But neither did she want to be a distraction.

Grim came back to her, gave one long rusty meow, butted her hand with his head and started purring. In her maudlin frame of mind, such a simple gesture of trust left her ready to weep. "You like being pampered, huh?" She drew him into her lap and began brushing again.

Already, giant fur balls rolled over the lawn like tumbleweeds. Many of the tangles had had to be cut out, so he had a few patchy places, but otherwise, he looked beautiful.

Cross, but oh so precious.

She cuddled him up to her face and hugged him.

A shadow fell over her.

Thinking Chris had returned with a bag for the cleanup, she tipped her head back, but instead it was Jackson. He stared down at her, expression enigmatic except for his eyes. Burning bright with sensual need, they left her scorched.

Caught up in her own disturbing analogy, Alani whispered, "Hi."

"Hey." He knelt down beside her. "What'd the vet say?"

"So far, so good. Tomorrow, Chris will take him to her office to get the results of some blood tests, and if everything is as good as she suspects, he'll get a few shots. But he's parasite free, ears clean, eyes clear. All he needs is lots of love."

"Looks like you're giving him that."

The cat abandoned her to high-step, back arched, tail lifted, over to Jackson. He wove in and around Jackson's legs, purring loudly in that raspy voice of his.

Grinning, Jackson scooped him up. "My man, you're looking real slick." He ran a hand along the cat's back, found a knot of fur and reached for the scissors.

So gentle, he cut out the tangle without a single complaint from Grim.

The setting sun shone on Jackson's face, in his bright green eyes, gilding his blond hair and emphasizing the clarity of his astounding good looks. Jackson was a man who could make women melt by appearance alone. Coupled with his protective streak and generous nature, he devastated her senses.

Cupping the side of his face, Alani drew him toward her for a kiss. She thought of everything he'd done to her, how he made her body burn, and she badly wanted to reciprocate.

"Mmm." Noses touching, he asked, "What was that for?"

"I want you." She sighed. "I've wanted you since that aborted seduction in the car." The words left her mouth, and she laughed. "That's a lie. I wanted you long before that. In fact, it's getting harder and harder to remember when I didn't want you."

Arrested, he gazed into her eyes a moment, then looked around, probably trying to figure out how they could work it.

She smiled. "Sorry. Chris will be back in a minute. He's going to help me clean up the fur mess."

"Here." Jackson set the cat in her lap and started gathering up the fur.

Knowing he shared the physical need with her left Alani's mood lightened. "In a rush?"

"After what you said? That kiss?" He chased down a rolling ball of fluffy fur. "Damn right."

Seconds later, Chris showed up. Jackson took the bag from him and shoved everything inside.

Watching him, Chris said, "Let me guess — you're in a hurry?"

"Something like that."

"Jackson." With him being so blatant about things, Alani couldn't keep the heat out of her cheeks. "I was going to help Chris get the cat settled —"

"He can do it." Expression imploring, Jackson appealed to Chris. "You can do it, right?"

Rolling his eyes, Chris said, "Yeah, sure. Who am I to stand in the way of true love?"

Both Jackson and Alani froze. Jackson

cracked first. "You're the man, Chris. Thanks."

"I've pretty much already got everything ready, anyway. The vet suggested keeping him separated from the others, but the girls are dying to say hi, so maybe I can take him down to my place now."

Alani looked to the front door and saw Tai and Sargie looking out, big brown eyes hopeful, their noses pressed to the screen.

She laughed. "They are such big, sweet muffins."

"Liger is more undecided." Chris smiled back at the dogs. "But then that fat cat doesn't stir himself for too many people, so why would he bother with another animal?"

"If Priss hears you call him fat, she'll skin you."

Chris laughed. "Actually, Trace is more defensive of him now than she is."

"Yeah, that's great. Good for Liger." Impatient, Jackson scooped up the cat, stroked him a few times, whispered in his ear, then handed him over to Chris. "Thanks."

Pretending great distress, Chris put a hand to his head. "First you want me, now you're giving me the brush-off."

Jackson gave him a light shove. "I said I needed someone like you." He reached for

Alani. "Besides, Dare would never give you up."

"Course he wouldn't. I'm too valuable."

Alani hesitated. "You'll let me know if Grim has any problems?"

"I will, but don't worry. He'll be fine." He gave Jackson a level man-to-man stare. "Don't do anything I wouldn't do." And with that, he walked off.

Jackson stood there a second. "What wouldn't he do?"

Tugging him toward the house, Alani said, "Knowing Chris, it's all fair game. And right now, that works just fine for me."

"Much more talk like that," Jackson murmured behind her, "and I won't last."

"We have the rest of the night." The dogs had left the front door to follow Chris, so as she led Jackson through the house, they ran into no one. She propelled him into the room they'd use. "I'm interested to learn more about this quickie you mentioned, but —"

His mouth landed on hers. She found herself backed up to the closed door, his hips pressed to hers, his hands on her breasts.

Oh, my. He really was impatient.

Alani ran her hands over his wide, hard back, down his spine and onto his sexy muscled backside.

He jumped as if pinched. Rearing back to see her, gaze hot, he whispered, "You little tease."

Did her touch really cause so much reaction? Infused with confidence, Alani smiled. "I'd like a turn."

Still with his hands on her breasts, his thumbs teasing her nipples, he asked, "At what?"

"Being the . . . aggressor."

As they stared at each other, she felt the rise of his erection and his body heat.

When he said nothing, she gently pushed away from the door. "Let's switch positions."

"Yeah, okay." But for once he seemed clumsy. Eyes narrowed with sensual intent, he watched her. "Woman, what are you planning to do?"

"Nothing you haven't done to me."

He sucked in a ragged breath. "Yeah."

"Nothing I haven't already done — except that you don't remember." She gazed up at him. "And you didn't let me finish."

Another breath. "Okay. Sure. If that's what you want."

"I want you, Jackson." She opened his belt buckle.

In a rush, he shifted, reaching back for his

holster as she slid the belt free.

Alani held out a hand, and he surprised her by placing the holstered gun in her palm. It was heavy but warm from his body. She set it, with the belt, on a chair beside the bed.

Avoiding Jackson's gaze, knowing he had the power to throw off her plans with but a look, she concentrated on his jeans. The snap opened easily.

"Careful now," he told her.

And he held his breath as she eased the zipper down over a solid erection. Slipping her hand inside the open jeans, she stroked him. The feel of him through the cotton boxers excited her.

She wanted more.

She dropped down to her knees.

Jackson rasped, "God, woman." His big hand settled in her hair. "Gotta say, you look good down there."

"That's what you said the first time." She smiled. "Let's get off your boots so I can get you naked."

He didn't reply, and when she looked up, his long fingers worked through her hair. His chest labored, and color rose on his high cheekbones.

"You gonna blow me, darlin'?"

That was the plan, but she hadn't expected

him to outright ask. "Let's play it by ear."

He massaged her scalp. "Let's play it by tongue."

So suggestive. And since when could a hand on her head make her insane with need?

Since Jackson, obviously.

She turned her attention back to his boots, unlacing them and, when he lifted a foot, removing them. She peeled off his socks.

Even his big feet were sexy, she thought, especially with the way he braced them apart in anticipation of what would come.

Alani looked up the length of his tall body and came back to her feet.

"You're killing me here."

"A big, strong guy like you can take it." Catching the hem of his shirt, she drew it up his torso. His skin was hot, and other than a sprinkling of body hair, smooth and sleek over iron muscles and long bones. Leaning forward, Alani kissed his chest, lightly bit a pectoral muscle, teased her tongue over a flat nipple.

His head went back. "If I come in my pants, it'll be your fault."

She stalled. "Is that a possibility?"

Eyes closed, face flushed, he grinned. "Nah. Least, I hope not."

"Good." She got the shirt up more, and then let him strip it off over his head. Spreading both hands on his chest, she said, "Because I want to taste you this time."

While he sucked in air, she went back to her knees and tugged down the jeans. When the denim bunched at the bottom of his thighs, she leaned forward and kissed him through his boxers. "You smell really good, Jackson." Hands on his hips, she opened her mouth over him, teased along his length with her teeth. She nuzzled lower, where his scent was stronger, and her stomach did a somersault.

"Know what, babe?" He shifted uneasily. "That'd feel even better if we both got naked."

Knowing he'd rob her of her chance if she disrobed, Alani shook her head. "Just you." She tugged the jeans down the rest of the way, and as he stepped free, she pushed them aside. "Now the boxers."

"Hell, yeah." Without a modest bone in his body, Jackson stripped them off. He stroked her head. "You wanna come up here and kiss me?"

"No, I think I'll do my kissing from down here." He pulsed with life when she wrapped her fist around him. "Jackson?"

Tense from his toes to his eyebrows, he

said, "Hmm?"

"Tell me if I do anything wrong." And with that, she leaned forward to lick away a salty drop of fluid from the head.

"Yeah, su —" Cut short on a gasp, his reply ended with a groan.

Liking that reaction, Alani licked him again, all around and down the shaft to the base.

Breathing hard, he cupped her head in both hands and urged her closer. "Open up, Alani. Let me feel your mouth."

Even now, when she hoped to wrest away the control, he managed to easily seduce her using no more than his honest need.

"Like this?" She parted her lips around him, drew him in.

"Ah . . . fuck. Yeah."

Kneading her hair, he held her still while easing farther into her mouth. It excited her unbearably, to hear his breathless groans, feel the growing tension in his muscles, breathe in his heat and the scent that was purely Jackson.

He put one hand over hers where she held him and, in a gravelly rasp, instructed, "Squeeze me. Like this." He showed her how to move her hand in counterpoint to her mouth. His thumb slid over her face. "Suck on me. Let me feel your cheeks hollow out —"

And when she did, he praised her with, "Good. Too good." He groaned. "Damn, I can't wait."

She slid him free, licked again, drew him back in.

His knees locked. "That's enough, Alani. Enough."

He tried to tug her away, but she didn't want to stop. This time, she wanted everything from him.

"Alani . . . baby, it's now or never." Another groan, raw, broken, and: *"Too late."* Cupping his hands around her neck, he drew her close and growled out a strong release that shook his big body.

Alani stayed with him as he continued to groan and tremble, and then he eased her away with a broken, breathless laugh.

"Yeah," he murmured, "that helped."

On her knees looking up at him, Alani asked, "Helped with what?"

"All that ails me." He put his head back against the door, drew in several laboring breaths and blew them out slowly. "Now."

Her whole body throbbed with a sweet, expanding ache. "Now what?"

"Now you." He caught her under the arms and scooped her up. "I hope the sandwiches filled you up, because I have a feeling we'll be missing dinner."

On the ragged edge of need, Alani said truthfully, "That works just fine for me."

Chapter Twenty

Hours later, judging by the limp way she rested beside him and the deepness of her breathing, Jackson assumed she slept. His whole body still buzzed with sensation. He knew sex. He knew pleasure.

God Almighty, what he got from Alani was something else.

He wanted to sleep, too, but he couldn't quiet the upheaval of his thoughts as they bounced from Arizona and Alani, now and the future, danger and . . . love.

For most of his life, he'd made a point of not wanting anything that he didn't know he could get.

But now, he wanted a lot.

And there wasn't a single certainty to be found.

When Alani's gentle fingers moved over his chest, Jackson realized that she'd only been catching her wind. He took her hand as it started to wander down his body. "Not to cut into your bragging rights, babe, but I'm spent. Even for me, that was . . ." Profound? No, he couldn't say that to her. "Draining."

"Mmm." She curled into him. "For me, too."

How could he make her understand that the last few hours with her only made him want more?

Like everything.

He kissed her forehead. "Sleep."

"I don't know if I can. Not yet." She half crawled up over his chest. "What are we going to do?"

They hadn't turned on any lights, and as the sun had set, darkness filled every corner. With the drapes closed, not even moonlight filtered in.

But he knew how she looked. He knew her small, plump breasts were against his chest, her pink nipples now soft, her pale hair tumbled into sexy disarray and her mouth swollen from too many kisses.

The beauty of her, of having her with him like this, left his heart full.

The uncertainty of the future cramped his brain.

"Do?" he asked while trailing a hand down her spine. "About what?"

Two beats of silence warned him before

she said, "Arizona." And in a rush: "We have to figure out how to help her."

His blood ran cold. "There is no *we.*" He turned, putting her under him. "You've got nothing to do with it."

Voice soft, a little wounded, she said, "No?"

"No." But realizing how that might sound, he clarified, "I'd like you to meet her. I hope that you'll like her. But she's into something."

"How do you know?"

Because she was always into something. He shook his head. "If Arizona needs help, I'll help her. But you'll keep your little nose out of it."

"So I have no part?"

"Not in this." Not in anything dangerous.

"Then what?" Defiance filled her tone. "Sex?"

"Definitely." He was sexually satisfied to the point of exhaustion, so they both knew the way he parted her thighs and settled between them was no more than taking a dominant position.

Not that it did him much good.

"You hardly need my input for that."

"I need your participation." He bent and kissed her before she could shun him. "And I want you to help me decorate, to pitch in with Grim."

"Such important jobs."

He racked his brain. "I like your company. I like talking with you."

"Well I want more." Alani shoved against his chest. "I want to *help*."

Jackson caught and controlled her hands. Thrusting his face down close to hers, he said, "You can help by not getting in my way."

That cut her. Though she remained pinned beneath him, he felt her disengage in every other way. "I see."

He struggled for a breath and put his forehead to hers. "Nah, baby, you don't."

"Get off."

"Already did. How many times?" Teasing wouldn't win her over, but it'd give him a second to think. "Did you keep count this round?"

"Yes, but it doesn't matter. So you're a sexual dynamo or something? So what?" She bucked up against him and almost got away. He quickly resettled her. "I don't care!"

"Yeah, I think you do." She'd even bragged about it. When he'd started this erotic campaign to numb her with so much physical gratification that she wouldn't be able to hold back, he'd expected some excesses, but he'd surprised even himself. "Otherwise you wouldn't have mentioned it to the wives."

Breathing hard, she went still. "I didn't know it was unusual."

Imagining how Priss and Molly must've taken her claims, he had to laugh. He didn't doubt that Dare and Trace were carnal men, but yeah . . . he was sort of going for the gold lately. "God, woman, you screw with my composure."

"Oh, poor you." She shoved at him again. "Now get *off* of me."

Instead Jackson released her hands and slowly, gently, cradled her close. He rolled to put her atop him. "You really want to help, baby?"

As if sensing a trap, she went motionless. He felt her breath, her uncertainty. He felt her body on his, the beating of her heart, the shifting of her thighs.

"Yes."

Sliding his hands down to her adorably rounded ass, he snugged her in close. "Then don't push me away." Her skin was so soft, so silky and warm. He closed his eyes against all the ways she affected him. "I can't sleep. I should be dead to the world, but my brain won't stop buzzing."

Her fingertips moved over his shoulder, then up to the side of his throat. "Jackson . . ."

"Talk to me."

Voice soft with understanding, she asked, "About what?"

Everything. Hell, he'd brought her to climax over and over again, and while he loved the way she groaned and the sexy sounds she made while tightening all around him, she hadn't made a single avowal of her feelings.

"How about . . . ?" *Whether or not you want me for more than sex?* That sounded lame even to him.

"What?" Overflowing with empathy, she stroked his jaw. "You can talk to me, Jackson, you know that."

"Okay." It seemed like a good idea to start over. "I was wondering, if this all ended tomorrow —"

She stiffened. *"Us?"*

"No!" Jesus, why would she think such a thing? "I'm talking about the danger. Once we get it resolved . . . then what?"

The silence grew deafening until his heartbeat sounded in his ears and his chest hurt.

"I guess . . ." Leaving that thought unfinished, she scooted to the side of him and sat up. He heard her sigh, felt her vulnerability. "I guess I wouldn't need your protection anymore, would I?"

She'd always have it, whether she wanted it or not. Sitting up behind her, he wrapped his arms around her, surrounding her with his determination. "Would you stay anyway?"

"You mean here?" She twisted to see him. "At Dare's?"

"No." Damn, but this was tough. He wasn't used to analyzing his words, to thinking about the ramifications to things he might say. Determined to get it all out, he drew her back down to the bed and loomed over her. "With me."

Shocked confusion had her breathing faster. "At your house?"

"Yeah."

"You'd want that?"

Right now, at this particular moment, he wanted that more than anything. Curling up to sleep with Alani each night, waking with her snuggled warm at his side each morning and making love to her at every opportunity . . . what wasn't to like?

Making himself perfectly clear, Jackson said, "Move in with me."

"Oh." Near to hyperventilating, she said again, with more meaning, "Oh."

Oh, what? Was her reaction shock or lack of enthusiasm? He didn't know, and at the moment, he didn't care. "Move in with me," he said again, with more insistence.

"Why?"

The question threw him. He gripped her shoulders and gave her a gentle squeeze. "What do you mean, why?"

Pragmatic, she said, "You asked me to live with you. I want to know *why*."

He hadn't expected an inquisition, but maybe he should have. Nothing with Alani would ever be simple.

The right words to convince her burned his throat, but they'd sound like melodramatic crap, and he wasn't ready to go there yet.

He bent and kissed her hard. "I want time with you. Time without all the interference, without threats and the constant moving from one place to another. I want to be alone with you, without tripping over your damned brother or Dare."

She shrugged. "Where I go, they usually show up."

Yeah, he knew that, but at his place they'd have a lot more privacy. "If you're there with me, you can help me finish my house. You have great taste."

"No more naked lady statues and wall art?"

He felt her weakening and grinned. "Not

unless it's a picture of you."

"Not in this lifetime!"

"Spoilsport." He kissed her. "We could swim, go boating. Decorate, cook. And we can get Grim acclimated to his new place."

"You're saying we could have . . . fun?"

"Yeah." *Fun* pretty much described how he felt about his time with Alani.

After she thought about it, she lifted up to kiss him sweetly on his bottom lip. "And if we're under the same roof, we could have sex whenever we wanted."

He locked his jaw and said, "Sunup to sundown." Not that he could be lukewarm about unhindered sex with Alani. But it meant more than that to him, so he needed it to mean more to her, too.

"I never thought of myself as the type of woman to shack up." She gave a delicate shiver. "It sounds rather *salacious,* doesn't it?"

The phrase insulted the hell out of Jackson. Did she see this only as an opportunity for more experimenting? "I wouldn't call it that."

"Then what?"

Was she egging him on? He couldn't tell. "I want us to live together. You don't have to call it anything else."

"I like the idea."

"But?"

She touched his jaw. "With my job, my brother, our separate responsibilities, how would that work, exactly?"

Jackson concentrated on the simplest problems. "I'm not that far from your office, right? When I'm not off on a case, we could bounce back and forth, maybe stay at your place two days a week so you could catch up."

"I suppose I could work off the computer the rest of the week, ordering and organizing."

"There, you see? Problem solved." Hoping to seal the deal, he kissed her again. "And your brother might as well get used to it, right?" He stared hard through the darkness, wishing he could see her face. "What do you say?"

"Well . . ."

As time stretched out without her replying, he felt scraped raw from the inside out. He'd never before asked a woman to live with him. He'd rarely ever asked a woman to stay over at all.

Finally he couldn't take it; his temper snapped. He stretched up on stiffened arms and glared down at her. "Jesus, woman, are you doing math? It was a simple enough —"

"Yes."

His heart dropped and then exploded in frantic pounding. "Yes?"

She slid her arms around his neck, and he heard the smile in her voice. "Yes, I'll move in with you."

Relief obliterated his exhaustion. Alani kissed his shoulder, shifted her legs under his, and crazy as it seemed, he felt himself getting hard again.

He caught her mouth with his own and went about devouring her. Tomorrow, he'd tell her about the plan to head back to his apartment. And before they left Dare's, he'd explain that Arizona would always be a part of his life. He'd tackle the danger and her brother.

Tomorrow.

One way or another, he'd work it all out so that Alani would remain his.

Arizona decided to call Jackson at four in the morning.

Like most normal people, he was probably expecting the call to come at a more reasonable hour. And now that he had a new squeeze, she'd just bet he was all cozy under the sheets with her right now. Normally, she'd give him a little more time.

But it wasn't to be.

After catching a few hours of shut-eye, she'd gone out on the hunt again. Tooling around the truck stops, she'd asked too many questions and deliberately stirred up suspicions.

Finally she'd gotten a bite.

No idea if one of the cars trailing her was owned by the same yahoos in the silver BMW. But maybe. Until she got them, every last one of them, she wouldn't feel complete. She'd remain only a piece of a person. A brain, a heart — but no soul. No real substance.

That thought made her laugh. Having no substance meant she couldn't be hurt. When was the last time she'd felt like a normal person?

A lifetime ago.

No wonder she couldn't remember much about it. Even with Jackson trying so hard to help her fit in, the truth won out: she'd been forever changed by her experiences. The past had helped to shape her into a force of vengeance.

Jackson had killed the ones who hurt her, robbing her of the revenge she'd desperately wanted.

But if it hadn't been for him, she would have died.

So she paid it forward by helping others

who would be abused by traffickers. Somehow, somewhere, it had to make a difference.

To someone.

Pulling up to the front of another bar, in plain view of passersby, she put the car in Park. Windows up and doors locked, she sat back and stewed on the plan. Jackson would want to help her, but in this, he couldn't.

Not this time.

She needed a safe place to set up. Having no personal residence of her own, she'd have to make do with someone else's digs.

Girlfriend's? That might work.

But she was more familiar with Jackson's apartment. If she got him out of there, then she'd have a clear field.

Guilt nudged at her resolve, but she shoved it aside with ruthless determination.

She dialed Jackson.

It didn't surprise her that his cell rang only once. Jackson might sleep, but even then, he remained on alert. He was the most amazing man she'd ever met.

"Hey, sweetcheeks. It's me."

As if he hadn't been sleeping at all, he said crisp and clear, "Where are you?"

Watching every car that passed, every man who peered at her, Arizona laughed. "You're a broken record, you know that?"

"I want to see you." Rustling in the background interrupted that command. She heard Jackson shush a sleepy-voiced woman.

His new honeypot.

Arizona curled her lip. "Am I interrupting?"

"No. Where are you?"

Relentless. "Actually, stud-o, I'm heading out to meet you."

Paying no attention to the pet name, he asked, "Now?"

Arizona could almost picture him looking at the clock. "No time like the present, right? Unlike *some* people, I don't have a warm body beside me to keep me lazing in the bed."

He ignored that, too. "Where?"

One car moved past slowly, and even though Arizona couldn't see into it through the windows, she tracked it until it went out of sight. Her senses prickled. Déjà vu? She didn't recognize the car, but she recognized *something.*

Absently, she said to Jackson, "I was thinking of the all-important backup plan."

"How long?"

Even with the car out of sight, her senses continued to prickle in an alarming way that somehow had nothing to do with danger. "When did you become a man of few words?

Or is it that your little tootsie is listening in?"

"How long, hon?"

Oh, how that voice did her in. Jackson was the only man she knew who treated her like a very special kid sister. Even her father had never shown her that same simple acceptance. But then, her father had been a weak, sick fool. He hadn't deserved her mom.

He hadn't deserved her.

Jackson wasn't weak. And unlike most men she knew, he didn't want her as a woman. He only wanted her as a . . . responsibility. Sometimes a friend. But never anything sexual.

It confused the hell out of her. It also freed her to show all the affection she wanted to give. To Jackson.

He wouldn't misunderstand. He wouldn't take advantage of her own weakness. Pressing a fist to her heart, she cursed low.

"Arizona?"

She shook her head to clear it of overly sentimental slush. "Let's say a couple of hours, give or take fifteen minutes, okay?" She was less than half an hour from his apartment, but she had the sudden urge to cause a little chaos. Violence always cleansed the remorse.

She flexed her fingers, clenched a fist and continued, “Later, baby.”

He tried to protest, but she shut the phone and ignored it when he called back. What was she? A child who needed constant supervision?

If he knew what she planned, he’d have a conniption, and that’d ruin half her fun.

Pausing at the open door to the bar, she peered past the smoke and darkness and saw the same depressing sights as always. Men slumped at dirty round tables. Others hung over the bar, cradling their drinks like lifelines. Some staggered about, and a few even looked sober. But it wouldn’t last.

She needed to do nothing more than walk in, and one of the foul bastards would get grabby.

It never failed.

Anxious for the relief of mindless violence, she started in — and a noise to her right grabbed her attention. Something moved, the scratching of sluggish feet, metal scraped, paper rustled.

Curious, she headed toward a dark alley that ran between the bar and a closed novelty shop. Out of nowhere, a man appeared beside a trash bin. Tall, strong. Shoulder propped against the brick wall, head held just so.

On the ground nearby lay a crumpled body.

Well, well, well. What had happened here?

Arizona tucked in her chin and studied the scene. Thanks to a faulty streetlamp, she couldn't see the man's face, couldn't read his expression.

But it didn't matter. On a gut level, she recognized him all the same.

Affecting a stance — arms crossed, hip cocked out — Arizona smiled. "You stole my wallet."

"Yeah, I did." Spencer dug into his pocket, produced the slim wallet and, holding it out in front of him, started toward her.

The urge to flee came alive inside Arizona. Her heart raced, and her palms went damp. Pride demanded that she hold her ground. She nodded at the fallen body. "Is that one dead?"

"He was following you. I knocked him out." His big shoulder lifted. "I got him good, but I think he'll live."

"Oh." Closer and closer he came. "Why'd you do that?"

"Knock him out?"

"Yeah." She curled her lip. "What's it to you?"

"Hell if I know. Seemed like a good idea at the time." He kept stalking closer.

"You weren't playing the hero, were you?" One gallant in her life was enough; she couldn't stomach two do-gooders.

"God forbid," he said with mocking good humor that rubbed her raw. He was so damn big, so imposing.

She kept herself still with sheer grit. When he was less than ten feet away, she snapped, "That's far enough."

Hands out to his sides, he stopped. "Take it easy, okay?"

No, it wasn't okay. But she needed her wallet back. Her phone, too, if he had that. "Why don't you just —" He tossed her the wallet.

Stupidly, she made an automatic grab for it, and he was on her.

She swallowed back a shriek of surprise as he locked her against him with the same damn hold he'd used before. Her back to his chest, her toes off the ground, his strong arms around her.

Helpless.

She ground her teeth together but said nothing. Damn it, she knew better. What was it about him that blew her edge?

"This is better, isn't it?" He didn't wait for her to answer; he backed them both deeper into the shadows and finally stopped near the alley entrance. "Now, I have some questions for you."

"Go fuck yourself."

He tsked. "You kiss your momma with that dirty mouth, little girl?"

The jibe cut deep. "She's dead, so that'd be pretty damned gross, wouldn't it?" The hurt closed in on her, making her eyes burn. It wasn't easy, but she tried not to pant.

Silence thrummed between them, until he said quietly, "I'm sorry."

Oh, God, he *sounded* sorry. The urge to struggle nearly overwhelmed her, but she knew it wouldn't do her any good. She had to wait for an opportunity.

In steady, even breaths, his chest expanded against her back, lulling her . . . comforting her.

Robbing her will.

Where his muscled arms crossed over her body, he squeezed the tiniest bit — almost like a hug.

She hadn't felt a hug in so damn long . . .

She hated it. She hated him.

She bided her time.

He'd make a mistake. They all did.

Sounding accusatory, he whispered, "You really shouldn't be here." Against her backside, she felt the rise of his excitement.

The tiny thrill she felt was surely confidence. "Perv."

Warm breath brushed her temple. "That's justified." Voice hoarse, guilty, he said, "I'm sorry for that, too." His nose touched her hair, he inhaled —

Taking swift advantage, Arizona delivered a brutal head butt that made his arms go slack. This time she turned more quickly, and her knee landed with precision.

Mouth open, expression blank for an instant in time, he said, "That was . . ." Groaning, he dropped hard to his knees and rasped, "Unnecessary."

"*You* shouldn't be here." Hands fisted, body alive with rampant and conflicting sensations, Arizona railed. "Why are you? What are you up to?"

He held himself and groaned.

What he'd wanted with her, she didn't know, but she wasn't an idiot. He was far too big, too skilled and strong for her to take on. Any second now, he'd regain his breath.

And after crushing his boys, she imagined his good will would be long gone.

Making a strategic retreat, she snatched up her wallet and ran back to her car. In seconds she was locked inside. Seconds after that, a grim smile in place, she fired up the engine.

Spencer hit the passenger door window

with a furious curse, but she shoved the car in gear and stomped the gas pedal. In the rearview mirror, she saw him jump away from the car to keep from being run over.

Her tires squealed. Rubber burned.

She couldn't get far enough away, fast enough.

He wasn't like the others, and she wanted no part of him.

But not for a very, very long time had she felt so . . . awakened. The numbness of pain and betrayal and hatred that usually pervaded her soul and kept her going against exhaustion both physical and mental, now waned under a strange pulsing heat. Her arms tingled. Her stomach fluttered.

Ah, God. Not good.

No way would she meet Jackson at the designated spot, not when trouble followed her. It'd take her another hour to get close. He wasn't in town, she knew that.

Instead of hitting up the abandoned warehouse as prearranged, she'd go to his apartment. She'd hole up there until she knew for certain that she'd thrown anyone who might be tailing her.

And if she couldn't be sure, well then, she'd call it off. Jackson would know what to do.

Unlike her, he never fucked up.

Unlike her, he was really something else. Something good. Funny and noble and possessed of an innate honor forever out of her reach.

She would always do her best to help keep him that way.

Chapter Twenty-One

Being surreptitious, Jackson checked the phone. The code showed calls from both Dare and Trace, confirming that not a soul had followed them from Dare's home to his apartment. He perused the parking area and saw mostly familiar cars. At six in the morning, few people were around.

"When are you going to meet Arizona?"

"I don't know." He struggled with his conscience. Alani wanted him to confide in her. She didn't have a clue that he, Dare and Trace were deliberately keeping her in the dark.

It didn't feel right. Sure, she knew Arizona had called. She knew he'd try to help her.

She didn't know that she had an unwitting role in setting a trap.

He turned to look at her. "She'll call again."

"And then you'll go to meet her at a secret place?"

He couldn't answer. He didn't want to lie to her.

"Alone?"

He reached for her hand. "Let's get inside, then we'll talk."

She held back. "That sounds ominous."

"Everything's fine. I have some explaining to do, that's all." He didn't want to betray Trace or Dare, but more than that, he didn't want to betray Alani's trust.

This morning she'd dressed in another of her classy outfits, and it turned him on. There was something about the understated wrapping on such a sexy package that stirred him on a gut level.

He knew how she looked under that demure sundress.

He knew how she burned for him.

Keeping watch as they crossed to the front door of his ground-level apartment, Jackson listened to the clicking of her low heels on pavement, the distant whine of a siren, the chatter of birds in the trees.

Somewhere out there, Trace and Dare had set up, Trace ahead of him, Dare behind. She would be safe.

"Here." He handed her the front door key while he turned to study the surrounding area. He knew the location by heart, every possible vantage point, every place to hide.

Only an idiot would live somewhere without knowing, and he wasn't an idiot.

Big trees shaded the apartment complex, offering concealment. He scrutinized each and every one.

Shaking her head at him, Alani unlocked the door. Jackson stopped her from going in, reaching in around her to turn on the light switch.

This was where he'd first made love to her.

Sensations bombarded him — and judging by her expression, they hit her, too.

"Come on." A hand at the small of her back, he brought her inside, then relocked the door. "Wait here."

Doing a quick, cursory check of the place, he ensured their privacy. He knew Dare and Trace had been through his place with a fine-tooth comb, but they'd left his belongings undisturbed. Few would ever know they'd been there.

Jackson saw the subtle signs. Too bad they hadn't found anything to help with the identity of the woman who'd drugged him.

When he came back into the living room, he found Alani standing beside the door, her face flushed, her gaze warmed with expectation.

"Memories?"

She nodded and looked beyond him to the hallway that led to his bedroom.

Rather than approach her, he propped a shoulder on the wall. "Bad?"

"Not at all." Gathering herself, she looked around. "Your apartment amuses me, Jackson."

He surveyed the decorations that mostly consisted of the naked female form. He now knew that none of them held a candle to Alani. "You weren't amused before."

"I was jealous then."

His gaze zeroed in on her. "Of artwork?"

"Of your interest in other women. Of your experience."

"Yeah?" He rubbed the back of his neck, shrugged. He couldn't very well deny that for most of his life, he'd been a glutton and then some. "I told you. Sex made some shit easier to deal with."

"It was an escape mechanism. I know." She dropped her purse on a table and came to him, sliding her hands up his chest and around his neck. "Now, I have to admit that I appreciate your experience."

"No kidding?" He looped his hands around her narrow waist.

"Of course." Her smile held new self-confidence. "After all, I've been the beneficiary of all you've learned."

"All I've learned? Not yet." He dragged her in closer. "But I'd be happy to show you —"

His phone made a quiet beep.

Shit.

Keeping her close, he said, "Hold that thought," and drew out the cell to see the code.

Visitor.

At this time of the morning? He took Alani's arm and drew her away from the living room and into the kitchen. "Stay put."

"But —"

Pressing her up to the wall, he kissed her hard. "Someone's coming up. Don't move. Promise me."

He saw it in her eyes: she wanted to ask a million questions. But instead, she nodded. "All right."

Amazing, sensible, understanding Alani.

He hesitated. She'd almost sidetracked him with that teasing confession, but he had to come clean with her, and soon, especially now that she knew he had gotten the code. "We'll get to that talk in just a minute, okay?"

She nodded. "Be careful."

Jackson turned to go back into the living room, turning out the lights as he moved. With the sun on the rise, an intruder wouldn't need the lights to see, but at least the apartment would be in shadows.

He'd just reached the door when he heard a quiet scraping sound.

His brows shot up. Someone was trying to pick his lock! So not a visitor, after all. But then . . . why hadn't Dare or Trace told him?

The lock clicked, so whoever wanted in had some skills.

Moving beside the door, he waited — relaxed, ready, even anxious — and as the doorknob turned, he jerked it open and yanked the "visitor" inside.

Of course, he saw right away that it was Arizona.

But she didn't see that it was him.

He dodged a fist, a kick, an elbow.

Damn it. He didn't want to hurt her. "Arizona!"

She paused in midswing, drawing up short of punching his crotch.

Jackson stared at her. Then exploded. *"Are you out of your freaking mind?"* What if it had been darker, or his reflexes weren't as good? What if he hadn't realized it was her? He might have struck her, and she was so fundamentally female that a shot from him would have put her out of commission — maybe for good.

She breathed hard. By small degrees,

surprise left her face, replaced with a blinding smile.

He saw her intent and thought, *Oh, hell,* seconds before she launched herself into his arms with a squealing, "Jackson!"

She didn't just hug him. No, not Arizona. She threw her legs around his waist, her arms around his neck and all but smothered his face in her boobs as she hugged him with all her strength.

His damned reflexes had him catching her by the ass so she wouldn't fall.

"I didn't know you were here." She kissed him all over.

"Arizona —" Aware of Alani, silent and watchful in the background, he tried to pry her away. "What are you doing here?"

She allowed him to set her back on her feet. Hands on her hips, she flipped back her long dark hair . . . and her smile slipped. "I didn't know you were here, Jackson." And then with growing accusation, "Why the hell are you forever switching cars?"

She looked frazzled and a little scared, when nothing ever scared her. "You know why."

Disgruntled, she crossed her arms. "Well, it makes it really tough to know when you're lurking around."

"Lurking in my own apartment?"

"I thought we were meeting at the warehouse!"

Just as annoyed, he leaned into her space. "But you came here instead and now all my plans are screwed." Uh-oh. He hadn't quite meant to say that just then. He looked up and found Alani staring at him with surprise, amusement, and if he didn't miss his guess, tenderness.

What the hell was there to be tender about?

Arizona followed his gaze, and her jaw dropped. "You have *got* to be kidding me."

He did a quick and unnecessary introduction, then cautioned, "Be nice, Arizona. I mean it."

"Right. Got it. *Nice.*" She nodded toward Alani. "So you're here, instead of there, because God forbid Girlfriend gets anywhere near the fire?"

Jackson bent down to blast her with his ire. "The same would go for you if you'd ever listen!"

She sniffed. "You weren't supposed to be here."

"Then why did you come here?"

"I wanted to be alone."

And just like that, his anger, his attitude and his heart all softened. Gruff, he insisted, "You're not alone. Not anymore."

"Yeah, I know. I get that." Almost as an afterthought, she added, "Thanks."

Jackson's eyes narrowed.

"But the thing is . . ." After glancing at Alani, she huffed in exasperation. "I think some dude might've followed me here."

Jackson's back went straight. Impossible. Neither Dare nor Trace had spotted a tail on her, or they'd have already let him know.

Almost as he thought it, the phone made a sound, and he knew, he just *knew,* what the message would be. He glanced at the cell and wanted to groan.

Another intruder, creeping in from the side of the complex.

"Get in the kitchen with Alani." He started toward the door.

"Yeah . . . not happening."

No. *No, no, no.* Brought up short by her stubbornness, he slowly turned to face her. "Arizona," he warned in a forceful growl. Her presence here at his apartment had not been part of the overall plan. He had to reconfigure with Dare and Trace, and the more he wrestled with her overblown bravado, the less control he had.

"I wouldn't have brought trouble to your door!" Arizona insisted. "But I thought you were elsewhere, and that you'd go straight to the warehouse. I thought I'd have time to clean up this mess by myself. I still can —"

Unwilling to waste more time, Jackson lifted her by her upper arms, ignored her protests as he carried her forward, and plopped her back down in the kitchen beside a very silent and wide-eyed Alani. *"Stay."*

"Jackson," Alani protested. "Really."

When he turned away, Arizona caught the back of his shirt. "Wait, damn it!"

He didn't have time for this. "It's all right, Arizona. Be quiet." And then to Alani, "Keep her in here."

"Ha!" Arizona shot Alani a dirty look.

Alani asked, "How exactly do you expect me to do that?"

Women. He sighed, gave an eye roll and ordered, "Stay in the kitchen. Both of you." He pointed at Arizona. "I mean it. Take one step out of here and I'll —"

"What?" she challenged. "What will you do? Send me to *college?*"

Of all the . . .

Alani cleared her throat. "I'm not a fighter, Arizona, so truly, I'd appreciate it if you stayed here with me."

Swinging around to stare at her, Arizona said, "Is that a joke?"

"No." She scooted closer to Arizona. "I'll

feel much safer if I'm not alone."

God love her. Jackson smiled at Alani, gave a nod of approval over her innovative persuasion and went to the door. Behind him, he heard Arizona grumbling.

But she didn't follow him.

Peering out the door of the apartment, he saw no one, so he slipped out.

He'd rather have a confrontation away from the women, so they couldn't be drawn into the violence. He took a step to the side of his door — and almost ran into a man.

They both took an aggressive stance.

Because they remained so close to the front door, Jackson knew the women could see them, but he didn't take his gaze off the man. If this had to happen in front of them, well, he trusted Alani to control Arizona. Somehow.

"Now just hold on," the guy said, his hands out, but his caution and suspicion obvious.

Jackson smiled — and the other guy, correctly interpreting that look, withdrew a gun.

Arizona said, "No!"

And Alani said, "Trust him."

Yeah, trust was an important thing, and it went both ways. He nodded at the guy. "You

"Then why?" Jackson put the blade of the knife to Spencer's throat. "What do you want?"

"To collect a few bounties, one in particular." Ignoring the knife, he spit blood to the side, then dropped his head back. "Badge is in my back pocket."

Eyeing him suspiciously, Jackson sat back on Spencer's thighs, keeping him immobile. "Get it."

At his ease, Spencer lifted a hip and dug out the badge. He held it up for Jackson.

Huh. Spencer Lark. Looked legit enough. "So you're a bounty hunter. What does that have to do with me?"

"Not a damned thing." Spencer came up to one elbow and glanced at Arizona. "But like the fucking Pied Piper, she's got a string of crooks dogging her heels. I want them." He gave Jackson a slick smile. "And they're here."

"Not yet they aren't."

"You're sure of that?"

"Very sure." Trace or Dare would have alerted him. "If you're saying they'll show up —" which Jackson hoped was the case so he could settle things "— then —"

In the next second, Spencer tossed him back while bounding to his feet.

Impressed — a little — Jackson said,

"You're fast."

Working his bruised jaw, Spencer said, "Not fast enough, apparently."

Knowing he was disarmed, Jackson gave him an opportunity to explain. "Let's hear it, but make it the short version."

"I've been trailing a trafficker for months now."

Gasping, Arizona said, "Me, too," making both men lock their jaws.

"I met Arizona at a bar where she shouldn't have been. The same bastards I'm after now were there that night. Thanks to her, they got away from me."

"You're blaming *me* for that?" Arizona demanded. "If it wasn't for you, I would have had them!"

Undaunted by her interruption, Spencer continued. "It didn't take me long to figure out that she uses herself for bait." Grim-faced, he glared at Arizona. "She knew they were following her, not the other way around."

When they both stared at her in disapproval, Arizona gave a negligent shrug. "That's my unique way of cornering someone."

Jackson wanted to pull out his hair. He felt sick. Defeated. How long had Arizona been playing that game? And how the hell had she survived so long? All that time, while he thought he'd made her safe, she been throwing herself into the path of destruction.

Correctly reading Jackson's expression, Spencer nodded. "You see my dilemma. I want the bounty —"

"But not with her as a casualty of the process."

"That's about it."

"Hold on." Keeping Spencer in his sights, Jackson withdrew his cell and put in a call.

Trace picked up. "I take it he's someone you know?"

"Not me, Arizona. He says he's a bounty hunter, maybe following the same people we want."

Wasting no time, Trace asked, "What's his name?"

"Spencer Lark."

"Give me ten minutes."

"Thanks." Jackson disconnected the call.

Laconic, Spencer asked, "This is an operation?"

"Something like that."

"Great." He again glanced around the area before zeroing in on Jackson. "So we can either continue with the pissing contest or we can get inside and make some plans."

Not for a second did Jackson trust him.

He didn't know him, but he sensed that all the treachery was coming to a head. "Already got a plan."

"Yeah, well, I hope it includes locking Arizona in a closet. Apparently that's what it takes to keep her out of trouble."

That was one taunt too many, and Arizona shocked Jackson by launching herself at the big man.

Rather than dodge her, Spencer appeared to anticipate the move. He caught her to him, swung her up, and Arizona ended up dumped over his shoulder.

When Spencer held her there, Jackson started to react, but seeing how careful he was with her and hearing no complaints from Arizona, he held back.

To Alani, the guy said, "Excuse me," and he carried Arizona into the apartment.

Shocked by it all, Alani met Jackson's gaze — and cracked a smile. "Oh, my."

"It needed only this." Never trusting things to be what they seemed, he ushered Alani back into the apartment, too. His phone made a sound, and he glanced at it to see a message from Dare.

Three simple letters. WTF?

He shook his head. Seriously. What the fuck was going on?

He couldn't wait to find out.

■ ■ ■ ■

Spencer stopped in the living room and dropped Arizona down to the couch. With alacrity, he backed away from her.

Alani could understand why. The younger woman appeared more than furious. And it didn't take a genius to know she had a very short fuse and the audacity to back it up.

Jackson drew her to a halt just inside the front door. He closed it, then leaned back on it. "Why the hell didn't you stay in the kitchen?"

Though the turn of events had been more than fascinating, Alani turned to Jackson. He had a lot to explain. "Arizona didn't want to stay."

He grunted. "If you start following Arizona, you're going to find yourself dealing with a lot of trouble."

So much frustrated affection filled his words that Alani smiled and leaned into him.

Perplexed, Jackson said, "I will never understand you."

"I know." She let out a sigh. "Jackson, why didn't you tell me this was all part of a grand plan?"

He surprised her by saying, "I should

have. I'm sorry."

Ever since Arizona had shown up, she'd been caught in a whirlwind of emotions. The way Jackson and Arizona interacted like siblings added new insight to his personality, emphasizing his big heart. He'd taken a wounded, abused girl and made her family.

How could she not love him?

Arizona certainly did. Alani glanced at her again. She was by far the most exotic and the most beautiful woman she'd ever seen.

Long dark curls hung down her back. Smooth caramel-colored skin contrasted sharply with light blue eyes, fringed by long, lush lashes. Tall and slender, but with Barbie doll curves, Arizona would turn heads wherever she went.

That is, if her "drop dead" attitude didn't turn people away.

It hadn't deterred Jackson, and it sure wasn't deterring Spencer, either. At the moment, he and Arizona were engaged in a furious, whispered debate. Their gazes were hot enough to set the apartment on fire.

She shook her head. "It's a lot to take in."

"Gotta roll with the punches. But yeah, I didn't see this one coming."

It struck her that Jackson might not be the one to blame this time. "It was Dare and Trace, wasn't it? They wanted me kept in the dark?"

"They worry about you." He cupped the side of her face in that tender, attentive way of his. "Doesn't matter now anyway. Arizona has thrown a kink in the works. Soon as Trace finishes his check on our newcomer, we'll have to reevaluate everything."

So now was Jackson's chance to come clean with her. Would he? "Everything being . . . ?"

Spencer moved away from Arizona. "I'm interested to hear this myself."

As if gauging Spencer's reaction, Jackson said, "I knew someone had been after us, but I didn't know who, and I didn't even know where to start. Then Arizona told me the same silver BMW that tried to run us off the road had been following her."

Spencer nodded. "The cocky bastards make it easy for me to spot them in that flashy car."

Arizona brightened. "So you were going to use me to lure them in?"

"No." Jackson scowled ferociously. "I would never do anything to endanger you."

She deflated.

Seeing Arizona's expression, Alani said, "Jackson loves you. Of course he wouldn't put you at risk."

Spencer quirked a brow while Arizona and

Jackson stared at her.

Leaning into Jackson again, Alani said, "You've never told her that you love her?"

Arizona looked so ill at ease that Alani was ready to clout Jackson if he didn't give the right answer.

"It's never come up, but of course I do." He wrapped an arm around Alani. "Like a kid sister."

Arizona rolled her eyes, but a dusky rose flushed her skin. Grudgingly, she admitted, "Love you, too."

Alani noted the lack of a qualifier for Arizona. Did she fancy herself in love with Jackson? Or was love just so alien to her that she couldn't separate one type from another?

"Great." Spencer relaxed again. "So if the drama's over, can we get back to the action?"

Nodding, Jackson took Alani's hand and led her over to the couch by Arizona. He sat down beside her. "I wouldn't set you up to be followed, but since you said they were following you anyway, it gives me an opportunity to trap them."

It all came together for Alani. "The best way to keep everyone safe is to end the threat once and for all."

"Forever looking over your shoulder,

dodging shadows. That's no way to live."

"It's worked for me so far," Arizona complained. "But whatever. Why don't I just go out there now and when they come for me, you can grab them?"

"No."

Spencer said, "*Hell,* no."

As if to sway Jackson, Arizona said, "I've got my gun." She lifted up one leg of her jeans to show a black nylon ankle holster fastened around her trim leg with Velcro. She patted it lovingly. "I'll be fine."

Livid, Jackson held out a hand. "Give it to me."

"What? No way." When Spencer snarled, it prompted Arizona to turn her cannon on him. "You can just be quiet! You have nothing to do with anything."

Too quick for Arizona to react, Jackson ripped open the Velcro and took the gun and holster from her. He thrust it at Alani.

With two fingers, she held it away from her body. "Um . . ." Though Trace had taught her to shoot, it still made her uncomfortable to handle a gun. "What am I supposed to do with this?"

"Just hang on to it for a minute."

"Oh." She looked around but saw no place safe to put it. "Okay."

Taking her compliance for granted, Jackson again caught Arizona's shoulders. "I have this under control."

Hoping to help him convince her, Alani said, "I'm sure he does. He's very good at this sort of thing."

As the only person squeamish about a gun, Alani got a lot of attention from the other three. Giving a lame smile, she got up to put the gun, holster and all, in her purse.

On the off chance Arizona decided to take it from her, she didn't want to be a sitting duck.

When Jackson's phone beeped, he eased out from between the women and moved away to check it. Everyone watched him, anxious for news, but Alani also watched Arizona.

And Arizona was busy watching Spencer with a sort of defiant uncertainty in her demeanor. That particular look told Alani so much.

Though there wasn't much difference in their ages, Jackson was right — a whole world separated them.

"Your name cleared," Jackson told Spencer.

Too restless to sit, Spencer prowled around the living room. "Must be one hell of an operation for you to know that already."

"I get by."

"You're not a cop."

Jackson smiled and, without bothering to reply, moved closer to discuss the situation with Spencer.

While they talked, Alani tried to think of a way to help Arizona. Angry tension radiated off her in waves, gathering force with each second that passed. The awful burden of her hurt kept her confrontational. Alani understood that natural protection mechanism — people couldn't very well disappoint Arizona if she didn't care enough to let them.

Insolence, bravado and antagonism hid a lot of pain.

But thanks to Jackson, Alani had finally moved on. Not once had she had a nightmare with Jackson at her side. He filled up her world so completely that it was impossible to dwell on negativity or fear.

He'd saved her.

Now maybe she could help him save Arizona.

Chapter Twenty-Two

They waited all day, and nothing happened. Jackson knew Dare and Trace were more than used to long stakeouts, but as the sun began to sink in the sky, his uneasiness grew.

Through codes, they'd stayed in touch, but kept actual phone conversations to a minimum.

Alani had long ago fixed food for everyone, and she kept refilling his and Spencer's coffee cups.

But Arizona didn't eat. She didn't talk.

What bothered Jackson the most was how she grew edgier with each hour that passed. He'd seen it before, how the strain built until it could break a person. Waiting for fate to fuck you over was never easy. Most people preferred to face an issue head-on.

For someone like Arizona, a woman driven to confront her demons, laying low would be a certain type of hell. He wished for some way to help her, but she'd rejected conversation with everyone, including Alani.

That hadn't slowed Alani down, though. She'd continued to chat at Arizona every so often as if she weren't being rebuffed. He admired her optimism, compassion and tenacity.

She looked up, caught him watching her and blew him a kiss.

Amazing Alani.

She hadn't shown a single sign of jealousy over Arizona. No, she got it. Really got it.

All of it, including Arizona's emotional wounds.

Jackson knew then, without a shadow of a doubt, that he loved her. And he knew with even more certainty that he didn't want to be without her. He needed her in his life in a million different ways.

She wanted to experiment and explore her newfound sexuality, so he wouldn't pressure her. But as soon as they wrapped up this sting, he'd show her how good a life together would be.

Arizona went to a window to look out. "How long are we going to do this?"

Calm personified, Jackson said, "As long as necessary. If it's getting to you, why don't you take a nap? I know you didn't get much sleep."

"Get real."

Yeah, he couldn't see Arizona dodging out to rest. "Then put on a movie, or grab a magazine or something. Might as well get comfortable."

As if it was somehow Spencer's fault, she shot him an evil look and stalked down the hall in search of reading material.

It was another hour before the call finally came.

Dare this time, not Trace, and he wasted no time sharing his news. "We have them."

Slowly, Jackson came to his feet. "Details?"

"Two carloads. Seven men. Loaded down with enough weapons to be a small army."

They'd come prepared. "Any problems?"

Dare ignored that to say, "Trace convinced one of them to talk."

Yeah, Jackson knew how convincing Trace could be.

"The head guy says you were the main target, but they wanted Arizona almost as much, and Alani, too, if it'd hurt you. They had a sniper rifle. If you'd stepped out again —"

"Or if you hadn't been keeping watch." One way or another, they wanted him dead. Too bad he didn't plan to accommodate them.

"The dumbasses set up about forty yards

from us. Trace picked off the shooters first, then I went in with his cover."

Jackson got such a rush when a plan fell into place. "Have fun?"

"Actually, yeah, I did."

Jackson glanced back at Spencer. The bounty hunter stood at the alert, willing to forgo the find if necessary but waiting for the verdict.

Jackson asked Dare, "Everyone still alive?"

"More or less."

"Perfect." Jackson covered the phone. "How good are you, Spencer?"

Looking even bigger than his nearly six-and-a-half feet, Spencer met Jackson's gaze dead-on. His mouth barely moved when he said, "I have very personal reasons for making sure they pay."

"Yeah? I don't suppose you want to tell me about it?"

"No."

Because it'd mean he could get back to loving Alani, Jackson accepted that. Speaking into the phone again, he said, "With a little help to ensure no one gets away, we could let the bounty hunter take them off our hands." And that'd leave them free to wrap up other details.

Dare had a few things to say about that — things Jackson wouldn't share with his audience. He met Alani's gaze, stared into her eyes and knew she'd be a problem. "We'll ensure he follows through."

Dare said, "You better be right about this."

Knowing himself to be a great judge of character, Jackson said, "I am." With the others listening in, he added, "I'll send Spencer on his way, then meet you at your place."

Arizona's shoulders slumped. Did she really think he'd abandon her?

He looked to Alani for help. As if she'd been waiting for him, she smiled, then leaned over to talk quietly with Arizona.

"There's one more thing," Dare said.

What now? "I'm listening."

"Tobin called Trace to share an interesting bit of info."

Jackson stiffened. It took Dare only moments to fill him in on the call, and the particulars obliterated any doubts Jackson had. "Got it." Since Jackson already knew where Trace and Dare were stationed, he said, "I'm sending on the bounty hunter, so try to make sure there's someone left for him to collect, okay?"

Dare laughed at that and disconnected the call.

Knowing the rest wouldn't be easy, Jackson walked over to Alani. "Looks like it's all settled."

Trembling with fury, upset, or both, Arizona stormed into the kitchen.

"This has been very hard on her," Alani said as if to defend Arizona. "Give me a minute to talk to her, okay?"

Fascinated, especially since Arizona left him floundering more often than not, Jackson asked, "What will you say?"

"That she should trust you, of course." She went on tiptoe to give him a quick kiss before rushing off after Arizona.

Humbled by her faith, Jackson stood there a moment before he realized how Spencer stared after Arizona. Like a man unsure of which goal to pursue, he looked very undecided.

"Make up your mind fast." Jackson would give him back his gun once they were ready to part ways. "I can handle it just fine without your involvement."

Pensive, Spencer said, "If I don't bring them in alive, I don't get paid."

Somehow, Jackson thought money didn't factor into Spencer's involvement. "That concerns you?"

Finally Spencer drew his attention away from Arizona. "Not really, no." Unflinching, he studied Jackson. "You?"

"Dead or alive, I want them gone."

Glancing back at Arizona one last time, Spencer nodded. "Good enough."

"Tread carefully." Jackson folded his arms over his chest. "She's been through a worse hell than you can imagine."

"You'd be surprised what I can imagine." Something in Spencer's voice told a deep, dark secret. Face devoid of emotion, he headed for the door. "I'll wait out front."

Just then, Jackson heard the argument erupt, and he went to investigate. Arizona tried to insist on leaving, and Alani was just as insistent that she not.

"You're going with us," Jackson told her, putting an end to it. He wouldn't have his plans screwed at this late date.

Defiant to the bitter end, Arizona squared off with him. "I have my own car."

"I'll have someone get it."

Her small body vibrated with tension. "I have stuff in my trunk that I need."

"Then we'll collect it first," Alani told her.

That didn't convince her. "I need my gun back."

To maintain control, Jackson refused. For now. Later, he'd probably feel better knowing she was armed.

It took a lot of coaxing and an inordinate amount of patience on his part to finally get Arizona out to the parking area. When she stomped ahead of them, Jackson caught her arm and drew her back.

Seeing Alani as the more compromising of the two, he whispered to her, "Stay behind me."

She gave him one startled look — and did as requested, urging Arizona to do the same.

And wonder of wonders, Arizona complied.

Even in the middle of a carefully wrought plan, Jackson couldn't miss the importance of that. Arizona might pretend that Alani had no impact on her, but like him, she'd already been drawn in.

Alani had that effect on everyone.

With the women cooperating, Jackson let out a breath, but he wouldn't be completely at ease until he got them both back to his place.

One look at Spencer, and he knew he felt the same.

"Give me back my gun."

They were out in the open, but darkness had fallen. His apartment complex had good security, and bright lights kept the immediate area well-lit. But that only made them more of a target to anyone hiding in the shadows beyond. It was a quiet area, far enough away from the actual building to make him uneasy.

As the women got into the car, Jackson handed over the semiautomatic to Spencer. "Don't you want to know where to collect your bounty?"

Pulling the slide partially back, he found a shell in the chamber, the gun still loaded. Satisfied, he looked around the area. "Something's not right."

Perceptive. But then Jackson had already guessed that. "Ride with us."

Eyes narrowing, Spencer said, "All right."

When Spencer climbed into the backseat with her, Arizona caught on. "What's going on? What's wrong?"

"Marc Tobin called." Neither Spencer nor Arizona asked for details, but Jackson supplied them anyway, keeping the explanation of Tobin's relationship to Alani brief and to the point so as not to embarrass her. "He remembered that one of the people who had him was a woman."

In the front seat beside him, Alani frowned. "A woman? Could it have been the woman I saw at your apartment?"

"The one who drugged me." Jackson hated coincidence. "They had him blindfolded, so he couldn't see her, but she was there while they worked him over. He says he could tell by her laugh that she was female."

Breathing a little faster, Arizona dropped back in her seat. "Her laugh," she repeated in a barely perceptible whisper. And then, voice stronger, "What did she look like?"

Jackson deferred to Alani. Something troubled Arizona, something beyond the idea that he could have been hurt. "Mid-thirties. Brown hair —"

"And brown eyes." Shooting forward in her seat again, Arizona struggled for breath. Spencer started to reach for her, but she already had her door open. She lurched out of the car and stalked several feet away.

Shit. "I'll get her," Jackson said to Alani, then opened his door and stepped out. He didn't approach Arizona, but then he didn't have to. She only went so far before turning and storming back. "Tell me what's wrong."

Her lips trembled, then firmed. Stopping short of reaching him, she stiffened her spine and jutted out her chin. "She was my height?"

Alani had gotten out of the car, too, but stayed near her door. She spoke to Arizona over the roof. "I'm sorry, but I really don't remember. I was . . . shocked to find Jackson with a woman."

Jackson never took his gaze off Arizona. "You know who it might have been?"

As Arizona squeezed her eyes shut, Spencer stepped from the car. "I do." He leaned on the car beside the open door. "Chandra Silverman."

"No." Arizona shook her head. "She's *dead.* Tell him, Jackson. They're all dead!"

Under normal circumstances, Arizona would never betray any aspect of his work, he knew that. What she implied was not something condoned by the legal system. But this wasn't normal circumstances, and Arizona edged on hysteria.

When he didn't reply, she grabbed his shirt. Almost pleading, she whispered, "She's dead, isn't she?"

His big hand wrapped around her fragile wrist, and with his thumb he soothed over her chilled skin. "I know of three men, Arizona. That's all."

She tried to shake him. "The bitch who ran the show?"

"Other than you, I didn't see any women that day." Jackson had a horrible feeling about things.

"But . . ." Arizona searched his face. "She was there. She was always there."

"Probably enjoying herself." Spencer ran a hand over his head. "She's more evil than any man I've ever met. And I know for a fact Chandra is alive and well, because she's the main one I've been tracking."

By small degrees, Arizona gathered herself. "All this time . . ."

"You thought she was gone?" Spencer asked. "Then who the hell have you been tracking?"

"Her lackeys. Her associates. Anyone who ever took part in her sick games." Wrapping her arms around herself, Arizona laughed. "God, this is a twist, huh?"

Spencer pulled her around to him. "Whatever she did to you, Arizona, she'll pay."

Arizona laughed even harder. "I thought she was dead, and that wasn't payment enough." She tried to shove away from him, but he only tightened his hold.

Alani walked to their side of the car. She leaned into Jackson. "I'm so sorry."

Arizona looked at her. "We need to get out of here."

Grim, Jackson moved Alani behind him. "Too late." A silver BMW, headlights off, pulled in and blocked them.

"Ohmigod." Alani clutched her purse against her chest. "It's the car."

Not comforting Alani was one of the hardest things Jackson had ever done, but he had to focus on that car. "Both of you, stay behind me."

Arizona snorted. "Spencer just booked."

Perfect. "He knows what he's doing." At

least, Jackson hoped he hadn't misjudged things there. "Show a little faith."

"I could —"

Alani interrupted her, saying, "We'll do exactly what Jackson tells us to!"

As the car stopped, Jackson backed up, forcing the women behind the car. "Alani?"

"What?"

Terror made her voice high and thin, torturing him. "I'm asking nice."

"Asking *what?*"

"For you to trust me now."

He heard her draw a deep breath, then another — and finally she smoothed her hand down his back. "I do."

One day, she'd be saying that in front of a preacher. "Thanks, babe." Smiling in satisfaction, Jackson stepped forward, more than ready to get the show on the road.

Taking Arizona's hand, Alani hunkered down behind the car. Her heart beat so fast that she thought she might pass out.

It was Arizona who whispered, "Breathe. I'm strong, but I'm not sure I can carry you if we need to run."

Under less dire circumstances, Alani might have laughed. "I won't faint, I promise."

"Glad to hear it."

God, she sounded like Jackson. In some ways, they were so much alike that it made perfect sense for them to be pseudosiblings. Alani was very glad that they'd had each other.

She peeked around to see what was happening.

As the BMW's doors opened and people stepped out, Jackson stood beside the driver's door, the epitome of confidence. Three men . . . and one woman.

Lousy odds, but when it came to handling bad situations, she'd put her money, and her heart, on Jackson. *Please, please, please don't let him be hurt.*

The woman held a gun loosely in her hand, her arm down at her side. And she smiled.

"That's her," Alani whispered to Arizona. "That's the woman who drugged Jackson."

"Chandra." Arizona stared at her with a laser beam of red-hot hatred. "If ever a person needed killing, she's it."

Smug, the woman — Chandra — stepped toward Jackson. "I wouldn't suggest you try anything."

Behind her, arms crossed, the musclemen waited.

"No?" As if bored, Jackson stepped away from the car — moving the danger farther away. "Why not?"

"Your backup is done for. They think they've solved everything." She shrugged. "Of course, that was just part of my plan."

"Yeah?" He took another step away. "What plan is that?"

"The plan to keep them preoccupied with others. The plan to set up all of you." Her eyes glittered. "The plan to get even, of course."

"Huh." With a lack of concern, Jackson said, "I'm surprised you came yourself. Even a complete psycho has to realize that's a risky move. Or is it just that you couldn't afford any more henchmen?"

"I wanted to see you die!" The outburst left her flustered, and she quickly collected herself again. And then, on a tittering laugh that sent goose bumps down Alani's spine, she purred, "You don't recognize me, do you?"

"Sure I do. You're Chandra Silverman."

Her expression hardened.

"They were good drugs, but they didn't stop my brain from working. You had to know I'd figure it all out."

"All of it? I doubt that." Chandra moved closer to him while the men held guns and watched. "I've always enjoyed an . . . elaborate revenge."

"How elaborate?"

The sinister smile widened. "For starters, I had decided to have you. Did you know that?"

"Damn, lady, that is cruel and unusual punishment."

"Shut up!" Again, she collected herself. Breathing deep, she looked him over, then cocked out a hip. "I would have had you, and then rendered you useless. For a man like you, that'd be the best revenge."

Quietly, Jackson said, "Even drugged, that never would have happened."

"Ha! You wouldn't have had a choice. Believe me, it would have been a done deal if that prissy little bitch hadn't showed up." Looking beyond Jackson, she murmured, "But she did show up, didn't she? She threw off my plans, so now she has to pay, too."

Hearing such a direct threat made Alani's throat go tight. Without saying a word, Arizona leaned into her, bolstering her.

Chandra continued to smile. "Tell her to come out from behind the car."

Succinct, Jackson said, "Dream on."

"There's nowhere for her to go. You realize that, right?"

"I realize a whole lot of things. Now you should realize how bad your planning ability is."

Chandra shook her head on a laugh. "I'm excellent at what I do."

"Yeah?" Jackson moved slightly closer to her. "That's why Marc Tobin is safe? That's why I took your men out of commission so easily? That's why you got busted that first day at my apartment?" He snorted. "Doesn't sound like good planning to me."

For a second, Chandra showed her anger, but then she merely laughed again. "Get her out here, or I'll shoot you."

As if he had all the control, Jackson said, "Why don't you tell me first what this is all about? Why me?"

"You stole from me." She shrugged. "One of my favorite girls, too."

Jackson's entire demeanor changed. Voice filled with deadly menace, he said, "You threw her away."

Pleased to get a rise from him, Chandra curled her mouth. "No, I tried to *kill* her. Those are two very different things." She waved the gun barrel at him. "You robbed me of my satisfaction, and you demolished my men."

"I've demolished a lot of your men. So what? They sucked anyway."

The guys watching took exception to that, and reached for their guns. Chandra raised a hand. "Not yet," she said. She looked beyond Jackson, and made brief eye contact with Alani. "She's back there with your girlfriend, isn't she? I followed her here, so don't bother denying it."

"She's no concern of yours."

"There's where you're wrong. I'm thorough. You said so yourself, if you recall. I destroy those who cross me. And that means I'll have them both, and you'll watch as they die." Keeping the gun on Jackson, she spoke toward the car. "Now, girls, why don't you come on out before I let my men dissect him?"

Knowing what she would do, Alani grabbed Arizona's arm. *"No."*

Undecided, Arizona chewed her bottom lip. "I have to."

Panic beat in Alani's heart. "Absolutely not."

Chandra heard their exchange, and laughed. "Step out or he's dead. The choice is yours."

Swallowing back a groan, Alani grabbed on to Arizona, but that only got her half dragged along when Arizona did as ordered.

"I'm sorry," Alani said to Jackson.

"That's all right, doll. No harm." He kept his back to her, his posture relaxed — and despite facing the armed lunatics, that helped Alani to be brave, too.

"Loyal little thing, aren't you?" Chandra said to Arizona.

Arizona smirked. "I'm surprised you can even say the word. Usually dead women can't talk. And you *are* dead — whether you realize it yet or not."

Oh God, oh God. Alani tried to think what to do.

"Still as mouthy as ever, I see." Chandra tipped her head. "Arms out."

Staring straight at Chandra, Arizona lifted her arms.

Chandra tsked in mock disappointment. "Weaponless? You're slipping. And here my men were so looking forward to disarming you."

"They won't touch her," Jackson promised.

"They will get their fill," Chandra countered.

"No." And he approached Chandra.

Stunned by the bold move, she ordered, "Stop right there."

"I don't think so."

Her jaw clenched, and she turned to aim the gun at Alani.

Heart stuttering, Alani shrank back — until Jackson moved into the line of fire. That scared her even more. But he stopped before Chandra fired, and now he stood oh so much closer to her.

Alani fixated on that gun. She hated guns, all of them, but to see one aimed at Jackson amplified everything tenfold.

"Let's get it all said, lady. Why did you drug me in the first place?"

"For one thing, I needed to search your place." She lifted a slender shoulder. "I figured you had to have a clue around somewhere that'd tell me where to find my property. Yes, I knew you took her. You didn't see me that night on the bridge. You never suspected that a woman could be involved, did you?"

He laughed. "I've known plenty of sick females. There's nothing unique about you."

"Think again." She stepped up to him, the gun held tight in her hand. Jackson just stared down at her, insolent, unmoved, showing not one iota of fear. "Most people would have gone after their property and been satisfied. But not me. I tracked you that night, and you've been a project of mine ever since. I have detailed plans for you."

"Works for me, 'cuz I hate unfinished business."

Hearing Jackson taunt a madwoman, Alani had to shove a fist against her mouth to stay quiet.

"Me, too," Arizona said. "And since the business is mostly between us, why don't you leave him out of it?" Pale, cold, in some way deadly, Arizona started forward.

"Don't you dare," Alani told her. When Chandra and her men eyed her with varying degrees of surprise, Alani forced herself to stop cowering. The nearly hysterical laugh almost escaped, but she managed to quell it. Hoping to infuse some confidence into her tone, she said to Arizona, "He has it under control. Can't you see that?"

Arizona waffled . . . and held back.

Jackson regained Chandra's attention by asking, "How'd you get in, anyway? I hate to think I let every crazy broad past the door."

Chandra trailed the knuckles of her gun hand down his body and over his fly. "Still don't remember? My, those were good drugs."

She caressed him — and Alani wanted to take her apart. She surprised herself with the ferocious inclination.

But it helped her to remember that she had Arizona's gun in her purse.

Oh. Did she dare? Would she be able to withdraw it without anyone noticing?

Holding her breath, she slipped her hand into the purse and easily located the heavy gun. The men had all their attention on Jackson, almost as if they feared him.

But they didn't see her as a threat.

Alani's knees felt weak, her stomach sick.

Chandra continued talking. "I knocked, and when you answered, I turned on the tears. It was an award-winning act, if I say so myself."

Arizona scoffed. "Men are so damn stupid about that stuff."

Chandra ignored her. "I told you that I'd been in a wreck and I felt sick and I'd lost my phone. You were so sweet, so gallant."

"I'm gagging here," Arizona said.

Expression unchanged, Chandra said to her men, "If she speaks again, shoot her."

Bravado in place, Arizona pretended to lock her lips and throw away the key.

Alani admired her so much, especially knowing how Arizona felt about Chandra. Was she the only one to note the pallor of Arizona's skin?

Hugging the purse, Alani slipped her finger around the trigger. Keeping the gun concealed, she turned it on Chandra and swallowed hard. Aiming at a target was one thing.

Shooting at a human being, even a truly vile person, was something altogether different.

"You went to get me a drink," Chandra said, "but you'd left a cola sitting there on a table in front of the television, so I dosed it." She shrugged. "Easier than I'd ever expected, given the way you shredded my men that night on the bridge. I'd watched from a safe distance away, you know. Even as I detested you for interfering, I admired your ability."

Again, she pawed his crotch. By the second, the idea of shooting her seemed less repulsive to Alani.

"After a couple of sips, you suspected something wasn't right, but —" Chandra smiled "— it was already too late for you."

"Not buying it." Jackson shook his head. "Two sips wouldn't have done me in."

"No, but it dazed you enough that I could get you with a hypodermic."

"Ah. Now, that I believe." He tilted his head to study her. "So you have a big operation?"

"Big enough." She did more stroking, then made a sound of pleasure. "Sort of like you."

Arizona snapped. "Oh my God, that is so freaking pathetic, you lecherous bitch! Can you only get near a man by raping him at gunpoint?"

Everything seemed to happen at once.

Chandra screamed, "Shoot her!"

In an incredibly fast move, Jackson sent the switchblade through the air to embed in one guard's shoulder, and almost at the same time he locked Chandra in front of him, her own gun now turned on the other guard, his finger covering the trigger.

Too late to pull back, Alani fired.

Multiple gun blasts sounded, so loud that they made her yelp and nearly stopped her heart. A window on the BMW shattered.

Her shot.

Chandra slumped in Jackson's arms — not her shot.

Even with the knife in his shoulder, the panicked guard reached for his gun, but didn't make it. He screamed as something hit his hand, sending blood spewing and making his gun drop. The other guard took one bullet to the shoulder, another to his thigh.

And just like that, the strained confrontation ended. The two goons and Chandra were no longer a threat to anyone.

Heart still hammering, Alani struggled to make sense of what transpired. Jackson stood as upright, as strong and confident as ever. Arizona, while dazed and panting, appeared uninjured.

What had happened?

Gun drawn, Spencer materialized from

behind the BMW. So he had circled around and was behind them the whole time? Alani knew by his fierce expression and rock-hard jaw that he was the one who'd shot Chandra. He paused to remove weapons from the fallen guards, then strode right past Jackson on his way to Arizona.

Shaking so badly she could barely stay on her feet, Alani looked around in relieved amazement. Bodies were down. Blood had splattered. Glass shattered.

She shivered . . . and her gaze came right back to Jackson.

He wasn't hurt, thank God. He didn't even look upset. The explosion of gunfire hadn't fazed him at all.

Gaze locked, he stared at Alani while lowering Chandra to the ground.

And then her brother was there, leaning over Chandra, searching her for other weapons, checking her pulse and finally, putting in a call on his cell.

In two big steps, Jackson reached her, scooped her up and carried her to the car to sit her on the trunk.

"Alani?" His voice was firm, in control, insistent. With a gentle hand, he cupped the side of her face. "Baby, you okay?"

She stared at him, her stomach recoiled, and she thrust the purse at him. It now had a giant black hole in it. "Are you *nuts?*"

A slow smile wiped away the worry on his face. "I don't think so, no."

She saw nothing funny in any of it. "You *provoked* her! Were you trying to get shot?"

"Dare, Trace and Spencer had things covered."

"They couldn't have kept her from . . ." She couldn't say it. If Chandra had pulled that trigger, it could be Jackson on the ground right now, bleeding out. Tears welled in her eyes and clogged her throat, but she blinked fast and took two deep breaths. "That was insanely dangerous."

"She didn't have her finger on the trigger. She wanted to toy with us more than anything else."

"You can't know that." And the truth of what he'd done shook her. "You wanted her focused on you, so she wasn't focused on Arizona or me."

"You think you know me pretty well, huh?" He kept touching her face. "Well, you're right, and I won't apologize for that, so don't ask me to. Besides, the odds of her actually firing here, in the parking lot of an apartment complex, were pretty damn slim."

But thanks to her nerves, *Alani* had fired. Oh, wow, had she blown his plans?

"Yeah," Jackson said, reading her expression. "We figured the first group that Dare and Trace nabbed was just a setup. It was too easy. And when Chandra had the gall to show up in the BMW, I knew she felt safe, like she had all her bases covered. She wanted to play, but she'd have put us in the car and driven to a more private location before executing anyone."

Horrid, horrid woman. "She's . . . dead?"

"Not yet, but I don't know if she'll make it." He gave her a stern stare. "She's not for you to worry about."

True enough. Alani nodded. "I hate all this covert crap."

Smiling at her, Jackson smoothed her hair in a now-familiar way. "God, I never forget details, but I swear, I forgot all about you having that gun. Probably because never, not in a million years, did I expect you to use it."

"I forgot you had Spencer's knife," she admitted. "I mean, I know yours is in your boot, but I didn't see how you could get to it, and with your gun in the harness . . . and that crazy woman aiming at you —"

"I know." He put her head to his shoulder, but she could feel his smile when he kissed her temple.

She punched his ribs. "How in the world

can you be amused?"

"You're alive and well. Arizona is fine." He hugged her. "And the men Dare has under wraps already told him where to find the rest of Chandra's operation."

She pushed back to see his face. "So we'll be able to free everyone?"

"No *we* to it, babe, but yeah, people are already on their way. Everyone will be taken care of, I promise." He kissed her, but the kiss ended with a laugh.

Insulted, Alani frowned at him. "What's funny?"

Still grinning, he shook his head. "Shit went south on me when that BMW showed up before we could get out of the lot. I wasn't expecting that. I was improvising, making plans as I went along, and then you shot that damn gun and I had no fucking clue what had happened."

"You didn't look surprised." She hugged him, reassured by his big warm body, his secure hold. "You are so fast."

Trace came over to them, but he spoke to Jackson, asking, "She's okay?"

Alani quit hiding against him. "She is fine." And then to Trace, "Where did you come from?"

"We were keeping watch." He tugged on a lock of her hair. "Dare has the other goons on lockdown, but he had clear shots if necessary. I was closer. No one would have let you get hurt."

"I was more worried about Jackson."

Trace gave a crooked grin, and nudged Jackson. "I wouldn't have let *him* get hurt, either."

Jackson nodded over at Arizona. She and Spencer were involved in a quiet argument. Arizona looked . . . well, shattered. Her eyes were red, her face stiff. "Trace, do me a favor and make sure she doesn't split, okay?"

"Being that you're preoccupied?"

"Something like that."

"I've got it. But you know, we really should cue in the bounty hunter, don't you think?"

He nodded. "Cops'll be on us in no time, and people are starting to gather."

Alani sat up straighter. "Go." Knowing they had to coordinate stories, she shooed him away. "Do whatever you have to do."

With a shake of his head, Trace walked off toward Arizona.

Gaze warm and intimate, Jackson touched her face. "We have so much talking to do."

The groan bubbled out. After all his efforts to avoid deep discussions, that sounded pretty serious. She had a few things to say to him, too, but she definitely needed to compose herself first. "No more cloak-and-dagger, please. I can't take it right now."

He smiled. "Nah, nothing like that." Sirens sounded. He looked at her mouth, gave her another brief kiss, and straightened away. "Wait for me in the car?"

"All right." Alani forced herself to her shaky legs and all but collapsed in the backseat. Seconds later, Trace got Arizona into the car, too. Seconds after that, he was gone.

Jackson and Spencer talked, but they both kept their eyes on the car, watchful, protective.

Really good guys.

Arizona stewed, but Alani couldn't just ignore her. "You're okay?"

"It should have been me."

Shaking her head, Alani said, "What do you mean?"

"I should have shot Chandra. I owed her. It was my right, not his." Gaze devoid of feeling, she stared out the window. "Spencer robbed me of my revenge, and I'll never forgive him for that."

It broke Alani's heart to think of what Arizona carried inside her, the hatred and need for retribution.

It was going to take a lot for anyone to really reach her.

"Someday," Alani whispered, "you might feel differently."

Arizona surprised her by saying, "Maybe." She rested her forehead against the cool glass. "But not tonight."

Chapter Twenty-Three

With Grim the cat sprawled in his lap, purring in his rusty voice, Jackson lounged back in the big easy chair Alani had chosen just for him. It went with his other new furnishings, made his place feel like a real home and still suited him. He couldn't remember ever being so comfortable.

Of course, that had as much to do with the fact that Alani was still with him, as with any of the furnishings.

With the danger behind them, he and Alani spent all their days together. Grim had settled right in, and Arizona . . . well, she was getting used to things.

Three weeks had passed since Chandra Silverman had died in the hospital. Spencer had taken in the rest of the cretins, and they were currently incarcerated on a list of charges a mile long. The best lawyer in the world wouldn't do them any good — especially with Trace pulling in a few favors to ensure that no one cut them any deals.

Busting up their trafficking ring had freed a dozen females of various ages and nationalities. And finally, Alani and Arizona were safe.

Life was good.

Trace admired a decorative dish on a side table — something else Alani had chosen. "So Arizona is adjusting to her new job?"

God, he hoped so. "Seems like." Jackson had given her an array of duties that she embraced with gusto. She'd visited them a few times, but by using the computer for her work, she could still live on her own. She threw herself into researching the backgrounds of small-scale, local-level traffickers.

Jackson didn't want her anywhere near far-reaching organizations with major muscle behind them. Those were for him, Dare and Trace to deal with.

"The house looks great," Dare said.

"Yeah. Alani did a terrific job, huh?" He could say that they were living together, except that Alani kept her own residence and only brought to his home the things she needed on a regular basis.

But he was working on that. Without pushing her too much, they'd had that serious talk. About exclusivity. He told her how precious she was to him, and he made it clear that he didn't want things ending anytime soon.

Once he finally won her over, he'd tell her that he wanted her to stay with him forever. He'd tell her just how much he cared. He would —

"When are you going to marry her?"

Whoa. The question from Trace came out of left field. One second they were complimenting his house, and then — *bam* — they dropped the bombshell.

But the truth was, Jackson had thought about it plenty. Every day, in fact.

It was what he wanted, so Jackson started to say that he'd marry her just as soon as he could get her to agree — but then he noticed that both Dare and Trace wore identical looks of challenge.

No way in hell would he let them think they'd forced him to the altar.

One way or another, he *would* marry Alani — but only because he wanted to spend his life with her.

Not for any other reason.

Definitely not because Dare and Trace felt like forcing the issue. Alani wanted time to play, to experiment, and he knew for a fact she was enjoying their time together.

She deserved his patience, no matter how

it killed him.

"Well?" Dare gave him a level look. "Let's hear it."

They actually expected excuses from him? *Pfft.* Did he look stupid? "It's none of your business."

"It's my business," Trace said.

" 'Fraid not." Jackson relaxed back in his chair while Grim pawed his shirt. "And you know your sister wouldn't appreciate you nosing in."

"I don't get you, Jackson." Dare shook his head. "I thought you cared about her."

"I love her."

They both did a double-take, and then they stared for a really long time.

"What?"

"You love her?" Dare asked with a slow grin.

"Damn, neither of you see her as a woman, do you? Don't look so shocked. I'm not a dunce. Alani's beautiful and smart and sexy and . . . of course I love her." What man wouldn't?

Trace said, "Well, hallelujah."

Before they got too carried away, Jackson said, "And for your information, I *will* marry her — but only if she loves me, too."

Dare opened his mouth, shut it, then snorted.

Trace rolled his eyes. "You're insecure? That's the holdup?"

"I never said that." But yeah, with her, in this, he sort of was.

"So you've told her you love her?"

Not exactly, but she had to know. Right? In every way other than saying the words, he'd shown her how much he cared.

Done with the conversation, Jackson said, "I don't want to rush her, that's all. She told me up front how she wanted things to be, so I'm biding my time and letting her have the space she needs. When she's ready to settle down —"

"I'm ready."

All three of them swiveled their heads around to see Alani standing in the doorway. She wore another killer sundress that made him want to ravish her. But then, no matter what she wore, he wanted to ravish her.

Usually she wanted him to. That was one of the beauties of having her close at hand 24/7.

Taken off guard, unsure what she'd heard or what she thought about it, Jackson said cautiously, "Hey."

She licked her lips.

Nervousness? Was her brother pressuring her, too? Jackson sat forward to put Grim on the floor. "I thought you were with the wives and Chris out back."

Her eyes looked huge as she watched him. Grim went to her and wound around her legs. "I was, but we're ready to start the grill so . . . I came in to get you." Absently, she picked up the cat and started petting him.

His big emerald eyes closed in bliss.

Jackson scowled. "You overheard." And now she felt on the spot.

She nodded, and without quite looking at him, her face tucked in close to Grim's neck, she repeated, "I'm ready."

Afraid he'd misunderstood, Jackson said, "For the grill?"

She shook her head. "To settle down."

Slowly Jackson came out of his seat. He wanted her to spell it out. "With me? Here?"

A smile twitched her lips. "I love you, too, you know." She met his gaze. "And I'm ready."

Damn, but hearing her say it made his blood burn and his pulse race. Blind to everything and everyone else, Jackson started toward her.

She held up a hand.

His heartbeat stalled. Now what?

After a deep breath, she whispered, "I could be pregnant."

Jackson tripped over his own feet. *"What?"* Hadn't seen that one coming. Hadn't even considered it, since he'd been so careful.

There was a thump, and when he looked back, he found Trace sprawled out in the chair he'd left. Dare stood over him, a wide grin in place.

Dismissing her brother and ignoring her outstretched hand, Jackson closed the gap between them.

His heart felt so big it hurt his chest. Barely able to breathe, much less speak, he whispered, "You're pregnant?"

"I think so." Talking fast, Alani explained, "That first night, you didn't . . ." Her gaze darted past him to her brother and Dare.

Impatience hummed in Jackson's veins. He needed to be alone with her. He needed to hear it all.

Pregnant. A baby. His and Alani's child . . .

His knees shook.

He turned in a rush. "Out."

Saluting him, Dare dragged Trace out of the chair. Together, both of them wearing subdued but satisfied grins, they sidled out of the room.

Jackson again set Grim on the floor, then cupped Alani's face with trembling hands. He searched her eyes. "I didn't use protection?"

"No." Her smile wavered with uncertainty. "I'm sorry, but I didn't even think about . . .

not until Dare mentioned the possibility to me."

His head swam. "*Dare* mentioned it?"

"That first day when they came by. You'd been drugged, so he said it was possible you hadn't even thought of it, and then I couldn't remember if you had every single time . . ."

Little by little, that day came back to Jackson. He'd been frantic to reach her, hammered over the fact that he couldn't remember what had happened, more than anxious to get her alone again so he could figure it all out. "Dare took you into the kitchen."

She nodded. "I'm late for my period. But I can't know for sure without a test. And with everything going on, well, I've been here and we've been having so much fun —"

"You were wondering all this time, but you didn't say anything to me?" He felt . . . well, sort of betrayed. But also elated.

She loved him.

She could be carrying his child.

A double whammy.

Going all stiff and affronted, Alani said, "Well, excuse me, but we had killers on our tail and we were moving from one place to the next and —"

And she'd had three weeks since then, but

probably wasn't certain of his reaction.

To let her know exactly how he felt about it, Jackson drew her in for a long kiss. When he lifted his mouth, she leaned into him.

"I'm so sorry, Jackson. I wasn't sure how you'd feel about it —"

"I love you." He tipped up her chin. "I didn't know anything was missing until I met you. I didn't know I could be so . . . satisfied."

"Sexually?" she whispered, sounding scandalized.

He had to grin. "That, for sure. But I meant with life. With every damned day." He lifted her off her feet and swung her around. "Damn, woman, but you make me happier than I knew was possible."

She smiled now, too. "And if I'm pregnant?"

"I hope you are." As he said it, he knew it was true. Alani, a baby . . . his own family. He nuzzled her neck, but when Grim complained, he bent to scoop him up again. "If you aren't, well hey, I'm willing to work on it. Whatever you want, honey."

Laughing, she put her arms around him. "Know what I want right now?"

"I can hope."

She poked him in the ribs. "I want us to go be with our family and friends."

Yeah, thanks to Alani, they were like family to him. The idea of that had never much mattered before. But now? He almost enjoyed Dare and Trace's overprotective meddling. "I get to tell your brother we're getting married, okay?" He frowned. "That is . . . you will marry me, right?"

"Since you promised me whatever I want, I'll insist on it."

Grim looked between them, gave a scratchy meow and began purring.

Jackson hugged her again. "I wonder if we'll be able to talk Arizona into attending the wedding?" Whether Arizona wanted to admit it or not, she was also a part of his family now. Alani wouldn't have it any other way.

"If we invite Spencer," Alani said, "I'm betting she'll be there with bells on."

Using the specialized, highly secure program that Jackson had given her access to, Arizona finished up her report. With a printout in front of her, she tilted back her chair and perused the details.

The words almost blurred in front of her. A sad story. But that was reality for you.

She'd finished all the work Jackson had given her, and then some. Plenty of scumbags would go down. Plenty of women would be safer for it.

She had no reason to feel guilty for her extracurricular investigation, especially when it had given her so much insight into Spencer Lark.

It still infuriated her that he'd robbed her of her vengeance. She'd worked so long and so hard to find everyone associated with Chandra, everyone who might have played a role in the downturn of her life.

No, she hadn't known Chandra still lived, but once she'd found out, well, it was her right, her duty, to take care of her. Course, with what she'd just learned, she knew Spencer had his own reasons for vengeance.

They had a few things in common.

Soon, she'd find out if it'd be enough to form an alliance. She needed someone like him. She needed someone with his ability.

He owed her. And one way or another, she'd collect.

ABOUT THE AUTHOR

Since first publishing in January 1996, **Lori Foster** has become a Waldenbooks, Borders, *USA TODAY*, *Publishers Weekly* and *New York Times* bestselling author. To learn more, visit www.LoriFoster.com.

We hope you have enjoyed this Large Print book. Other Thorndike, Wheeler, Kennebec, and Chivers Press Large Print books are available at your library or directly from the publishers.

For information about current and upcoming titles, please call or write, without obligation, to:

Publisher
Thorndike Press
10 Water St., Suite 310
Waterville, ME 04901
Tel. (800) 223-1244

or visit our Web site at:

http://gale.cengage.com/thorndike

OR

Chivers Large Print
published by AudioGO Ltd
St James House, The Square
Lower Bristol Road
Bath BA2 3SB
England
Tel. +44(0) 800 136919
email: info@audiogo.co.uk
www.audiogo.co.uk

All our Large Print titles are designed for easy reading, and all our books are made to last.